THE HUNT FOR LOST SOULS

GUARDIAN OF THE CORE (BOOK 3)

MICHAEL E. THIES

 Writer's Block Press

WRITER'S BLOCK PRESS

For information please contact: Writer's Block Press, 4266 Bonmaur Terrace, Slinger, WI 53086

 Writer's Block Press

Michaelethies@michaelethies.com

The Hunt for Lost Souls is a work of fiction. Names, characters, places and incidents originate from the author's imagination and are used fictitiously. Any resemblance to actual persons, living or dead, events, or locales is entirely coincidental.

Printed and bound in PRC and the United States of America. Published by Writer's Block Press. All rights reserved.

Family Crests and Badges by Melissa Thies

Map by Ben Hying

Cover by Scarlett Wang

ISBN: 978-0-9895668-3-4

Library of Congress Control Number: 2021921335

www.michaelethies.com

Contents

PROLOGUE

G uardian Edwyrd Eska stared at the twelve communication screens ahead of him. Each monitor showed a different lord or lady from a different nation. An awkward silence had persisted in the room for quite some time now. Patiently, he waited. He knew that telling them about the Twelve's civil war, how he had intervened, and the necessity in sealing the Twelve away and then scattering them across Gladonus would bring about a prolonged time of contemplation and speculation about what the future might hold. These were who they had prayed to; these were who they were used to answering to; these were their Twelve.

"So the Twelve are no more?"

How many times do I need to repeat myself? Guardian Eska remained stoic. "They are still *alive...* just not in physical form."

"Well, in what kind of *form* are they sealed?" Lady Liliana of Mistral asked.

"I choose not to disclose that information to anyone here at this time. I am sorry."

"Well, what information will you disclose?" Lord Vangle asked.

"Nothing more than what I have already told you concerning the Twelve. It is up to each of you to spread the information to your civilians."

"You are trying to make us look bad in the eyes of our civilians for your brash actions?" Lord Grime of Sereya squinted.

Eska could still see the marks on his neck from when Tundra interrogated him. A quick and subtle smirk came to his lips. "Lord Grime, if I had delayed my actions, Mount Volan would have been reduced to a molehill, and the moon may have even crashed into your own planet. There was no other way. Each of you must see that. I did not *kill* the Twelve, they are merely *sealed*, remember that."

Lady Aprah nodded her approval. "I, for one, thank you for saving Mount Volan, Guardian Eska."

He returned the gesture, but remained silent. The nations could show allegiance to him, but he could show none in return. It was the duty of a Guardian. A wicked, cruel duty that left many despising him and eager to voice their opinions. One such person was his old rival Victor Zigarda. If the past Trial contestant had wanted an opportunity to showcase Eska's inability to be Guardian, now was the time, but he remained unexpectedly silent, preoccupied for most of the virtual meeting.

"If there is nothing else, then I want to move onto one other order of business before this meeting is adjourned. Some of you may or may not know about the unfortunate situation that has befallen the Paens as of late. While I won't get into specifics here with you, I will notify you all that Hydro Áylan Paen is now the subject of an interplanetary manhunt." Eska surveyed all of the lords' and ladies' faces, their various expressions converted now into confusion. "I will be sending out my Hown to track him down. Martial Law is now enacted. Should they come to you seeking information, you would do well to oblige them of their request. Their authority now supersedes your own for the time being. If you catch wind of Hydro's presence, report it immediately to General Satorus or me. I am uploading the general's personal telecommunicator number into your databases as we speak, so you can contact him instantaneously." Guardian Eska pushed a series of buttons and each of the monitors flashed with the words *uploading contact information.*

"I have received it, my guardian."

"So have I."

When all of the families in power confirmed that they received his general's contact information, Eska continued. "That is all then for now. I wish you luck as your nations make this transition." Eska pushed a red button and one-by-one the screens powered off. He exhaled and massaged his forehead. *At least that is over.*

The door opened behind him.

Eska turned his head. "Ethen? You're up."

A crutch underneath his armpits, the conseleigh hobbled towards the center of the telecommunication chamber. "Te medicine in te apothecary has started to do its work. How did te meeting fare?"

"They are upset, as they should be. And Pirini Lilapa has done its job once again in sowing discord in the system. It is only a matter of time before all feel the effect of its aftermath, not just those on Onkh."

"I wish we could have done more. I wish it didn't have to come to tat."

"Aye. You did what you could. That is all I can ask from my conseleigh."

"It may be not my place to overstep, but I do think it may be wise to contact Luvan."

Eska narrowed his eyes. "Why?"

"He, like me, my guardian, was only trying to help."

"He disobeyed my orders."

"Tey were tall commands."

"Commands all the same."

"You told te lords and ladies ten about his dismissal?"

Eska shook his head. "I thought it best not to relay any more information than necessary at this moment. If they knew he was absent, then I would need to begin the replacement process. I do not have time for that. My focus is elsewhere."

"Elsewhere, my guardian?" Ethen stroked his conical beard.

A call came to the chamber. Duty forced Eska to turn back around. *Tundra's calling.* Pushing a green button to accept the call, he saw Tundra's face framed by the very commotion and chaos that vied for his attention. She was out of breath and spoke haltingly.

"Edwyrd, we found him. We found Hydro. He is in Mendeck. We chased him, but he evaded us. Should we try and locate him?"

"You are sure it is him?"

"Positive."

Eirek came into the picture now, panting.

"I gave him chase, but he cast Power that I couldn't overcome."

They were so close. Perhaps it's for the best they didn't find him. He may be too dangerous for them. Eska slunk his shoulders and stared at the communication panel.

"Should we give further chase to him?"

"No. Return here immediately. I need to have a word with both of you. Especially you, Eirek."

Eska stared at Eirek until his apprentice eventually looked away. *Does he know what I want to discuss with him?* He nodded towards Tundra and the communication ended.

"You are not going after him?" Ethen asked.

Eska walked out of the chamber, Ethen hobbling by his side. "No. There is more at stake than Hydro right now."

"Like what?"

In the lobby, Eska stopped. "Our apprentice. We are lucky he still has his life after a confrontation with Hydro. I will send General Satorus and a fraction of the Hown to Mendeck to hunt Hydro down. He is a lost soul. And a dangerous one at that. They will be best equipped for handling him. Right now, Eirek's training needs to be accelerated." Eska put a hand on Ethen's shoulder.

"I am hardly ready to do such a ting!"

"Then I suggest you get some rest in the apothecary. It's time he learns how to wield a weapon. You saw his performance during your trial."

Eska didn't wait for Ethen's response; he went outdoors, walking down the steps to the dirty earth, a façade covering what dwelt below, what he vowed to protect, until Gladonus was ready for it once again. The silver of the afternoon sky had turned purple, waning into darkness and nighttime, polishing the diamonds that filled the vast expanse.

"What do you search for up tere?" Ethen asked.

"Memories." Eska let the lie fall out of his lips. The truth was a secret best kept to himself and Vesel, his dragon.

"Memories?"

"Aye, every person has a star, Ethen. And the ones who aren't present with us today, their stars burned out many years ago. Like my mentor, Guardian Matthau Crevon." Eska looked back at Ethen for a brief moment and then returned his gaze to the stars and continued the lie. "I try to imagine how bright his star must have shone while he was alive. How bright one of the Twelve's stars must shine, even now. Sometimes even how bright my sister's star would have shone before she died. Then I try to think of how I could find my own."

"What would you do if you found it?"

Eska eyed Ethen curiously. He smiled. "Well, I would wish upon it, of course."

"Wish, my guardian? Isn't tat just a folktale?"

"Truly, we may never know. Unless we find our star."

"And tat seems highly impossible. How is anyone supposed to find teirs?"

Eska remained silent, looking at the stars.

Ethen yawned. "Well, I am going back to rest. Goodnight, my guardian."

"Goodnight, Ethen. Rest well. Tomorrow marks a new day. Tomorrow marks change."

Eska stayed outside a while longer. A silhouette flew above him. *Vesel is prowling.* Eska hummed, thinking about what the dragon searched for. Sustenance? Purpose? As his dragon scoured the land, Eska scoured the sky of souls. When his eyes at last fell upon his own star, he almost thought about calling to it and finally hearing its voice. Finally learning his true name and embracing its meaning. Finally knowing whether the stories surrounding the stars were more than just fables. Instead, he held his tongue, not wanting to call to it only to lie once more.

PART I - LOST

CHAPTER ONE

BROKEN

The cell wasn't dark, but it might as well have been. Ever since Zakk had come in and thrown the jewels at Zain's feet, gloom held him captive. *Gift...* His vision glazed over the gems strewn around him.

"Zain."

He ignored his father's voice.

"Zain. Listen to me."

Zain didn't want to hear. He put his hands around his ears and neck and pushed his head in between his bent knees.

"Zain... I'm possible. Right? You're possible."

I'm possible? Am I? Images of blood splattering in the great hall came back to him. His personal guard, Gerald, had died right in front of him, and the others were being harvested in the Blood Chambers, whatever those were.

Zain rocked back and forth, noticing now the absence of the feather that would have dangled below his neck, but even that had been taken away. *They took everything from me...*

"Zain, another sword can be made for you. But another will cannot be forged. You must hold on to the one I know you still have."

Zain stopped rocking. He removed his head from its burrow between his knees and turned to his father. "But my sword." Zain bent forward and picked up the jewels. They fell through his fingers one by one, a small clang of perpetual defeat.

"The sword is merely metal. The jewels are what I added to it. They are me and will always be me, and so you, too, will always have me."

The last jewel fell through his fingers.

Clapping.

Zain twisted his body. The prisoner in the cell next to him stopped clapping.

"Beautiful fuckin' speech. You should win an award for best fazer. But zese kids will only ever disappoint you. Zey never amount to much. Zey take and take and take, but never give. Zey only care about zemselves. Next zing you know, zey will leave you in here or dead..."

Zain remained silent for a little while, staring intently at the man with thick hands, like a mechanic's, and black, unkempt hair. The red light of the room caught him at such an angle to give him two faces, a crimson side as red as blood and a black side, unknown and dreadful.

"All you ever did was take."

"What would you know about what I've done?"

"Gabrielle told me how you molested her, you perverted piece of—"

"Get him up."

Zain twisted his body to the voice. Zakk stood before his jail cell. Two guards came around Zakk, blocking Zain's view of his lost friend. After they unlocked the cell door, they hustled him and got him to his feet, keeping a tight grip on his forearms. Zain didn't struggle; he knew it would be pointless to do so.

"What's going on?" Zain's father reached for Zain's hand but couldn't quite grasp it. Deep lines creased his forehead and his eyes widened at Zakk's sudden intrusion.

Zakk looked from Zain to his father. "Both of you are about to go home." Zakk twitched his head, signaling for the guards to hoist Zain's father up and then take them away.

Zain stopped before Zakk. "Home?"

"Isn't that what you wanted?" Zakk's gaze bore deep into Zain.

Nervously, Zain looked to his father, now escorted by two guards.

"What is this about?" his father asked.

"The apprentice came and said we had to release you."

"Eirek is here?" *We're free.*

Zakk ignored his question. "Take them away."

We're free. Side-by-side, Zain and his father were led out of the dungeons. *We're free.* The idea latched onto Zain, burrowing into his mind and consuming him. Paraded down another hallway after the dungeon, they eventually reached an egg-shaped door. A guard swiped his card, signaling the elevator to descend.

"Wait, my jewels. They're in the cell." Zain stopped and moved backwards, but the guards held onto him tight, pinching his arms.

"You'll get them later," one said, then pushed Zain into the open elevator door.

Together, the six of them entered. One guard pushed a button while the others faced them, hands on hilts.

From the speakers in the corners, the pod-shaped elevator spoke.

"You have chosen the Blood Chambers. Verification please."

"Blood Chambers?" The elevator jolted into action, causing a slight shift to Zain's posture. "Where are we..." Zain tried to move forward, but the guards suppressed him.

"Zain?"

Prickles crept up Zain's forearm, making their way to the back of his neck. He ignored the desire to look at his father, instead keeping his eyes focused on the guards in front of him, hands glued to their hilts, smug smirks on their faces.

Minutes later, the pod stopped. The door opened. A long hallway stretched before them. Snatched by each arm and shoulder, Zain and his father were marched down the long stretch of hallway. With each step the amalgam of copper and anesthetics became more poignant. Normally, Zain would fight. He would struggle. But with his father being marched down the same plank to the same fate, did it even matter? Was it worth putting his father's life in greater jeopardy? Still, Zain kept his shoulders up, his focus fixated and alert for whatever lay behind the pair of sliding doors at the end of the hallway.

The doors slid open. Two men wearing masks and labsuits of black and red appeared. Zain and his father were pushed inside, into their custody. The guards didn't follow.

Instantly, a nozzle coated Zain in a light mist from above. The temperature dropped, raising the hairs on his skin once more. The smell of metallic rot multiplied but was quickly overpowered by anesthesia. His eyes closed and he saw no more.

Zain awoke to a splitting headache and numbness in his arms. Puncturing his skin, tubes syphoned his blood, feedings the bags next to him. As consciousness came back to him, so too did the numbness spreading throughout his body. Blurs moved with his vision until he stopped, allowing the world to come into focus. Beside him, his dad was strapped to a different bed, tubes running out of his arms as well.

All around, Zain noticed pints of blood being collected from other unconscious bodies. He recognized some of them as Vangle's men. *Why is he harvesting all of this blood?* A sickness grew in Zain's stomach. The raw metallic overload hit his nose like the sulfur on Vatu Volcano. He wanted to retch. He tried leaning over the side of his bed, but bindings held him in place. His eyes widened. He yanked. They didn't budge. *I have to—*

Footsteps. Then two men looked down at him with long noses, crooked lips and furunculous faces. They examined him with dull grey eyes, a hint of amber within the only salient feature.

"Hmmm, look, Zall, this one is awake. And it's struggling. What its name?"

"Zain Berrese. I believe this one and its father were the ones Lord Zigarda mentioned. It's the one that provided most of the other blood here for us."

"It did quite the job. And look at its skin." The nameless man ran his hands over Zain's defenseless body. "It's so exotic."

Zain tightened his forearms and clenched his fists. He struggled and kicked, bucked his head and his body, but to no avail. The leather straps held him in place.

"Look, it's getting mad. Should we knock it out again?"

"No, not yet, Zall. I want to do something."

The nameless man moved away. Zall held a grin on his face as he examined Zain, feasting upon him with his eyes. While his partner was away, Zall ran his hands across Zain's forearms, up his shoulders, and clenched his chin. "Simply delectable." Zall licked his lips.

Zain cowered his neck as much as he could, trying to free himself from the man's scabrous hand. Upon the return of the other man, Zall pulled his hand away.

"Quit frightening it, Zall. It's my turn to play with it now."

"What are you going to do, Zarich?"

Zarich didn't answer. Instead, he fastened a tube to the bag of blood and poked a needle into his own arm. A loud moan of euphoria and ecstasy came soon after as blood flowed into Zarich's flabby forearm. With each second, the loose skin grew more taut. His face bubbled, white puss spilling from his boils. He pulled the needle from his arm and began to massage his face, spreading out the puss as if it was lotion. When he pulled his hands away from his face, Zain squirmed, his heart hammering in his chest. He yanked at the bonds on his forearms futilely, producing only a laugh from Zall. A cackle came from Zarich, an echo of one Zain knew too well. Before passing out, Zain took in the dark-skinned face looking back at him, the short, cropped hair and firm jawline. It was a face Zain had seen many times before. It was his own.

CHAPTER TWO

APPREHENDED

Z akk made his way to the throne room. While others ran about the hallways, mindless drones to the wailing siren, Zakk walked. He didn't like rushing things. It bred carelessness.

A beep.

The telecommunicator on his wrist vibrated. *Zigarda again? I'm on my way. Hasn't he heard of patience?*

Another siren wailed.

How urgent could it possibly be? In truth, this was only the second time he had heard the sirens scream. The first had alerted him to Zain's arrival before the slaughter, and its only purpose was to give people time to get organized. If this was another tedious drill such as that, Zakk would have to reevaluate the effectiveness of Zigarda's tactics.

A soldier in a black snakeskin suit rushed past, bumping into Zakk. "Sorry, Sir Shiren. Zigarda is calling us. Do you come?"

"In my own time." Zakk continued walking.

The man didn't wait for Zakk; he turned around and caught up with another group of individuals surely making their way to the throne room. *What is this about?*

Zakk bit his lip in contemplation as he ruminated on the matter at hand. Had Eska's apprentice and conseleigh come back? Perhaps. That is the only thing Zakk could think of to warrant such immediacy. But if Zigarda could manage living as long as the Guardian of the Core, then he could wait a few more minutes for Zakk's arrival.

In the throne room, Dr. Cere, Lord Zigarda, and both his receiver and advisor were present. Thirty snakeskin-suited guards assembled in three groups of ten stood near the exit. At the sight of his arrival, the alarm died.

"Why didn't you get here sooner?"

"I came as fast as I could," he lied. "What's wrong?"

"Prince Hydro Paen has been spotted here in Mendeck. You are to lead the capturing party." Zigarda pointed to the group of guards in the hall. "There is no time to waste."

Hydro's here. Zakk recalled the conversation with Numos. *How fortunate.* "Where?"

"Last spotted in the marketplace."

"I'll find him." Zakk walked away.

"Not without help you won't." Zigarda called him back.

Zakk halted. "That is why I have the other troops."

Zigarda coughed and cleared his throat. "You are not to bring him back dead. Hydro is more valuable than that." Zigarda nodded to his head scientist. "Genus."

The old man in a black lab coat stepped forward. From behind his back, Dr. Cere produced a device shaped like a metallic Y. "I take it you remember this device?"

Zakk gulped. Shivers crept along his neck as he remembered the blue noose of electricity that had been his reprimand for his blunder on Vatu Volcano during the fourth of Eska's Trials. With caution, Zakk took the device and inspected it. "It's short."

"Yes, it needs to be that way. Too wide and the shock will feel like a tickle. When the coils are denser and closer together, it will put Hydro into a state of temporary paralysis, allowing him to be captured."

"I will need to get close."

"Yes. Hopefully you have no problem with that."

"What am I to do against his Power until I can get close enough to detain him?"

"Half of the guards are versed in the language. They are at your front. Use them." Zigarda pointed to the guards in red snakeskin suits.

"Do not mess up again," Dr. Cere added.

"I won't."

"I know. To make sure of it, take these as well." Dr. Cere extended his other hand with a closed fist.

Zakk eyed the fist.

"Go on. Time is of the essence."

Zakk held out his own hand. Multiple mechanical insects fell into his palm. They looked eerily similar to the ones Dr. Cere had invented to put into action the first part of their plan: the corruption of the Core's asteroid, Hown. The mosquitos released there during the receiver's brief stint on the Core would transmit a virus to those on the asteroid. The asteroid itself was insignificant, but the Hown stationed on that asteroid were the best fighters in the system. Many Gazo students dreamed of being accepted as a personal soldier of the Core, but unless they were first in class academically, best in class physically, and emotionally adept, they wouldn't be accepted into the rigorous training program. Zigarda knew the Hown soldiers had to be eliminated first if he ever wanted a chance to take revenge on the Guardian of the Core.

"What do these do?"

"They will give you the chance to get close to him by gassing him out of wherever he is currently hiding. Guards in the grey snakeskin suits will help you activate them." Cere pointed to the last row of snakeskin guards.

Zakk put the flies in a pouch attached to his belt and walked to the front of the troops. From the front row of red guards, Zakk pulled four out of line to join him.

In the second row, Zakk took the largest of the black snakeskin guards and did the same with the last row of grey snakeskin guards. The rest he split up into three more groups of eight.

"To cover Mendeck as efficiently as possible, each group will use a hovercraft. If the target is spotted, immediately contact each group leader and then halt the target as best as possible without engaging. We do not want to lose him. Is this understood?"

All remained silent but swiftly nodded their head in compliance.

Zakk led them out of the compound. In a matter of moments, each group mobilized and began hunting for their prey. Hunting for Hydro.

Hydro's last known sighting had been in the market area, so Zakk decided it best for his group to look there first. Unlike most other days, the market was abandoned, save for a few stragglers unaware of his scouting party's arrival, for they were mesmerized by the large wall of Power that sectioned off the street.

Zakk furrowed his brows at the display of opposites working in tandem, seeing electricity crawl through the watery wall like eels. "Halt." Zakk hopped off and strolled forward to examine the barrier more closely. He wanted to touch it but knew better than to oblige his curiosity. "Can you fix this?" He asked, hearing one of the guards shuffle up beside him.

"It may take some time."

"Do it. We can get a trace on him past this wall."

He left, leaving the red snakeskin guards to use their Power. The stragglers had since departed, probably afraid of any repercussions that could befall them for loitering. Unfortunate, too, as Zakk could have gained more information from them. What he was left with was an array of detritus and some copper cures, silver spells, and golden bonds, and a few dead bodies of citizens unfortunate enough to be involved in the altercation. He plucked a golden bond up off the street and another one for good luck, and put them in his pocket. Bonds always came in two.

But the extra gold couldn't compensate for first-hand information. The coins couldn't talk to him and tell him how *that* happened. Zakk crossed his arms and tapped his foot, waiting for the Powerbearers to finish their incantations.

To pass his time, he examined one of the corpses close to him. He reeled back. Not because of any pungent scent or the blood painting the cobblestone street red, nor was he particularly remorseful that it happened to be a young woman who had been caught in the aftermath of the duel. He pulled back because the woman was cut in two. Severed.

Zakk shook his head and approached the woman's cadaver once more. To make sure he was seeing correctly, he yanked on her shoe, seeing how much of her body moved with his action. Only the lower half.

An Ether Weapon...

"We're done."

Zakk torqued back and examined the field behind the soldier. His face tightened and he narrowed his vision. "Let's go." He sauntered past the soldiers who fell in line behind him. This time, though, he made sure to have one hand on his hilt and the other holding tight onto the device given to him by Dr. Cere. Zakk knew his ordinary steel couldn't hold mettle when pitted against an Ether Weapon; the weapon had changed the rules of the game. Zakk would rather bring back a carcass than end up a carcass.

Eventually, the marketplace gave way to a plaza with a fountain in its center. Through his telecommunicator, Zakk ordered the three other exits that connected the plaza to other parts of the city sealed off. Stragglers vacated the premises after a brandishing of steel from the guards in black snakeskin suits.

"No sign of him."

"Yes. He is here. In one of those." Zakk pointed to the line of two-story duplexes located on one side of the plaza, much unlike the ones located on the skirts of the city.

"How do you know?"

"I was lost once, too," Zakk muttered to himself.

"What?"

"Nothing." Zakk shook his head and narrowed his focus on the only building with the lights on. "He's in that one." Zakk pointed to the one on the left.

"He wouldn't be stupid enough to leave the lights on."

"He isn't. Let's go."

If Zakk hadn't done the same thing during his time as an orphan before being adopted by Zain's parents, he wouldn't have guessed that house either, thinking it to be a family having dinner.

By the time he stood at the stoop of the duplex, another five guards not relegated to guarding the exits of the plaza joined his own party, making them ten strong.

"You two." Zakk pointed. "Open the door." Zakk stayed back, focusing on what would come next after the two guards in black snakeskin suits opened the door. The grey guard remained at his side.

One of the red guards pushed the door slightly ajar and reeled back. The other coughed and covered his nose. *Recent death.* Zakk didn't need to smell it to know how the musk bit one's nose.

Zakk split them into three groups, sending two inside to check the upper and the lower levels. He kept one grey and one red snakeskin guard by his side should Hydro try to escape.

Silence.

Anticipation.

When the first shriek came, the red guard to his right moved forward, wanting to enter the fray. Admirable, but foolish. "Wait." Zakk put his arm in front of the soldier. With his other hand, he reached into the pouch where he had put the electronic insects Dr. Cere had given him. Zakk turned to the grey guard on his left. "Hold out your hand." Zakk dumped the metallic insects into the open palm. "Unleash these."

The grey guard darted up the steps and bent down at the threshold of the building. Amidst more shrieks of death, the guard released the insects.

Gas flooded the house, making it impossible to see beyond the steps. And then the cloven body of the grey guard flopped back down the stairs. A shadow. The slightest movement. Zakk glanced up in time to see his prey leaping out of the toxic fog, intent on depriving Zakk of his head.

"Sorry. Not today." Zakk stepped to the side, yanking the red guard to fill his void, feeding the lamb to the slaughter, and drawing Dr. Cere's device. Hunter moved around the hunted, and with the practiced precision granted to him from sparring classes at Gazo's, Zakk jabbed forward with the device, catching his quarry in an electric noose.

Electricity surged through the man. The grip on his Ether Weapon failed, the real danger clanging to the ground. His arms swung frantically. Finally, after a moment of futile struggle, he collapsed beside his Ether Weapon.

Three of Zakk's men staggered out of the building, arms held over their mouths. Zakk sighed. It seemed none of the other men had survived. He returned his gaze to the prey at his feet, not wanting to think about the men he sacrificed to earn this dead weight of a body. Zakk took the Ether Blade into his own hand, marveling at its cloudy amethyst beauty, and wondered if he would ever have a weapon of such renown.

"Is that him?"

Zakk tore his gaze from the blade. He nodded. "Let's go. Zigarda is expecting this one."

Zakk began walking, dragging the limp body behind him. He didn't command anyone to help him; it would've been too much of a privilege for a prize who had killed so many. Where Hydro fit into their plans now that he was captured, Zakk didn't know. But Zakk did know a thing or two about justice. It was what a true Gazo's student lived by. Zain was currently receiving his. And as Zakk dragged the fallen prince back to the Web, he was receiving his own, now being nothing higher than the dirt on the ground.

CHAPTER THREE

INTERROGATION

L ights. Blinding lights. Like those of what the heavens of Axiumé must look like when the dead first step foot upon the celestial plane. That is what Hydro woke to.

He blinked and moved to cover his eyes. Iron scraped against his wrist. Slowly, his vision adjusted. Manacles shackled him to a metal table. In shock, he tried standing. The attempt was futile. His ankles were chained as well. He wiggled and squirmed, trying to escape from the shackles that bound him. They itched. And all Hydro wanted was freedom.

Across the room, a door opened. In strolled a man wearing a halfhat that pushed black hair to the right side of his face. "Hydro Paen, ve've been looking for you."

Hydro didn't respond.

"My name is Yuan Shimes. I am Lord Zigarda's receiver."

The name held an air of familiarity. His father had always maintained a strong relationship with Empora and, because of it, Hydro had encountered Zigarda's aides multiple times. However, something seemed off this time. Surely things had gone sour between their nations, otherwise Hydro wouldn't be seated at a metal table within a metal room.

"Where is Lord Zigarda?"

"He is vatching our conversation. Do you know vhy you are here?"

Hydro didn't answer immediately. He evaluated the receiver's composure. "Because of what happened on Acquava?"

The words brought back a flood of memories. His mother's shrills as she burned alive. The warm blood of his father splattering upon his face. Aiton's hopeless and confused eyes.

"Aahh!" Hydro shook his head free from the images and tried to stand. This time the table moved, causing the receiver to retreat towards the door. A hand touched his. "Anne?" The ire inside him died in the warm smile of the dark-skinned child who sat in her white dress on top of the table.

"*And* you are correct in zat regards. But vhy you are here and not in Guardian Eska's custody? You realize za Guardian of za Core is looking for you, yes? He vill send troops here shortly. I am sure."

I don't need to listen to him. Hydro rotated his neck and curled his fists.

"I see your eyes wandering. It won't matter. You cannot use Power here, not in this room." A smug smile spread across Yuan's face. Arms crossed, he tapped his fingers on his elbows, waiting for Hydro to respond.

Fire surged within him. *This fool will burn alive.*

Anne massaged his knuckles. *It is better they not know about us.*

Hydro relaxed and stared at Yuan. "I suppose I can't."

"Now, vhy are you in zis city?"

"I don't need to answer to you."

"You vill if you vant your sword returned to you. You vill if you don't want to be given into Eska's charge. You vill if you want freedom."

Hydro yanked on his shackles again, eliciting a slight smirk from Yuan. "Pa—"

Anne stroked his forearm now. *Easy, Hydro Paen. You will get it back. Play along with their questions, but do not reveal me. They will take me from you if they find out.*

Hydro exhaled, not finishing the incantation. "What should I say?"

"The truth vould be a good start to zis relationship." Yuan cocked his head to one side.

After a long moment in which he contemplated what to say, he turned back his attention to Yuan. The receiver either didn't notice his lack of eye contact or didn't care. Hydro clicked his tongue. "I was traveling."

"Traveling to where?"

"Chaon."

"Vhy?"

"I have unfinished business there."

"That business will need to—"

The door opened. A hooded man entered.

"Yuan, you may leave us. Hydro desires to speak to someone more like him."

"Lord Zigarda. Of course." Yuan bowed and left.

Zigarda took a seat in the chair across the table from Hydro and pulled back his black hood, revealing a boiled and marred face. Crags underneath his lidless eyes showed his age much more prominently when combined with the burns.

Hydro straightened in his chair.

"Do I scare you, Prince Paen?"

"No." Hydro feigned confidence by staring into his charcoal eyes, trying to win a battle of authority, only to lose by looking away. Anne had left him, making him feel more vulnerable than before.

Victor Zigarda waited for Hydro to look at him again. When this happened, he slid a smirk upon his lips and continued speaking. "Good. There is no need to be frightened. Your family and I have always maintained good countenance with one another."

"My family is dead."

"Yes. And murdered by you. But that doesn't have to sour our relationship."

Hydro stayed silent. He wanted to cross his arms, but the manacles at his wrist wouldn't allow him that luxury, so he reserved himself to tapping his fingers on the cool metal.

"I don't blame you for murdering your family. I understand the hardships you faced during the Trials." Zigarda drew a finger over his face to emphasize each scar and crag. "That is what being an effective leader does. They empathize with those around them. Forgive Yuan, but he merely wanted to toy with you. I, on the other hand, want to offer you what you crave most."

Hydro stopped tapping his fingers. "And what is that?"

"Freedom. Isn't that so?"

Hydro didn't respond.

"Did you know that I contended with Guardian Eska during his Trials? That I, too, was a Trials participant?"

Hydro nodded.

"I, too, was next-in-line to inherit my family's throne here on Empora, but, like you, I didn't want that. I wanted more than what this life could have offered me."

"What is that?"

"Immortality."

"You have lived longer than any other person without First Blood, I would say you have found that secret without being Guardian."

A wry smile crossed Zigarda's lips. "Oh, Hydro Paen, you have so much to learn about your family's wealth."

Hydro leaned forward. "Then tell me."

"In due time. In due time." Zigarda waved his hand as if hushing Hydro. "Tell me something, Hydro Paen. Why did you attend the Trials?"

"You already said it."

"You wanted more. You wanted freedom from the duty that would have bound you on Acquava, is that correct?"

Hydro gulped.

"You did it merely to spite your mother."

Hydro shifted in his seat. Still, he said nothing.

"Selfish reasons. And the wrong ones, I assure you. You would not have made a good Guardian."

"And your reason is more pious?"

"No. I am just as selfish as you are, wanting immortality and the Power that came along with being Guardian of the Core. However, those are *only* selfish reasons, not the wrong ones. I knew there would still be duty to maintain as Guardian. My reasons were based upon what I couldn't get here in Empora, your reasons were mainly a culprit of hubris, and that is why you lost."

"So did you."

Zigarda twitched his head. "I may have lost, but I fared better than you."

"I came in second." Hydro leaned forward.

"You came in third." Zigarda leaned forward, hands clasped together. "I've been informed it was Zain Berrese who truly won the competition, and then that man, Eirek Mourse, is it? Yes, he beat you."

Hydro shrugged back into his chair. He threw his gaze to the side. "Second. Third. What does it matter? We both lost."

"Aye, but I should have won. How could I have known that Guardian Eska could have unleashed Power that managed to overcome my own?" Zigarda snapped his fingers.

The door behind him opened and a small gas lamp was lit.

"*Palo.*" A blue flame danced upon Zigarda's hands.

Hydro's eyes watched the blue fire in awe.

The spell died, and the lamp was taken away.

"I can tell from your eyes that you understand what a blue flame means."

Only Professor Haruko, Hydro knew, could cast a blue flame. The users were very rare, but it was always a sign of extreme Power.

"How did Guardian Eska beat you?"

"I ask myself that question time and time again. How *did* he overcome my Power? He cast Power with the might of his bonded animal."

"Well, then, that's no surprise. He is bonded to a dragon."

"Aye, it *should be* no surprise, Hydro Paen. I know a dragon's Power, especially with fire, is well beyond any blue flame I can cast. The problem is that Edwyrd showed up to those Trials alone, without his animal. How he managed to tap into his animal's Power planets away is something I have yet to truly understand, but he did it, and I lost, and now I have a permanent reminder of what that loss looks like and feels like."

"Why are you telling me this?"

"Because we are alike, you and I. We both lost Trials that were meant to be ours. And we went back to a family dishonored and dejected." Zigarda stood up now and walked around the room, hands behind his back, spilling a story all the while. "When I went back home, my father found my face disgusting. And, to be honest, I couldn't agree more with him. Eska had severely wounded me in that last battle, when the..." Zigarda paused. He shook his head. "Never mind. Anyway, even though I was the eldest and the most capable of my family, because of my disfigurement, my father decided to pass the birthright onto my younger brother, Kalvin. While he could cast Power, it wasn't like mine. While he was certainly skilled at talking, he didn't have it in him to break hearts. He was a people pleaser." Zigarda turned to look at Hydro, boring into him with the lidless, charcoal eyes. "Those types of individuals are the worst. Telling you what you want to hear but never really expressing their own opinion. I knew that if the rule of Empora went to him, the strides Empora was making towards being an inter-planetary force would be lost... so I killed him." Zigarda paused, hands behind his back, turned away from Hydro, as if he were lost in profound nostalgia.

"How did you do it?"

Zigarda turned around with a grin on his face. He pushed his hand forward. "A knife, through the ribs in the back. After my own father's funeral, of course, I would never kill my father..." Zigarda paused again and held Hydro's stare for a long moment before continuing his circling of the metallic chamber. "The others who held ties to the throne fled. To where, I didn't really care. It is too long ago to really remember. And I still really don't care to this day, seeing as my debt was paid. But, afterwards, I did what lords do."

"And what is that?"

"Their duty: rule. And so I began networking with others. I first made allies with the Shangkun family in Chaon. And then, with the development of interplanetary travel, I decided to expand my...," a devilish grin came to his lips, as if he had thought of something clever, "*web* of influence to other families in power on other planets. Lord Grime in Sereya. My connection with your family started with your father's father, Áylan."

"You knew my grandfather?"

"Why, of course. He was just beginning to build the Acqua Roads to better interconnect all provinces of Acquava and he needed the expertise of Empora."

"Why not go to Gar? They are closer and more advanced in technology now."

Lord Zigarda hunched over the table. "At this time, Gar didn't exist, not yet anyway. But even if they did, Hydro Paen, I believe you answered your own question. Who would want to deal with a Garian, anyway?"

"How do you know that?"

"Little birds flutter to my ear every once in a while. Well, perhaps, not so little." He corrected himself with a slight grin. "But even Lord Grime tells me they are savages, and isn't that true?"

Hydro found himself nodding in agreement, even though he hadn't meant to be so compliant. Whether Zigarda said that to get him to his side, or if he truly did despise Garians, Hydro didn't know. But he had to admit that Zigarda, while physically uncharismatic now, had a way with words and would have been lethal in his prime.

"And so Empora lent expertise and knowledge to the construction process, and in return Empora became wealthier, certainly, but the wealth in bonds and spells and cures didn't concern me as much as rumored water I had heard about while on Acquava."

Hydro tilted his head. Even he had no idea of what Zigarda spoke.

"At first, I was interested in the Katarh flower. I'm sure you know it and its properties?"

Hydro nodded. "It heals... burns," he pushed out, realizing why Zigarda wanted to connect with his family.

"Yes. That is one of its many properties. Sadly, however, my face was beyond repair. And, also, I was advancing in years. After hearing about this from your grandfather's adored—"

"Elias?"

"Yes, that is the one. I became rather disheartened. However, upon a return visit one time to check on the progress of the roads, your grandfather took me aside and gave me a gift of good faith. A bond between friends." Zigarda stood behind Hydro now and in his left hand he held a blue liquid, the brightest color Hydro had ever seen. "He gave me this. Do you know what it is?" Zigarda swirled it around in its tube.

Hydro blinked and shook his head.

"It's youthwater. And it is your duty now to get this for me."

Hydro frowned. "And how would I get it?"

"Only lords of Acquava can cross the Watery Path safely, and although your brother now rules, he is not the true lord while you still live."

"And if I were to cross the Watery Path for you, where would I find this youthwater? I have seen the chambers and have never noticed water of this hue."

"The goddess Pearl. Her life force supplies the pool at the top of her throne with the proper reactant it needs to produce the youthwater."

Hydro grinned. And then that grin turned into a guffaw. And if it hadn't been for the chains holding him stationary, he would have fallen over in a rage of laughter.

"What is so funny?"

"Pearl will not be supplying any life force to anyone or anything for a while," he said through bouts of laughter.

"That is where you are wrong. Guardian Eska locked her away at the Meeting of the Twelve, keeping her life force intact while she remains inactive."

Hydro laughed. "You... fool... Eska did no such thing... because Pearl is dead..."

"Impossible."

"It is very possible. I sliced off her head myself." Hydro reined in his laughter as he saw the look of mortality cross Zigarda's countenance.

"Do you know what you have done?"

"Yes. Killed a false deity."

"You... you..." Zigarda coughed. He took out the vial of blue liquid and took a swig of its essence. He recovered instantly. "You pompous—"

A door swung open behind Zigarda. For a brief second, Hydro heard an alarm wail. When the door closed, the sound vanished. Yuan rushed to Zigarda's ear.

"Are you certain?"

Yuan nodded.

"Where is Zakk? Send him." Zigarda flicked his hand, ushering Yuan to leave, but then changed his mind and pulled on the sleeve to stop him. "Tell one of the shifters to come in."

Yuan nodded, bowed, and left.

Zigarda turned back to Hydro, a disturbingly satisfied smirk spread out across his face. He exhaled deeply. "You try to rile me up, Hydro Paen, but it matters not. What you've done only means we will require your services now more than ever."

"I am not interested. I have business in Chaon."

"That may be, but you are not in the best position for bargaining, Hydro Paen."

"Pearl is dead. I told you. I cannot get you this youthwater."

"No. You can't. And although a slight inconvenience, I will find a way to overcome it. That is what successful people do. My plans, I realize, have changed, but my goal still remains."

"And that is?"

Zigarda smirked but ignored the question. "I offer you the chance to satisfy your need of adventure, Hydro Paen. I offer you your freedom. If you don't accept, I will notify the Hown currently looking for you and within the hour you will be under Guardian Eska's jurisdiction. How does that sound to you?"

Hydro tried crossing his arms, only to jingle the chains attached to the table. He lowered his arms and ignored Zigarda's brooding eyes. He hoped Anne would appear to him, but she remained invisible, offering him no guidance.

"The strong and silent type are you, Hydro Paen? Well, if that last reason isn't good enough for you, then perhaps I will have to up the stakes a little bit. Accept this offer and you will have the chance to save your brother from certain disaster."

Hydro's eyes bulged. His he tried to break free from his bonds but failed once again. "What have you done with Aiton?"

"Nothing. Yet. But do not help us and I am afraid that Acquava may suddenly lack Empora's allegiance, and in the coming months that support may be crucial to dissuade those interested in rebelling against a prince orphaned so young and a family name ruined by a monstrous son."

Hydro leaned back in his chair. He tilted his chin upward. "All of our houses are loyal."

"Yes, it certainly was like that underneath your father's rule, but there was a time, Hydro Paen, when not all of Acquava had such a fashionable view of your lineage."

Hydro's shoulder slumped. He didn't look away, though.

"I see you don't understand... let me explain it to you. Empora's first capital was Rydel. Do you know where Rydel is?"

"Near the sea."

"Yes, it is, and because of its location, the capital had to move. Do you know why?"

Hydro studied Zigarda. After a little while, he shook his head.

"Because of the sea. When you think of the seas and oceans on Acquava, what do you think of?"

"The sea is free... lawless... ruthless..." The words came without much effort.

"And that is exactly what the sea is. No one owns the sea. It is the truest idea of freedom and lawlessness there is, and it was these things that seeped into every man who came overseas to this land. It made them ruthless and disrespectful of our land and Rydel was laid siege to many times. Now, tell me, is there more land or water on Acquava?"

"Water."

"Yes, water that makes many men think they are free to do as they would. Why do you think your family has continued living in power for so long? Or why your father would potentially upset the royal houses by marrying a commoner."

Hydro's gaze bolted to the man. His skin prickled.

"Yes, I know about your mother's birth."

I always wondered why Father had no qualms about marrying her. Hydro spent a long while surveying Zigarda, calculating his next words. "So, this is about blackmail? You intend to force me into your charge?"

A wry smile ever present on Zigarda's lips, he shook his head. His charcoal eyes gleamed in satisfaction, as if a fire were slowly being rekindled from the ashes. "No. I've already cornered you into my charge, you just haven't accepted it yet. This is about more than that, Hydro Paen. This is about change." Zigarda raised a hand and snapped his finger.

A moment later, the door behind Zigarda opened and a woman with wisps of thin, uneven grey hair entered. Her face was anything but beautiful, full of pores and wrinkles. She held the same charcoal eyes like Zigarda, but flakes of amber hid in hers, making her slightly more pleasant to look at, if only by the one trait. She strode towards Hydro, pausing ever so slightly when she laid eyes upon his own. Keeping her stride as best she could, she dragged a hand up his exposed forearm, along his shoulder, disappearing behind him, fingers never leaving him, as she trailed the back of his neck in the exposed spot between collar and hair and then down his right arm, until she came back alongside Zigarda.

Hydro choked. Other than her clothes, the woman had transformed into his exact doppelganger. "How.... How..."

"Adventure breeds change. And I offer you that adventure. The adventure to understand who you truly are deep down inside." Zigarda pointed to the heart of Hydro's doppelganger. "It's the chance to embark with me on a path that will change this system of Gladonus forever."

"And if I don't?" Hydro forced himself to sound resilient, if only for the sake of his own pride.

Zigarda scoffed. "As if you have any other choice, Hydro Paen. But I will amuse you all the same. If you don't, not only will you be given over to Eska's custody, but I will send her to Acquava. She will return as you to finish what you already started there."

"And what is that?" Hydro still gawked at the woman, himself, whoever it was, next to Zigarda. Its eyes flicked to Hydro's right. Hydro turned his gaze as well; Anne had reappeared, sitting cross-legged on the table next to him. *Can she see her?*

Zigarda's voice pulled him from his thoughts. "The utter destruction of your family's namesake and lineage."

Hydro hung his head. He didn't need Anne's touch to tell him what to do. There was one person he cared about more than any other. It was time to admit defeat and let his bravado fail. With a sigh, he pushed out his concession. "What is it you will have me do?"

CHAPTER FOUR

ESCAPE

A larms rang.

Drowsiness dissipated into total consciousness. Zain blinked. His ears piqued. Sirens screamed. *What's going on?*

Feeling came back to him, first in his fingers as he gripped the air, then in his feet as he wiggled his toes. The stolen blood soon didn't seem significant.

He blinked again. The two shifters who had toyed with him had now moved to the sliding glass doors.

Zain tightened his abs and raised his body up, glancing down. The bindings on his wrists and legs were leather, nothing more. He tugged at his wrist, noticing they hadn't been refastened after his initial attempt at escaping. They weren't as tight as they should be, but not loose enough for him to slip a hand through. Yet. To solve this problem, he rubbed his hand on his leg. Friction would create warmth which would lead to sweat, which was otherwise impossible to obtain in this temperature-regulated room. While he rubbed, he kept watch on the two at the glass door. One had disappeared. To where, Zain didn't know. He didn't have time to think about that now, though.

Rub. Pull. Rub. Pull. He repeated the process until his hand became raw and sweaty enough to slide it out from its fastening. Without hesitation, he unfastened the other strap and yanked the tubes from his arm.

The screeching sirens stopped.

Zain paused halfway through freeing his feet. He looked up. The shifter saw him. *Shit.*

The shifter yelled something in a foreign language and the other shifter came out from a room and also observed Zain. He darted back into the room while the other shifter maneuvered through the rows of donors to reach Zain.

By the time the man tried to crowd the bed, Zain had freed his feet and kicked the man in the face, sending him reeling backwards into another bed. Zain got off the bed and pounced on the man, taking advantage of the confusion. He punched the man and immediately regretted it. His fingers cracked. A sharp pain stung his arm. Zain recoiled from his mistake.

The man pushed Zain off and then rushed him. Without taking time to establish his balance first, the result was sloppy and indirect. Almost like a matador leading a bull through a curtain, Zain maneuvered to the side, then grabbed the charging man around the neck with his forearm. Momentum took them to the ground. To control the struggle, Zain wrapped his legs around the shifter's lower body while continuing to apply pressure to the neck.

Amidst the lapse of breathing and the frantic hands clawing at the floor, footsteps shuffled towards Zain. The flailing stopped. The other shifter stood in front of Zain, looking from him to the body of his limp colleague, then approached cautiously, a syringe in his hand. Zain released his forearms, sliding his arms to the man's back in stride with the other's cautious steps.

One step. Two steps. Three.

Now.

As fluid as a flowing river, Zain pushed the unconscious man on top of him towards the other, allowing Zain to get into a crouching position as the other stepped back. Zain rushed forward and swiped with his left arm, knocking the syringe out of the man's grasp. With his right hand, he clawed the man's face, pushing him down and back.

Zain landed on top of the man's back. He grabbed the man's head and bashed it into the floor.

Once. Twice.

Screams. Pain. Struggle. The sickening sound of skin slapping against the floor. The crunch of cartilage as, first, the nose broke, then that of the skull shattering, and with it, blood splattering over the tiled floor, pooling around the man's broken face all the way to Zain's knees. When it was finally over, Zain crawled backwards, as if trying to escape the reality of what he had just done.

One breath.

Two breaths.

Blood soaked his hands and his clothes.

Three breaths.

Zain took a moment and closed his eyes, leaning his head back against the metal frame he slouched on. Something ruffled his hair.

Feet.

The others! Zain bolted upright. He maneuvered around the side of his father's bed, yanked the tubes from his father's arm, and then loosened the bindings.

When finished, he proceeded to do the same to the men from his party. Others lay in the same comatose state as well, but Zain didn't have time to help; he didn't know how long it would be until someone would enter the room.

Zain maneuvered back to his father and shook him by the shoulders. When that failed, he slapped his father's cheeks with growing intensity until his father's eyes finally fluttered awake.

"Zain? What's happening?"

"I'm not sure, but we need to go. Now." Zain yanked his father upright.

"Argh." Zain's father put a hand to his forehead.

"The dizziness will pass. You need to move your body. It's the only way to get your blood pumping again."

"Okay. Okay." Zain's father crawled off his bed and noticed the mess on the floor. "Zain! Did you do this?"

"They were going to kill us."

Zain didn't wait for his father's response. Instead, he went to a refrigerator located in the back corner of the holding room, looking for anything to aid the recovery of his men. Surely there must be something. If there had been a drug to make his blood clot to stop his attempted suicide when his party was first betrayed, then there had to be a drug to reactivate the body.

To Zain's good fortune, the refrigerator was carefully organized, and the labels were in readable terms. *Blood clotter. Blood thinner.* Zain read the labels. *Where is.... A ha! Blood inducer.* Inside the transparent pull-out shelf, he found a cluster of syringes already filled with some sort of liquid. *Perfect.*

"What are you doing?"

Zain grabbed as many syringes as he could and returned to his father. "We are getting out of this place."

"Who? What are those?"

"Medicine for the soldiers who came with me."

"You shouldn't have come for me, Zain. I was forced to—"

"We've already talked about this. I don't want to hear about it anymore. What's done is done."

Zain took one syringe and went to the first of his men, Interested Issac. Although he didn't know all the basics of injection, he knew enough to look for a vein. He stuck the needle into Issac's arm and pushed down with his thumb.

"Zain, those jewels are meant to lock away the Twelve."

"The Twelve deserve it." Zain moved onto another of his comrades.

"Why are you of so little faith?"

Zain paused over the arm of Nimble Nyrin. He looked back at his father. "You already know the answer to that." Zain returned his gaze to Nyrin's limp arm. He shook his head and pushed down with his thumb once more. "This isn't the—"

Doors opened.

Zain let go of Nyrin's arm and turned around. Two men in black snakeskin suits entered the facility. *Shit.* Without hesitation, Zain rushed towards them. As Zain put himself between them and his father, one guard said something to the other and left, leaving Zain to face the man alone. *Shit.*

The guard drew his sword. Zain paused two sword lengths away and examined his opponent's footing and posture. Shoulders hunched forward. *A lunge.* Zain stepped backwards as the man swiped forward. His foot hit something. He looked down. *The syringe! That'll have to do.*

Again, the guard lunged, faster than Zain expected, almost as if the suits gave him increased agility. Zain managed to wheel an empty bed in front of him. The sword clanged on the metal arms. Zain rammed the bed into the man, pushing him back slightly. It wasn't much; there was no momentum to help Zain, but it was enough to allow him to grab the syringe. He held it behind his back, hoping that the distraction of the bed veiled his action.

Zain maneuvered around the bed, keeping his focus on the man's body. The man swung downwards. Zain dodged. He punched the bicep of the man's sword arm, causing him to drop the sword. Snaking his arm around the man's neck, Zain crashed his knee into the man's stomach, then injected the serum into the exposed neck. The man wrestled loose, but as soon as he stood up, he wobbled like a drunkard and then collapsed.

"Is he dead?"

Zain spun back around. Interested Issac was sitting upright on his moveable bed. The others Zain injected were awake, too.

"I'm not sure. We need to release the others. Take the syringes and inject them into our men. We need to move."

"Okay."

While the three he had injected so far dealt with the others, Zain scavenged the man's limp body, finding a black keycard similar to the one he had seen used earlier. Shoving it into his pocket, he then hustled over to reclaim his sword. When he turned around, he noticed all the others had been rejuvenated.

"Where will we go?" Giant Garie asked.

"Once we escape the compound, everything should be easier. We can lose them in the streets. Follow me." Zain led the men out of the Blood Chambers and to the elevator door.

Zain swiped the card, opening the door.

"How will we even get that far?"

Zain wished he knew the compound better. He did know, though, that past the throne room there was an exit to the outside streets. He was about to push the button when he remembered his father had spent sixth months here.

"Dad, did you learn of any other exits?"

"There is an entrance in the back. It's underground. Zigarda had me transported through that while I went on excavations to collect the jewels for him."

"Do you remember how to get there?"

"I... I think so." After a brief moment of indecision, Zain's father pushed the button for *Courtyard C.*

"We need weapons," Nimble Nyrin said.

"No time for that. One of the guards escaped. I'm sure he will warn Zigarda."

Their pod shot downwards.

"But if they do try to stop us, how will we defend ourselves?" Nimble Nyrin asked.

"I have a sword." Zain pointed to his hip. "But I think something big happened." Zain crossed his arms over his bloody chest. "Alarms rang earlier. They woke me. Let's hope that means there won't be as many patrolling."

"What do you think it was?" Interested Issac asked.

"It doesn't matter. Nothing does now, besides our escape. We need to contact my uncle and tell him what has happened."

Zain turned to Issac. "That is why every minute counts. While we have a moment, everyone think. We need some place to turn. We need a plan once we make it outside the compound."

The pod stopped. The door opened. Empty courtyards.

"Let's move."

He stepped out into the openness. The same red clouds still hung in the air, keeping him from knowing if it was day or night. He didn't make it more than ten paces when a voice froze him.

"Zain!"

Zain turned around and tilted his head to the voice. A figure in a black snakeskin suit accompanied by guards stood on the second level across the courtyard, and though the visor was down, Zain didn't need to see a face to know Zakk's voice.

Keeping his eyes on his former friend, Zain yelled out to the others. "Move. Now. Follow my father, I'll buy you some time."

"Zain there's no way—"

"Issac, go. This is my fight." As hurried footsteps retreated behind him, the tension in Zain's shoulders eased.

"This is certainly not a fight you will win, Zain." Zakk jumped down from his vantage point.

A flash of silver. Two flashes. Zain stepped to the side of one and ducked under the other one. Then a third came. He batted it down, too focused on the action to see or hear anything else. *A dagger?* Zain's eyes bulged. *Where did the others land?*

"Stop," Zakk said, one hand extended to signal to the guards. "This is between Zain and me. Do not act unless I say so."

Zain let his shoulders sink. He looked behind him, wondering how far his party had progressed, and his heart jumped into his throat. *Dad!* His father lay on the ground with two daggers in his torso, one imbedded in his stomach and one near his heart. Zain began rushing to his father's side. He didn't get far before Zakk was in front of him.

How is that—

"Where do you think you are going? We still have unfinished business."

Peering past Zakk's shoulder, he yelled out to Issac and the others. "Go! Now!"

Zakk drew Viper and pointed it at Zain. He knew the sword well. It had been the weapon Zakk used at every tournament in Gazo's, rightfully named for the split tip at the point of the blade.

One of the guards called out. "Should we go after them? They're getting away."

"They aren't important," Zakk shot back to his comrade. "They have no place to go and no weapons."

Zakk's hubris worked in Zain's favor; it eliminated the others from the equation and would allow his party time to escape. He knew this confrontation was coming; he had known it since he betrayed Zakk before the Trials. Seeing no other possibility, Zain inhaled deeply and drew the sword he had stolen.

"Is this finally the revenge you've wanted?"

"Because of you, I missed the Trials."

"It seems like you were there regardless of my actions."

Zakk spat on the ground between them. "I lowered myself to nothing more than a stowaway."

Zakk lunged forward, faster than Zain anticipated. Although he managed to deflect most of the strike, the sword caught a part of his shirt and tore a seam. *That was close. He's faster. Just like the guard in the Blood Chambers. It must be the suit.*

Zain inched back a few feet. He would need more time to react. To help with this, he moved sideways in a circle, forcing Zakk to do the same to stay aligned with him. All the while, Zain kept an eye on Zakk's body, scanning for the slightest of movements that would force him to react.

Feet forward. Shoulders hunched. Zain shuffled back as Zakk lunged towards him. He deflected the strike and brought his elbow to Zakk's head, sending him sideways to the ground. Unaffected, Zakk used the momentum to roll into a crouching position.

Slowly, Zakk stood. He twisted his neck and let out a slight laugh. "All that time in the jail cell hasn't affected you, Zain. Good." Zakk flipped the sword and swung downwards.

Zain blocked. A little. The force threw him off balance. To avoid losing the grip on his sword, he stepped backwards. Zakk capitalized on Zain's sloppiness and sliced downwards, cutting the skin on Zain's forearm.

Zain shook his head, ignoring the pain. *What kind of suit is this? He's stronger, too. I won't be able to stave him off much longer. Where is everyone?*

He shuffled back a few steps, awarding himself a little distance and readying for another defensive. Zakk charged. Swipe. Block. Slash. Duck. Zain wheeled back. Pain came to his face. Then more to his stomach. Zain hit the ground. *I didn't even see that—*

Zakk didn't allow Zain a moment's rest. Before Zain knew what was happening, Zakk leaped in the air and brought his sword down. With a desperate lurch of his arm, Zain got his sword up just in time to deflect the killing blow.

Anger. Pain. Vengeance. Zakk's eyes held them all. But there was a glint of something else there, something Zain couldn't define. It brought words to his mouth. "Zakk. Stop this."

Zakk buckled, grunting in pain.

Not wanting the opportunity to go to waste, Zain pushed the sword away with his own and then swept Zakk's feet from under him. Zakk crashed heavily to the ground, hand reaching for the throwing knife lodged in his left hamstring.

Two hovercrafts had appeared. Zakk's guards hesitated, then sprang into action. Zain dashed over Zakk to his getaway. Nyrin extended his hand and helped Zain into the hovercraft while it pulled away. His father lay bleeding on the bench, cloth pushed into the wounds.

Zain turned from the scene towards Zakk, not wishing to acknowledge the weakened state of his father. He watched as Zakk pulled the knife out of his hamstring and flung it to the ground, his gaze fixed on Zain and full of ire. Men gathered around him. He shrugged them off and stormed back into the compound.

No one had won.

And Zain believed no one ever would.

CHAPTER FIVE

C-BOT

Zigarda glanced towards the mirror in the room and nodded. Soon after, an old man in a black lab coat entered to join Zigarda and the *thing*. Hydro didn't know what to call it, though it had reverted back to the form of a hideous woman. When the man entered, he didn't say a word, only laid a handheld crystal mirror on the table and then casually strolled towards Hydro. With surprising strength, he tilted Hydro's neck to one side. His eyes widening, Hydro struggled.

"Be still." The old man pushed Hydro's shoulder down and held his neck at an even greater angle, forcing Hydro into compliance.

"Who are you?"

"This is Doctor Cere. He hates Garians just as much as you do."

"Why do you—"

A poke. Multiple pokes.

The man walked to Zigarda's side and laid a syringe on the table, now filled with red, next to the mirror. "Because of how much respect they showed to that blue-haired wench."

"Conseleigh Iycel?"

"I knew her as Lady of Sereya. Before she became conseleigh. But, yes, her. I worked for her at that point. You may have seen this device before?" Dr. Cere held up his hand and wiggled his index finger, drawing attention to the crystal blue ring around his finger. "I invented this. It keeps the body cool. Very useful when foreigners find themselves on planets such as Pyre."

Mouth agape, Hydro looked at the man. *He invented that?* The ingenious device was very popular among the wealthy Acquavans who could then travel to the Pyre nations in comfort.

"What else have you invented?"

"Oh, many things, Hydro Paen. Some you know about...," the man picked up the crystal mirror and showed it to Hydro, "and other things that are one of a kind. My genius, though, like Victor's disfigurement, wasn't accepted by others. We were rejected. Like you. And that is why I believe we will get along rather nicely, for we have an affinity for dejection and being misunderstood when we all want the same goal."

"What is that?"

"To see our projects through to completion. That is what all geniuses do. Tundra Iycel will go down with Eska one way or another. One poison for two lovers. They share the same fate." Dr. Cere walked to stand behind Hydro once more.

"You know about them?"

Lord Zigarda cocked his head. "And you do as well?"

"Before I left the Core, I saw them share an embrace. I never gave it much thought until just now."

"Hydro Paen, you certainly interest me. Good. I love meeting first-hand witnesses. It will prove valuable."

"What do you—" Hydro jerked his neck. "Owh." His neck itched. He rubbed it on his shoulder. "Why did you steal more?"

After returning to Zigarda's side once more, Dr. Cere smiled. "All good things in time, Hydro Paen."

Lord Zigarda laughed. "Every drop we get ensures our success and your compliance." "What do you mean?"

Zigarda took one of the syringes from the table and examined it. He handed it to the woman on his left. "She will be going to Acquava."

"I already told you, I am yours. There is no need for that."

"I beg to differ. She will keep a good eye on your brother for you while you are on your assignment, and if you happen to not cooperate, or if you happen to fail, well..."

Hydro looked from Zigarda to the woman who smirked.

"Understood?"

Face placid, Hydro nodded.

"Good." Zigarda turned to the woman. "You may leave us now. Assemble your things and get ready for a voyage to Acquava. You will go with Genus. Tell the guards to come back in."

"Yes, my lord."

Lord Zigarda waited a moment and stared delightfully at Hydro. "We are going to let you out of those chains now. I hope there will be no problem."

Hydro remained mute. His gaze darted between the two men and then to two black snakeskin-suited guards who entered the room. One undid the cuffs around his feet, and the other removed his manacles.

Hydro stood up, stretched, and massaged his wrists. "When will I get my sword back?"

"Soon. First, we have business to discuss. Follow us." Zigarda turned on his heel and left, Dr. Cere following suit.

For someone so old, Zigarda didn't hobble as much as Hydro expected. Zigarda kept pace with the doctor beside him, walking in front of the two guards who had released Hydro and who shepherded him through the hallways. Even without his sword, he could overpower the guards next to him and probably the man in the lab coat, but he wasn't sure about Zigarda. What did any of that mean, though, when his brother's life would be threatened if he disobeyed?

The alarm he had heard while in the holding chamber had died. Footsteps, like a small militia mobilizing, replaced it. Up ahead, at an intersection, a black man, the same one who Hydro had encountered after being forced out of the abandoned home, stood at the front of twenty-five soldiers. The footsteps ceased.

The man examined Hydro and then switched his gaze to Zigarda and Dr. Cere. "He's left the premises. We have troops assembled to find him."

"What are you doing here? Hunt them down."

"Yes, my lord."

"Who is left?" Dr. Cere asked.

"A few leftovers of his party. His father, too."

"Unfortunate. Kill them all. It no longer matters if they are alive. Take a shifter with you and that woman's blood. It may prove useful."

"Yes, my lord." The soldier turned on his heel and left.

Zigarda continued walking, hands behind his back. Dr. Cere took the opportunity to talk to Zigarda about what they had learned from the soldier who stopped them. Both, Hydro observed, made no attempt to quiet their voices while Hydro trailed behind them, enveloped by the two guards on either side.

"The shifters need a lesson in carelessness. Their barbaric rituals are what allowed this to happen."

"Yes, perhaps. This may be a good opportunity for us to use the woman's blood, though. Things will still go according to plan. Adaptability is key to any success. You know that, Genus."

"If only all leaders thought like you, Victor."

"I'm glad they don't, otherwise—"

A chubby man with curly hair ran up to Zigarda from behind, not stopping until he was had overtaken him. The group stopped.

"My... lord...," the man said, bent over with hands on his knees.

"What is it?"

The man composed himself and flashed his eyes at Hydro. Hydro recognized him instantly. It was Zigarda's advisor.

"I have news."

"I assume you would, otherwise you wouldn't be stopping us. What is it? We are busy."

The advisor took in another gulp of air. "Hown ships have just entered Empora's atmosphere. They are en route."

Zigarda muttered something under his breath and turned back to Hydro. "Well, that certainly didn't take long."

"What should we—"

Zigarda waved off the man. He continued forward to the door at the end of the hallway. "Guards, go with Edwyn. Gather others and start transferring the bodies from the Blood Chambers into Doctor Cere's ship. He will be leaving here shortly after we are finished with this one. If those Hown come here and I'm not back, stall them for as long as you can. Prince Paen, come. Time is of the essence." Zigarda snapped his fingers.

Hydro obeyed, not knowing what else he could do. The oval-shaped door opened, and next thing Hydro knew, he was propelled upwards to the courtyard.

Outside, white light from the poles around the courtyard pushed the red upward to look like clouds. It gave Hydro a clear view of the notorious Web, which looked more like three separate prisons than an estate for a lord. They didn't enter any of the other domes, though; instead, they went towards the black obelisk that cut up into the sky from the courtyard's center, its head vanishing above the crown of clouds.

Hydro gave a curious glance at the two elders in front of him. "You must feel confident that I won't hurt you to send your guards away like that."

Zigarda smirked. "Come now, Prince Paen, we both know those guards wouldn't have made a spell of significance if you actually wanted to do us harm. You've had your chance to strike us down already, but you haven't. No, I think you are intrigued by what I am offering you, and that is why you will not harm us."

Hydro crossed his arms. "I don't have my sword, and you are threatening my brother."

Zigarda chuckled. "Yes, well, there is that, too." Zigarda turned around and placed his hand on a waist-high pedestal. "And the fact that the Hown are now closing in on your position. Tell me, how were you found?"

Beep.

"Scan complete. Identification verified."

Two steels doors pulled back, revealing the innards of the obelisk.

"Conseleigh Iycel and the Commoner saw me."

"That explains it then. Follow me."

The lights in the chamber flicked on one by one, activated by their motion. First it was only the ground floor, but then the lights above activated, and the ones above that, until the room was awash in light. As each level of light activated, Hydro saw the reason this facility was obscenely tall—at its center stood a creature of metal. A machine the size of interplanetary transports.

The construct stood at least four stories tall and had wings like that of a steel butterfly that extended past its head another two stories. Its head contained glass windows for eyes. Large metal arms and legs made its mechanical figure almost human. *What in Abaddon's name...*

"How... how—"

"Is this possible?" Zigarda finished Hydro's question. "It is possible because I have the resources to acquire the parts needed to bring Doctor Cere's brilliance to fruition."

"But... what... what is it?"

"Genus, would you care to explain?"

"I told you, Hydro Paen, some of my inventions are one of a kind. This is one of them. Its name is C-Bot. Made from various alloys, the frame is regular steel, but the extremities of the machine are all made of copious amounts of zircha steel."

"Zircha?" Hydro tore his gaze from the monolithic robot to Dr. Cere. "So it can morph?"

"Yes. It's a polymorphous machine. In this mode, it is a self-functioning combative machine, wielding enough weight and power to crush people into oblivion and turn towns to dust. It can also transform itself into an interplanetary transport vessel, allowing breach of any planet's atmosphere. Finally, it can eject parts of itself, the extremities, which can then morph into personalized hovercrafts and ships for smaller transportation needs."

Hydro's gaze wandered up the height of the machine once more as he realized the intent behind the doctor's words. "You want me to pilot this. There are codes and licenses I would need."

"Of course. All the documents you could ever need have been doctored and uploaded to the C-Bot's mainframe. You will use the left arm for when you travel the planet of Onkh. The right arm for Pyre. The left leg for Agrost. And the right leg can be used for here, if you should need it. Although, I am fairly certain you'll be able to fly on this planet without restrictions."

"Why?" Hydro took another look at the machine, still trying to fathom its workings.

"Because it is already below atmosphere control. The Atmos won't be guiding it to a docking hub at it normally would when the atmosphere has been breached."

"But the other planets, how will I get past the Atmos?"

"Inside the ship is a hologram projector. When you go for identification, stand before it and it will plaster a new face on you and even alter your speech as you are processed."

"It will alter my face?"

"And your voice. Only virtually, of course. You are not a skinchanger, but I had the idea for it while working alongside them here at the Web."

"Where did they come from?"

"You ask too many questions. What you should be most concerned about, Hydro Paen is the jewels you are required to procure."

"You are sending me on a hunt for jewels?" Hydro couldn't control his laughter.

Zigarda shot Hydro a deadly glare. "Not just any jewels, Hydro Paen, godstones."

"What do you mean, godstones?"

"These jewels contain the life force of the Twelve... well, besides Pearl. They are lost souls. And you are to hunt them down." Zigarda paused for a moment, then continued. "A Guardian's Power derives from the gods. When they die, his Power diminishes, and when his Power diminishes, he is finally weak enough to be attacked."

"Why would he have been foolish enough to leave himself so vulnerable?"

"He didn't. The jewels are scattered throughout Gladonus. Normally, we wouldn't be able to trace them, no one would be able to, and if one happened to be stumbled upon, well, then it would merely be a spectacle for the eye. Rather clever on Edwyrd's part. However, I am more so."

Hydro stared at him in disbelief.

"You doubt my prescience? Well, let's just say a man with foresight informed us of events that may happen during Pirini Lilapa."

"Foresight? Like a soothsayer?"

"Of sorts, yes." A smirk spread apart Zigarda's cracked lips.

Hydro spat on the ground. "They never know what is true and what is false. All they give are lies. They shouldn't be—"

"I do not care what issues you have with seers or soothsayers or those who claim to have foresight. What I care about is the retrieval and the destruction of those jewels. And that, Hydro Paen, is where you come into play."

"How?"

"Your blade, Purge. It has already killed one of the Twelve and with it you will destroy the other eleven."

"This machine cannot do that?" Hydro waved his arms at the machine.

"No. It cannot." Dr. Cere reentered the conversation. "Despite its physical prowess, and the ability to transform, it is still only made of zircha, meaning if it broke a jewel, the god inside would still be alive. If your blade, however, sliced through a jewel, then the god inside would die."

"Eska will start to become suspicious when he notices his energy being syphoned."

"That is why you must collect them all before destroying any. And after each jewel is collected, you will report back to me."

Hydro furrowed his brows and crossed his arms over his chest. "How long do I have?"

"Until those Hown soldiers find you or two months, which ever comes first. I assume it shouldn't take longer than that considering the tracker inside the machine."

"Tracker?"

"Yes." Dr. Cere nodded. "Inside C-Bot, on the panel next to the driver's seat, is a radar device giving off locations for each jewel. It is also mobile, making the task of finding them that much easier. After you find each jewel, click the button located on the panel and it will send a signal informing us you have retrieved another jewel." Dr. Cere handed the mirror and the vial of Hydro's blood to Zigarda. "Victor will be using this crystal scry to know your location at all times."

"Crystal scry?"

"I would have expected you to know how this device works."

Hydro shook his head.

Dr. Cere squeezed a slight droplet of blood onto the crystal mirror, causing the surface to ripple out like waves. Eventually, the ripples stilled, dissolving into an image of the crystal mirror.

"It shows what I see?"

"Yes, precisely. Whatever you are looking at, Victor will be able to see as well. It will help inform us of your whereabouts and that you are, indeed, completing your quest."

"I will use this after each jewel you find," Zigarda said. "Call me paranoid, Hydro Paen, but I have little faith. I prefer seeing things with my own eyes. If too much time passes before I see you have retrieved a jewel, I will have the shifter go to your brother. I am rather impatient now that you have ruined my source of youthwater."

Hydro wanted to retort but thought it best not to give into Zigarda's goading. "Eska will become suspicious when he realizes the jewels are being hunted."

"I am unsure how cognizant Eska remains of where the jewels actually are. But even if he did find that his jewels were being hunted, he cannot find you."

"The Hown."

"They only know you are here because of Conseleigh Iycel and the apprentice. If you stop dallying and leave, they will have no idea where you went," Zigarda said.

"How do you know——"

"Because since the incident with your family, I have learned that you remain untraceable. Even by your own brother. This intrigues me. While I know not why this is, when I heard of it, I knew that you would be the perfect individual for this mission."

"You are doing this just for revenge on Eska?"

"Hydro Áylan Paen, you have so very much to learn. While revenge is sweet, it is the Power of the Guardian of the Core that I want."

"Powers that will be syphoned when I destroy the jewels, yes?"

"If it comes to that, sure. But, even so, it is the reimaje on the Guardian's head that is his most prized possession."

"What do you mean, if it comes to that?"

"Alternatives, Hydro Paen. Any successful idea has contingencies. You truly never did listen in your father's council sessions, did you."

Hydro remained silent.

"You will find Purge waiting for you in the cockpit."

Hydro harrumphed and looked away.

"Do not delay. Your brother is counting on you."

"How do I enter it?"

"The ladder is there." Dr. Cere extended a bony finger. "Better get to it. But before you go, one more thing. Take this." He extended a closed fist.

Hydro eyed it cautiously but placed his open hand underneath nonetheless. A capsule the size of one of his knuckles fell into his palm. It was black and unexpectedly heavy.

"Eat this should you get caught by the Hown."

"What is it?"

The doctor thought for a moment, then said, "Consider it your last resort."

"What do you mean?"

"What do you think I mean?" Dr. Cere arched his eyebrows and stared at Hydro.

"A suicide pill? But then——"

"If you get caught, your mission ends anyway. I assume you will want to die before you face the Guardian of the Core. This way you end things on your own terms. Keep it safe. Don't swallow. Make sure you bite into it. Don't chew it unless you have no other option."

Hydro gripped the black capsule between his thumb and index finger and rotated it in front of him, trying to see inside, but the opaque cover didn't allow him to glean anything. He put the pill in a separate pouch attached to his belt.

Exhaling heavily, Hydro left the two men and went over to the ostentatiously tall ladder. He grasped one rung, feeling the cold steel bite into his hand, then began the climb. One hand after the other, endlessly climbing, to a path and a future that remained so unknown.

CHAPTER SIX

HUNTED

The wind howled as Interested Issac drove what remained of Zain's party through the congested city streets of Mendeck. Zain leaned on his father. Applying pressure to the wounds with Nyrin, he tried his best to not let his concern show. It failed.

"Zain, I will be fine... Don't... don't worry." His father managed a smile.

Zain couldn't smile back. Instead, he gave a glance at Nyrin and then back to Issac, who was driving. So far, he had done a good job of avoiding those sure to be pursuing them.

"Zain, we're almost there."

Zain craned his neck, glancing at the hill that led out of the depressed city. *We made—*

Crash.

Not them.

Ahead. The other hovercraft.

The sound split his ears.

The second hovercraft spun around and slammed into a streetlight, but not before being bludgeoned by two other vehicles in the streets. The impact catapulted one of Zain's men from the ship into a nearby light post. He didn't move again.

Issac increased their speed, bypassing the wreck. Zain left his father, stood up, and gripped Issac's shoulder. "Turn around. We need to help."

"We'll be caught."

"Those are our brothers. They need help!"

"Zain, your father," Nyrin shouted from behind.

Zain resisted the urge to look back. "My father's a fighter; he will be fine, but they need our help now."

"I don't agree." Issac continued driving forward.

"I didn't escape Zigarda's compound with my men to see some of them fall into his hands again. I don't care if you agree. Do it. Now." Zain picked up one of the knives they had taken from his father's body and made sure Issac saw its edge.

Grimacing, Issac complied and turned the hovercraft around. As they sped towards the wreckage, Zain scanned ahead. Only two of his men remained on their feet: Giant Garie and Dominating Dominic. Capable fighters, but they wouldn't last long against the barrage of men slowly encroaching on them.

Sirens screamed. Farther up ahead, two more hovercrafts advanced on their position.

We will need to make this fast.

One block away.

Dom wheeled back, caught by a blade. Garie jumped over a handrail to his fallen companion's aid, parried a sword slice, and stabbed the attacker in the chest. Garie locked eyes with Zain. He heaved Dominic onto one shoulder.

"While turning, drift into the stationed car. It'll throw Zigarda's men off balance."

"Zain, that'll leave us vulnerable."

"Not if we're quick." Zain turned back to the two other soldiers who had escaped with him. "Nyrin, Michel, hold my father down and get ready."

The men nodded.

Zain sat in the co-pilot's seat. The scene had changed. Garie had maneuvered himself and Dom to the top of the pile of crashed crafts. And there was a third figure. Helping them. A woman with long black hair. Her clothes looked familiar, as did her frame. Zain frowned. *Is that...*

"Zain?"

Issac's voice brought him back. "Do it. Now."

The hovercraft turned, then drifted. Zain squeezed the metal frame in front of him, locking out his arms, bracing for impact. When it hit, two of Zigarda's soldiers fell from where they climbed.

A groan of pain burst from the back of the hovercraft and Zain looked back to see his father's face contorted in agony.

"Take care of him. I'll be back." Zain hopped over the railing and onto the pile of wrecked hovercrafts.

At the top, he joined in the fray with the other three, immediately putting his sword up to block an attack and then kicking the same man down the wreckage.

"Zain?"

He took the woman's forearm. "Gabrielle?" He turned to the others. "Get in. We need to move now."

Zain helped Garie and Dom across the wreckage and into the hovercraft. Issac sped off as soon as everyone boarded, leaving the incoming onslaught of soldiers behind.

"What happened to Dom? Are you okay?"

"I'm fine, yeah. But I turned around and noticed..." Garie nodded toward Gabrielle who sat across from him in her Gracie's uniform. "I saw her uniform, so I called out to her for help. I... I didn't think she could help, but she did. She killed the man who wounded Dom, and then we went to the top and held them off until you came. I... I don't know what to say..."

"Zanks would be a start," Gabrielle said.

"I don't even know your name," Garie said.

"Gabrielle Ravwey. You are a Gazo's student, I take it?"

"No," Zain broke in. "They are the King's Guard; they traveled with me to get my father." Zain glanced towards his father. Michel and Nyrin had helped sprawl Dominic next to his father on the floor of the hovercraft. Both competed in the race for survival.

Sirens wailed.

Gabrielle went over to Zain's father and pressed her fingers on his forehead. "Zain, your fazer will die. He has a fever now, too. He needs medical attention."

"Zain, where are we going?" Issac asked.

The skirts of the city encompassed them now. The monoliths of buildings that had swallowed them in the city's stomach now gave way to smaller buildings— houses, though hardly deserving of the name. At the beginning of the hill, the city road gave way to a dirt red road. Like a tongue, it led them out of the city's mouth.

"Zain?" Issac repeated the question.

"We already discussed this. We go to Gracie's."

Gabrielle bolted upright and put a hand to her chest. "Gracie's? You are bringing them there?"

"Gabrielle, we have no other choice. The women there are trained. They can take care of my father and Dominic. Please?"

"Zain..." Gabrielle closed her eyes and looked away. "Let me check, okay?"

"Okay."

Gabrielle walked to the edge of the hovercraft, back turned away from him.

The wind howled past, obscuring Gabrielle's voice. As she busied herself with communications, Zain focused on his father on the hovercraft floor. After a few minutes, Gabrielle came back to crouch down beside Zain.

"So?" Zain flashed her a glance.

"It will be okay."

"Good." Zain refocused his attention on his father. "What were you doing there, anyway?"

"Zigarda. He wanted to see me for an interview on how za Trials went."

"Now? It's been months."

"Yes, well, I can't say I expected much more." She laughed and flicked her wrist.

"How did you find us there?" Zain kept one hand steady on his father's neck, feeling for his pulse, and the other on the wound near his heart.

"I heard the crash, and I ran over to see. Zat's when I saw he was in trouble, and Zigarda's men were closing on him." Gabrielle tilted her chin towards Garie. "I don't know why... but I somezing led me zere... like faiz... and I zought maybe zis was my chance to see you again, so I joined za fray."

"Your school; I'm sorry for dragging them into this."

"It will be fine, Zain. Everyzing will be taken care of."

"What do you mean?"

"You. Your father. I will take care of you."

Zain smiled. He looked towards Gabrielle. The wind blew her hair in front of her face, obscuring it. With a gentle hand, Zain pulled back her hair, closed his eyes, and leaned in to kiss her. The kiss went cold and unreciprocated.

"Gabrielle?" He opened his eyes. Shocked eyes of grey and amber stared back into his own. "You're..."

Zain never finished his sentence. Gabrielle butted her head forward, crashing into Zain's. The unexpected move sent Zain backwards, crashing next to where Dom lay. His head rang.

A wail broke through the clouds of raucousness and pandemonium.

Another one reached the same crescendo.

Thuds. Grunts. Steel singing against itself. Zain rubbed a palm on his forehead and shook his head, trying to rid himself of the dizziness.

He blinked.

And blinked again.

The woman, Gabrielle, or whoever this person was, now kneeled on the ground of the hovercraft, arms locked by Garie and Nyrin. Close to her lay a dagger coated in red. She licked her lips. A smile slowly spread across her face that now boiled and oozed in a white puss. The puss seeped over her skin, sinking in, and replacing Gabrielle's face with the face of his father.

"You can't kill your father, can you, Zain?" The man laughed.

The two holding the shifter let go in shock. The shifter took the opportunity and pounced on Zain, grabbing the nearby dagger and bringing it down. The hovercraft jerked. The dagger pierced Zain's upper chest. The shifter lifted it up again and brought it down, but Zain caught his arms. His father looked down on him in anger and rage and lust and passion.

The man fell to the side, tackled by Dominic, who groaned with the effort. He grasped his neck and fell to the floor, eyes staring wide at nothing.

"Aahh," Dominic grasped his neck and fell to the floor.

Metal clinked, wet with red. The shifter reached for it again, but the other two had regained their balance from the sudden jerk and apprehended him once more.

No!

The shifter laughed. "Are you going to kill me now, Son?"

"You're not my father."

"Why sure I am. Look." He laughed and laughed and laughed.

Zain yelled at the clouds above. He found the sword that had been tossed about the hovercraft and plunged it through the man's chest. Blood sprayed his face, but he welcomed it like rain to a parched man. It tasted right. It tasted warm. It tasted like justice.

Zain dropped to his knees, now eye-level with his doppelganger father.

"I may die...," the man coughed blood to the ground, "but the shifters will rise again. We will have our revenge. He said it was time. Ajid volintasey fuan." He tilted his head to the sky and laughed. Slowly, his face changed back to one of pores and boils and crags. His eyes glazed over.

Zain stood. The others released their grip, letting the skin changer fall on its face, joining Dom's lifeless body.

Dad! Where's my dad? Zain pivoted, ignoring the pain starting to swell in his chest. He kneeled over his father's body and shook him.

There wasn't any movement.

"Dad? Dad, wake up." Zain shoved harder.

Still he lay unresponsive.

A fresh red wound at the center of his chest explained why. Zain unbuttoned his father's shirt and put pressure to the wound, trying to stem the bleeding. "Dad! It'll be okay. It'll be okay!"

Nyrin came over and put fingers underneath his father's chin. "Zain, I think he's gone. There's no pulse."

"No. That can't be. That can't be." Zain took his own fingers and felt for a pulse. He felt it. It was there. He knew it was.

"Zain... he's..."

"Don't! He's not. He's not. Dad, you're going to be fine." Zain shook his father's body, trying to rouse him but to no avail.

Someone tugged on his arm.

Zain torqued his neck. "What?"

Giant Garie stepped back. "We're here."

Zain shifted and looked past the large man. Gracie's Academy obscured them in shadows. Around the hovercraft, women were staring at them and every minute more and more were coming out to observe the disruption.

Within moments, an older woman entered the scene. White hair, cropped at the back and only coming to her ears near her face, bespoke her age. Despite the hairstyle, the lack of wrinkles on her skin and the still-vibrant blue eyes made it appear time had forgotten to take its toll on her. A black dress skimmed her figure and a purple scarf around her neck and shoulders flaunted the color of the academy.

She pointed towards Zain. "You. What is your name?"

"Zain Berrese. Ma'am, you have to help. My father, he's been injured. There's been an attack. Shapeshifters have—"

"One thing at a time, Mr. Berrese. What is one of Gazo's doing here?"

"I..." Zain gulped, realizing now that they were never expecting them at all. The endorphins from his body had begun to fade. Pain crept into his upper chest. He put his hand on it, feeling the wet blood, almost forgetting his stab wound. "Aahh..."

"You're injured?"

Zain nodded. "We've been attacked. My father... please help my father."

"Angeline and Perrine, run to the apothecary. Get a stretcher for Mr. Berrese's father and bring back an ointment for wounds."

"Yes, ma'am." Two women bowed and left.

"Ma'am, I'm a friend of Gabrielle Ravwey. Please, I need to speak with her."

The woman stared at him for a moment. "Camila." A girl rushed to the woman's side. "Go get Gabrielle."

The girl darted off, maneuvering through the throng of women.

"I hope you have a good explanation for all of this ruckus, Mr. Berrese."

"I do."

"How many of you are there?"

Zain leaned against the hovercraft for support and placed one hand over his chest as the pain settled deeper and deeper. "Four." Zain shook his head. "Five, ma'am." He grimaced.

Someone tugged Zain's shirt, causing him to turn around.

"What is..." His voice died. Off in the distance, other hovercrafts were approaching. Reinforcements had come, and his explanation would need to get a whole lot better.

CHAPTER SEVEN

BLIND FAITH

The flower she spun between the tips of her fingers hadn't begun to wilt—it had only been two days. But it would. Like anything that didn't receive the proper attention, it would die. A shame, too. It was a pretty flower from a man Gabrielle had fallen for while playing the game of her expertise, the one Gracie's trained its students for—manipulation. It wasn't just swords that won battles. Words, swagger, and confidence also won battles, and Gabrielle had all of them. That was why she was still undefeated.

But that man had nearly beaten her, had nearly usurped her barriers, until he faltered at the Trial's climax when she needed him most. A different man, though, had demolished her barriers, had risked his own life to save hers, yet there had been no word from him. *Why are men so confusing?*

A knock came at her door.

Eirek? Does he bring word of Zain already? Just the day before, he had visited her, claiming the contestants of the Trials were in trouble, but so far, Gabrielle had experienced nothing. He had told her he would visit Zain in Mendeck, so perhaps it was him again, back with information.

She set the flower down on the couch and then went to open the door. A younger student, Camila, stared back at her, panting, hair frazzled as if she had just run up all four flights of steps to reach her.

"Yes? Is somezing za matter?"

"The headmistress requests your presence out front."

Gabrielle creased her brow. "Why?"

"Visitors. For you."

Gabrielle stepped forward. "Visitors? Who?"

The girl retreated a little. "A man and three others. I think one of their names is Zain or something like that."

Zain? Gabrielle pushed aside the girl and left her room. *After all this time? Could it be true?* She hurried down the steps and out into the eerily vacant hallway. She glanced at her telecommunicator. *Why isn't anyone in class?*

When she passed through the revolving doors of Gracie's lobby, she halted, stunned at the mass of women gathered outside. It seemed that everyone from the school was here. She pushed her way through the crowd at first, but when people recognized it was her, they moved out of her way willingly.

"... certain of this, Mr. Berrese?"

Upon hearing the voice of Headmistress Carla Sonetta, Gabrielle strained her ears, trying her best to ignore the susurrus of students around her. Gracie's Academy totaled two thousand students. Not a large academy by any means, but it was the best one. They didn't accept just anyone.

"As much as I can be. My father..."

"Zigarda's men come... need..."

"Put me in a situation that is quite delicate."

"I am sorry for that, but—"

"Zain!" Gabrielle finished bypassing the crowd of students. She grabbed his shoulders. Her eyes widened. Breaths caught in her throat. Blood soaked his outfit and oozed through gauze that had been tapped to his chest. She smoothed her hands over his wounds, feeling him tense up as she did so. She looked into his eyes, finding only flecks of relief amongst the apprehension and anxiety that ate away at him and added weight to his breaths. "Zain, what happened?"

Carla Sonetta crossed her arms and gave both of them a piercing gaze. "Your friend puts this Academy in danger. He make claims about shapeshifters and godstones and plans to lock up the Twelve."

Gabrielle did a double take at the unusual vocabulary that came out of the headmistress's mouth. *What is going on?*

"Miss Sonetta, Gabrielle, I... I don't... there is no time to talk now, but I have been to Abaddon and back today, and I swear I am not lying."

Lady Sonetta scoffed at the comment. "We all know Gazo's students don't pray to anything."

"Enough of your prayer bullshit... that doesn't mean I'm any less truthful."

"Prayer is a confirma—"

Gabrielle touched Carla's shoulder, and she stopped. "He may not believe in our ways, Lady Sonetta, but I believe him. He wouldn't lie."

The headmistress faced Gabrielle, eyebrow raised with the same quizzical look Gabrielle had come to know well. It was a long look of steady examination. To ease the other woman's tension, Gabrielle put a hand to her forehead, hoping the initiation of the Old Prayer would quell her suspicion. Her headmistress put a hand to her forehead as well, and together they said the prayer.

After, Carla Sonetta turned to Zain and his men. "Get off the hovercraft and get behind us."

They complied, and moments later, four hovercrafts carrying five soldiers each reached their doorstep. Gabrielle recognized one—Zakk Shiren.

What is he doing? Is he working for Zigarda now?

"Headmistress Carla Sonetta, my name is—"

"I know your face. I just don't understand why you're here... with *them*."

If Zakk was irritated by the headmistress's interruption, he hid it well and continued in a polite manner. "It seems that some men that were being held in our custody have escaped into your Academy."

"And of what, may I ask, are these men guilty?"

"Conspiracy against Lord Victor Zigarda. They will be tried by the lord himself."

"Hmmm," Carla hummed. "I have heard something different." She walked forward and put a hand on her hip.

"Whatever he has told you is a lie, I can assure you. Look at his neck, do you see that scar?"

She turned around and squinted towards Zain. "Yes, what of it?"

"I gave him that—"

"Liar!"

She shot up her hand, motioning for Zain to remain silent. "Continue."

"As I was saying, I only barely managed to hold Zain back as he tried to attack Lord Zigarda months prior. Since then, he has been awaiting our sentencing since, which was to be given tomorrow."

"How... *inconvenient.*"

"Yes. Very. Hand him over and no harm shall come to the school."

"And if we don't?" The hand on her hip slid down to her sword handle.

Zakk noticed the move but didn't react. "If you don't, Gracie's will be stripped of its funding. All of these girls you have taken in will be forced to return home, no longer being eligible for temporary residency in Empora."

"Your words are empty, Mr. Shiren. Lord Zigarda controls nothing of our funding and seeing as we have the winner of the latest weapons tournament in our midst, one even your old school has failed to win, I doubt the senate will see us as any sort of failure. No, Mr. Shiren, our school will very much remain open." She walked forward another step.

"I will not let you insult me or Lord Zigarda." Zakk's hand moved to the grip of his sword.

"Are you threatening us?" Carla Sonetta inclined her head and drew her hand upward in a pointed finger.

Gabrielle knew the signal. Everyone in the crowd who was able would now have their hands on their hilt. Gabrielle itched to hold hers, but she had left it in her room.

"Look around you, Mr. Shiren, what hopes do you have of winning? The odds are against you."

Zakk didn't betray any drop in confidence. On the contrary, he rebuked the headmistress's words. "You are really going to let even your young ones die? I thought Gracie's was more *decent* than that."

"And what hopes do your twenty men have against our school of two-thousand?"

"*Twenty-five men,*" Zakk corrected. "Of high caliber. I trained them myself. I can only count six for you, Lady Sonetta. Half of your women haven't even reached puberty. The other quarter I doubt can hold a sword, and the last quarter, well, I highly doubt they are as skilled as you hope. Are they all ready for war?" Zakk withdrew his sword, the two tips at the top gleaming like a snake's tongue.

Carla remained silent at the counter. After a moment's pause, with hands behind her back and an ever-watchful eye kept upon Zakk, she paced in front of him. "Tell me, how confident are you in your sword skills, Mr. Shiren?"

"Ask the man behind you."

She waved her hand. "I do not care what he thinks. I care about what you think."

"I have yet to face a challenge. I am Zigarda's lead soldier. I train the others."

"Confident then?"

"Yes." Zakk nodded.

"Let's settle this one-on-one then." Carla stopped in front of Zakk and drew her sword.

Zakk chortled. "You?"

"No. I am nearing seventy now. I admit, I wouldn't be much of an adversary for you. A different story in my younger years."

"Then Zain?"

"No."

"Then who?"

Carla turned around and pointed the sword. "Gabrielle."

Gabrielle jumped. Everyone behind her clapped. She gulped.

Zain stepped past Gabrielle. "What are you doing? This is my fight. Gabrielle doesn't need to—"

"Mr. Berrese, you may say the words, but you do not mean them. If this was truly your fight, you wouldn't have led these men here to our doorstep. And your story intrigues me. I want to hear more. I don't trust what would happen to you should Zakk lose."

"You don't think I am a man of my word?"

"No, I do not. Do not take it personally, either of you." She pivoted her gaze between Zakk and Zain. "I believe no man from Gazo's. It will be Gabrielle, Mr. Shiren. You can accept or reject the offer. Which will it be?"

A cheer rose around Gabrielle. Hands pushed her forward blindly, oblivious to the stakes of this contest. A tournament had rules and regulations, and although injury was possible, it was highly unlikely per the regulations each combatant had to follow in the scoring system. But the faith Lady Sonetta showed her only strengthened her own. She stepped forward, past Zain, ready to accept the extended sword.

Zain grabbed her shoulder. "You can't do this. This is my mess."

She smiled. "Zis *is* your mess. But you helped me out of my mess once upon a time. Now it's my turn to help you." She removed his hand from her shoulder and walked away.

"Gabrielle, stop."

"What?"

Zain pulled her close and whispered in her ear. "He's wounded on his left side, expect him to keep more of his weight on his right."

Gabrielle nodded and tried to leave, but he held her back once more. "Also, the suit Zakk's wearing, the suit all of them are wearing, I don't know how it does it, but it increases their speed and strength."

Turning slightly, she gave a furtive glance to Zakk, surveying his suit of black snakeskin. *Interesting.* She turned back to Zain and squeezed his hand. "Zank you." She kissed his cheek and then left him to stand beside Carla Sonetta.

"Do you accept?" Carla asked.

Zakk's smirk had creased to nothing but a flat line. A furrow had formed in his brow as he fixated on Gabrielle, surely assessing all the possible outcomes. They had never faced one another, but they knew each other through the winner's circles at tournaments. Neither of them looked behind at those they championed, already fully cognizant of the stakes of this duel.

Zakk clicked his tongue and crossed his arms over his chest. "What is the contest?"

"You two, alone, with no help from anyone. No wards. No Power. Only skill. The first to yield loses. If you win, Mr. Shiren, you will leave our ladies alone and take Zain Berrese and his company back to Mendeck. If you lose, you will leave here with your men, and you will never return to threaten us again. If Zigarda wants to keep his title as the longest reigning lord, I suspect he will agree."

Mouth still closed, Zakk moved his tongue across his front teeth. "Fine. Have it your way. It makes no difference."

"Cockiness breeds over-confidence, Mr. Shiren; it will corrupt you. Someday you may see the light, assuming you survive this first..." Carla turned to Gabrielle. "Are you ready?"

"I don't have my weapon here. It is in my room."

"Take mine. I have been meaning to give it to you, anyway. Now is the perfect time."

"Headmistress... I... I... can't..."

"You must. You have earned this blade, Gabrielle. No one else can say they have won a weapons tournament on the Core. No one else can say they are undefeated. And no one else has taken to our beliefs and supplication like you have. Whether you know it or not, you have shaped this school." She extended her hands, offering the sword fully.

Gabrielle took the rapier in both her hands. She tested the weight with a few practice thrusts. It was top heavier than the sword she lost in the fourth trial, but it would do. It had to do. In truth, it was never the sword that was a part of her, as much as it was the dagger she kept in the garter around her leg. She never removed that. Ever.

After dispelling any nervousness with a deep exhale, she stepped forward into the unencumbered space meant for her and Zakk. *If he is anyzing like Zain, it will not be too difficult. But if zat armor of his really does improve his speed, zis may be more interesting.* She scanned his footing. *Right foot first. He's left handed.* She then scanned the ground, counting paces. *Five.* If this was a regular duel, it would've been fine, but Gabrielle retreated three more; she would need the extra distance to respond if Zain's warning held truth.

Gabrielle stabbed the ground with her rapier. Hands clasped on the hilt, she bowed before it and repeated the traditional Gracie's prayer to herself, concluding with, "Ancients, please let me win to keep zose I care for safe. Ancients, to zis I pray."

"No amount of praying will help you. Zain and I have unfinished business."

She opened her eyes, stood, and drew the rapier out of the ground. She blew a lock of hair out of her eye. "You Gazo's brutes are all za same. You need manners in decency. In time you will see. As for Zain, he still has unfinished business wiz us." She tucked her loose hair behind her ears and stepped forward with her left foot in front. Now she was ready.

Carla Sonetta stepped in between both of them, arms raised. She exchanged glances with both. "The contest ends when the other declares they are bested, is this understood?"

Gabrielle nodded her head; Zakk mimicked her.

"Very well. You may begin." Carla Sonetta stepped away, leaving just the two of them.

And just as with any duel, Gabrielle forgot about the others watching. It kept her focused. Ready. Alive.

The wind blew. She waited. She would let Zakk strike first in order to gauge his speed. He didn't move from his position. *He's not as careless as Zain. Interesting.*

"What's wrong, are you afraid to lose?" Gabrielle smirked and twirled her sword.

Zakk chuckled. "I'm simply savoring the moment before I defeat the undefeated Gabrielle Ravwey." Zakk bent his neck to one side, then the other.

"You men are all za same. Talk but no action."

"You'll see. I'm different."

"Zen show me." Gabrielle didn't let her eyes close.

Zakk rushed her, sword in front like a lance. The extra paces let Gabrielle prepare. She parried, swiping his sword to the left. Momentum carried his sword overhead, and Gabrielle raised her right shoulder to block. Her knees bent. She kept her sword above her, resisting Zakk's strength. She tried not to frown. *Zain was right.* When she couldn't hold the stalemate any longer, she jumped back two paces.

Zakk advanced.

Steel sung, chorused by grunts of determination. Compared to others she had faced, he certainly was faster. Arm fully extended, keeping the rapier at ninety degrees, she held back the celerity of his strikes by keeping him at a distance. It was easy enough to parry each incoming attack and then lash out with a flick of her wrist. But she couldn't maintain this forever. Each blow she parried sent ripples down her forearm, and her shoulder was starting to ache.

Duck. Parry. Strike. Strike. Block.

The two circled each other in rounds of offensive and defensive bursts.

"You're tiring."

She was, but she didn't dare admit it. "I'm simply enjoying watching you zink you can win." She returned his smirk.

The line of Zakk's face flattened. He lashed forward. Gabrielle reacted. He pushed her sword aside and surged into her, shoving a shoulder into her chest. She fell back two steps, but maintained her balance. He swung down at her; she rolled to the right and sliced at his left thigh. It connected, tearing through the snakeskin.

Zakk's knee buckled, but he spun around on the momentum and swung outward and upward. This caught Gabrielle by surprise, and she barely had time to protect her neck. The movement resulted in a sloppy and awkward grip, causing Gabrielle to keep her grip on the sword only thanks to the inner guard.

Zakk pushed himself to his right foot and lunged forward. Gabrielle barely blocked. Her grip weakened. She spun around, buying herself time. She repositioned her grip with two hands and brought her sword upwards to meet Zakk's. The collision rebounded her to the ground on all fours. The forceful impact broke her grip. The sword skidded away from her. She reached for her dagger, but before she could seize it, Zakk kicked her stomach.

She spun onto her back. Her back arched, and she inhaled deeply. She scrambled back to all fours, trying to reach her sword. Zakk followed her. Another blow to her ribs forced her onto her back once again. With one arm, she held her stomach. Zakk stood above her now, sword to her face. She felt the two tips of his blade touch her lips. She had never tasted steel like that before. She didn't like it.

"Say you're finished."

Gabrielle breathed heavily; she closed her eyes. *Ancients please...*

"Say you're finished." Zakk shoved the tip of his sword farther into her lips.

While focusing on Zakk, she slid her other hand down her side. "Never."

Zakk chuckled. "Suit yourself. Consider this duel over." Zakk raised his sword and plunged it downward.

Gabrielle pulled the dagger from her garter and brought it to her face, just in front of her nose. She was fast. She blocked the attack.

Almost.

When the sword came down, Gabrielle's dagger caught it in between the tips of his blades. But with her weakened arms, it only slowed the attack. It couldn't stop it.

Her eyes erupted in pain. They teared. Or bled. She couldn't tell. The world no longer appeared around her. Skies became shadows. Vision became visceral. Pain became present. Endorphins empowered her to persevere.

She kicked her leg upward. Zakk moaned. She had found her mark. Next to her, a thud. Something brushed against her legs. Everything was dark now. Dark like night. She pushed herself up and took two paces. Instinct, faith, and muscle memory. She felt for the braids of his hair. *There!* She pulled back on his hair and, with practiced precision, brought her dagger to his neck.

"Gabrielle!"

Carla's shout jerked Gabrielle's arm upwards as she halted her movement, but the blade still broke the skin. She felt blood, but only a trickle.

"Gabrielle!"

She twirled her head. *Why can't I see?*

"You don't need to do this."

Gabrielle exhaled. Her endorphins ebbed. *Why can't I see? I need to go. I need to leave.* She brought the dagger back to his throat, tip prickling his skin in the right spot this time. "Do you forfeit?"

Zakk struggled.

Gabrielle pulled the hair back harder and pushed her foot into his left hamstring. Zakk grunted.

"Do you forfeit?" She pressed the dagger deeper into his neck. It would take so little to end his life.

No response.

"Do you forfeit?" She shifted the dagger across his neck, let him feel the edge.

"Yes... yes. I'm done."

Gabrielle stopped and shoved his face down. *Why can't I see?* She stepped around the shadow of his body. She didn't know where she wandered, but she let her feet take her. Her cheeks became wet. Maybe they already were, and she just hadn't noticed it. A pair of arms took her in and cradled her in their warmth. Her head pressed against someone's chest. She whimpered. *Why can't I see?*

CHAPTER EIGHT

A STORY TO TELL

A nxiety and apprehension ate away at Zain as he watched the events unfold before him. , As Zakk's sword had descended, Zain had tried to push his way through the crowd, but Carla Sonetta had stopped him from interfering. And now he stood stoic with shock, unsure what course of action he should take. The last thing he had seen was a blend of blood and tears blemishing her cheeks. Now she was hidden from view by a circle of academy women. Zain glanced at Zakk, who still knelt, his fingers tracing the line of wet blood just underneath his chin, lost in the reality of his own defeat.

"You forfeited. Take your soldiers and leave. Never bother us again."

The headmistress's voice pulled him from his thoughts. Face scrunched, Zakk spat on the ground and pushed himself up from his left knee. He turned around and walked away, not sparing another glance at his adversaries. "We leave."

"But Zigarda wants him dead." One of the soldiers pointed a knife towards Zain. Zakk offered no response.

"It seems Zigarda will have to claim his life another day." Carla called back from her group of women.

"To Abaddon with that." The man ran forward and threw two daggers when in range. The first went into Zain's ribcage. Grunting, he stumbled backwards and dropped to his knees. The other came for his face. Nyrin batted it down and stepped in front of Zain. Down on all fours, Zain yanked the dagger from his ribcage and threw it to the ground.

The sea of women drew their steel.

Zakk's men did the same.

Zakk cocked his head but made no move to join his party. Up and down, his shoulders went. He spun around and skulked past his soldiers to the outlier in front. Before the man had time to react, Zakk brought his sword against the man's neck in one fluid slice. The body collapsed, and the head rolled on the ground, stopping at a point halfway between him and Zain.

Zakk turned back to his troops. "Does anybody else feel like disobeying orders?" He pointed his sword at all of them.

Every soldier who had drawn a sword now returned it to its sheath.

"We leave. Now. Zain will get to keep what pitiful life he still has." Zakk took one last look at Zain before he maneuvered past his troops and boarded a hovercraft. His men followed, and as they disappeared into the horizon, Zain heard the swords behind him return to their sheaths.

Carla Sonetta turned around. "Melody..."

"Yes, Headmistresses?" A girl called.

"Take Mr. Berrese here to the apothecary and tell the senior adored to report to my office with her tools and medicine. The rest of you, go back to your rooms. Classes are canceled."

With the help of Issac and Garie, Zain got to his feet.

"What about Gabrie—"

"She is going to be treated privately with me. I suggest you deal with your own wounds in the meantime." She inclined her head towards his ravaged chest. "And your father—"

"Dad. Where is he?"

"In the apothecary. Exactly where I said he would be after we took him from the hovercraft. Now, go."

Zain spared a glance at Gabrielle, who still cried into the shoulders of her headmistress.

"This way, sir," said a quiet, mousy girl in her teens.

Zain followed her, Issac, Nyrin and Garie at his side.

As they walked through the halls of the academy, Garie said, "Zain, you know your dad is—"

Issac grabbed Garie's arm and shook his head, ceasing his comrade's comment.

Zain halted. "My dad is what?"

Garie blinked and stumbled for words before finally saying, "Is family. Like Dom was. I hope he's healed."

"I'm sorry about Dom. He saved my—"

"Melody, what are they doing here? Where are you taking them?"

Zain twisted his head. A pair of young girls stood in front of their guide. One crossed her arms over her chest and the look on her face was hostile. Zain heard murmurs from other girls and women in the hallway as they watched the confrontation unfold.

"Headmistress Sonetta wanted me to guide them to the apothecary."

"They don't deserve to be here." The girl flicked her eyes from Melody to Zain.

"That is for the headmistress to decide, Malysen."

Malysen maneuvered around Melody and came straight to Zain. She poked a finger into his chest. "Miss Gabrielle got hurt because of you. Why did you come here?"

"I..." Zain gulped.

"Why don't you leave and go back to where you belong? This is a place for *decent* people, not Gazo's people."

An older woman ended the short chastisement by taking the girl's hand and leading her away. "Come on, Malysen. They aren't worth it."

Melody turned around. "I'm sorry about that, sir."

Zain's heart prickled the same as his skin. Could he do anything right? His lead had caused men to die in Mendeck. His lead caused Dominic's death. And by his lead, Gabrielle, Gracie's star student—the symbol of the school—was now hurt, perhaps blinded.

Zain swallowed. "I should be the one who is sorry."

Melody shook her head. "No. We of Gracie's should be more decent than that. We preach forgiveness here, although it can be difficult at times to do so. Follow me, we are almost there."

Zain obliged and was led farther into the academy. Stares and whispers followed him and his companions, haunting every step taken in this foreign haven.

Melody left after transferring Zain's party into the care of two middle-aged adored.

The first, a short blonde woman, didn't bother to hide her reaction to the wounds in Zain's torso. Her eyes went wide as she said, "Dear, we must get you looked at immediately. Come. Come."

The second adored dragged Zain by the hand to an apothecary bed. He sat upright, his feet dangling off the side, just barely touching the floor. Both adored put on gloves and worked in tandem to dress his wounds with anesthetics.

Zain grimaced at the sting, his breath hissing through clenched teeth.

The blonde continued dabbing his chest with an antiseptic towel. "Yes, dear. That is to make sure the cut is cleaned. We don't want it getting infected. We're going to stitch it up now."

"When can the stitches be removed?"

The second adored pushed her long brown hair over her shoulder and threaded a needle with suture. "No need. These are absorbable sutures. They will dissolve on their own as the body heals." She poked his chest and started threading the needle and suture through his skin. When she finished, she leaned back. "There, good as new. Your name?"

"Zain Berrese."

"Berrese, you said?" The brunette arched her eyebrows.

"Yes."

"And it's your father in the other room?"

"Yes. Where is he?"

"And another one, correct?" Issac asked.

"Yes, both are there." The blonde answered. "We need to know what is to be done with them. Come."

The adored led them to the bodies. Each occupied a bed. They were dressed in white elastic garments that stretched to be suitable for any size person. There was no evidence of the smears and spatters of blood Zain had last seen on them.

Strolling around to one side of Zain's father, she glanced at a tablet and put it down on a small desk beside her. "What do you want done with your father's body?"

"What do you mean? What else can be done for them?" Zain asked.

"Well, nothing, besides figuring out how to deal with their bodies. They were both dead upon arrival here."

Zain's eyes bulged. He shook his head, a roar in his ears. "What do you mean, dead? My father isn't dead." Zain's gaze shot to his father, scanning him up and down. He was breathing. Zain saw it. It was barely noticeable, but it was there.

"Unless you and I have different definitions of what life is, Mr. Berrese, your father is dead."

"Dead?"

"Dead as in, no longer alive. No breathing. No pulse. Nothing."

"Noth—"

"Take his hand in your own if you don't believe us."

Zain gulped. He stepped forward. Eyes fought back tears. "Dad?" He whispered. He reached out a hand, but then stopped, his fingers hovering over his father's. "I can't."

"Then here." The blonde adored came alongside him and gently pushed his hand together with his father's.

Cold.

Deathly cold.

"No. No. No. No." Zain shook his head.

A hand came to his shoulder. "I'm sorry for your loss, Mr. Berrese."

Zain crashed against the bed, his body draping over his father's, wanting nothing more than to transfer his warmth to his father. "There must be something you can do."

The brunette adored chuckled. "For death? You have wishful thinking, Mr. Berrese."

"Zain." Another hand came to his shoulder.

Zain twisted his body. "Issac, did you know?"

"Zain, we've tried to tell you, but you wouldn't listen."

"I..." Zain gulped as his words threatened to choke him.

"What can be done for the bodies?" Issac asked.

"Many things. What would you like done?"

"Is there a crematory here?"

"There is."

"Perhaps it's best we collect their ashes."

"If that's what you—"

"No." Swiping at the tears on his face, Zain forced himself off his father. "No. How long can you preserve the bodies?"

"It depends on the alchemy used. Certain combinations of ointments are more effective than others. Given the supplies we have on hand, at least a few months, I would say."

"Can you do that?"

"You don't want to bury them immediately?"

Zain shook his head. "Not here."

"Zain, what are you doing?" Issac asked, taking half a step toward Zain before hesitating.

"Giving my father the proper burial he needs."

"In an ideal world we could, but Zigarda is hunting us. When Zakk returns and admits failure, who knows what else Zigarda will do to get to us. The bodies will be a burden we can't afford to carry."

"Do what you want for Dom, you knew him best, but my father—"

The brunette adored cleared her throat. "Mr. Berrese, there is another thing we can do that may be of interest to you."

The blonde adored raised an eyebrow as she looked at her colleague.

Zain cocked his head. "Tell me."

The brunette smiled and glanced nervously down at her clipboard. "Well, excuse me if I am being overly presumptuous here, but your father, he is *the* Berrese, correct? As in Berrese Jewelers?"

Zain nodded slowly.

"I... well, I thought as much. Everyone knows the cuts of his stones. My husband bought me a Berrese for our wedding a decade ago." She flashed a cut diamond on her hand, the bracelets on her wrist jingling as she did so. "Truly, I am sorry for your loss, Mr. Berrese, but I think I may know of a way to honor him best."

Zain arched an eyebrow. "And that is?"

She pointed the clipboard at Issac. "As your friend said, cremation, but not just any cremation. We would take his ashes and turn them into a jewel. The process is called *cremain*."

Zain frowned. "A jewel? You can do that?"

The blonde adored smiled. "Janice, brilliant idea."

Janice continued, "Many things are possible for those who have studied the adored arts. It's a relatively new method of cremation here, but I believe this is an appropriate situation for it."

"What kind of jewel would it be? How much does it cost?"

"I will have to discuss that with Headmistress Sonetta and Cynthia, our supervisor, but if that option is available, would you like it?"

"Yes," Zain said.

"Very well then. And for the other body?"

"Normal cremation will be fine," Issac said.

Janice nodded. "Hilary and I will begin filling out the paperwork and notify the headmistress of your intent. You all can stay here and pay your final respects if you wish."

The two women left. A hand came to Zain's shoulder. "Zain..."

Zain shook his head. "It... it doesn't matter, Issac. With everything that's happened, I must have not been able to comprehend what you were trying to say." He looked down at the still, silent faces of Dominic and his father. *Two more men lost. How many more will die because of me?* Zain sighed.

"Don't worry about them. They are in a better place now." A second hand squeezed Zain's shoulder as Nyrin joined him. "If you hadn't acted as you did, we would still be in those Blood Chambers."

"Thanks, Nyrin. Issac. Garie." Zain turned to all of them. "Let's just...," Zain paused, "let's just take a moment to show our respect."

Zain clasped his hands together and bowed his head. The others followed suit. He closed his eyes, taking a moment to remember the fallen who had already given their lives for his cause: Dom, Quiet Quint, Broadened Barry, Gerald, his father. When he opened his eyes, he took his father's hand one last time and held it as the cold transferred to his own fingertips.

"Let's remember to appreciate what we have. The dead would not wish us to dwell on what has been lost."

"Even if that's family?"

"Dom was family, too. We are all family," Garie said. "Family sticks together. We are there for one another."

Zain felt a knot of shame form in his throat. Had he been there for his family? For any of them? Or had they only been there for him? "We should leave. There's nothing else that can be done here." Zain turned on his heel and exited the apothecary.

"Zain? What's the matter?" Issac hurried after him. "That was abrupt."

Zain shook his head and kept walking. "It's nothing, Issac. I need to see how Gabrielle is doing and speak with Carla Sonetta."

"I'll come with you."

"Okay." Zain slowed his pace as he realized he didn't know where the headmistress's office was. To his fortune, Janice appeared from another room in the apothecary. "Excuse me," Zain called.

She turned and smiled. "Mr. Berrese. We just finished the paperwork. I'm going to deliver it now."

"To Carla Sonetta?"

"Yes."

"I need to speak with her as well."

"Follow me."

Zain followed the adored as she led him back the way he had come and at last down to a circular lobby. She rapped on the open door of an austere, large office at the rear of the lobby. Within, the headmistress glanced up, her gaze narrowing slightly as she saw Zain. "Yes, Mr. Berrese?"

"We need to talk. I... how is Gabrielle?"

The headmistress's gaze shifted to the adored and Zain's men. "I believe we do need to talk, Mr. Berrese. But alone. The others can wait in the lobby. I'll call for someone to take them to the guest quarters."

Zain turned around. "I'll see you guys later, okay?" The three men nodded.

"We'll be waiting," Issac said.

Zain faced the headmistress once more and entered the office, seeing now that Gabrielle lay on a couch across the room. Carla Sonetta, Janice, and another adored stood over her, mostly obscuring her from view. Zain closed the door behind him, ready to face the repercussions of his actions.

"Gabrielle?" Zain choked out the words, unsure if she would even want to hear his voice anymore.

"Zain?" She shifted at his voice. "Is that you?"

The three women parted to allow Zain access to Gabrielle. He moved to her left side and sat on the arm of the couch. The other adored sat alongside Gabrielle, while Carla Sonetta and Janice stood.

Zain put his hand on Gabrielle's. "Yes, it is. How are..." Zain swallowed hard as she turned her face to him, giving him a full look at the damage. Gone were the brilliant blue irises, replaced with clouds of grey and ruptured red veins. "...you?" he forced himself to finish the question.

"I... I..." She couldn't complete her sentence as more tears came.

"You musn't cry Gabrielle. I know it is difficult, but crying vill only negate ze effectiveness of ze ointment."

Gabrielle sniffled and tried to compose herself. "I'm sorry, Adored Blois."

"Cynthia, dear. Please. In a time like zis, zere is no need for formalities."

Gabrielle sniffled and moved a finger to her cheek.

Cynthia grabbed her finger before she could touch her eye. "Remember, ve must let ze ointment do its work."

Gabrielle winced.

"Mr. Berrese, it's best if you follow me and let Cynthia work with Gabrielle," Carla said. "Come along." She nodded toward an adjacent room, then withdrew, Janice following behind her.

Gabrielle squeezed Zain's hand before he left, but he couldn't find any words for her. He went into the inner office and closed the door behind him.

Carla Sonetta had sat in a chair behind a mahogany desk. Painted on the wall behind her was a long stream of words in a flowing script that read like a prayer. It ended with the words, *"Ancients, to this we pray."* Another wall held a trophy case brimming with plaques and awards won at past tournaments.

She set a tablet on the desk and looked at Zain. "Janice tells me you'd like your father cremated into a jewel. Is that correct?"

Zain nodded. "If it is possible."

"I don't see why it wouldn't be possible. Nothing is impossible, isn't that a saying you Gazo's men always repeat?"

Zain stood upright, hands clasped behind his back. "That's because it's true."

"I offered the suggestion, Headmistress." Janice bowed her head. "After learning that this was *the* Berrese from Berrese Jewelers."

"Yes. It would certainly be most fitting for your father. Wouldn't it?" Carla Sonetta crossed her arms. "Ashes to ashes as our faith says." She leaned forward. "But *you* don't believe in our faith. You're a lost soul. All you have managed to do is sow discord and your actions have now caused Gabrielle to lose her vision. Do you understand that?" Her face grew stern and her voice harsh. "She will never be able to see again. And it's because of you."

Zain swallowed and tried not to show his discomfort. *A lost soul?* Was he really so hopeless? As she continued her diatribe, each sentence struck his chest harder than the last. What could he say that would make things better? There was nothing he could say. He knew that. Words were water, anyway. Guardian Eska had taught him that, had tested that during his Trials. But Zain needed some way of showing the headmistress that he wasn't completely lost. That he wasn't beyond redemption. And then he remembered Melody's words in the hallway.

"Forgiveness."

"What was that?"

"Your faith preaches forgiveness, doesn't it?" Cautiously, Zain looked at Carla Sonetta. Though still stern, her face had lost its sharpest edges. "It's about being decent. And, well, perhaps I have never learned because I have never been given the opportunity to be as decent as the women at Gracie's. But maybe you could forgive me and teach me what it's like to have faith?"

Carla Sonetta leaned back in her chair, her posture suddenly stiffening. She opened her mouth, closed it again, then finally cleared her throat before speaking.

"Well... I must say that is rather unexpected." She glanced at Janice, who had remained silent beside the desk, then back to Zain. "Do you mean the words you say?"

Zain nodded. "Yes," he confirmed.

"Then let it be so. Janice, you may proceed with the cremain process for Mr. Berrese's father. One act of good faith deserves another."

"Very well, Headmistress." She curtsied and left.

When the door closed, Carla Sonetta beamed. "Where do we begin?"

"I've never really known how to pray."

Carla Sonetta cocked her head. "Well, I suppose that is an acceptable place to start, considering the circumstances in the other room. Very well." She stood up from her desk and maneuvered around it to stand in front of Zain.

"What do I do?"

She grabbed Zain's hands and put them together. "First, you put your hands together like this. Then, say whatever it is you want to wish for; don't worry so much about what that is right now. You will find your voice in time. But it's important how you end the prayer."

"How is that?"

She pointed at the words on the wall behind her desk. "Ancients, to this I pray."

Zain opened his mouth but couldn't force anything to come out.

"You don't have to do it now. Do it when you feel ready, but remember to keep your hands like this and to end your prayer thus."

"But I want to do it now."

Carla Sonetta offered him a smile. "Okay, then let's pray for something together."

Unable to come up with better words, Zain sighed, then said, "Please heal Gabrielle. Ancients, to this I pray."

The headmistress opened her eyes. "That will do, Mr. Berrese. It's best if you close your eyes when you pray, but what you said is a start." She returned to her chair. "Please, take a seat."

Behind him, a knock rapped on the door.

"Come in."

Cynthia walked in and shut the door behind her, leaving Gabrielle alone in the other room.

"An update? Good news, perhaps?"

Cynthia sighed and shook her head. "I'm afraid not. The damage is permanent. Ve have managed to numb ze pain, zough, and stop ze bleeding."

Carla Sonetta pushed out a breath. "Well, I suppose that is a reason to be thankful."

"What more can be done?" Zain asked.

"Besides eyeglasses to help her eyes in ze light, nothing. A miracle vould have to happen for eyes like hers to see again."

"And the eyeglasses?" Carla Sonetta asked.

"Ve don't have zem here, but I can put in an order for zem in Rydel."

Carla Sonetta put a finger to her lips and leaned back in her chair. Brows furrowing, she bit down on her nail. "That may be our best course of action," she said to herself. She looked at Cynthia and nodded. "Very well. Lead Gabrielle to the apothecary so she can rest there for the night and then contact Rydel."

"Very vell, Headmistress."

Cynthia left.

Zain turned back around. "What did you mean?"

"By what?"

"Best course of action?"

She sighed. "Mr. Berrese, while it is nice that you want to find faith, it does not negate your actions. Moreover, the repercussions of those actions that will come swiftly here."

"Zakk left. You said that Zigarda would be a fool to shut you down."

"Aye, that is true, but if your information is valuable enough to send a squad of people to kill you, Zigarda may act foolishly. He may have nothing else to lose." She sighed and waved her hand in the air. "But perhaps I am rushing to conclusions. Regardless, Mr. Berrese, I think it's time you told me your story."

CHAPTER NINE

1NFORMED

E irek stood alongside Guardian Eska on the veranda. Mountains loomed in the distance. By Guardian Eska's request, no one else was present. And since dismissing Tundra from his chambers shortly after their return, there had been only silence. Eirek had kept quiet, waiting for Guardian Eska to speak, but now he wondered if he was expected to say something.

A breeze fluttered by them, lifting up Guardian Eska's cape for a slight moment before it fell down to rest upon his back once more. Eirek tilted his face to the sky. Eska's dragon prowled for game in the distance.

"You know...," Eska began, "fate is certainly an interesting thing. No matter how you try to avoid it, it finds you, and you are either amused by its humor or bedeviled by it."

Eirek didn't speak, hoping that Guardian Eska would continue opening up to him. Since his acceptance as apprentice at Coronation, he hadn't actually had much, if any, alone time with his mentor, so this was a rarity he welcomed, especially considering the circumstances of which they now spoke. He had spent a month and a half training his ability to use Power with the Sages, and the routine of his training had been disrupted by the untimely death of Lord Paen and the Meeting of the Twelve that followed. Then came Pirini Lilapa, and the aftermath had given Eirek no time to re-assimilate into his life as apprentice, instead forcing him to mature at an accelerated rate—or die by his inability to do so.

For the first time since their brief conversation after Coronation, Eirek stood alone with his mentor, hoping to gain even a modicum of knowledge from him.

"I choose to be amused by it." Guardian Eska turned to him. "Because it is unnecessary to torment yourself over something not in your control." Guardian Eska removed his grip from the railing and pointed to the sky. "Do you see Vesel flying?"

Eirek nodded.

"Before I became apprentice, Eirek, I lived in Nova in the capital, Steorra. I had a father and a mother and even a sister who was as inquisitive as I was. We were strong. To live in Nova, you have to be. One day, Alicia, my sister, went too far away from the city's shields. When I came home after my training with Garrett, my parents asked me if I had seen her. She hadn't returned. Fearing her safety, they sent me out after her, knowing that I had a better chance of surviving due to my training.

"Using my ability to track her through her blood, I was able to sense her, and I located her inside of the Dragon's Ruins. My sister could use Power as well, a fortunate development as our parents couldn't cast. Surrounded by five dragons, she had cast a stone shield to block their fire and their flight advantage, but when she saw me, she lost focus, and the barrier collapsed. A dragon swept in and tore through what little defense she had and killed her.

"My sister died right before my eyes. The dragon then turned his attention to me and we stared at each other for a long while. The other dragons perched on top of the ruins of bones or took to the sky, eagerly awaiting what would happen between me and the alpha male that stood before me.

"He roared and from his mouth spewed silver flames. Still affected by the loss of my sister, my attempt at raising a shield was feeble at best, and so the fire crumbled my shield and drenched me in flames. But at that moment something incredible happened. Instead of harming me, the fire spoke to me. It told me the dragon's name: Vesel. And then the flames died. Vesel stood there, as stupefied as I was, an intense silence between us.

"I walked up to him and called out his name, and he responded to me. Then he unleashed a roar and flapped up into the air, scaring off all the other dragons. He used one of his companions as an example and flung him down to the earth, sending the body crashing into a few pillars of bones. The others fled. The quick skirmish allowed me the time to examine my sister and grab her body.

"That was my first experience with my dragon, Eirek. It seems that fate wanted to grant me tremendous Power through bonding with a dragon, but the very same dragon that killed my sister."

Eirek blinked a few times, taking in the story. He had no idea Guardian Eska's life was rife with such intricacies.

Guardian Eska searched for Vesel. Upon failing, he turned his attention back to Eirek. "I could have let my first encounter sour my relationship with Vesel for the rest of my life, but I chose to accept fate for the humor it chose to show me that day. This is because I had a strong mentor, Eirek. Garret Omyon convinced me that sometimes hardship is necessary for the greater good, and I can see now that it was. I won my Trials because of the strength Vesel gave me, strength that, in turn, my sister gave me with her sacrifice. If she hadn't ventured out that day, I may never have found my bonded animal. I may never have become the Guardian of the Core. When fate seemingly takes away everything from you, as it did your uncle, know that it is not without a purpose. And I think you realize that, somewhere deep down, I think... *I hope* you realize that."

Eirek dug into his pockets and pulled out the two objects inside: a golden bond and a slip of paper. Eirek showed Eska the paper.

"What is this?"

"The last message my uncle left for me before he died."

"AVF?"

"Ajid Voluntasey Fuan," Eirek recited.

"Do you know what that means?"

He nodded. "My uncle told me before I left for the Trials." Shifting his weight to his elbow, Eirek leaned his frame against the balustrade. "My uncle was killed by the Other, wasn't he? He was killed by the Third Ancient."

"I believe that he was, yes." Eska handed the note back to Eirek. "Did you ever ask yourself how your uncle knew such arbitrary and extensive knowledge?"

Eirek shook his head. "He was always full of surprises. I guess it never crossed my mind. It makes sense now, though. Now that I know he was Galan." Eirek paused a little before asking, "What does that make me?"

"It makes you a descendant of the Ancients, Eirek. Galan, or as you knew him, Angal, was never your uncle, for Galan had no brother. He is your oldest forefather."

The information should have astonished, but Eirek merely felt himself nod. At this point, he didn't know what else could shock him, and since finding out what the letters meant in Mendeck, he had begun to think that fate was having a larger role to play in his life than he would have liked. He should have guessed it the moment Angal pushed him to partake in the Trials.

"What really happened to my parents? Where are they? Angal told me they died."

"That is something only Naydeia would know. I'm sorry."

"But how could they have been killed? Who could have killed them? How am I not dead?"

"Since learning your heritage, Eirek, I have wondered that myself. Although I don't have the specifics, my speculation deals in logic. When Galan and Naydeia had a child, that child must have contained nearly pure Ancient blood as well, but not as pure as their own. In fact, every subsequent offspring in that lineage must have had a constant dilution in their blood until you. My guess is upon the realization of the blood they carried, perhaps they went against the wishes of their mother and father and tried to find the Ancient and take revenge for what it did to Bane and Lyoen."

"Why would they do that?"

"Pride is the simplest answer. Knowing that you descend from Ancients can be too powerful of an aphrodisiac to some. It may have caused them to perpetuate their own self-prophecy and abandon their reclusive lives." Guardian Eska strummed his fingers on the balustrade and then looked at Eirek. "Or, perhaps events such as the Plague during the third Pirini Lilapa killed them, or the Burning and the Branding in the first. My guess is that it has been consistently easier to find the offspring of Galan and Naydeia because of the diluted blood. While Galan and Naydeia's blood made it nearly impossible for them to be traced and hard to kill if found, their offspring could have easily fallen victim to past Pirini Lilapas or other misfortunes."

"Is that why I've never met them?"

"You haven't?"

Eirek shook his head.

"Can you recall any memories of them?"

Eirek opened his mouth and then shut it. "No. Actually, I can't... Why can't I?"

"What is your earliest memory?"

Eirek bit his lip and thought back. "I... I guess I never really thought about that. My first memory was when Angal was taking me to the Mourses' house. He dropped me off there and told them to raise me. He told them about my parents' deaths."

"But you never really met your parents?"

Eirek blushed and shook his head. "No. I never did."

Guardian Eska opened his mouth and then closed it. He moved his hands behind his back to stop the movement of his cape as the breeze increased. "We may never know the true reason why that is, Eirek, but my guess is that perhaps Galan could have been your father. If he was your father, then that is perhaps why you have no recollection of others in your life besides him and the Mourses."

"Why would he say he is my uncle, then? Why not tell me—"

"Because the truth killed off many of his other sons or daughters, most likely. The same reason why he left you in the hands of the Mourses, I imagine. If the Third One were to find you and him together, then it truly would be the end of a purer Ancient lineage. This is most likely the reason why he separated you from contact with your mother—to preserve the bloodline."

"But he showed the world who he was. He sang songs and told stories to royalty. He didn't keep a low profile at all."

"No. It seems that he did not, but he never revealed his Power, did he?"

Eirek thought about it for a second, then shook his head. He snapped his fingers. "It makes sense now."

"What does?"

"Cronos told me something while on the Sacred Passage. He told me that Lyoen was female. I thought she was male until he told me that. Is he correct?"

"He is. Lyoen has many names. The Mother. The Alchemist."

"During my last trip to Syf, though, Angal said Lyoen was a *he*. And... and he even mentioned the Other in his song, too."

"He mentioned the Other?"

Eirek nodded. "The Clayses questioned him immediately."

"And?" Eska put a hand underneath his chin.

"He dismissed it immediately as just a story. But, I... I think he was trying to tell me something. Without me knowing it, he was hinting at who I am. What my blood represents. And, I think now I understand why he called Lyoen *he*. He didn't want to reveal his true knowledge to people. To me."

"That would make sense, and it would be very smart of him. In fact, if I may add to your theory, Eirek, I think he fancied playing for royalty and the powerful because it allowed him the chance to manipulate them as needed. You have to remember, Eirek, that Galan was the most-talented person in the Adored Arts next to his mother, Lyoen. My guess is that everything that you don't remember is because of him. The willingness of the Mourses to take you in is because of him. The Clayses recommending you for my Trials, I imagine, is also his doing. Throughout your whole life, he has safeguarded you from a distance and has steered your life to this very moment, all without telling you of your true lineage." Guardian Eska scanned Eirek. "So, again, I say you let fate bedevil you or amuse you. Which one will it be?"

Eirek put his hands on the railing and looked outward, trying to see what Eska saw past the swelling desert that eventually led to mountains and the green grasslands beyond. Thinking about everything that led him to this moment, Eirek chuckled.

"What is it?"

"I shouldn't be here right now. Zain Berrese should be, but he denied it. Perhaps this is another way of fate playing with us."

Eska grinned as well. "Perhaps it is."

Eirek looked up towards Eska. "So what happens now?"

"Now it seems that the prophecy is being fulfilled."

"The prophecy," Eirek muttered.

"Do you know it?" Eska asked, taking Eirek away from further speculation.

Eirek nodded. "He recited it to the Clayses after he had finished telling the story about the Ancients."

"Is that so? What did he say?"

"He said that the Smiths had sung the prophecy."

"The Smiths?"

"Yes. Who are they?"

"I do not believe any of them are still alive, although if Galan mentioned that the prophecy came from them, then perhaps there is at least one still alive, as the prophecy came about after the Great War. The Twelve heard it and then passed that knowledge onto my position, starting with the first Guardian, Jorey Raule."

"How many were there?"

Eirek listened intently while Eska explained that each Ancient had created four powerful beings to serve as their personal council. Ancient Lyoen created the Smiths, Bane the Sages, and the Other the Four Creatures of Legend. After a confrontation between Lyoen and Bane, Lyoen offered up one of her Smiths in recompense for a transgression. This betrayal caused the Smiths to flee Gladima.

Eirek took a moment to let the information sink in.

"Why doesn't the Third One have a name?"

"Supposedly it does, but we will never know it. Before being locked away, Bane cast a spell on him or her to rob it of its name so that no one ever spoke it. I have had a suspicion for some time that Pirini Lilapa is the Other's work."

"What makes you think that?"

"It is the anniversary of the day the Ancients perished, so it also happens to be the day that the Third One is strongest. That is why there is always a disaster of epic proportion on that day. The first anniversary saw the Burning and the Branding. Hordes of books were destroyed, most likely erasing any trace of its name. Throughout the centuries since, its name has been slowly forgotten. I am unsure even those with First Blood remember how to spell it or say it anymore. Now it is just called the Other."

"But the Great War wasn't started by him... or it...," Eirek flailed his hands, unsure how to address the mysterious entity, "or whatever. It was started by Bane and Lyoen. Surely they are more of a threat than *it* is. As Guardian, who are we protecting from escaping?"

"All of them. Bane. Lyoen. The Other. Desmós. If Gladima were reopened, that prophecy would become fulfilled. Repeat the prophecy again for me. Tell me if the last line is something that you would want on your conscience."

Eirek repeated the prophecy:

> *"Chosen will be blood from all five domains.*
> *Hope they will bring through chaos, anger, and pain.*
> *Twelve will lose favor, four will regain form.*
> *Bringing with them more death than the Great War."*

A thought came to his mind, but Eska spoke before he could ask.

"The Great War, Eirek, nearly eliminated all of those with First Blood. The force of the Ancients battling was so great that it took what was once your planet of Agrost and thrust the nation of Mistral up into the sky. It broke the continent of Acquava into the islands they are now. Another war of that magnitude would destroy the galaxy.

"The Twelve, in their younger, more power-lust days, knew this. That is why they created the Guardian of the Core position. What they didn't know, however, is that their life source was tied to Gladima. As it continued suffering a perpetual state of neglect and devolution, a part of them suffered the same fate. And as they gloated and touted their strength around the planets, failing to acknowledge the Ancients or the land that gave them such prowess, the more they changed. Your uncle, or Galan, may have aged, yes, but he never transformed like the Twelve, probably because he kept his faith in the Ancients. I'm guessing if Naydeia is ever found, she would look the same as well."

Eirek understood now. At least, he thought he did. "What will the five be chosen for?"

"The Trials." Eska bobbed his head and looked outward.

"But it never says that. It merely says: *Chosen will be blood from all five domains.*"

Eska inclined his head towards Eirek and fixed him with a piercing stare. "What else could it refer to?"

"My uncle... Galan..." Eirek shook his head. "Angal... Angal thrust riddle upon riddle on me ever since I could remember. Not a time went by when we were together that he wouldn't pose me another riddle."

"This is not a riddle, Eirek."

"No, but it functions just the same. The word play is there, open for interpretation. *Domain* in this case means planet, and we know that by the number five in front of it, correct?"

Eska nodded his head haltingly.

"There in itself is an interpretation. Therefore, perhaps what we've interpreted as *chosen* is wrong. How do we know it *is* concerning the Trials in the first place?"

"The reimaje." Eska pointed to the black cloth tied around his head.

Eirek sunk his shoulders. "What do you mean?"

"This reimaje contains every thought and memory of its previous wearers, Eirek. That is why it is so powerful. I have seen the Twelve, long before they were the deformities you saw. I saw them tell the first Guardian about the prophecy and instruct him why he must choose carefully. Not only so that the Twelve could retain their Power, I assume, but also to stop a second Great War from happening."

Eirek pondered Eska's words. "Was the first Guardian chosen through Trials as well?"

"Of course. Every Guardian has been."

"How were the contestants chosen?"

"The Twelve chose from the most willing on each planet."

"And the prophecy came after?"

Eska nodded.

"Then it can't be the Trials," Eirek stated. "Otherwise, the very first selection could have already led to the Twelve's demise."

"Well, what else could it be if not the Trials?"

Eirek took time to think, reciting the lines to himself a few more times. He extended a finger into the air. "Gladima."

"What?" Eska cocked his head.

"What if this prophecy refers to returning to Gladima?" Eirek waved his hands to stop Eska's question, not wanting to be interrupted. "It can be inferred that the Twelve here in the third line are the Twelve that *have* recently lost favor. The four that are mentioned after it perhaps are the four that you mentioned earlier: Bane, Lyoen, the Other, and Desmós. All of them are connected with Gladima. The Twelve wanted to return there, the Other and Desmós certainly want to be reunited there as well. And, as you mentioned, if those four were to be at their full strength again..."

"Then a second Great War would happen." Eska finished Eirek's thought. He remained silent and scanned his apprentice with a newfound appreciation. "So, then, what exactly are they chosen for?"

"Perhaps the *five* mentioned are key players involved in the reopening of Gladima. Influential in whatever second Great War may come to be."

"So who may the five be?" Eska frowned. "How would they be chosen if not by me?"

"Well, perhaps they *were chosen* by you."

"But the—"

"Perhaps it's not only for the Trials. You choose your conseleigh as well, correct?"

"Correct." Eska's eyes grew. "Are you assuming that perhaps the five are a combination between contestants and conseleigh?"

Eirek nodded his head. "It could be. Whoever the five are, you would already have a mixture of choices between conseleigh and contestants from the other four domains, leaving me for the fifth domain, Gladima. A domain you never intended to select, and one that never could have been selected if not for Angal."

Eska strummed his chin with one hand, keeping the other behind his back. He paced back and forth on the veranda. "That may make sense. I hadn't elected anyone from Pyre, but Riagan is from there."

"Actually, my guardian, I... I believe a contestant you chose was from Pyre, too."

Eska waved off the comment. "Impossible. I made certain to elect an individual from Mistral instead of a woman from Pyre because I feared the prophecy being fulfilled."

"But, as you said, fate has a sense of humor."

Guardian Eska pivoted on his heel to look at Eirek. "Then who else is from there?"

"I believe Cain Evber."

"Evber is from Epoch. That is where his family name is from. They have been ruling there for nearly six-hundred years."

"But I don't think Cain is blood to the Eybers."

"What do you mean?"

"When Conseleigh Iycel and I observed him and his father at Castle Thoth after Pirini Lilapa, I had a hard time noticing the similarities between the two. Both wore glasses, sure, but the height difference and body structure are very different. Also, before he left the Core, I saw him in the lobby, and I spoke with him. He... well, he seemed lost, as if he didn't know who he was anymore. He was not the same man that came with me to the Core. And, unlike the others, I noticed that he didn't sweat while on Pyre. Is that normal?"

"I noticed that as well." Guardian Eska clasped his hands behind his back. "And to answer your question, no, that is not normal. The only people who do not sweat while on Pyre are those who hold blood from there, or who have a type of ring to keep them cool. I thought Cain the latter, as he did wear many rings on his fingers. Now that you mention the other things, though, perhaps..." He stopped. His eyes glowed.

The communication ended a few minutes later. "Who was that?"

"Conseleigh Rorum. He has just received an important call from Carla Sonetta." Eirek looked to Eska blankly.

"It is Gabrielle's headmistress at Gracie's Academy. It appears Zain Berrese has just shown up on her doorstep with some rather important news for me."

"Zain? Tundra and I just came from Empora hours ago."

"I know. This is quite unexpected indeed. We can finish our conversation on the way to the telecommunication room."

"Okay." Eirek followed Eska back through his room and to the raised platform that was the only way to and from the third floor.

While the platform lowered them, Eska put a hand on Eirek's shoulder. "Do you believe Cain knows yet?"

"I think he is lost and confused."

"Yes. This situation would be quite difficult for anyone to comprehend. Will you help him then? If he truly is from Pyre, then I believe he may be one of the five mentioned in the prophecy."

"I can try my best. Who do you think the others are?"

"I suspect Hydro will have a role to play in all of this with that necklace he carries. He is from Onkh." They passed the second level. Guardian Eska continued, "Perhaps Zain, somehow. He was my original choice for apprentice until he turned it down. But who could Agrost be. It can't be you or Cain any longer. It surely cannot be Peter Koluma."

"Who is he?"

"The Trial participant who never showed up."

"Luvan," Eirek said.

"Lu..." Eska couldn't finish his thoughts.

"He coordinated the first trial, correct? And isn't that where Hydro picked up the necklace?"

Eska laughed and shook his head.

"What is it?"

"Apprentice Mourse, you'll learn soon enough."

The platform stopped on the ground floor where Tundra Iycel and Ethen Aprorum waited.

"Learn what?" Tundra asked.

"How some of us are fit for fate." Eska walked past them, and as he did so, his two conseleigh turned on their heels and followed alongside. Not slowing to talk, Eska said, "Ethen, do you want to tell me the meaning of this? Zain Berrese, are you sure?"

Eirek hustled to keep up with the fast pace of the party.

"Tat is what Carla Sonetta told me."

"Tundra, did we not tell Lord Zigarda to send him home?" Eska stopped at a small podium before the telecommunication chamber and put his hand on the scanner. The doors opened.

"Yes. And Apprentice Mourse and I did tell Lord Zigarda, but I do not believe we ever saw the real Zain, Edwyrd."

Eska traveled past the doors into the circular chamber filled with twelve large screens. Only one of them was powered on. The word standby flashed on it. Eska stopped behind the main control panel and turned to them. "Why wasn't this mentioned before?"

"The appearance of Hydro caught my attention," Tundra said.

Eirek nodded. "And our conversation never revolved around Zain or the fake Zain that I saw in Zigarda's keep."

"How do you know it wasn't Zain?"

Eirek explained how he had put questions to Zain and how the answers didn't match what Zain's mother had said before they left Ka'Che. Tundra chimed in about the sword that Zain had carried at his hip; it wasn't the long sword he had received during the Trials that required it to be strapped over his back.

"Very well. Let's see what Mr. Berrese has to say." Eska turned back to the control panel and pushed a button. Simultaneously, the screen that had been flashing *standby* revealed Zain Berrese.

"Guardian Eska, Eirek, Conseleigh Iycel and Aprorum. It's nice to see you again."

"You as well, Mr. Berrese," Eska said. "My conseleigh tell me you have important news to tell me."

"Yes, sir, I do. Recently, my father and I just escaped Zigarda's compound."

"Escaped?"

Zain nodded. He proceeded to tell the story of his betrayal and his encounter with the shapeshifters. He ended on the sad note of his father's death.

"The shapeshifter said something to me before it died."

"What was that?"

"*Ajid voluntasey fuan.* I probably mispronounced it. It was something like that. What does it mean?"

Eirek glanced furtively at Eska.

The Guardian remained focused ahead. "I am unsure myself."

Eirek looked down at the floor to hide his surprise. *He lied.*

"Is there anything else, Mr. Berrese?"

"What are you going to do about any of this?"

"Nothing as of now."

"But—"

"I assure you, the jewels are safe."

"My father made those jewels trackable. Zigarda will be able to hunt them down."

"Be that as it may, he cannot release the Twelve without them all being present. I imagine a few of them will be quite impossible for him to manage."

Zain threw his hands at the screen. "What about his Blood Chamber? Who knows how many shifters he has out in the universe!"

Eska's neck tightened. "While employing shifters is cause for concern, it is quite a hard allegation to pin properly onto him, for they are almost impossible to distinguish. Unless it is in direct regards to my position as Guardian of the Core, I am not allowed to interfere in the happenings of other nations. I hope you understand."

"What about Gabrielle's blood! How did he have blood from Gabrielle? Zigarda infiltrated the Trials somehow. Isn't that cause for action?"

"Yes. And action will be taken, I assure you, but everything in its own time, Mr. Berrese. Patience is necessary sometimes." Guardian Eska shifted slightly and clasped his hands behind his back. "Is there anything else?"

Zain's zeal died away. "No. There's no point, anyway." Zain slouched. "You never end up helping the people that need help."

Tundra stepped forward. "Zain Berrese, how—"

The connection ended.

Eirek gulped. *Did he just disconnect with the most powerful person in the system?*

"And that is why he wouldn't have made a good Guardian." Tundra threw her arms at the screen.

Ethen remained stoic with one arm crossed over his chest. The other picked at his conical beard. "Tat is certainly not surprising."

"What do you mean?" Tundra pivoted.

"His sword. Too aggressive. I noticed ta jewels when Eska examined it."

"Ethen speaks the truth. In my choosing him as the apprentice, I knew his training could change him. Anyway, it doesn't—" Eska stopped his thought as a call came on his telecom screen. It didn't even finish ringing before Eska connected the caller. "General Satorus. What news do you have?"

"We found the alleyway where Conseleigh Iycel and your apprentice spotted Hydro. We followed the chase to an open courtyard where we saw a slew of bodies."

"Bodies?"

"Yes. Zigarda's men by the sigil on their suits. The suits, however, I've never..." The general coughed into his fist. "I've never seen suits quite like them."

"What do you mean?"

"Skin-tight compression suits like snakeskin."

"What is so odd about that?"

"Well, the lack of protection they offer. Our zircha steel had no problems in piercing the armor on the remaining cadavers. It makes me believe there is a special unseen function, otherwise no soldier would openly wear less protective gear."

"And what of Hydro Paen?"

"Yes, that is what I was getting to. We have scoped the perimeter; he isn't around. The dead bodies, though, my guardian. Some of them are severed in two. That means..."

"An Ether Weapon," Eska completed the thought.

"Yes. Precisely. We know Hydro Paen has one on his person. The carnage here makes me believe that they found him, and my guess is that Zigarda's men outnumbered him and subdued him. Whatever the special function of the suits are, it could make such a thing possible."

"So you believe he is in the Web now?"

General Satorus nodded. "I do. Do you give us permission to search the Web?"

Guardian Eska grinned. "Complete authority. Let Lord Zigarda know you have reason to believe he is harboring the prince and then search the entire compound."

"Very well, my guardian."

"And while you are there searching the compound, make sure you ask to be taken to the Blood Chambers. It has recently come to my attention that Lord Zigarda may be harvesting blood and employing shifters."

General Satorus turned his head. "Should we be ready for an altercation?"

"You should be ready for anything."

"I will report back to you after we have finished our investigation."

"Good."

The connection cut.

Eska beamed at his party. "It seems this may work out better than planned. If we can catch Zigarda red handed in blood harvesting, especially blood of the Trials participants, then there is cause for me to strip him of his title. What a welcome relief that would be."

"What about the jewels?" Eirek asked. "Zain just said Zigarda is seeking them. Doesn't that already prove he wishes to overthrow you?"

"It is one man's word against another if I don't have actual proof, Eirek."

"You don't trust Zain?"

Eska shook his head. "It isn't that. I do. But what was the answer to the riddle I posed for you at the end of the Trials? What is it that we see every day?"

"Equals." Eirek sighed.

"Correct. While I may not like Zigarda, and while I may favor Mr. Berrese more, I cannot allow myself to be swayed by biases. If Zigarda wants to hunt down the jewels, he can, but as I said to Zain Berrese, some of them will be quite difficult to obtain, even with any sort of tracking device. And if he does find them all, he will not be able to release them without help from Cronos or me."

"So what now?"

"Now we wait for General Satorus's report. Perhaps this will be easier than imagined. If it doesn't conclude favorably, then I will need some time to think about what to do next. The hunt for Hydro. The syphoning of Gabrielle's blood.

All of it is, well, rather much. I admit that even I need time to process everything that has happened recently. For now, though, Apprentice Mourse, I suggest you take a rest in whatever way feels most comfortable to you. Tomorrow you will begin training with Conseleigh Rorum. It's necessary that we continue your training where we left off before Pirini Lilapa. Things are bound to get physical."

A nervous weight building in his stomach, Eirek glanced at Conseleigh Rorum.

The conseleigh with tanned skin held a gleam in his eye as he plucked pieces of his beard. "Tat would be my pleasure."

Eirek swallowed.

CHAPTER TEN

THE HUNTERS

E ven though Zakk didn't speak to anyone accompanying him on the return journey, it didn't mean he had a moment to himself. On the contrary, his thoughts wrestled with him. *Why didn't she yield? How did she keep fighting? I should've won. Why didn't she kill me?*

The Red Cloud hung over the city of Mendeck like a scab on earthy flesh. Seeing it, and knowing that the people of Mendeck worked tirelessly to produce it, Zakk reflexively brought his fingers to his neck, feeling the first line Gabrielle had cut, a little above the jugular. It now took on the form of a scab itself—a coagulation of old blood and new blood. Then he slid his fingers a little lower, touching the second mark, the one that would've ended his life if he had not forfeited. As quickly as he touched it, he pulled his hand away. His confidence couldn't afford to waver.

The same streets were still filled with the same shit. The wreckage site had been nearly all cleared away. Survivors and scavengers still walked about the area; the former trying to make sense of the situation, and the latter trying to make a quick coin by selling the detritus that remained. The former, Zakk knew, wouldn't receive the answers they searched for; answers were hard to come by in a city like this. Sometimes that was a good thing. Zakk had been deprived of very important answers all of his life, yet somehow he managed. They would too, if they were strong enough.

Victor Zigarda's Web sat at the heart of the city. But upon approach, Zakk noticed more activity than normal. Off in the distance, he slowed, observing the unfolding scene.

Men in black uniforms, at least thirty, entered the compound, led by Zigarda's receiver. *Hown?*

Zakk had never actually seen the Hown before, but he had learned about them while attending Gazo's Academy. It was every student's dream to be selected to be a Hown. And while Gazo's Academy was far superior to other schools, only a small percentage of those individuals were ever deemed good enough to be invited into the Hown regiment. The last one Zakk had heard of was a man named Oliver

Thane, who had graduated from the Academy years ago. He had been the Gabrielle Ravwey of Gazo's, undefeated in all his tournaments. Zakk wondered then if Gabrielle would have ever been offered a position as a Hown, given her record. Well, certainly not after their altercation. How did she manage to overcome him after what he did to her? His hand went back to his neck. *Why didn't she kill me?*

"What's wrong?"

Zakk twisted his head. The other hovercraft had pulled alongside him. Zakk thrummed the wheel for a moment, biting his lower lip and furrowing his brows in contemplation. "We wait here."

"Why?"

"Orders from Zigarda," Zakk lied. He didn't need direct orders from the lord to understand how precarious the situation was, and if Zigarda was to go down, Zakk did not want to be along for the ride. Most likely they were there to investigate Hydro's appearance in Mendeck, but he wondered what they would find when they searched the Web. How well could Zigarda actually cover his tracks? Only time would tell.

"How long?"

"Until I say we can go back in. Let's move our hovercrafts somewhere less conspicuous." Zakk maneuvered his hovercraft to an alleyway and parked it at an angle where he could just see the front gates of the Web.

There he waited. And while he waited, he found himself fingering the new scab over and over again, wondering why in Abaddon she hadn't drawn the dagger across his throat after what he had done to her.

Hours passed. Eventually, though, Zakk saw the Hown leave the Web, enter their hovercrafts, and drive off toward a different part of the city. But he didn't go back immediately. He knew better than to be too impatient. After waiting another half hour, he activated the anitron on his hovercraft and flew back to the Web. This time, though, Zakk used the private entrance at the rear.

He deposited his hovercraft and wandered into the throne room. Victor Zigarda was deep in conversation with his receiver and advisor. Upon noticing Zakk's arrival, Yuan leaned into Zigarda's ear. Zigarda shot a furtive glance towards Zakk, but continued discussing something with his council nonetheless.

When he finished, he gave his full attention to Zakk. "You're back. Please tell me you have good news for me."

"I..." Zakk didn't want to admit his shortcoming yet. "How did the meeting with the Hown go?" Zigarda opened his mouth, but Zakk continued. "I saw them outside. Decided it would be best to wait for their departure."

"Well, that is certainly a very keen observation. Good. We managed to clear out the Blood Chambers before they arrived. Dr. Cere took the patients with him to Onkh to the base in Sereya."

"So they found nothing?"

"My boy, I would not be here right now if they had found something, would I? In this game of Power, you always have to be one step ahead. Now, tell me, how did things conclude with Zain?"

"I... Zain is still alive." Zakk didn't cower his gaze. Back straight, chest up, he faced the incredulous stares from the three others.

"What do you mean *he is still alive*?" Edwyn asked.

"We made it to Gracie's Academy where the shifter said they were headed, but the Academy stood at their defense."

"And you and your men couldn't handle a school of girls?" The advisor laughed.

"Vat can you do right?" Yuan threw his hands up in exasperation.

Zigarda waved his hand, silencing the others. Those two didn't matter. Zigarda was the only one that sent shivers up Zakk's arm. Him and the shifters. Until this point, Zigarda had remained silent, fixated on Zakk with a look that he couldn't quite read. Zigarda walked towards Zakk, slowly, steadily, never blinking.

Zakk braced, tightening his muscles for whatever would follow.

Closer, Zigarda crept. "Did you not have it in you to kill him? I thought that is what you wanted, revenge? Revenge on the family that abandoned you. Yet you seem unable to truly do what is needed to be done."

"We would have died trying to take on the entire school; we were only twenty-five men against an academy of two-thousand." Zakk moved his hands behind his back, close to his hip, just in case.

Never dropping eye contact with Zakk, Zigarda continued forward. "Yes, well, Zain and his father would be dead right now. Sometimes sacrifices need to be made..."

His preparation didn't matter, though. One flick of Zigarda's hand and Zakk found himself unable to move, his feet now locked to the floor underneath of him. With another wave of Zigarda's hand, electricity pulsed through Zakk's body. Without the ability to use Power, he was helpless to Zigarda's fury.

He crumbled to the floor and twitched in and out of consciousness. Senses impaired, he tried to decipher his surroundings. Jolts still ran through his body, causing him to kick and spasm sporadically.

Minutes passed. How long? He didn't know, but eventually, the buzzing in his ears subsided; his vision returned. He saw himself, looming above. He blinked, trying to make sense of it. Then he groaned and put a hand up to his head as a wave of pain pulsed in his skull. He blinked again. The figure of himself was still there before his eyes. A movement to his left drew his attention, and he saw the repulsive and furunculous form of a shapeshifter.

Shouting wordlessly,

Zakk crawled backwards, realizing at last what was going on.

The shifter Zakk laughed. "It's always fun playing with Common Bloods, Hevar."

The other shifter stroked his elbow. He stepped forward and placed a hand on his partner's shoulder. "They are quite hysterical, Asher."

Zakk bolted to his feet. He looked around. The throne room was empty but for the shifters. "Where... where is everyone? What do you want?"

"Zigarda sent us. We leave tomorrow to start our trek to Ka'Che. He said it's good to get some information on the people we are going to be impersonating."

Zakk bit his lip and glanced from one to the other. To think that these men could steal bodies and cover up their own dreadful disfiguration by using blood or mere touch, made his skin prickle with disgust and fear.

"You didn't study them while they were in Zigarda's dungeon?"

"We know what they look like." This time the man to the right spoke. "But we want to know more: their habits, their nuances, their motivations." His doppelganger moved forward. "To be successful, it is not enough to be solely in someone's skin." The man grinned. Face-to-face, Zakk saw himself touch his head. "It is crucial to be in their mind as well."

Zakk clenched his fists. "Get out of my skin!"

"Of course." The man retreated and reverted back to his ugly self. The small smile flattened. "Now, tell us."

Zakk went through what he knew of the two Berrese men. How Zain usually blundered and was less of a tactician and calculator than Zakk. How Laron was married to a woman named Brisine and how he would always kiss her on the hand before the lips. How Zain was motivated to be the best, but Laron found purpose in providing for his family.

"That is all, then?" The man with the two knives asked.

Zakk surveyed them. He realized that the shifter called Hevar carried two knives. Asher wielded a sword. "No, you will need to be Zain." Zakk pointed to Asher.

"And why is that?"

"Because Zain carries a sword, and he carries it on his back. Laron isn't a fighter, so you will need to hide your knives until you are ready to make your move."

The two men smirked at one another and nodded. "And this is why we talked to you. Anything else?" Asher's eyes gleamed.

"I failed. Zain and his father are still alive. They are surely going to send word back to Lord Vangle before you both arrive."

Hevar chuckled. "Normally, you'd be correct. But the telecommunication system in the castle has already been compromised. Nothing but Ka'Chean calls are allowed to go through to Lord Vangle. You see, human, we shifters don't *fail* in our missions." Hevar smirked. "Now, is that all?"

Zakk held back his glare, preferring to clench his hands behind his back instead in order to not let his anger show. "No. One more thing. There are two ports in Pelopon. One underneath the castle, in a cave by the bluff. And one in the town. You will want to use the former. They will be expecting you there."

"Anything else?"

"No."

"Before we leave, Lord Zigarda commanded us to tell you to go clear out the dungeon and meet him in the armory. The Web is being evacuated."

Evacuated? "What for?"

"War."

Zakk watched the two men leave. He pursed his lips, considering correcting what he had said, but now there were too many other things to think about. In truth, they would want to use the port in town. The other one was only for Vangle's ships; it would raise suspicion to dock there. After a moment's consideration, he decided to make his way to the dungeons, not caring enough to say anything else. After all, they never failed. And as shapeshifters, their life was a lie. So what difference would a couple more lies make?

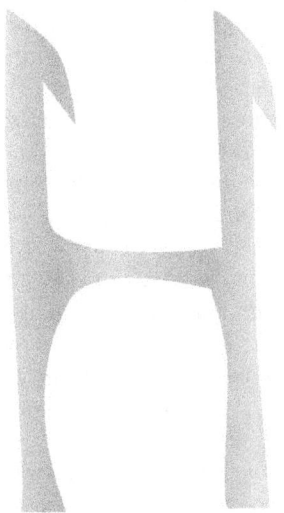

INTERLUDE - CAPTAIN'S LOG

The team, led by General Satorus and me, tracked down Hydro Paen's position to a courtyard in a residential area of town. Following upon Conseleigh Iycel's advice, we wandered the streets through which she and the apprentice gave chase and came upon the courtyard where another altercation occurred. This one involved Lord Zigarda's men, identified by the sigil we found on the dead bodies.

Upon surveying the house, we found nothing but more bodies. More bodies and what appears to be some sort of mechanical fly. There were two of them. According to results from tests conducted in the ship, we've gathered that their purpose was to fumigate the house, hence the reason why the casing of the fly was open and void of anything inside, just a faint, lingering odor that is repugnant to the nose. So repugnant, in fact, that it put me into a fit of coughing, more so than usual. I do hope an infection isn't spreading among the men. I have noticed most of the soldiers in this regiment suffering from similar symptoms.

In good news, the rash on my neck has appeared to stop swelling, presumably thanks to the preventive measures I took to curtail the need to scratch at it. I do hate mosquitos, and I'm sure one bit me while on Hown. Why the Ancients ever created such insects is beyond my comprehension.

I digress. I suppose my thoughts haven't been as calculated as of late. I admit to being rather foggy. It must be the pace of this hunt and the implications of it. How Hydro has managed to elude everyone for so long gives testament that there is something else at play here. What that something else is, though, I have yet to understand.

Under speculation from General Satorus, we went to the Web. There was no sign of Hydro there. We had searched the compound thrice over, in multiple groups. The man wasn't there. Nor was there anything special about the Blood Chambers that the general and I examined personally. It was merely a queer name for an apothecary, as stated by the adored who worked there.

In the dungeons we found prisoners of Zigarda, and, after running a facial recognition on each of them, found that each had been properly sentenced. There is no harm in keeping those people there. They deserve their punishment for the acts they committed.

A last-ditch effort led us to the telecommunication chamber where we demanded to see a record of Lord Zigarda's call logs. Although a little reluctant at first, he agreed. His hesitation suggested tension on his part, but none of the calls were recorded, so we could only see who he called, when he called, and the length of the call. We asked about each entry in turn, and for each entry, Lord Zigarda had an answer.

General Satorus is reporting all of this information to Guardian Eska as I record this. It is my duty to keep personal records of our hunt for Hydro Paen, while it is General Satorus's duty to report to Eska directly. What this lack of information brings with it, though, I cannot say. We are once again back at ground zero. While we have a crystal scry used for determining an individual's location, we cannot use it unless we have some of Hydro's blood, and that is something we do not have. Yet. Although... although an idea just came to me that I must share with the general. Yes, I do believe there is a way that we can track Hydro. Not all hope is lost. We will bring him to justice.

For the honor and glory of the Guardian of the Core, Edwyrd Eska, this is Chase Arwayn signing off.

PART II - SEARCHING

CHAPTER ELEVEN

THE FIRST JEWEL

I n front of Hydro stood a monolithic beast, similar in size to the machine Hydro now sat inside.

Deimos.

When the beast saw him, folded wings tucked behind its back expanded, spreading slowly to their fullest length. Hydro's skin prickled. The hairs on his forearm lifted. The beast attempted to take flight only to be held in place by massive chains locked around its feet. The chains shuddered and dragged against the thick columns that held them. But the chains, Hydro was quite certain, were the least of the beast's concerns. A line of Power emanated from each of the twelve columns, and they wove together to form a large sphere of Power that was both black and transparent. It was this encompassing force field, Hydro assumed, that really locked Deimos in place.

Hydro thrummed the panel in front of him. "Why did you bring me here?"

A male voice, toneless and mechanical, said, "A jewel is here. It is close. You must find it."

Hydro glanced to the mobile radar sitting on the chair next to him. "Are you certain?"

"Sensors indicate yes."

Hydro clicked his tongue. *Of course. This is a rather enticing spot for a jewel after all.*

Without another thought, Hydro snatched the radar and exited the ship.

Alone, and the only soul on this vast plain of ruin, Hydro strolled around the caged beast locked within the black sphere of unfathomable Power. Deimos's colossal form and seething anger made Hydro's jaw hang slack. Behind the beast, a massive tail, similar to that of a dragon, swept back and forth on the ground. Wings of electric blue flapped lightly, like a slow heartbeat. Thick arms corded with muscle were held in place by even thicker chains lashed to two of the pillars. Instead of fingers, the beast had five long, granite-like talons.

When Hydro finished circling the perimeter of the beast, he saw Anne standing in front of it, silently looking up, seemingly unafraid. "Anne?"

She spared him a glance and then continued looking upwards. *Magnificent isn't he?*

Hydro stopped alongside of her. "This is Deimos, yes?"

Yes, he is.

"What is he?" Hydro scanned the beast up and down.

Deimos looked at him, but only for a moment before flicking its gaze back to Anne when she spoke.

His creation. His last child.

"He can see you? Why can he see you?"

Because we share the same blood.

"What do you mean?"

We are family, Hydro Paen.

"You and this?" Hydro pointed to the beast.

Yes. All of us are related in some way.

The radar beeped and vibrated, reminding Hydro of his task. Again, his purpose had been made foggy, this time by Anne's mesmerizing voice. It bound him, like nothing else ever had. Well, perhaps besides his love for his brother Aiton.

He sighed. Although he was a man without chains, he still didn't have freedom; he still needed to complete this system-wide hunt for jewels to protect his brother. Hydro took another lap around the beast, this time keeping his eyes to the ground, glancing occasionally at the radar. He was going farther away from it. The jewel had been closer to where Anne was.

Back in front of the beast, he clasped his hands on the top of his head and looked up and around. A shimmer atop one of the pillars caught his eye. Hydro took a step forward and spoke. *"Maa."*

The earth underneath him pushed him upward, understanding his desire. He rose until he had created a spire equal to the height of the pillar. There, thirty feet above the ground, an onyx jewel sat on top of the pillar, its blackness absorbing whatever sunlight shone on this place. Anne stood on the spire as well.

"How did you get here?"

I am everywhere you go, Hydro Paen.

Hydro frowned but said nothing. He picked up the jewel and twirled it between his fingers. Even through the blackness of the polished gemstone, hazel eyes reflected back to him.

The tremor of distant vibrations worked through the spire and into his feet. Hydro bit his lip and looked away from the jewel. He couldn't explain why his senses were more acute, but they were. He assumed it was the necklace. Just as it gave him the ability to cast Power with no natural source present, it also, he felt, increased his senses. He had first experienced it the night he left the Core when he could see clear as day, even though it was the grave of night.

Where is that coming from?

Deimos had lost interest in Hydro and looked westward. Hydro followed its gaze. A large group traveled in the distance, only visible due to its sheer size. Thousands upon thousands walked the ground carrying banners of Chaon. *Is Chaon going to war? Why?*

Because the past doesn't forget.

Hydro flinched, aware he hadn't spoken out loud. To his left, Anne had reappeared. "You—"

We are now one, Hydro Paen. I know what you think.

He twitched his lips. "What past?"

A past that started with the Conquest long ago... when those with the Power to bond were persecuted and killed.

Hydro remained speechless.

The Power my master made has no equal and soon everyone will know.

Hydro turned his attention back to the black sphere of Power that sat before him. "Power greater than this?"

This is only the Power of the Guardian of the Core.

"And the Twelve, you forget." Hydro turned the jewel over in his hand once more.

Both are inconsequential compared to the type of Power I of which I speak.

The chains rattled again. Deimos stared at Hydro once more. Unblinking. Unmoving. The intense fixation froze Hydro in place. Coldness overtook him, making him quiver.

"Why would Eska place a jewel here?"

Because no one comes to this place. They are all afraid that Deimos will escape. That's why the soldiers kept their distance.

Hydro looked down at Anne. "And will he escape?"

Not while the Guardian of the Core lives. Or the Twelve. Bonds are only as strong as the person or people who bind them.

"Eska bound these." Hydro examined the onyx gem in his hand once more. "Does that mean these won't be released until Eska dies?"

They will never be released. Zigarda tasked you with destroying them and if you want a chance at challenging Eska, you must. You have always wanted that, right?

Hydro peered into the jewel. His gaze lingered there in the depths for a long moment. Then he closed his hand around it. "Yes. And that commoner he named Apprentice."

By the end of this adventure, you will have the chance to do both, I feel.

He pulled his eyes away from the jewel and realized Deimos hadn't released his attention. Now, though, the beast's vision wasn't fixed on Hydro's face, but had moved slightly lower, as if Deimos could see what Hydro wore under his tunic. Its eyes flicked towards Anne for a moment before returning their chilling, unwavering, searching, waiting gaze to Hydro. The necklace pulsed under his shirt. It warmed him. Kept him safe from Deimos's glare.

CHAPTER TWELVE

A LONELY NIGHT

F ire. Close enough to scorch his face. Yelling. Loud enough to numb his body. Silhouettes danced beyond the fire. Steel sung beyond the fire. Only confusion stood beyond the fire.

Water lifted its orange and red veil, revealing only pain. Pain as Aiton's father fell to his knees. Pain as Aiton's brother plunged sword through flesh. And even more pain as each looked at Aiton, caught in the act.

Aiton jolted upright. He turned over onto his forearm, his heart still pounding, his mind still remembering, reliving and regretting ever seeing it. The nightmare had returned to him—after a week without it—it had returned. *Why?*

Even with blankets wrapping his body, Aiton shivered. He looked to the night sky. *Brother. Father. Mother.* He sighed. For a time, he thought about his family, but then those thoughts slowly drifted away and soon Aiton's mind held only emptiness. An abyss and solitude that he didn't want to give into.

He had passed out immediately after being led to bed by Korth. His day had been exhausting, filled with hearing the requests of his citizens, a meeting with his council, a Power session with Professor Haruko, and an odd visit from a dignitary of the Roil province. Each had taken a toll on him. And now another nightmare had stolen from him any peace he may have found. What more could he go through?

Unable to sleep, restless in bed, he threw off the covers and walked out of the room. His feet carried him to the door to his right—to his sister's room. At the threshold, he waited. He wondered if he should enter. This is where he had found his brother crying. Why had he been crying? Why? His palm felt the door first. Then his fingers. One hand. And then both. Using his left hand, he twisted the doorknob and pushed open the door with his right.

Darkness enveloped most of the room, but a sliver of light now penetrated it. Aiton followed it to a full-length mirror in a seashell frame. Light reflected off the mirror, showing Aiton what else lay in the darkness.

Aiton left the light's protection and embraced the darkness. In all of his life, he had never been in this room save the time he saw his brother in tears, laying on the floor next to the bed. What could have been so terrifying that it brought his brother even lower than his knees? That it brought tears to his brother's face?

In the darkness, Aiton found a desk. On it was a picture locked inside a seashell frame, a jar full of sand, a pearl necklace, and a sea-blue hair ribbon. Aiton grabbed the picture and walked back into the light and sat down at the head of his sister's bed.

His fingers traced over her small face. *Anya.* Black hair, like their father's, fell past her shoulders. She had been smiling, revealing perfect white teeth, as white as her gown. Pearls hung around her neck.

"Sister... you really were beautiful."

Aiton had never seen her. She had died before he was born, but now, in this room, he couldn't help but wonder what she would've been like. *Would you have been able to cast Power? Could you have?* No one had told Aiton much about her, besides her aptitude in reading and dancing. Other than that, she was an enigma to him.

He sighed and left the picture frame on the bed. He pushed himself off and followed the shard of light out of the room, closing the door behind him.

No soldier was outside this time, dead and lying in a pool of blood. No screams or the singing of steel. There wasn't chaos and hate and pain. There was only silence. Well, actually, that wasn't true. As Aiton stopped before his brother's door, he heard something higher up on the third level.

Attracted to the sound, Aiton bypassed his brother's room and his own. With each step, the noise grew louder. As quietly as he could, he climbed the staircase, hoping to not betray his presence.

"...*who* he is marrying."

Aiton stopped. From his position on the steps, he could just make out the top of Professor Haruko's head. On all fours, he climbed another step, making sure to keep hidden in the shadows.

"Lauren Puwl."

When Aiton heard Korth's voice, he abandoned his quest to get as close as possible, retreating one step when he saw the top of Korth's shaved pate. Korth was more observant than others. Aiton controlled his breath and strained his ears. This location would have to do. He didn't need to see them to recognize who said what.

"She isn't exactly the prettiest of the Puwl family, is she?" Darien scoffed.

"But she is the eldest and next in line," Haruko added.

"It's a political play. That much is obvious, but I am more worried about why he chooses to do this now. Hekter Sigurd has been single since my time at the Academy nearly ten years back, before the late Paen recruited me for private lessons. And there have been plenty of others for him to marry, even Axyel's niece on Talyn isle was an option."

"I think it's related to the moons and Hydro," Darien said.

"And... " Haruko paused. "Aiton still couldn't cast today. I think Hekter sees a weakness in the Paen name now and wants to take lordship for himself."

Aiton's heart pounded. His breathing intensified. He resisted the temptation to crawl up the stairs and expose himself.

"The little lord seemed upset when I took him upstairs."

"Did you let that messenger see?"

"No. Of course not. He came while Aiton and I trained, but I made sure the lord's training concluded at his presence."

"Good." Darien sighed. "Strategically, what do you think of the move, Korth?" he asked.

"You and Ignis are right. The other names you mentioned would have been suitable candidates. All are pretty and fair, but Symeria has the second largest portion of Acquavan soldiers after ours here at the capital. With a marriage to the Puwl family, they would control the spaceport, a potential obstacle for aid from other nations, and it puts them in a position to block any traffic from the north, meaning we would need to rely on our forces from the Summer Isles, Hart Isles, and Talyn."

"Do you think it wise to attend this wedding?" Haruko asked.

"Hekter won't be stupid enough to try anything at such a public event. I imagine all the marquises will be there. And if he is a man of propriety, Conseleigh Iycel will have at least been invited. If she is there, nothing will happen," Korth said.

"And if she isn't?" Darien cut in.

Korth spoke after a few moments of silence, ignoring the question. "This may just be an attempt to shake us and ascertain our resolve."

"That's true. But, still, we need to account for the fact that this will eventually become a threat. Especially if Aiton can't cast. Do you think he is..."

Aiton held onto his breath. He closed his eyes, trying to block the tears.

"I... I am still unsure. He is only going on ten, but he should show signs. Most boys or girls would have by now."

Aiton sniffled. He hiccupped.

"What was—"

Aiton scurried down the steps, taking care to clear his face. He rushed back into his room, closed the door, and hopped into bed. He brought the covers over his face and wiped it clean, then worked to regulate

his breathing. The door to his room creaked open. Aiton ignored the urge to look, keeping focus on his breaths and pretending to be asleep.

"He's still asleep."

Aiton heard Korth whisper.

The door closed.

Aiton exhaled. And sniffled once again. He clenched his hands into tiny fists and pummeled his bed. Tears came to his eyes, but he snuffed them out. He would never let them fall, no matter how weak the past made him feel.

He wouldn't be able to fall asleep, at least not right away. He looked at his hands. His brother had taught him casting Power was the only thing that ever really mattered, and now Aiton understood that. If he could cast Power, none of his council would think it necessary to talk about him in the shadows and silence of night. *Why can't you cast? Why don't you work?* He contorted his body and saw a glass of water on his nightstand. *"Vesi!"*

Nothing.

He tried again.

Nothing.

"Work! I command you to work." He slapped his hands together with numbing force. Eventually, he gave up and brought them over his sobbing face. "Why don't I work?" Snot and tears worked their way into his tired palms.

After his fit subsided, he looked up to the night sky. Only blackness looked back at him. *Does your star still shine, Brother? Or are you up in Axiumé right now with Mother and Father? Are you—* He stopped; he didn't want to think about that possibility. He blinked and sighed. He wondered why they called it night's grave, for a grave was full of dead people, but the sky was full of life and light. It was full of wishes. And, hopefully, it was still one star brighter.

CHAPTER THIRTEEN

RYDEL

Hunched back, hands covering his face and his nose, Zain leaned forward in the chair. He fidgeted with the newly adorned ring on his right index finger, the cremain, the only thing left of his father. He had been hunched over examining it for half an hour now and hadn't stopped touching it since receiving it earlier that day when they evacuated Gracie's. The adored who worked in the academy gave it to him. Normally, he would have liked the fact that it looked like a garnet, for the dark red and black reminded him of his Gazo's uniform; it reminded him of the Ka'Chean banners. But now, it only reminded Zain of his father's sacrifice and those awful blood chambers. Perhaps that was the reason why he continually played with it around his finger as if he was constantly unsure whether it fit or not.

To take his mind off of his predicament and his father, he stood up and walked around the waiting room, hands clasped behind his back, trying to walk out his thoughts while ignoring the others in the waiting room of the apothecary. Many of them were the Gracie's students that remained. Not for him. For Gabrielle. And only for Gabrielle. Carla Sonetta had made that point very clear to him before she went in to see how Gabrielle fared in yet another attempt to correct her impairment.

The apothecary was adjoined to the spaceport. Its main purpose was to serve those leaving or arriving from other nations or planets in the system. As a result, its peak hours fluctuated vastly with the cycles of the intersystem transport. Zain could see all the inter-planetary transport traffic through the large window that sprawled across the waiting room. The ships departing and arriving were little more than a distraction for Zain. It helped him ignore the stares in the room and the unintelligible whispers that he knew were about him, but it did little to calm his actual anxiety.

He took his hands down from his face and hung them between his legs. Immediately, his fingers began fidgeting with the ring on his right hand. Zain sighed. *Dad... I failed you. How many more will have to suffer due to me?*

A hand came to his back. "Zain, you okay?"

Zain twisted his body. He exhaled. "It's nothing, Issac. I'll get through this."

"We're here for you."

Zain nodded. He stood up and made his way to the large window. Leaning his head against it, he closed his eyes, letting his senses die to the vibrations from the sporadic departures outside. He put his hands together in prayer. Under his breath he whispered, "Ancients, if you really do exist, let Gabrielle be okay. Let her vision return to her. Ancients, to this—"

A new tenor to the whispers around him alerted Zain. He shifted off the window to see all the remnants of Gracie's Academy standing at attention. Zain looked to the doorway. There stood the headmistress, arm linked with Gabrielle's, who now wore a pair of black sunglasses.

Zain stalked forward. "What did the adored say?"

Carla Sonetta shook her head.

Zain's heart plummeted. "Gabe..."

Gabrielle sniffled. "It'll be fine, Zain. It will." She smiled. "What do we do next?"

Is she... Zain couldn't read her face. Was it her faith that made her strong, or was her strength merely a facade? Zain sighed.

Carla Sonetta cleared her throat. "Well, Mr. Berrese?"

"We have to board a ship set for Pelopon. As soon as possible."

Carla Sonetta glanced past Zain at the windows that reflected the settling dusk. "Impossible tonight. We will have to try first thing in the morning."

"Where can we stay?"

"I have a contact in Rydel. The family is trustworthy. They have been a part of Gracie's since its inception."

"They have room for all of us?"

"They should."

At Carla's advisement, they left their hovercrafts at the spaceport nearby the apothecary, then rode two large public hoverbuses to the center of Rydel. Carla Sonetta rode in the first one with a group of students, and Zain rode in the second one with Gabrielle and his team of survivors: Nyrin, Garie, and Issac. When the headmistress and her group of women stepped off at a registered bus stop, Zain led Gabrielle by the arm and exited his bus as well.

Flushed with lights, the square in the center of the city still bustled with life. Musicians played cheerful melodies and dancers frolicked near a fountain in the square's center, all trying to procure a few more coins before retiring for the night. Ignoring the distractions, Carla led them away from the square and up a slightly inclined cobblestone road. Zain followed, moving through narrow streets made crowded by the size of their party. Eventually, they stopped in front of a two-story wooden house enclosed by a forked metal gate. Parts of the building had been renovated to rectify damage and aging, and one section on the right wing of the large compound was a new addition that boasted a facade of stone instead of wood.

Carla Sonetta stopped before the gate and pushed a button. A moment later, a woman's voice greeted them in Emporian. Carla Sonetta responded in kind. Then silence lingered once again until a man's voice came through the speaker. Lights flared up in the home and Zain saw two faces peeking behind the curtains of the windows, as inconspicuous as could be. Carla Sonetta continued speaking to the man in Emporian, but her voice sounded urgent and stressed now.

Another long stretch of silence passed.

Finally, the gates opened, and the headmistress ushered everyone through before entering herself. No one dared to walk up the steps to the home, though, until she did so. Before she reached the top step of the estate, the front door opened and an old man and woman stood together in the light of their entry. Carla Sonetta walked inside and, without a moment's hesitation, proceeded to kiss both of them on their cheeks. The sea of women that had been waiting patiently before the house swarmed the estate. Zain and his party entered last, where Carla Sonetta stopped them to have a word with the old couple.

"Gabrielle, Zain, this is Cabal Sendel and his wife, Esther. They will host us for the night."

"It is a pleasure to meet you. Especially you, Gabrielle." Cabal held out his hand.

Gabrielle blushed. "What do you mean?"

Cabal didn't respond for a second. He paused, as if rearranging his thoughts. "It's nothing," he decided. "Carla has told us so much about you, though, and your accomplishments over the past years with Gracie's."

Gabrielle bowed a little. With Zain's help, she took Cabal's outstretched hand. "Za pleasure is mine, Mr. Sendel. You have done so much for zis school."

"It is but a legacy of my forefathers, please."

Carla Sonetta turned to Zain. "Zain, in the times before and after the Great War, it was the Sendel family that helped build Gracie's Academy to what it is today. Did you know that?"

Zain shook his head.

She turned back to the old man and his wife. "Zain comes from Gazo's Academy in Ka'Che. I don't think they ever tell the whole origin story over there."

"It is certainly quite the tale," Cabal said, nodding. "But a tale for another day. Set your things down and get comfy. We do not have much space here, but we have bedrooms for at least Gabrielle and Carla. Esther can show them."

"Follow me."

The women disappeared up to the second floor.

"Zain, I have one spare room for you, if you'd like. My son Clark doesn't live here any longer. He's moved to the south."

"How about the rest of my men?"

"The three of them are welcome to any floor space or couch that hasn't been claimed by the women yet. There is room in my study, I believe."

Zain turned. "Garie, you're larger than I am. You can have the bed."

"Are you sure, Zain?"

Zain nodded and smiled.

"Well, if you insist, Z.Z."

"Let me show you the way then, Garie."

After Cabal had shown Garie to the extra room on the second floor, he came back down the steps and led Zain, Issac, and Nyrin to the study. There, Zain leaned back on a cushioned bench below a window. Issac took the couch, leaving Nyrin with a chair with a separate footrest. Putting one of the pillows from the couch behind his back, Zain settled his hands on his lap and looked towards the midnight sky. Although he couldn't see the stars due to the glare of the city lights on the window, he still managed to see the moons, and tonight they called to him more than other nights. He didn't know why.

The other two said *goodnight* and Zain repeated it back on instinct. His mind had already drifted elsewhere, to Gabrielle and Carla Sonetta. Her last comment about the withheld information regarding the foundation of Gazo's and Gracie's Academy interested him. What was the real story? Why hadn't he been told the whole thing? What did that mean for him?

As he ruminated on that, he caught himself fidgeting with the ring on his hand yet again. The red of the garnet caught his eye, as it always did. This caused him to finger the scars on his palms. Then, slowly, his eyes drifted to his left forearm. He was tempted to roll up his sleeve, knowing doing so would call forth the past, but he had promised to no longer dwell on that. On Ava. So he resisted the urge, though this did nothing to keep his current predicaments from gnawing at him. His mother was in danger, and attempts to contact her had failed. His father was dead, now nothing more than a cremain jewel on his finger. And Zakk was just as lost as he was. With all of his missteps and wrongdoings in plain sight before him, would praying even make a difference against all the wrong he had committed in his life? Were the Ancients watching him now?

Zain sighed.

He shifted his position and used the cushion as a pillow and laid down flat. He brought his hands together and laid them on top of his chest, fingers locked together. For a long time, he didn't speak; he just stared up at the glare on the glass above him, wondering what he should say. Finally, he decided he needed to say something. "I don't know how this whole thing goes. I don't really know what I'm supposed to say. I'm just supposed to say something to you, I guess. But I feel lost right now. What is the true story of the founding of Gazo's Academy? I don't know how you can tell me or show me that, but I pray that you do. I feel unsure of everything, I guess. And why didn't you heal, Gabrielle? She tells me prayers work, but I've never seen any prayer answered. Maybe you can show me that, too. Maybe you can prove me wrong. Ancients, to this I pray."

Zain put his hands to his side and closed his eyes, wondering if the Ancients even heard him.

"Zain, we have a problem."

Groggy and exhausted, Zain blinked into consciousness as hands shook his shoulder. He groaned as he took in Nyrin's face and look of concern. Blinking again, he noticed Carla Sonetta standing behind Nyrin, cross-armed. Locked to her arm was Gabrielle, and Cabal stood on her other side, looking down, forehead creased as though deep in thought.

Zain bolted upright. "What is it?"

"I went down to the docks this morning to procure your ship for Ka'Che and asked a sailor about voyage to Pelopon. He said his ship was headed there but has no room left. I asked why and he mentioned to me that a mandate came in late last night requiring all ships prepare to sail to Pelopon with Marquis Crine's troops."

Zain looked from Cabal to Carla Sonetta.

"Another sailor gave me the same story. By the time I had approached two more, some Emporian soldiers were already making their way to the docks. The fourth one told me he even heard rumors of ships ferrying Lord Zigarda's men."

Zain jumped to his feet. "Zigarda is here?"

"I left to come back here after I heard that."

"What time is it?"

"It's already nine," Carla Sonetta said.

The study door opened and Esther walked in. "Cabal, there are two men outside asking for entrance into our compound."

Every head in the room turned toward Esther.

Cabal held up his hand to his wife. "I'll be right there." To everyone else, he said. "Wait here." They exited together.

"Zigarda is here, Zain. Zigarda!" Issac paced around the room. "Do you think they know we are here?"

Zain bit his lip. He didn't have an answer; luckily, he didn't need one. Carla Sonetta spoke.

"Maybe. But, then again, maybe not. The apothecary at the spaceport had to record our visit. Our hovercrafts are there as well, yes. But there is also footage and records of Gracie's students boarding the intersystem transports. With the hovercrafts abandoned there, they may think all of us left the planet. That is our best-case scenario."

"And our worst case?" Issac tilted his head.

"I believe that is being checked on right now," Zain said. He put his hands behind his head and paced.

"What will we—"

Nyrin was cut short when the door opened.

"I managed to buy some time, but they will be back," Cabal said, "probably with Marquis Crine himself. I hope Lord Zigarda doesn't show."

"What happened?" Carla asked.

"Empora is searching for you and your students."

"It's because of us." Zain lowered his head.

"Zain, we made za choice to help you. Do not feel bad."

Zain lifted his head. Were his emotions so obvious, or was Gabrielle that perceptive, even when blind?

"A group of your size all going to one place is hard to miss. I'm guessing word went out that you may be here, no doubt encouraged by my presence at the docks earlier and footage of your arrival yesterday."

"Cabal, what can we do?" Carla Sonetta asked.

"I have a plan." Cabal stepped away from his wife to the desk in the corner of the room. After rummaging through a drawer, he pulled something out and stood before Carla Sonetta and Gabrielle. "Gabrielle, hold out your hand." Cabal placed a token in Gabrielle's hand.

What is that?

"I... I don't understand." Gabrielle felt the coin with her fingers, trying to identify it through touch.

Carla Sonetta grabbed the coin from Gabrielle. "Cabal, is this..."

He frowned. "It is."

Zain came to stand alongside the headmistress. On one side of the coin, the image of an embossed scorpion dominated the scene, its tail arched and ready to strike. A small spider hung from a small strand of thread directly in front of the tail.

Carla whispered something to Gabrielle and handed back the coin.

Gabrielle gasped and turned her face toward Cabal once more. "Za resistance. You are a member?" She fingered the coin more carefully now, feeling each embossed groove.

Cabal nodded. "My family has been a member since Zigarda took control of the throne from his father. Gabrielle, when Carla forced you to end your relationship with Guy, it was upon my advice."

Gabrielle dropped her mouth and turned her head to the headmistress, then back to Cabal.

"Do not be angry with her for doing such a thing. It was for the good of Gracie's Academy, to which my family holds much deeper ties. I knew such an open relationship between the Scorpions' leader and the Academy's star student would put too much unwanted attention on the Academy.

"My family's clout in Empora's early years has kept Gracie's funded, open, and thriving. That kind of open affiliation, though, may have ended that, despite the reputation my family possesses." Cabal turned his attention to Carla. "It is that reputation that is giving me a moment's reprieve before they demand entry, but only a moment, and you and your women have to leave by then. The coin I gave Gabrielle will grant you an audience with the resistance. Ride east to Terran. There, you will find a pub called *The Brew Frontiere*. A man named Rune will find you there." He tightened his jaw, and with serious eyes, he exchanged a glance with everyone in the room.

"How?" Issac asked. "We don't have hovercrafts and there is sure to be more security everywhere."

"You're correct. You won't be able to use the city's buses again." Cabal nodded. "To the east of my building, though, there is a waiting station for taxicrafts."

"Taxis? There are more than sixty of us, Cabal." Carla Sonetta sharpened her voice, clearly opposed to the idea.

"Taxicraft..." Zain muttered to himself. "No. It can work." He snapped his fingers and arched his eyebrows. "I took one on the way back from the Core. For the right amount of money, they can take us anywhere."

"Mr. Berrese, most of the Academy's money was used buying the transport fares for the women who aren't with us now."

Cabal spoke quietly. "I have money I can spare you, Carla."

The headmistress shifted her head, her discomfort clear.

Zain took a step forward. "Cabal's plan will work. Any taxi will be more than glad to take us to the spaceport—"

"No," Cabal said, shaking his head. "You should take the taxi all the way to Terran. Zigarda will be alerted to your presence again if the hovercrafts are moved from the spaceport."

"Cabal is right. They can be easily tracked."

"Taxicrafts will be your best bet right now because they aren't mass public transport. I doubt the drivers have been alerted to look for us yet. Marquis Crine will be slow to announce such a disturbance to radio. He won't do so without Lord Zigarda's confirmation. An accusation against Gracie's is serious. Our reputation is not insignificant and such an act will have implications in the senate. Zigarda will want proof first. He may be a ruthless leader, but he isn't careless."

"Will there be enough?" Issac asked. "We'll need seventeen taxicrafts at least, assuming each one has space for four."

"We can only pray," Carla said. "I will go inform the others and start grouping them."

Zain felt nervous energy building in his stomach.

"I'll go tell Garie," Nyrin offered.

"And I can help organize the groups," Issac said.

"Carla, I will go ready some provisions for your group." Esther bowed out of the room, followed closely by Nyrin, Issac, and Carla.

Cabal

approached Gabrielle and placed a hand on her shoulder. He glanced from her to Zain, then offered a wry smile

. "I never thought I would have the pleasure of having students from both academies in this house again at the same time. Truly momentous, considering how things were left."

"How were things left?" Zain asked without meaning to.

"In a schism of death..." Cabal said. "At least, so I've heard. I have to go make some calls now, Gabrielle, to tell the Scorpions of your impending arrival."

"Guy will know I'm coming?" she asked.

"Do you want him to know?"

Gabrielle shook her head. "I know him. He would do somezing brash if he knew I was coming."

"Then I will only mention Carla and Gracie's."

"Zank you."

Cabal bowed his head and left.

After the door closed, Gabrielle turned to Zain. She extended her hands. "Zain, would you like to pray with me?"

Zain hesitated, thankful Gabrielle couldn't see his unease. "I... I don't really understand how still."

"Zen take my hands and just listen."

Zain eyed her hands cautiously before accepting them. Gabrielle rubbed his knuckles with her thumbs. "What is zis?"

"It is a cremain. Your headmistress gave it to me."

The pleasant smile dropped from Gabrielle's face as her lips parted in surprise.

"My father. He died. Before the incident with Zakk."

"Zain, I'm so—"

Zain shook his head. "No. It is I who should be sorry for all of this. And what I put you through. Gabrielle, you lost your vision because of me."

"If it means you find faiz, it will be worz it."

Zain cocked his head. "What do you mean?"

"Headmistress Sonetta told me you asked her to teach you to pray."

Zain blushed. "I... I still don't really understand it, in truth. I don't know what to say or if it even matters with all the wrong I've done in my life."

Gabrielle put a finger to his lips. "Zain, who you are before you find za Ancients isn't za person you are after. Zey forgive all who are earnest in seeking zem. Pray and you will see. Seek zem out and you will see."

"Can you show me?"

Gabrielle smiled. "I would be delighted." She cleared her throat and squeezed his knuckles. "Ancients, hear my prayer. My mind is yours, free to zink as you zought." She brought her left hand up to her forehead. "My body is naked and pure, free to fight even za darkness of night." She clenched her right hand into a fist by her heart. "Take my soul, uncovered and untainted, free to bind." She brought both hands together near her lips, kissed her hands, and then reached back to grab Zain's hands. "Never let us forget zat you give za air we breaze; never let it grow stale. Never let us forget zat you drench us in za flames of Freyr and Lugh to keep us warm, even when zings seem cold. Never let us forget zat you make solid za water, which helps us stand. Never let us forget zat you feed us, spiritually and physically, wiz your words and grains zat you give us." Gabrielle forced Zain's hands upward, making sure they were in the position she taught him. "Ancients, guide us how only you can guide us. Keep us safe; protect us. Remove za guilt zat chains us to our past. Be our shields in zis time of uncertainty and tribulation. Ancients, to zis I pray."

Gabrielle let hands fall, bringing Zain's hands down in the process. She leaned on her tiptoes and pecked him on the cheek. Then she stood back and smiled at him. Zain's heart beat unsteadily and he looked at her in awe. And even though he could see everything, he still felt blind and wondered what Gabrielle saw.

CHAPTER FOURTEEN

MUSE

Wind rushed past her face, flinging her black hair behind her. She didn't squint; the sunglasses covered her eyes from the breeze. But even with the protection, she couldn't see. It had been almost a week now since the incident. To keep herself from going insane in the world of blackness that now enveloped her, she recalled, with all the vividness she could muster, the sight of things that mattered to her. Of places she would never forget and of people who meant the most to her, those whose faces she might never again see, but whose image she didn't want to lose: her mother, Carla Sonetta, classmates, those she had met during the Trials. And Zain. Whenever she thought of him, a slight smile formed on her lips. He had wanted to start practicing prayer, and that was already a huge step in the right direction. *From faith to faith, as it is said.*

But then Zain's face would fade, replaced by another, one she was surely going to meet soon enough—Guy Smith. Gabrielle rubbed her thumb across Cabal's coin, feeling the embossed scorpion. She sighed.

"What's wrong, hun?"

She turned her head to her friend's voice and felt Perrine squeeze her hand. She had agreed to ride with her east to Terran. In an effort to be less conspicuous, some students rode with strangers, having paid the taxicraft drivers extra to continue onward to Terran. Similar precautions also split up their group so that prominent figures in Gracie's Academy wouldn't ride together. So although Carla had wanted to accompany Gabrielle, she rode in a different taxicraft with three other students.

Since leaving the other two passengers at the spaceport an hour before, it had been just her and Perrine. The driver didn't talk, for which Gabrielle was thankful. She wouldn't be able to make conversation. If she couldn't even hold on to her own thoughts, what hope did she have holding a conversation for the hours required to get to Terran?

"What do you mean?"

"Well, you've been quiet for a while. How are you holding up?"

"I... I'm fine, zanks. I was just zinking."

"About what?"

She opened her mouth, then shut it again, not sure if she was ready to share. Perrine had been Gabrielle's first roommate at the Academy, and they had known each other for fifteen years, grown up together. But Gabrielle wasn't sure the other woman could really understand her. Could anyone? No one else lived in this world of blackness; she was alone.

"If you don't want to talk, that's fine. Just know that I'm here for you. Everyone is here for you."

Gabrielle felt another squeeze. She smiled, nodded, and squeezed back. Time passed. How much, Gabrielle didn't know. *Couldn't* know. While she couldn't see the suns, the heat on her face never dissipated, which probably meant it was midday or a little past.

"I can see the mountains finally."

Gabrielle imagined the looming Frontiere Mountains slowly coming into view before her. On a particularly good day, one could see them from Gracie's Academy if they were on a high enough level, but she lived in the opposite wing that only pointed to the north, to Mendeck and the Red Cloud.

"We will be passing the junction of the Great Bridge soon. It looks like we will get there without any trouble."

"Do you zink za bridge junction will be monitored?"

"All we can do is pray."

Perrine said a shortened version of the prayer, causing Gabrielle to smile. It was nice to be around someone with faith. Eventually, she hoped to share the same feeling with Zain, but she knew the path to faith was long and arduous, consisting of trials and tribulations that broke many. But it delivered purpose. She believed that more than anything.

Zain, however, had only just begun. What tests would the Ancients throw his way before he would realize his purpose? Even she had yet to realize her own purpose, but she had faith there was such a purpose; otherwise, she surely wouldn't be in the back seat of a taxicraft with her first roommate—she would have succumbed to the crueler realities of life.

Gabrielle joined in on the last line and said, "We pray to get zere safely. Ancients, to zis we pray." She kissed Perrine's hand and released it, feeling, at least for a moment, a bit of peaceful release. "I appreciate your company, Perrine. Zank you."

"Gabe... I... well, I appreciate yours as well."

Another brief moment of silence passed. Gabrielle bit her lip. "Can you walk on water?"

Perrine choked back a startled laugh. "What kind of question is that?"

Gabrielle heard a snort that must have come from the taxicraft driver.

Gabrielle leaned over and whispered. "Ignore him, Perrine. I want to know, zough. Please." Gabrielle felt out for her hand, but found it only after mistakenly squeezing her friend's thigh.

"I..." Perrine's voice quivered. "I haven't tried again since failing the first time after I learned the prayer."

"But why?"

"I don't want to explain."

"Why not?"

"Gabrielle, please don't make me."

"What is it? You can tell me. We're friends." Gabrielle squeezed her hand and then rubbed the top of it with her other. A smile came to her lips, even if it was a little forced.

"I..."

Pause.

"What is it?" Gabrielle rubbed her hand on top of Perrine's even more. There was something wrong. She could feel it now.

"I never tried again because of you."

Gabrielle leaned back, taking in the information.

"There. I said it."

"Me?" Part of her wanted to keep the next question to herself, but it escaped her lips. "But why?"

"Because I was always envious of you. The girl who walked on water after her first two years at the Academy. The woman who has never been beaten. Still has never been beaten."

"I don't understand."

"Gabrielle, you were Headmistress Sonetta's favorite student. You still are. If we didn't need to be so discrete, she would be riding in this taxicraft right now with you. Am I right?"

"I don't know—"

"It's true. No one else refers to her by her first name. Only you. For me it's always *headmistress.*"

"But—"

"Because you *are* Gracie's Academy, Gabe. You *are* the lifeblood of the school, whether you know it or not. The women who are here now, the women who are going to Terran to help you with Zain's situation only do so because of the courage you show in not abandoning him. You know that, don't you?"

Prickles climbed Gabrielle's arms despite the warmth of the sun. A shudder shot through her spine. She drew in a shaky breath and put a hand to her forehead, trying to make sense of her friend's words. Her comparison. *Is that why Carla gave me her sword? Does she think I represent Gracie's? Does she think that even now? Do others look at me the same way?* The thoughts that consumed her made her temporarily speechless. Enough so that Perrine spoke again.

"I... I was worried that if I couldn't do it... couldn't do it like you, who had already accomplished it, that I wasn't meant for Gracie's. That I wouldn't belong there. So..."

"You never did." Gabrielle finished. It died on the wind as soon as it left her mouth.

"No. I never did."

Gabrielle had known that others in the Academy looked up to her. That had never been a secret. But she had never understood the extent of it. The realization made her speechless.

The hovercraft remained silent until the taxicraft driver spoke. "Ladies, we're at the junction between the road and the Great Bridge."

"Za main road."

"I know. There seems to be traffic up ahead though."

"Is that usual?" Perrine asked.

"Don't usually take long rides like this, miss. I couldn't tell yah."

The speed of the taxicraft eventually died to nothing more than stop-and-go traffic. "It seems like there is some sort of accident or stopping point up ahead," the driver said

"Can you go around it?" Perrine asked.

"Not anymore."

She turned her head away and pretended to look out the window. She tucked a strand of hair behind her ear before turning to Perrine again. "Can I ask you somezing?"

"Sure, what is it?"

A pang pressed on her heart. With a deep breath, she found the strength to ask. "If you are so afraid, why are you helping me now?"

"What do you mean? Because Zain needs your help and you are unable to."

She twisted her lips. "What do you mean by that?"

"I'm sorry. That didn't come out right. Let me try again. Uhmm... Well... now that you're... well... you know."

"Blind?"

"Yeah... I... I feel more capable... I feel as though now it's my time to help Gracie's, and that means helping you, Gabe. I... I... feel as though if I can help you, I can prove to myself that I am competent enough to be a Gracie's student."

Gabrielle ruminated about those words for a few minutes. Could this be it? Her purpose? Was she here to help others to grow? She bit her lower lip and drummed her fingers against the side of the taxicraft like little patters of rain.

"Ladies, it looks like they're stopping everyone at the halfway toll. Some sort of inspection."

Gabrielle's neck tightened. "How many until it's our turn?"

"Seven. Maybe more."

Gabrielle turned to Perrine. "Are you wearing anyzing zat mentions za Academy?"

"Nothing... but... they'll recognize you, surely."

"How do you mean?"

"You're our most famous student. If Zigarda is checking for someone, it would be you or the headmistress."

And this is why we split up.

"You two ladies in trouble or something?"

"It's nothing," Perrine said. "Five now, Gabe."

"Hey now, ladies, I don't want any trouble or nothing here."

"There won't be," Perrine said, her voice stern. "They aren't looking for us."

"The worry in your voices says otherwise, miss."

"Just be casual and normal. We will double your fee, understood? Three now, Gabrielle. Driver, understood?" Perrine's voice escalated with each sentence.

"Understood. Casual."

Gabrielle mumbled the prayer to herself, hoping for smooth passage. "Never let za air we breaze grow stale, drench us in za flames we..." She stopped. "Za flames we use." She mumbled again. Her face grew hot. Without the wind cooling her skin, the heat from the suns intensified. *That's it.* She slapped the leather seat in excitement. "Perrine, where are the suns now?"

"Southeast."

"What hour?"

"Your two, why?"

"I have an idea."

"I hope it works because we're next."

Gabrielle swallowed down her nerves. Out of habit, she reached one hand to her garter and the dagger concealed there. It had saved her life and won her battles more times than she had fingers.

"Where this taxicraft going, sir?" The voice, brisk and bored, floated through the window to Gabrielle's ears

"Terran," the driver said casually.

"And who you got with you?"

"Don't know their names. Just a couple of women I picked up."

"Where are you coming from?"

"Rydel."

"And where are you going again?"

"Terran, sir. Is something the matter?"

"Nothing that concerns you. Roll down your windows please, we'd like to examine the passengers."

"Sure, sure."

Gabrielle heard her window lower even more. Her heart raced. Footsteps approached.

"Names please, ladies."

"Madison Vinet."

"Alexa Ahumada." Gabrielle shook her head slightly at her error. She should have used something less obvious than her mother's maiden name. Her fingers tapped the side of her left thigh.

"Identification?" A second voice, this one hoarse and coming from Perrine's side of the hovercraft.

She felt Perrine move next to her.

"I don't know where it went off to." A slight squeal hung in Perrine's voice.

"Your identification, madam."

Gabrielle looked around toward the voice on her side of the taxicraft. "Uhmm..."

"My friend forgot hers as well," Perrine said. "Why do we even need our identification? We aren't the ones driving." Perrine giggled.

"That's confidential, miss," said the man with the hoarse voice.

Gabrielle resisted the urge to swing her head back towards the sound. Instead, she kept her head forward, focused on the man who surely was observing her to her right. Gabrielle breathed, continuing to keep her pulse slow and steady.

"Can you take off your sunglasses, Alexa? We need to check faces."

Gabrielle ignored the knotting in her stomach and thought about her movements strategically. The trick would be not to let this man truly see her eyes. With her right hand she removed the glasses, put her forearm over her eyebrows, and looked up at the man as if shielding her vision from the suns' rays.

A moment passed.

Then two.

Gabrielle felt the need to grab the hilt of her dagger, but she resisted temptation.

Another moment passed.

Taut with suspense, she forced a smile to her lips. "Za suns are so bright today, I can hardly see. Can I put my sunglasses back on?"

"Yeah. Go ahead. All clear."

Gabrielle put her glasses back on and returned her right arm to her lap, leaving the left one by her thigh.

"Have a nice day, both of you," Perrine said. When safely out of earshot, she continued, "That was clever thinking, Gabe. I know why you asked about the suns now."

Gabrielle forced a smile. "Yeah."

"See, driver, nothing to worry about. Take us to Terran now."

The taxicraft started again and steadily regained its speed. The traffic stop would set them back a little for time, but there were no other major junctions between there and Terran. It would be at least another four hours before they arrived, and the ride would give her much needed time to consider what had just happened. Even though they had made it past the checkpoint, webs of doubt stuck to her. If she had withdrawn her dagger, what would've happened? If it wasn't for Perrine, where would she be now? Was she really as valuable as everyone thought she was? And the more she thought, the less certain she was of anything.

CHAPTER FIFTEEN

THE MEN FROM THE SOUTH

Even though it was foolish for her to do so, every day Brisine had been watching the sea, waiting for her husband and son. Ever since the news had come nearly a week ago that her son and her husband would be returning from Lord Zigarda's prison, she clung to the hope of seeing them again. And not just in holographic form, as she had been limited to for so long. She had heard from them sparingly, once when they had departed Liom to sail west, and later merely as a recorded message in which they expressed how much they missed her. She remembered how Laron had even pretended to take her hand and kiss it before blowing a kiss to her lips. Just the way he used to. She would relish that touch again soon. But for now, all she could do was wait.

Brisine sighed. It wasn't a sigh of regret, though, or worry, it was one of longing. She often caught herself spending countless hours just watching the sea, feeling the breeze rushing past and ruffling the hems of her dresses. The last few days, though, the communication had gone as cold as the stone that fortified the castle walls. That was to be expected, though. Not much happened in the open waters besides kraken duels, and she preferred her husband and her son not to get mixed up in one of those.

As always when she got tired of looking at the sea or when her stomach rumbled, she wandered back within the castle walls, had lunch with her brother and the other members of his council, and then passed her time by meandering around the central courtyard or its serpentine passageways. She had grown up in this castle, that was true, but since marrying at the age of twenty-one, she had lived in Stel for a little over thirty years, revisiting her childhood home only once or twice a year.

For her, it was too spacious. Too many nooks and crannies one could dally in for days on end, and while this had been amusing in her youth, she found it to be a little overwhelming in her mid-age.

So far, the day had played out in the exact same monotony as the preceding ones, but that all changed in the flap of a falcon's wing. She had been finishing the usual lunch with her brother, his family, and the other dignitaries he kept in his council when a man she didn't know told her brother of an urgent call in the telecommunication chamber.

Abraham paused for a second and wiped his mouth, but then continued eating. When the man restated the urgency, however, his brows had furrowed, and he had tossed down his linen and strode out of the chamber, leaving everyone to wonder what the news could be. Brisine hurried after him.

Within minutes, they had traversed the serpentine walls with a receiver's grace and stopped inside the telecommunication chamber. Two technicians were within, one sitting at a monitor and the other standing, arms crossed, making small talk with the person on the telecommunicator screen, a man Brisine knew to be Ryder Scarus, Marquis Brryn Ropis's receiver from the major southern city of Callumbra. A quite unexpected guest, indeed. So unexpected, in fact, that her brother cocked his head and blinked, as if making sure he was seeing who he thought he saw.

The doors closed behind them.

"Sheamus, thank you for fetching Lord Vangle."

The man named Sheamus nodded and returned to his seat at the main control panel.

"My lord, Receiver Scarus is here with urgent news from the—"

Scarus broke in. "Lord Vangle, Callumbra is under attack."

Abraham coughed. Brisine even did a double take at the words. Everything seemed off kilter all of a sudden.

"There is no time to waste, my lord. Callumbra is under attack. It started within the past hour."

"By whom? Where is Marquis Ropis?"

"The marquis is gathering forces and preparing to stop the Chaons."

"Chaon is invading us?"

Receiver Scarus nodded. "Yes. They came upon us just before mid-day."

"In the middle of the day, that makes no—"

"It makes perfect sense, my lord," Lukas Vangle said, edging forward from the back of the telecommunication chamber. He was Abraham's lead guard—and elder brother, if truth be told. But since he could not cast Power, the throne had passed to Abraham upon their father's death years back. "Because it is so hot in the south at this time of day, many of the men take a respite from the heat, preferring to busy themselves with eating or catch some rest in the shade. Many would not be as prepared as you think."

"And that is exactly what happened," confirmed Receiver Scarus.

Abraham blinked his eyes and put a hand to his forehead, massaging it, trying to make sense of all the information. "What kind of numbers are we looking at here?" He gestured with his hands.

"Fifty-thousand. Maybe more."

"Fifty-thous..." Advisor Errion Vesk's voice tapered off. "My lord, that is—"

"Substantial. Overwhelming," Lukas cut in. "They must have forces gathered from their port-side cities. That's the only way to mass such numbers so quickly."

"It doesn't matter how they have this many people. What matters is what will we do, my lord," Receiver Scarus said. "We need more men if we are to keep control of Callumbra."

"Are reinforcements from Redview and Berson on the way?"

"Yes, we called them to come to our aid before contacting you, but they are both minor cities. They won't amount to much help. Most of their forces are already living within Callumbra."

"Have they taken the spaceport yet?" Lukas asked.

"Not at this moment. We are holding that as the highest priority."

Abraham crossed his arms. "Good. Continue holding it. We will send aid. It'll be best if our ships can land within the area of the spaceport."

"Thank you, my lord. How many can we expect?"

"Half of our strength."

"Only half?"

"That should be more than sufficient, Receiver Scarus. We can never leave the capital unprotected. If you need more soldiers, contact Marquis Moxxie."

"Then I will do so, my lord." Receiver Scarus bowed. "Good day, my lord. Thank you for helping."

"The falcon always watches."

The communication cut.

"Lukas, gather the other generals. Have them spread the word in the capital. Soldiers in reserve should make their way to the spaceport immediately. I want you to gather another thousand troops from within the castle walls and ready them for battle in the south as well."

"Should I go as well?"

Abraham didn't respond right away. He bit his lower lip for a moment, mulling over his thoughts. "Yes. You will be my voice down in the south. I grant you all the authority to command the battle as you see fit. We cannot afford to lose Callumbra, do you understand?"

"I do, Brother."

Brisine's heart swelled. She didn't often hear the two talk like that, but when she did, she knew they transcended duty and stepped into a familial bond.

"I will begin preparations, then. We will take off by nightfall." Lukas shook his brother's forearm.

Abraham pulled his elder brother close, resting their foreheads together for a moment. "The falcon always watches."

"The falcon always watches," Lukas repeated.

"Lukas," Brisine cut into the show of brotherly love, "stay safe down there."

"Of course, little sister." He smiled and left without a moment's more hesitation.

Lord Vangle paced the telecommunication chamber with hands clasped behind his back, ignoring the quiet conversations among his receiver, advisor, and other family members in the room. Brisine just watched as he paced, knowing that he was determining his next course of action. He had become a lord again. And was taking steps to maneuver through this difficulty efficiently.

"Quinn..."

"Yes, my lord," said the man in charge of the telecommunication chamber.

"Pull up Lord Kapache. I wonder if there is a way we can solve whatever dispute caused this without bloodshed."

"On it. Sheamus."

"Already on it, Captain." The man who had retrieved them earlier nodded and turned to the panel and screens arrayed before him.

One.

Two.

Error. Cannot connect.

Brisine blinked and shook her head. *Error?*

"Error? What does that mean, *error*?" Abraham asked, his voice growing tighter with tension.

"I don't know..."

"Try again."

"Yes, my lord." Again the man scrolled through the list of contacts, found the telecommunication number of Lord Kapache, and dialed—to the same result.

Quinn went over to the control panel and did it himself, only to receive the same error message on the screen. Frowning, he pulled up a meticulous network of backend jargon that Brisine couldn't begin to comprehend.

"My lord, we will figure out what is wrong with the communication system. Until then, be patient."

Abraham sighed. "I have no choice but to be. Make sure to get this chamber up and running to full capacity. I want to speak to Lord Kapache." Abraham turned back to the others in the room. "Kylan, are you understanding just how difficult it is to be a lord?"

"Yes, Father."

"Good. I wouldn't wish it on you." He sighed again. "What's next? They always say bad things come in threes. Surely there has to be one—"

At that exact moment, a beep came from a device on the wrist of Abraham's receiver. He accepted the call and a holographic face of a guard spoke to him. "Receiver Mansen, Conseleigh Katore is here to see the lord."

"Conseleigh Katore?" The receiver's eyebrows arched, and he looked at the others in the room.

"Yes, sir. He says he needs to speak to Lord Vangle."

Abraham nodded.

"Very well," Receiver Mansen said. "I will come pick him up."

The communication cut.

"And that is the third. How perfect. Owlen, bring Conseleigh Katore to the throne room. I'll see him there."

"Yes, my lord."

"Quinn, inform me when you solve this fiasco."

"Yes, my lord."

Without another word, Abraham left and made his way to the throne room. Silence lingered in his wake until curiosity got the better of Brisine and the others. They followed the lord once more, waiting for the third tiding of bad news.

The doors to the throne room opened, and the receiver entered with the silver-haired man, Luvan Katore. He stood eye-level with Brisine and wore a yellow silk-threaded vest. A golden band on his finger told her of the vow he was committed to, and pierced lightning bolts studded his ears, but he wore no other jewelry.

Her brother rolled back his shoulders and cleared his throat. "Conseleigh Katore, this is most unexpected."

"Sorry to be a bother to you, Lord Vangle."

"It's a welcome distraction right now. Please." Abraham gestured for Conseleigh Katore to come closer. "Do you bring more news of Zain?"

Luvan tilted his head slightly. "No. No, I'm afraid I don't. Other business calls me here." He exchanged glances with all of them.

"So what is it, then? What brings you to Castle Semson? Why not Conseleigh Iycel?"

Luvan raised an eyebrow. "Typically, it would be Conseleigh Aprorum who would be treating with you. Is this to whom you refer?"

"No." Abraham shook his head. "Conseleigh Iycel arrived here just last week. She told us Conseleigh Aprorum had suffered an injury during the Meeting of the Twelve. She came here with Apprentice Mourse."

Luvan's face remained stoic. "She is currently busy training Apprentice Mourse in combat and Power until Ethen is healed." Luvan chuckled. "So much can happen in the span of only a few days."

"Or even a few hours." Abraham chuckled to himself. He shook his head. "Anyway, go on, what brings you here?"

"Well, I must confess something to you. I am not here on behalf of Guardian Eska, but rather an important matter concerning the Guardian."

A frown brough a shadow to Abraham's eyes. "Continue."

"There will be a meeting in twenty-one days at the Hall of Voices in Mistral."

"What does this meeting concern?" Errion Vesk asked, arms folded.

"It's concerning the abuse of Power Guardian Eska has recently demonstrated."

"You mean his decision to seal the Twelve?"

"*That...* " Luvan turned his attention to Abraham. "Among other things."

"*What* other things?" Errion asked.

"Broken vows. Brash decisions. To just name a few. Come to the meeting and you will hear more." Once more, Luvan glanced around at the assembled faces.

"Do the other conseleigh know of the hearing?" Errion asked.

"No. I fear the others are too close to the Guardian. They cannot see such things as I see."

"Does Guardian Eska know?"

"Unless the lords and ladies back my statements and my case, there is no reason to draw attention to such a thing. Only you, as a collective, have the authority to overturn his guardianship. If you find my narrative and evidence substantial, we can proceed to the next step."

"Very well," Abraham agreed.

"Then I take my leave. I will see you in three weeks."

"Wait, Conseleigh Katore!" Abraham held up his hand to call the man back to the circle.

"Yes, Lord Vangle?"

"You mentioned all the lords and ladies will be attending."

"Yes. My partner and I are disseminating the information now. There is no written evidence of my visit here today, just verbal for the time being in order to keep it as secretive as possible. I hope you understand."

Abraham waved off this statement. "Yes, surely. Have you visited Lord Kapache yet?"

"No. You are my first here on Myoli. My next stop will be Lord Zigarda."

"Hmm. Never mind then."

"Is it concerning the spaceships I saw being readied?"

"You have very good eyes, conseleigh."

"That's what we conseleigh are, the Guardian's eyes. And his ears if he has sense enough to listen."

"It seems he doesn't."

"Not for a while lately, I'm afraid. Anyway, it isn't in the Guardian of the Core's nature, nor that of his conseleigh, to interfere in the happenings of other planets, so I do wish you the best of luck in your situation."

"This war will not take long to quell. The falcon always watches."

"So I've heard." Luvan nodded his head and left with Receiver Mansen.

Abraham closed his eyes, breathed in deeply, and exhaled. "What a mess," he said, eyes still closed.

Errion asked, "What do you make of this hearing?"

Abraham opened his eyes. "I have no opinion yet. My mind is scattered."

"Yes, but Conseleigh Katore is acting alone in this. It doesn't feel right to me. And did you notice there was no C on his vest?"

Brisine had thought nothing of the object's absence. "Perhaps he simply forgot it?"

Errion frowned at her. "Maybe, but there may be something more that we don't know. I advise that we speak with Guardian Eska."

"No."

"Why not?"

"His actions *have* been questionable," Abraham conceded. "Conseleigh Katore is smart in spreading the word of this meeting personally. If I were to contact Guardian Eska, it would be my word against his. It would make me look brash." Abraham strummed his chin. "If we don't get this damn telecommunication chamber up in time, it will give me a chance to see Zalos in person."

"That is a long time to wait, my lord."

"Yes. Much too long. That is why I would rather do it virtually. Errion, would you go check on the status of the telecommunication room?"

"Of course, my lord." He bowed and left the lord's chambers, leaving only Lord Vangle and his immediate family in the room.

"All of you here, listen," Abraham said. "I want you to know that should we fail to stop Chaon in Callumbra, should the war come north, should it reach Pelopon, I want you to not be here when they come. Kylan, you would take my spot in this meeting, and Shayna, you would go with him. Bri, I believe it'd be best for you to go along as well."

"Abe, what about you?" Shayna asked. She approached the throne and took her husband's hand.

"I cannot abandon the castle. Not during a time like that. If the battle goes poorly, I must be like a commander on a sinking ship. Duty binds me in place." He spared all of them a glance. "This stays between us, though."

"Laron should be back by the time the meeting occurs," Brisine said. "I could take him and Zain with me. They could stay with Jamaal."

Abraham nodded. "That would be a wise thing to do, Bri. A wise thing to do."

The room stayed silent for a while, upended by Abraham's troubling words. Hands knotted together close to her breasts, Brisine lost herself in visions of the castle overrun by flames, the walls caving in, and all of them in tombs of castle stone as the Chaons claimed their home. The home that had raised her with stories and lore from the grandparents and caretakers assigned to her. The place where she had grown up until her marriage. All of it laid in piles of rubble and remnants should war come to pass. The only thing to break the heavy silence in the room was the door opening and the return of Abraham's advisor.

"Good news finally, Errion?"

The advisor shook his head. "Still malfunctioning, I'm afraid, my lord, but it seems they've pinpointed where exactly the problem is occurring."

"A step in the right direction, at least. Come, let us examine the problem." Abraham pushed himself off his throne. "Kylan, come join me. It'll be good for you to see this. Shay, Bri, remember what we talked about."

Brisine exchanged a look with her sister-in-law and nodded. Shayna offered her support and love before Abraham exited the room with his eldest son and his advisor.

In the silence left behind, Shayna sighed and looked at Brisine. "Well, hopefully things won't unfold that way."

"Lukas is going to the south. He is a good tactician. I know they will stave off the Chaon forces at Callumbra."

Shayna smiled. It seemed forced. "Of course."

"Shay... truly, it'll be alright."

The woman's composure broke. "What do you know of that?" She sniffled. "My husband just..." She launched herself forward into Brisine's arms.

Brisine held onto her sister-in-law, smoothing a hand over her hair. "He is acting as he should. Men are betrothed to duty. We women as well."

"What is our duty?"

"To support our husbands and the difficult decisions they have to make."

She sniffled into Brisine's shoulder. "Power isn't worth all the headache."

Brisine kissed the top of her head and rubbed her back. "It never is." She said the words to comfort Shayna, to appear strong, but in truth, Brisine wondered if Shayna spoke with conviction or out of fear. She had never seen her sister-in-law so distraught before, and Brisine believed it was only because of the tides of misfortune had swept them up in its current.

While Callumbra was on the precipice of war, Pelopon was still safe for the moment and would be for some time. And while that comforted her a little, she remembered Luvan's words. Things could change in just a matter of days. Her daily monotony had been dismantled in mere hours. She wondered what more would change in the weeks ahead. Surely Laron and Zain would be back before things escalated. Until then, she could only wait and worry, searching for them in the closing of her eyes and the light of her memories, for she would much rather be wrapped up in her thoughts than the castle walls that felt ever more constricting with each passing breath.

CHAPTER SIXTEEN

A LESSON IN FAITH

Hands clasped together behind his back, Zain paced his cell in the *Terran Traveler*. It was the most expensive hotel in the city, and as such, offered the most security. It was only a temporary solution to their problem, though. And a very temporary solution at that. The fact that they had to purchase supplies for their upcoming journey, coupled with the high price of a single golden bond per room per night at the hotel, meant that Gabrielle only had a few days to find the man called Rune. It was he who was to guide them to the rebellion, the only place right now that would offer Zain and his party asylum. Shelter was likely. But if Gabrielle was as convincing as she thought she was, there was a chance the rebellion's leaders would choose to aid Zain in stopping Zigarda's quest to overthrow Ka'Che.

As the most wanted man in Empora, Zain wasn't allowed to leave his hotel room. He hadn't even been allowed to be seen at the front desk. Instead, several Gracie students had ushered him in through a door at the back of the hotel once the party had picked up their key cards. Carla Sonetta, recognizable as the headmistress of the illustrious Gracie's Academy, was in a similar position as him, confined to her own room while her students served as her proxy. The faith she showed in them was remarkable, and Zain wondered if he would ever have faith like that. He wished he could see her now and continue learning more about Gracie's ways compared to Gazo's, but he dared not leave. It would only mean trouble. For now, he waited, pondered, and worried.

And he did all of this alone. Garie shared the room but had stepped out to gather supplies for the journey ahead. To minimize attention on their large party of one hundred and thirty-five individuals, while Gabrielle searched for Rune and their pathway to the rebellion, the others had been tasked with gathering supplies and information at set intervals and in small groups.

Eventually, even pacing exhausted Zain, so he sat down in a chair next to the window and looked outside, his gaze roaming over—but not really seeing—the greenery of the park that occupied much of his view. The copper statue of a man with abnormally large feet in the middle of the park had ceased to be a point of even minor curiosity for Zain. He slumped his shoulders. *What would Gabrielle do?*

He knew the answer before finishing his thought. He brought his hands up to his lips. "Ancients, hear my prayer. My... my mind is free to... free to." He bit his lower lip, trying to remember how the prayer went. "Free to think as you think. My soul is pure, even in..." He sighed. His folded hands collapsed. *There are too many words. Do I really need to remember all of them?*

A rustle at the door announced Garie's return. Zain watched as he loosened the drawstring bag on his back and let the contents spill out over one of the beds. "Finished with the first round of provisions."

"How is it out there?"

"Nothing too abnormal if you ask me."

"You didn't spy anyone?"

"I never was much good at that. Issac would know better than me. He's always had an eye for that kind of thing. Nyrin too, even."

Zain pursed his lips. He returned his gaze to the window. "Yeah. You're right. Did you wander by the Brew Frontiere at all?"

"No. Even if I could, I wouldn't, its on the opposite side of town, closer to the mountains."

"Yeah. That's right."

"You okay? You seem a little off."

"I just..." Zain exhaled again. "I just don't want to be locked up in here anymore. I've had enough cells these past few months to last me a lifetime."

"Well, at least this isn't Zigarda's dungeon or his Blood Chambers."

Zain squirmed. He stood up and plopped down on the bed next to the provisions and began idly picking through the pile. "Yeah. I guess you're right."

"But really, Zain, what's bothering you?"

"I feel useless here. You at least have a job to do. I am like a caged animal, and I'm the one that got everyone into this—"

A knock sounded on the door.

Zain sat up straighter. Garie put a hand on his sword, gesturing for Zain to move out of view of the door. Hand on the hilt of his sword, Zain stood and put his back to the wall, every inch of him tense as Garie looked through the peephole.

"It's Gabrielle and the other one. Perrine, I think."

Zain eased his muscles and nodded. Moving away from the wall, he said, "Let them in."

Garie opened the door, and the two women entered.

Once the door was closed, Zain spoke. "You're back. How did it go?"

"I'll let Gabrielle tell you. I'm going to inform the headmistress." Perrine nodded at them and left.

"I'll give you guys some time alone," Garie said, following her out..

"Well?" Zain repeated after the door had closed again.

Gabrielle shook her head. "Nozing."

"Nothing. I thought he was supposed to be there. You have the right place?"

"Yes, Zain. Of course. Well, I assume Perrine knows how to read. But we couldn't find him."

Zain led her to a chair near the window. "What does that mean?"

She sat down and tucked strands of hair behind her ears. "It means we are running out of time. But it's not only zat..."

Zain took a seat across from her and cocked an eyebrow. "What do you—"

"Zere are scouts looking for you, Zain. We ran into some at za bar."

"How do you know?"

"A feeling. Zere was a man. An *odd* man."

"Odd? How do you know?"

"I told Perrine to introduce herself and flirt wiz him. Ask him some questions to see if he was a supporter or not."

"And?"

"He answered wrong."

"How was he supposed to answer?"

"Zat doesn't matter. But Perrine told me he had been looking at us za entire time. Zain, he was onto us. He followed us outside, but I had Perrine lose him zrough za park. I will try again tomorrow."

"You can't." Zain reached for her hand. "That was already close enough."

Gabrielle smiled. "Zain, it will be okay. I have faiz. Za Ancients led us here."

"Cabal led us here."

"But he didn't have to. He risked a great deal in leading us here and giving us zis." Gabrielle removed the coin she had received from their host in Rydel from her pocket and turned it through her fingers.

"I can look. I'll find him."

Gabrielle shook her head. "No. You already know zat you cannot go. It's safer for you here."

"But I can see!" Gabrielle pulled back. Zain's stomach lurched. "Gabe, I'm sorry." He massaged her knuckles with his fingers. "What I'm trying to say is that it's only a matter of time before Zigarda knows we are here, regardless of if I stay in the hotel or not. And we can't afford a long stay here."

"I know, Zain. So does Carla. We will leave za day after tomorrow if we are not successful."

"Then I wish you best of luck tomorrow."

"Don't wish." Gabrielle turned her body to face Zain. "Pray. Have you?"

"I did in Rydel."

"How about here? Last night."

Zain didn't say anything.

It was Gabrielle's turn to offer his hand a reassuring squeeze. "You will form za habit in time. It's only natural. Do you remember za words at least?"

"I tried today, actually, but I couldn't remember. That's why... Why do we have to remember them, anyway?"

Gabrielle chuckled a little. "You Gazo's men are all za same."

Zain arched an eyebrow. "I don't..."

"Once upon a time Gazo said za same zing to his mozer when she didn't let him practice wiz her and his sister." Gabrielle shifted in the chair, squaring her shoulders to him. "If you don't have za passion to memorize zem, zough, zen what makes you believe you are going to have za passion required to use zem properly? It's like wanting to wield a sword wizout mastering za footwork, no?"

Zain's face grew hot. "You're right."

"I know I am." Gabrielle smirked. "Let's say zem again, so you remember." Gabrielle squeezed his hands. "Are you ready?"

Zain returned the pressure. She let go of his hands and began saying the prayer again, one line at a time, accompanying her voice with gestures. Although she couldn't see, Zain repeated each movement and echoed her words.

At the end, Gabrielle straightened her posture once more and cleared her throat. "In za second part of za prayer, we personalize our petitions. Ancients, please brighten my understanding. Allow me to see even in zis time of darkness. Put zose people in my life zat I need. Guide me in za way only you can. To za Ancients, zis I pray." Gabrielle smiled. "Your turn."

"Ancients, please help me to remember your words. Please help us escape this city unharmed. Please let my mother be okay. Let me somehow contact her before it's too late. Is that good?"

Gabrielle nodded. "You have to remember to close out the prayer."

"Oh, right. To the Ancients, this I pray."

"Zank you for trying, Zain." She leaned forward, felt for his face with her hand, then pecked his cheek with her lips. She pinched his chin, smiled, and sat back down. "It is still rough, but hopefully zat helps you remember."

For once, Zain was thankful Gabrielle was blind so that she couldn't see the warm flush he could feel in his cheeks or the way his mouth hung open slightly. He pulled himself together. "I will get it soon enough."

Gabrielle nodded and turned her head towards the window. "Zain…"

"Yes?"

"Are za city lights on yet?"

"They are coming on now."

"Are zey amber?"

"Look more orange than amber."

"Zat's a shame, zen. Zis city looked beautiful wiz an amber glow." She didn't say anything for a while. She sat down and placed her hands on her lap.

"Gabrielle?"

"Yes, Zain?"

"That statue in the center of the park. What is it?"

"He was za founder of za city. One of the indigenous Terrans, or mountainmen. Tourists come to zis city and rub his big feet."

"Why?"

"For good luck."

"Does it work?"

"No. Zere is no such zing as luck. Only fate and faiz."

"Fate? You believe we cannot control destiny?"

"I believe zat za Ancients steer us in za appropriate paz for our life, but it is ultimately our choice to decide to wander zat paz. Does zat make sense? All zings happen for a reason, we just have to have za faiz to see zat."

"All things?" Zain muttered, unable to look away from the glasses on Gabrielle's face.

She didn't answer, but perhaps she hadn't heard him. He had hardly heard himself. He settled back into his chair and looked out to the park. When Garie and Perrine returned and the two women left, Zain continued looking into the square and wondering if he would ever accumulate the amount of faith Gabrielle had and see that everything happened for a reason. And, if he did, what kind of Power would that grant him? What purpose would he aim to serve? Moreover, would it be worth the hardship he knew he would have to overcome to obtain it?

CHAPTER SEVENTEEN

THE BREW FRONTIERE

"What do you see?" Gabrielle asked, hunched forward. "Is zere a guy wiz glasses."

"A guy wiz..." Emilia's voice tapered off. "A few of zem."

Gabrielle tensed. "Any of zem smokers?"

"One."

"Is he by himself?"

"No. Wiz a group of ozers. Why?"

Gabrielle shifted her body, putting her left leg up on the bench and keeping her right leg hanging. Turned this way, she only showed her hair and back to the public while keeping her face towards the wall of the booth.

"Go get a menu. Two of zem."

"Okay."

Emilia left. Her abrupt departure wafted the scent of her lavender perfume to Gabrielle's nostrils, a much more pleasant smell than the smoke lingering in the bar. She returned a moment later, shuffling a thick cardboard menu to Gabrielle's elbow. She took it in her hands and pretended to read. "You do the same," Gabrielle said as she heard Emilia sit down once more.

"I zought we were looking for someone not ordering somezing."

"We are hiding. Zese will suffice for now." Gabrielle controlled her breathing. "What do you see?"

"Groups. A family. Two, actually."

"Any single people?"

"No. Well, za bartender."

Perhaps it's a group. It is the resistance, after all. Gabrielle held her head in one hand and pretended to look at the menu with the other.

"What shall we do, Miss Gabrielle?"

Gabrielle sighed, trying to figure out how to answer the recent graduate. Emilia was one of the newest trainers Gracie's had to offer, but still a woman who had yet to have an official trainee. She had passed the physical requirements and the Adored requirements to be a mentor, but as far as Gabrielle knew, she had yet to complete the Walk. The Walk was the most difficult element as it tested spiritual strength, something that one gained through faith, not through a textbook or class. Gabrielle wondered how much of it the woman had. She must have stood out in some way if Carla Sonetta had selected her to accompany Gabrielle after Perrine's failure in identifying the man known as Rune the day before. Gabrielle's glasses had hidden her identity so far, so she hadn't been compromised yet. Nor could she afford to be. As she was in possession of Cabal's coin, she was the one that could verify their legitimacy to Rune. If only Gabrielle could see. If she had her sight, she was sure she would have discovered the man already.

Gabrielle tapped the menu on the table. She gave it back to Emilia. "Go get us boz drinks. It'll decrease suspicion."

"What should I get? Zere's a lot to choose from here."

Gabrielle wouldn't know; she couldn't see. "Whatever sounds good."

"I'll be back."

When Emilia left, Gabrielle put her elbows on the table and massaged her temples. *What am I not seeing here?* She laughed to herself. She hadn't even meant to make such a joke. *Everything. Obviously.* She reined in her laughter and sighed.

"Pretty giggle you got there."

Gabrielle tensed. She ignored the urge to move around. "Who's asking?"

"I'm not asking. Just a comment. Can I sit?"

Before Gabrielle could object, the man sat down next to her. Smoke lingered in the air. "You look familiar. Have I seen you somewhere before?"

With a silent gasp, she tucked in her chin, causing her black hair to fall over her face. Was it the man from the day before? She had no idea of knowing, so she thought back to the description Perrine gave her the day before, trying to think of something clever to say to identify him. "It depends. Do you have your glasses on today?"

"Have them on every day. Helps me spot pretty ladies like you."

It is him. Gabrielle giggled. Her right hand reached for the dagger she kept in her garter. "I'm not pretty." She shook her head and gave a little nervous laugh, hoping to play the part.

"I'm sure you got a lot of men fighting over you. Or do you do the fighting most of the time?"

"Alexa, who's your friend?"

Gabrielle turned to Emilia. "I don't know, Elly. He hasn't introduced himself yet. He was just leaving."

"Mayka. Pleasure is mine. Take care, ladies. I'm sure I'll see you around."

Gabrielle gulped. *He is definitely one of Zigarda's men.* Gabrielle strained her ears to make sure the man had retreated. When she was sure that he had, she let go of the hilt of her dagger. A soft plump and two thuds reverberated on the wooden table. Gabrielle turned her attention to Emilia.

"Keep an eye on him. Is he za one wiz others?"

"Uh huh."

"Zat man was in here yesterday. Perrine spoke to him. I zink he is working for Zigarda."

"How do you know?"

"I just do."

"Should we go?"

Gabrielle shook her head. "No. We are obviously not leaving zis bar. He has ozers wiz him now."

"Zen..." Emilia's voice trailed off.

"Zen we have no choice but to find Rune."

Gabrielle tapped her feet and bit her lip. She began to move her hand to her lipring but realized she had taken it out that morning to try to appear less conspicuous and different from the day before. Obviously, that tactic had failed. She should have changed sunglasses, too, but she only had this pair. To cover her false move, she picked up the glass that Emilia had set in front of her and took a sip. She immediately put it back down again.

"Too sweet. What is zat?"

"Beehive Honeybrew."

"What did you get?"

"Za same. I like honey." A clank came to the table. "Zis is good. A shame you don't like it."

"I prefer a bite."

"Za barman recommended za Scorpion's Sting."

Gabrielle's ears perked. "What is it?"

"A shot, I guess, zat has a scorpion inside. I told him it was too early for zat."

"Do you still have a menu?"

"I can get one." Emilia walked away. She returned a moment later. "Here." She pushed it towards her.

"I can't read."

"Oh, zat's right. What do you—" Emilia cut herself short. "Gabe, zat group is leaving."

"All of zem?" Gabrielle leaned forward. She grabbed the beer again and took a drink, wanting to appear natural.

"No. One is still at za table."

"What is he doing?"

"Drinking a beer and chewing on nuts." Clank. "He keeps looking over here."

"Ignore him for now. Where is zat drink on za menu?"

"Uhmm... let me find it... Ah, here it is. Liquor section. Zird drink from za bottom."

Gabrielle froze. "Zird?"

"One. Two. Zhree. Yep. Why?"

It's the bartender. How to... "He recommended zat drink to Perrine and I yesterday. Do you know how to say cheers?"

"Yes. *Boire.*"

"Boire," Gabrielle repeated. She picked up the pint glass and finished it clean. "Take me to za bartender."

Emilia took her by her arm and they went to the bar area. With one hand on her glass, Gabrielle felt around with her other hand until she found the edge of the bar, and then she set her mug down.

"Finished already," a man's voice said. "Do you need another one?"

"No." Gabrielle shook her head. "We need somezing stronger."

"We got a Krine Brew bitter as it—"

"No. We need somezing stronger. Not bitter. What do you recommend?"

"The most popular is the Scorpion's Sting. I'm not sure you ladies can handle that, though."

"We'll give it a shot."

The man laughed. "A shot it is then. Coming right up."

Although Gabrielle couldn't tell what was going on, she knew it must have been something dramatic, for Emilia tugged her arm.

"Gabe... Gabe..." She pleaded in a hushed whisper. "It's a..."

"What?"

"A scorpion. It's..."

Gabrielle heard a muted clank. "Here you go. No better way to start the week. You must have had some weekend."

Perhaps it's better that I don't see. Gabrielle reached forward, fumbling with her fingers until she came upon something squishy. "What's zis?"

"Lemon, you take it after."

"And za shot?" Gabrielle's hand sought the glass.

"Here."

"Elly." Gabrielle turned to her companion. "Let's do zis."

"I... I can't!"

"Scorpion's already dead. Safe to eat. Don't worry."

"Elly," Gabrielle warned.

"I..." Emilia breathed in and out. "Okay."

"One... Two..." Gabrielle smelled the agave coming off the liquor and the citrus. It would be sour. She prepared her taste buds. "Zree."

Gabrielle pushed the shot back in her mouth and swallowed, not wanting to bite down on the solid entity that also entered her mouth at the same time. Swallowing hard, she fumbled for the lemon and put it in her mouth, cringing a little at the aftertaste.

"Zere." She coughed and slammed down the glass triumphantly.

Emilia replaced her glass as well, although the clang hers made was only a shadow of Gabrielle's. "What is in..."

"How much?" Gabrielle asked.

"First one is on the house. You two were brave."

"And za second one?" Gabrielle reached for the coin Cabal had given her and slid it to the bartender.

"This is more than enough to cover it. Another one coming right up."

"Gabe!"

Gabrielle scrunched her shoulders as Emilia let her name slip, hoping the stranger hadn't heard. "Where is he?"

"Who?"

"The man from before"

A moment of silence. "He's looking over here."

The bartender placed two more shots on the bar. "Here you go, ladies."

Gabrielle hesitated.

"Something the matter?"

"*Someone,*" Gabrielle corrected, arching her eyebrows.

"Nothing a shot won't fix. Take it. I guarantee you'll feel better."

For a moment, Gabrielle questioned her instincts, but she pushed that aside and grasped the second Scorpion's Sting. Open-mouthed, head tilted back, she swallowed the shot whole and put the glass down, less triumphantly than the first time. She felt a little dizzy. Emilia couldn't stop coughing. A hand came to rest on Gabrielle's.

"I zink I'm going to be sick."

"You probably are. Not everyone can handle two Stingers. Miss, take your friend to the bathroom before she throws up. We're doing some renovation in there, so be sure to choose the third stall."

"Where is za—"

"Up the ramp, turn right and go down the hallway."

Gabrielle hoped that Emilia was paying attention. She interlocked her arm with her friend's and started moving.

"Oh, don't want to be forgetting this, miss."

Gabrielle heard something slide across the bar. She reached out blindly and found it after a few attempts. *The coin?* She could tell immediately by the embossing. "Zank you." She nodded. Gabrielle walked away again, this time shaking Emilia. "Get yourself togezer. We need to—"

Emilia coughed. She stumbled her way across the floor, Gabrielle holding on and hoping that her compatriot had enough sense left in her to make a path for both of them. After the slight ramp, Gabrielle turned right, but let Emilia lead them. Soon enough, she heard a door swing open and a floral scent overtook the smoky air of the bar. *This must be the ladies—*

"We're here." Emilia let go of Gabrielle's arm. "What do we do?"

"You need za bazroom? I zought you were going to puke."

"*Life is a play.* Isn't zat one of our mottos?"

Gabrielle's mouth dropped. "You mean…?"

Emilia laughed. "Did I fool you? I zought you were za master at zat."

Gabrielle snickered. "I zought so, too." She chuckled.

"What did za bartender gave you?"

Gabrielle showed the coin. "I received zis in Rydel. I zink za man we need is za bartender."

"Now what?"

"Is zis bazroom under renovation?"

"No. Looks normal."

Gabrielle's smiled to herself. "Za zird stall. Let's go zere. What do you see?"

Emilia took her by the hand and brought her along. With a slow and steady creak, the bathroom stall door swung open. "Nozing, it's just a stall."

"Where is it?"

"Za zird one."

"But where compared to za ozers?"

"It's za last one."

"Za walls?"

"Lavender."

"Za toilet?"

"Normal. Sit down."

"Are you—"

"Wait." Gabrielle heard a slight hitch in Emilia's voice. "Zat's odd."

"What is?"

"It has two mezods for flushing."

"What do you mean?"

"A button on za top and a lever on za side."

The toilet flushed. Running water rushed to refill it.

"Za top one doesn't work."

"Check za ozer stalls." Gabrielle waited as Emilia moved between the stalls.

"None of zem have side levers. Only top buttons."

"But zis one doesn't work?"

"Probably why zey had to make a side lever."

Hmmmm... "How big is it?"

"About zis big." Emilia paused. "Oh, it's about za size of a bond."

"Try placing zis in zere." Gabrielle handed her the coin.

"Are you sure?"

"Yes. Try."

"Okay."

Although Gabrielle couldn't tell what was actually happening, she heard competing sounds. Firstly, all three toilets went off at the same time and then she heard grating and a shifting as if a stone or brick wall moved against itself.

"Gabrielle!" Her arm was yanked. "Zere's... zere's a staircase."

"Let's go. Get za coin."

Emilia led her around the toilet and to the open space. Then they descended a staircase slowly. It wound around until Gabrielle finally could feel her heels on cement instead of the wooden steps she had clacked upon.

"What's here?" Gabrielle asked.

"Nozing. Just large vats. It smells funny."

"Zat's yeast. It must be za brewing area."

She felt vibrations. Heard sound from up above.

"Gabrielle, za door behind us is closing. We are going to be trapped."

"We were already trapped."

Nothing.

Stillness.

Gabrielle felt the squeeze of Emilia's hand on her arm.

"What's going to happen?"

"We wait and see."

An hour passed. Maybe more. Maybe less. Gabrielle had lost track of time, and even if she could see, she doubted there would be a way to tell the time down in the cellar. It warmed her to know that at least Emilia wasn't just sitting in darkness, for she had told Gabrielle that there were dim lights spaced about the rectangular cellar. But at last a flurry of footsteps caused both of the women to stiffen as a new presence arrived.

"Good. You found it." Gabrielle recognized the bartender's voice.

"What is zis place?"

"The start. Are there others?"

"One hundred and thirty-three," Gabrielle said.

"Quite a lot of people. Where are you staying?"

"Za Terran Traveler."

"Expensive."

"Cannot put a price of safety."

"No, you cannot. Which is why you both will need to stay here. I will find your companions after I close the bar and send them here in small groups over the course of tonight and tomorrow. Give me the coin."

Gabrielle handed over the coin. The man had firmer hands than she would have thought possible for being a bartender. It was almost like he had farmer's hands, which probably meant he was as muscular as his heavy voice portrayed him to be.

"And zat man from upstairs?"

"I know them. That man with the glasses. Mayka. Half-indigenous, half-Emporian. A mixed blood. He and his friends are scouters. They shepherd people across the Frontiere Mountains for money. If they've got their sights on you, you can't leave here. You're safe, but I'd guess they are waiting to follow you outside."

"But if we never leave, won't they notice?"

"I'll take care of it."

"How are we going to escape?"

"By going under the mountains." There was a smile in Rune's voice.

"Under?"

"I'll explain more later. I have to go get back to work."

Gabrielle and Emilia waited for another long while, passing the time by swapping stories from Gracie's. But Gabrielle couldn't forget the question that had been gnawing at her.

"Why haven't you completed za Walk yet, Emilia?" she asked at last.

Gabrielle detected a slight hesitation before Emilia answered. "I haven't had za chance."

"What do you mean?"

"I just graduated not even a week after you returned from za Trials."

"You have had monzs zen."

"But I haven't had za spiritual mindset to make an attempt. I don't want to fail in front of za ozers."

"Is zere anyzing I can do to help you?"

"Your presence is already enough, Miss Gabrielle."

"Stop it." Gabrielle shook her head. "It is our adversity zat builds our faiz. I have just had more zan ozers..." Gabrielle's voice tapered off as memories of her father surged in her mind. She sighed. "Can I share somezing wiz you?"

"Sure."

Gabrielle heard Emilia shift on the floor of the brewing room and then felt the other woman's hands on her own.

"Faiz is about perspective. Even now I am grateful for my life. I know zere is some purpose zat I'm supposed to serve. Even now. Blind as I am, I am grateful."

"What are you grateful for?"

"For life. Zhrough my heartaches. Zrough za Trials. Zrough my blindness. Za Ancients have kept me alive. What is zere not to be zankful for when so many ozers don't get to see za next day? Do you ever reflect on what you are grateful for?"

"Sometimes."

"Do it more often, and you will grow your faiz. Zere is always somezing to see and notice, even if you live in darkness." Gabrielle chuckled.

"What is it?"

"My prayers. Za Ancients heard zem again."

"What did you pray for?"

"To be guided in a way zat only zey can do. To have people be put into my life for some reason. I know zat zere was a reason Carla Sonetta chose you to accompany me today. A reason why we are here right now. Why zis man is—"

The door opened. More footsteps on the stairs. More than one pair. *They're here!* Gabrielle pushed herself off the ground, alert.

"Gabrielle, you're here. You're safe."

Zain.

Before she knew it, Gabrielle was wrapped up in a hug. Lips came to meet hers. She didn't pull away. Instead, she leaned into the kiss.

When he released her, Gabrielle asked, "What are you doing here?"

"When you didn't make it back, I was worried."

"Frantic is more like it, Zain." Garie's voice. "You were pacing all over the room."

Gabrielle blushed. "I had to stay here. The man from yesterday was watching for us."

"It doesn't matter. You did it. We are here."

Zain wrapped her in another embrace.

"Who is wiz you?"

"Just my men."

"Za ozers?"

"I'll be sending them over here in groups, miss." Rune's voice again.

"Oh, right." Gabrielle blushed. She had forgotten in all the excitement of Zain's kiss and hearing Zain's voice again. "Zen all we do is wait." She reached her hands to Zain's shoulders and worked her way down his arms in search of hands. When she found them, she rubbed her thumbs over his knuckles. "Do you believe me now?"

"About what?"

"Prayers. Zey work." She smirked.

"I think I am starting to."

While Gabrielle and the others waited for more of the women from Gracie's to arrive, she told Zain how she had discovered the identity of Rune.

"You ate a scorpion?"

"Two scorpions," Emilia corrected. "We ate two."

Zain laughed. "How did it taste?"

"I've had better." Gabrielle smiled and leaned forward. Her lips found his once more.

"Gabe. You did it. It was the bartender."

Gabrielle nodded. "It was."

"How did you know?"

She told the story again for each new group that arrived every hour. She didn't know exactly how much time passed, but the six simple meals Rune provided helped her keep track until at last the final group arrived and Gabrielle was swept up in the warm embrace of none other than Carla Sonetta, who had overseen the departure of each group and waited until the final one to make her escape from the hotel.

After a brief reunion, Carla called for order in the crowded cellar and instructed for everyone to listen to Rune for direction.

"Thank you, Carla. We have no time to waste. Come with me. Come on. Come on."

Gabrielle was taken by the arm, guided by someone she didn't know, though by the hint of lavender in the air, she assumed it was Emilia. Guided down another flight of steps, her support stopped her. A mighty creaking sound filled the room.

"The Scorpions built this underground passageway to take you directly to our base in Soeco on the other side of the mountains. The journey takes two weeks or so, so I am glad to see you have come adequately prepared."

"Are there any stopping points along the way?" Perrine asked.

"There are small rest areas and a few larger outposts, but once you enter, you stay underground until the end, understood?"

"Understood," Carla said.

Gabrielle began moving forward, but Emilia held her back. "Are zere lights in zere?"

"Every two hundred fifty feet or so there is an electric sconce, but it'll mostly be darkness. I hope you aren't afraid of the dark."

Gabrielle pulled Emilia forward, hoping her confidence would give the young woman strength. "I live in darkness. Let's go."

CHAPTER EIGHTEEN

A WEB OF CONFUSION

L uvan took his first steps inside. Stillness and silence clung to this place like spiderwebs, lingering and catching Luvan quite off guard. He shouted out greetings, only to hear himself reply. Footsteps and heavy breaths were his constant companion, as well as a web of intrigue weaving through his mind. *What happened here?*

Hands akimbo, he stood before an ostentatiously large throne. It rose to the height of a glass ceiling that acted like a second floor above, as if Lord Zigarda preferred to treat with the higher-ups and look down upon everyone else. A circular staircase at either side of the room led up to the glass floor. *How peculiar.*

He folded his arms over his chest and tapped his forearms with his fingers. *Is anyone even here?*

It had been Senator Numos who suggested the plan to spread word about a meeting to overthrow Eska politically. Luvan had laughed off the idea of overthrowing Eska by force, for he had witnessed Eska's prowess first-hand; however, the plan the senator offered made sense. If the families in power gave approval to Eska when he was apprentice, then it is also in their ability as a collective unit to rebuke him throughout the span of his guardianship.

As Senator Numos explained: Why should the families of today live with the consequences sown by the families of yesteryears?

Luvan didn't have an answer for that. He had agreed to bring the message to Myoli and Pyre while Senator Numos visited the families in power on Onkh and Agrost.

But Victor Zigarda seemed to be absent. As Luvan strolled through the compound looking for answers, he realized it had been evacuated. But why?

He didn't know the answer to that now, but he hoped further searching would produce something. When he had arrived the day before, no one had answered at the gates. It was only after Luvan picked a lock at the back of the compound that he gained entrance to the complex. In addition to teaching Luvan in the ways of knives, his father had also taught him how to pick locks, and while he certainly didn't need to use the skill often, he was glad to have it in his repertoire.

Inside the Web, the courtyards had been emptied and a tall obelisk in the center had been cleared out. Strangest of all was the lack of detritus within the Web. If it had been a rushed evacuation, surely there would be remnants. But there wasn't. In truth, though, the lack of a keycard had prohibited him from seeing much of what the Web offered. Technically, he supposed, he could still get anywhere without a keycard, but there was a reason why Zigarda's compound had been notoriously called the Web; it ensnared people, each of the three sections its own separate web.

He had tried to gain access to the telecommunicator room, but the room was secured with a hard-wired identification panel. *A shame.*

After another hour of walking in solitude, he found himself wandering the dungeons on the assumption that Zigarda wouldn't bother emptying his cells. He was much too cruel to consider letting people go. To Luvan's surprise, the dungeon had been evacuated save for one man. Long black hair covered his face and he clutched at his stomach even in sleep as if in pain.

Luvan approached the cell. "What's your name? Where is everyone?"

The man jolted awake. His chains rattled. "Who are you?"

"I asked you first."

"Lucien."

"Where did everyone go, Lucien?"

"Zey left."

"Yes, I am quite aware of that, but to where?"

"How am I supposed to know? I've been locked in here."

"What happened?"

"A bunch of zose soldiers came."

"Soldiers? Describe them."

"Black outfits. An H on zeir chest. Stocky sons—"

"Hown?" Luvan muttered.

"Yeah. I zink zat is vhat I heard someone say."

Luvan put a hand to his chin. *Hown? Here? Has Zigarda been incarcerated? Had Eska finally brought the man in? Why? Why now?* In all his service to Guardian Eska, not once had he ever known Eska to call upon the services of Hown, so why now? *What is so imperative that—*

"Are you going to let me out or just stand zere tapping your feet?"

Lucien's question brought him back. Luvan shook his head and surveyed the man. "Why didn't they release you?"

"Beats me."

Luvan frowned. "How long have you been down here alone?"

"Don't know. Two days." A loud rumble from Lucien's stomach gave credence to this.

Luvan brought out his knife, picked the lock, and opened the cell. He didn't know what the man had done to deserve the chains, but leaving him to rot was something Luvan could not do. "Let's get you out of those things." Luvan went over and crouched down before the man. In the flickering red light the dungeon offered, Luvan saw a rough jawline that needed shaving, dark blue eyes, just a shade brighter than the black hair. The man seemed familiar, but where Luvan may have seen him, he didn't know.

Once he picked the manacles, Luvan stood up and sheathed his knife. "Lucien, is it?"

The man got to his feet and dusted off his clothes. "Zanks. I would have done it myself if I didn't have zose manacles on me."

Luvan raised an eyebrow. Had he just let loose a thief?

"I'm a mechanic. Know my way around all sorts of gadgets."

Well, that's certainly interesting. "Could you hard-wire a hand panel lock and bypass the security protocol?"

"Don't know unless I see it."

"Follow me."

"What's your name?"

"The man who just set you free. Let's go."

Luvan led the mechanic to the communication chamber and observed as he studied the hand panel. Lucien tapped it slightly and sighed.

"What does that mean?"

"Shouldn't be too hard if I had za equipment."

"What do you need?"

"Pliers. Screwdriver. Knife."

Luvan snatched his knife from the sheath, spun it into the air above his head, and caught it effortlessly. "A knife will have to be enough." He extended it to the man, hilt first.

The man eyed it cautiously, suitably intimidated. If the mechanic harbored any ideas about betraying his rescuer, he might think twice.

Arms crossed over his chest, Luvan leaned against a metal wall and watched the man do his work. Not even half an hour later, the door to the telecommunicator slid open by itself. Luvan entered and told Lucien to follow.

"I want to make sure everything is working here before I let you go. The knife." Luvan extended his hand.

Lucien complied. "A good blade. Where'd you learn to pick?"

"My father." Luvan pushed a button on the control panel. "Taught me a lot of things."

"Zat's what fathers do."

"Are you a father?"

"Yeah."

"What does your son do?"

"Daughter."

"My apology. Daughter. What does she do?"

"Don't know. Been locked up too long. She hasn't visited."

Luvan tapped his foot, waiting for the telecom screen to warm up. "What did you do to end up in there?"

"Taught her too many zings."

"Your daughter?"

"And wife."

"That's a crime?"

"I guess a hands-on mezod isn't best for everyone."

The screen turned on. "It's working, Lucien. You can leave. Thank you for your help."

"Zank you for za opportunity to see my family again. I zink zey've missed me."

Luvan didn't waste time responding; instead, he scrolled through the logs as the man walked away. Luvan noticed a flurry of calls all made within the same day, within minutes of each, really. Acquava. Sereya. Mistral. And here in Empora. By clicking on the ID code, Luvan was able to glean the exact destination of each call. Marquis Puwl in Rhemu. Lord Grime of Sereya. But his eyes widened upon seeing Senator Numos of Mistral on the list.

"Senator Numos..." Luvan pursed his lips and cocked his head. His posture slumped, and he brought a hand to his chin. *What is the senator doing mixed up with Lord Zigarda? Is Zigarda the one behind the plan and Numos merely his mouthpiece?*

Luvan drummed his fingertips. It wasn't so much of the possibility of a connection between the two that bothered Luvan—no, it was the fact that the senator had chosen to keep him in the dark. Why?

He turned off the computer and left. It was clear that Lord Zigarda most likely already knew about the meeting. It would be futile to try to reach him. Instead, Luvan would go to Chaon next, a nation that he hadn't stepped foot in for thirty-two years, and he hoped that it wouldn't leave him spun in a web of confusion yet again.

CHAPTER NINETEEN

THE CRYSTAL SCRY

E irek and Conseleigh Rorum stood upon the stone court painted in the likeness of Eska's sigil. Although he still rose at dawn to eat breakfast, he had been instructed that he no longer needed to run to the Gamrol Cliffs and back. Instead, before getting into swordplay, Conseleigh Rorum made sure to improve Eirek's conditioning through a series of high intensity movements such as pushups, jumping lunges, and Eirek's least favorite, burpees. It didn't matter how long it took Eirek, but he wasn't able to start weapons training with Conseleigh Rorum until he finished one hundred of each exercise. By the end of it, his body trembled with exhaustion and he could hardly hold a weapon or stand straight.

"It's necessary to improve your conditioning because it will lead to less fatigue in an actual battle, Apprentice Mourse."

"Running was so much easier," Eirek panted, bent over.

"Surely, but less pragmatic. Tere often won't be times where you will need to run continuously for a long span of time."

"Then... why did they... make me do it?"

"Stand up and put your hands behind your neck. Expand your ribcage. Walk around. It will help."

Eirek took the conseleigh's advice.

"I suspect maybe tey dislike you for someting." Conseleigh Rorum stroked his conical beard.

"Ugh." Eirek waved his arms around, trying to loosen his body.

"Are you ready?"

"I don't think I will ever be."

"Ten tere is no better time to start." Ethen strolled forward to the apprentice and handed him a sword, hilt first.

Eirek accepted it cautiously. "But I have my own."

"You have an Ether Weapon, Apprentice Mourse. I do not suggest we start with such an advanced weapon so early."

Advanced? Eirek glanced down at his own sword slung to his hip. "Are you sure?"

"Quite positive. You forget I was a weapons master before a conseleigh. I will leave Guardian Eska to practice tat wit you." Ethen drew his own weapon. "Now, first tings first. Tere are several different types of sword movements we can use: slash, jab, lunge, strike, sweep, swing." Ethen demonstrated each movement. "Tere are also defensive techniques such as parries and counters. We will discuss tose later. Today, however, we will relegate our practice to simple slashes so tat you understand ta eight angles we can strike from." Ethen came to stand alongside Eirek and swung his sword downward, over the top of an invisible opponent. "Tis is a vertical slash."

For the next hour, Ethen went over the other angles utilized in fights. Eirek swung his right arm in a repetitive motion, practicing all eight strokes until he could no longer hold the sword.

"I..." Eirek panted. "I can hardly lift it anymore."

"Ten use your left."

Eirek frowned as he jerked his head up to eye the other man. "Huh?"

"Since you can no longer use your right, use your left."

"But I'm right-handed. I've never..." Eirek shifted his sword from right to left. Even motionless it felt clumsy, and his first attempts at slashing accentuated this awkwardness even more.

"Know yourself from right to left and left to right before you focus on winning ta fight."

"Who said that?" Eirek took another awkward slash with his left under the watchful eye of Conseleigh Rorum.

"It's a Gazo's mantra. Did you forget I trained tere before being weapons master for ta Lord of Chaon?"

"No," Eirek lied. He swung again. "I can't. It's too awkward."

"It's only awkward because you are not used to doing it. In time, it will feel natural to you. Tis is a fundamental part of Gazo's training, you know."

"So Zain can use both sides?"

"I suspect so. I saw him do it briefly in ta Trials tournament. I imagine Gracie's taught Miss Rawvey the same."

Eirek slashed again. And again. Soon enough, he became bored with the repetitiveness. "When do we move onto something else?"

"When you can no longer hold the sword in your left arm either." Ethen's eyes gleamed.

At lunch, Eirek stared at the chicken, potatoes, and vegetables on his plate. Then he looked at his utensils. Then back to his food. Then to his utensils.

"Eirek, aren't you going to eat?" Guardian Eska asked.

"I..." Eirek tried raising his arm. "I don't think I can. My shoulder. My arms."

Guardian Eska guffawed, which set off immediate mimicry from the conseleigh who sat close by. "Ethen, I am proud to see his progress."

Ethen dabbed his lips with a napkin before speaking. "Aye, he still has a long way to go, but he gave it his best efforts today."

"And that is all we can ask of you, Apprentice Mourse."

Eirek took the fork in his hand and grimaced. He managed a slight smile at Tundra and the others and began eating.

When he had managed to stave off his hunger, if not quite eat his fill, Eirek followed Ethen outside to the stone court once again. "We continue?"

"Of course."

"But I can't even lift my arms anymore."

"Ten you will lift your feet." At the center of the golden and crimson stone court, Conseleigh Rorum turned around, hands behind his back.

Eirek tilted his head in confusion.

"Warriors still standing do not stand still."

Eirek exhaled. "Is that another Gazo's mantra?"

Conseleigh Rorum chuckled but shook his head. "No. Tis one comes from ta Hart Isles in Acquava, actually. I like it all ta same. No good warrior, Apprentice Mourse, will ever just stand in place. No battle will ever just be stationary. You will constantly be moving around and adjusting yourself to ta terrain, so now tat your arms are tired, it's time to tire your legs. We will practice your footwork." Ethen shuffled two steps forward and then two steps back. "This is called a shuffle, and warriors use it all the time in battle. We can advance, retreat, and move side-to-side. Tat is what I want you to practice." He demonstrated the different shuffles. "Your turn."

Eirek shuffled forward with ease while he found shuffling backward, slightly more difficult. Side-to-side was a nightmare, though, until Ethen shuffled alongside him and suggested the idea of kicking one foot into the other to make it more seamless. For at least another hour, Eirek continued this pattern of going forward, backward and then side-to-side, keeping his hands behind his back all the while to challenge his balance and core.

"Good. You have ta basics down." Conseleigh Rorum held up his hand. "Hardly ever will a battle be so easy. You will have to contend with offensive strikes or perhaps even Power. Let's try tat now. I will control Power and you will dodge it. *Maa.*"

Before Eirek knew it, his body was elevated on a pillar of earth.

"Congratulations, Apprentice Mourse, you've already died." Ethen chuckled. The pillar of earth retreated into the ground.

Eirek blushed as he regained his balance and footing.

"Let's try again. *Maa.*"

This time Eirek shuffled to the left, avoiding the spire emerging under him. He moved forward. Then backward. Then forward. Left. Left. Right. Left. Forward. Backward. Forward. Forward. Soon enough, Eirek got into a rhythm of avoiding the small earthen spires that Conseleigh Rorum created. He enjoyed the exercise and the practicality of such a drill.

As if understanding his enjoyment, Ethen sent four pillars at once. They surged upward with rumbling force, surrounding him, trapping him.

Darkness.

"Hey!" Eirek pounded on the earthen walls.

As swiftly as they had appeared, they vanished. Conseleigh Rorum stood immediately in front of Eirek, arm outstretched, within inches of his stomach. "You would have died, again. Twice." Ethen cocked his head to one side.

"There was no place to go."

"Ten you make a space."

"What do you mean?"

"He means that you need to use Power to your advantage sometimes."

Eirek spun around. Arms crossed, Guardian Eska stood at the entrance to the stone court, Tundra by his side. Eirek felt heat rising in his cheeks. "How long have you been there?"

"Long enough to see you die a few times now." Eska laughed and then advanced, Tundra strolling alongside him.

"What Ethen is trying to tell you is to be proactive, not *reactive* to the situation."

"I..." Eirek shook his head. "I don't understand."

"Ethen, are you ready?"

"Of course, my guardian."

Eirek flung his head around to Ethen, who now shuffled on the stone court, same as Eirek had been doing, avoiding small spires that rose up to ensnare his feet. This continued for a few minutes, but soon Ethen was posed with the same trap as Eska surrounded him with earthen barriers on all sides. Instead of succumbing to it, Ethen turned the pillars into a climbing route and avoided the entanglement altogether. No sooner did he land then a stream of water came to meet him from the manmade river that cut through the pathway to the estate.

"*Maa.*"

Ethen swiped his arm across his body, raising a small earthen shield in front of him before the water could douse him. With left arm forward, he rolled out of the grasp of a small hill that was encroaching from behind and into another that was rising up before him. Using the momentum of the roll, Ethen pushed off the small mound before it could fully form, somersaulting in the air and landing neatly. His legs gave way and he fell to one knee, grimacing.

The spells stopped.

"Ethen, are you alright?" Tundra asked.

"Leg is still sore from the incident with the Twelve." Huffing, he looked to Eirek. "Tat is what being proactive means." He strained to put a smile on his face.

Guardian Eska offered Ethen his gloved hand and brought his aide to his feet. "Ethen, Tundra will take you to the apothecary. You're to let Adored Amiti treat you."

"Guardian Eska, I am fine."

"Fine, but not in the condition I need you to be in. I will take over from here. And the subject of being proactive seems to be a fitting spot. I have a test for the young apprentice."

Eirek felt his stomach twitch with nerves as Eska's eyes washed over him. He stayed silent.

"Follow me, Eirek. There is a problem to solve, and I need your brain." Eska turned on his heel and walked away.

Alone with Eska in his chamber, Eirek looked at himself through a handheld crystal mirror. "What is this?"

"It's called a crystal scry. It was invented by Dr. Genus Cere when Tundra was lady of Sereya."

"What does it do?"

"Allows you to spy on people. As long as you have a little droplet of their identity."

"Their blood?"

"Precisely. Go ahead, try it."

Eirek looked around for something sharp. Finding no other object, he reached for his weapon.

"Here." Eska handed him a knife. "It's much better if you cut yourself with a normal blade. You may cut too deep with an Ether Weapon."

After laying the crystal mirror down on a wooden table, he looked up at Eska. "How much is needed?"

"Don't be overzealous. A droplet is plenty. I just want to demonstrate the mirror's functionality first before I pose to you the situation."

Eirek nodded. He poked his finger and let a tiny droplet fall to the crystal surface below. The jagged parts of the mirror dissolved, washing out like ripples in a once-placid pond. And there, in the mirror, he saw himself. He saw the mirror within the mirror. When he moved his head, the image in the mirror also changed.

"Do you understand how it works now?"

"It sees what I see."

"Very good. Yes. That is its purpose. Do you know why it was invented?"

Eirek shook his head.

"Hmm. I thought you would have."

"Why is that?"

"Because of a question you answered during your Coronation. Do you remember Lady Aprah's question?"

"I'm sorry. I... wait a minute... didn't it have to do with technology and Power?"

"Correct. And how they can exist side-by-side? Many people see technology and Power as equally subversive to one another. Each one trying to be better than its counterpart, the new usurping the old. You seemed to have a different view."

"I believe they co-exist," Eirek said. "Without Power, some amazing technologies would be lost."

"You are absolutely correct. What Power do you think this replaces?"

"Blood bonding?"

"Close enough. Blood bonding is the process you and I went through before Pirini Lilapa. One that we will undergo again soon enough. But being able to actually trace that person's blood, and thus their location, that actual process is blood scrying. Do you understand?"

"I do."

"Good. Now for your test."

Eirek shifted his stance. Wanting to make sure he gleaned everything, he put down the mirror and focused on Guardian Eska.

"Imagine you are one of the Hown. You have been informed of Hydro Paen's location, but it seems that he has outmaneuvered you."

"Hydro isn't in Mendeck?"

"No. I'm afraid not. I received word from the Hown a few days ago and we went back to ground zero in our search. However, just before retrieving you from Conseleigh Aprorum, I received another call from them. They've found a solution."

"They're going to use the mirror?"

"Yes."

"So they found some of Hydro's blood?"

"No. They haven't."

"Then..."

"This is the challenge, Eirek. How can you find someone who doesn't want to be found?"

"Well, you have to trap him."

"That comes after finding him. How do you find him?"

"Through the mirror."

"Yes, but we don't have his blood. How could we use it without that?"

"Well, what about his brother?"

Eska remained stoic. "From the funeral, we know already that his brother can't sense Hydro. The family has had no success thus far. What would make this any different?"

"Because it wouldn't rely on Aiton. The mirror would be objective."

Something shifted in Eska's face. "Explain."

"Well, even after we bonded blood, it took a while for me to actually understand how to sense you or the other conseleigh. Even now I still have difficulty with it."

"And why is that?"

"Because it is a type of Power I am not used to controlling yet."

"Exactly." Eska beamed. "I am unsure if you know this, Eirek, but Aiton has yet to cast his first spell of Power. Rumors in Acquava say he is Denied."

"I didn't cast my first spell until after Coronation."

"Yes. And I had never seen a fire glow like it. It was impressive. There is still time for Aiton to cast, surely, but let's pretend that he can't. How then would this crystal scry bypass that?"

"Well, it wouldn't rely on Aiton's Power or lack thereof. If Aiton truly can't cast Power then he could never sense his own brother's blood, anyway. The crystal scry would only rely on his blood, and he shares a percentage of the same blood with his brother because of their relationship."

"Exactly."

"But wouldn't the Hown only see what Aiton sees, not what Hydro sees?"

Eska smiled a little. "Excellent question. Very good, Eirek. That is exactly what would happen. After all, it is Aiton's blood we are collecting, not Hydro's, so the scry will be more attuned to what Aiton sees. But what if Aiton weren't to see anything? Then the Power of the scry would have no choice but to reach out to the alternative, if weaker, trace of blood. In this case, Hydro's."

"So Aiton will have to keep his eyes closed while it's being used?"

"Yes. A few of the Hown will stay with him to ensure his cooperation while coordinating with those hunting Hydro."

"Don't those methods seem a bit extreme? Aiton will have to give up his brother. Is it even legal to request his blood? Have you considered the repercussions of that? How that will affect him?"

Eska stood up from his throne of velvet and walked over to Eirek. He placed a hand on his shoulder. "Under normal circumstances, I would never condone this, but this situation is far from normal, as you know. And sometimes that is how life is, Eirek. Cruel. Remember the story that I told you about my sister?"

Eirek nodded.

"I never imagined trying to find her would in turn lead to her demise, nor that she would die right in front of me or that Vesel would be the one to kill her. But fate, as I mentioned to you before, is funny. You can let it amuse you or bedevil you. I am here today, standing before you, as Guardian of the Core. I am stronger because of her sacrifice. And while Aiton may not see this action as necessary now, he will grow stronger because of it. That is what all adversity and difficult decisions do—they make us stronger.

"Better than most, I understand what will be asked of Aiton. He is a good child, and I'm sorry that it has to come to this. But if Hydro is allowed to remain on the loose, then the whole system is in danger. And that is something I cannot allow. Do you understand? When you're Guardian, you will have choices to make. Choices that will offend many. Like the choice I made on Mount Volan. But you have to stand behind your words and not second-guess yourself."

Eirek sighed. "Those who are standing don't stand still."

"What was that?"

Speaking to the floor, Eirek said, "It is an Acquavan mantra Conseleigh Rorum taught me today."

"I know the words. I didn't know Ethen taught you that."

Eirek looked up and nodded. "Right before we practiced evasive techniques."

"And it is a good mantra to carry with you in life. Especially when making decisions, Eirek. Wait too long to make a decision, and the decision will be made for you. You will be reactive, not proactive, and as Guardian, that is something we cannot be. To waver is to die."

"I understand," Eirek said without really acknowledging his own words. His thoughts were elsewhere, stuck in the nostalgia of his uncle abandoning him. Well, Galan abandoning him in order to keep him safe from a distance. If he hadn't, if he had raised Eirek as he had raised Eirek's parents and the other lost siblings, then Eirek would likely be dead.

"That is all. I will see you at dinner, Eirek."

"Okay."

Shoulders slumped, he began walking out of Eska's chambers.

"Eirek," Eska called. "I'm proud of you. Good job."

Normally such a comment would excite Eirek, but today it did nothing to remove the weight crushing his shoulders. And it wasn't even his own weight. But knowing Aiton's predicament and thinking about how the final confrontation against Hydro would go made Eirek realize that life was indeed cruel. After all the events in his life, would Aiton still be able to stand at the end of the day? Would either of the Paens still be standing by the end of this?

CHAPTER TWENTY

THE SINKING SEA

From the cockpit of Dr. Cere's C-Bot, Hydro saw Mount Klaff increasing in size and clarity with each passing second. A part of him wanted to take the machine above the clouds and see what shape it held beyond its stem-glass appearance, but he didn't. That would be cheating. Also, it would ruin the mystery. Sometimes it was better not to know and simply let imagination run loose. Knowing things was complicated and his need for knowledge was what had led him to his current predicament.

His eyes drifted to the north. Qotia sat by the port, only noticeable for its large bell tower and the circular wheel, calling to all those who desired knowledge of the Adored Arts. But then his gaze shifted to the east. *The jungle.* He clicked his tongue and crossed his arms, brooding. The jungle was rife with memories. *Hmmmm.*

Hydro switched off auto-pilot and took control of the machine, steering it towards the green lump, pulling it away from its current trajectory.

Immediately, alarms started ringing.

"Switch back to auto-pilot mode."

"I have unfinished business with someone. The jewel can wait."

The ship made an attempt to enforce auto-pilot, but Hydro overruled it, intent on visiting the jungle where his life had started to spiral out of control. Zigarda had derailed his plans to meet with the three-eyed prophetess who called the lush stretch of green home. But no longer. He had his father's Ether Weapon now. He was stronger now. Now, she would pay.

"Turn back to jewel course."

"After this."

Hydro searched for the Brown Sea, knowing that the village would be near. Finding it, he scanned for an alcove where he could safely leave the ship while he took care of unfinished business. Taking the nearest alcove he could find, he lowered the ship to the north of the Brown Sea.

Relying on muscle memory, he set out for the village. There was no need to run this time. No chaos. No snakes or other venomous creatures. Still, even though he walked like a man who had been to Abaddon and back, he kept a constant hand on the hilt of Purge, waiting for something bad to inevitably happen.

When he found the Brown Sea, he surveyed his surroundings, trying to determine if he was on the correct side or not. To aide him, he looked for the drowned pillars and the five separate areas of devil's-sand that he had seen the first time. The first of the five pillars seemed far away, much farther than he remembered, meaning that he was already across the sea and on the correct path.

Pivoting on his heel, he turned to the west and continued walking, taking in the new sights. The first time he had made this journey, he had been unconscious. The second time, he had been chased by a village full of lunatics. What would it be this time? Surely all bad things came in threes. For the moment, though, he breathed in the untainted and pure forest air, taking in the silence and the serenity of the moment.

Branches shook. Leaves rattled. Hydro stopped.

In front of him stood a tiger, recoiling from the jump it had just made.

Hydro braced himself.

It is only me.

Hydro felt soothing warmth crawl over his body. Anne had appeared alongside him. *Anne?*

No, Hydro Paen. Here. It is I. The tiger growled.

Hydro ignored Anne's tug on his hand. The tiger prowled forward, circling him, keeping its eyes on Hydro. Hydro's gaze flickered between the tiger and Anne constantly.

Why do you look to your side, Hydro Paen? No one is there.

He lies, Hydro. I am here.

Hydro kept his attention on the tiger. "Who are you? Why can you talk to me?"

My name is Ritam. I am yours if you will have me.

Hydro's pulse quickened. Anne yanked on his arm.

You are already bonded, Hydro Paen. To me. I am more Powerful than him. Ask him what he can give you. Do it.

"What do you offer me?"

The tiger roared. *I bond with the person, not their greed. True bonds never give away their secrets. We test to see their worth. Is he leading you astray?*

Hydro tightened the grip on his blade. "He?"

Anne cut in his mind, blocking Hydro's ability to hear the tiger and pulled on his hand once more. Hydro looked down at the girl with black hair in her white dress.

This animal doesn't know what it's talking about. Delusional. She flung her free arm around, as if this made her point.

Do you trust me, Hydro Paen? The tiger crouched.

Who is he to trust? He wants to kill you. Look at him. Swing!

Before Hydro knew it, the tiger pounced on him—or tried. Castle training kicked in, activating Hydro's reflexes. He pulled out his sword and swung across. The tiger was cut in two, but the front half still collided with Hydro and pushed him to the ground. Claws ripped through fabric and along his collarbone. Blood spilled across his torso. He pushed the weight off as fast as he could and got to his feet.

Quickly, he patted down his neck. He felt no wounds. He ran his fingers over the necklace that dug into his skin, his fingertips feeling some new abrasions on the necklace, as if the tiger scratched at it with purpose.

Hydro swallowed. "Did I just..."

Very good, Hydro Paen. Your training has saved you. Anne tugged his hand, interrupting his thoughts. Warmth filtered into him again, but less powerful than before. The same as Hydro had always felt since first wearing the necklace.

Hydro ignored her. Blood on the Ether Blade soured his thoughts, so he put the blade away and retreated from the mishap. He walked away in silence. Anne kept him preoccupied, not giving Hydro a moment of introspection.

Why are we here, Hydro Paen? We have to collect the jewels.

"I have business with the seer."

You will die if you see her like this.

"Like what? I have my father's blade now. I have you, don't I? Didn't you say you were powerful?"

I am powerful, more powerful than her, but you haven't obtained all of me yet.

Hydro stopped and tapped his foot. He crossed his arms. "And when do I receive all of you?"

I already told you.

Hydro huffed. "Tell me again."

When you are free of the man you know and embrace the truth of the man you may become.

The words jogged his memory as he thought back to the Trials. "Well, perhaps she can help with that. She seems to know things." Hydro continued forward, now dead-set on reaching the village.

In time, he reached the village he had woken up in months previously. Dark-skinned villagers went about their day. His presence drew looks of surprise and suspicion, but Hydro moved through the village without engaging with them, keeping his hand on the hilt of Purge. He didn't know what they were really capable of, but right now, none of that mattered. The only thing that mattered was answers, and he would get those one way or another.

He stopped outside the starseer's tent, half expecting her to be waiting for him. Taking a deep breath, he pushed aside the beaded curtain and entered.

No one.

"Is she away?"

He surveyed the room, noticing the absence of the crystal orb on the high table. The bed in the corner was tidy, clean from nonuse. There were gaps on the bookshelf where books had been removed. He inspected further, but found nothing that would explain the seer's disappearance.

"Where have you run off to?" Hydro clicked his tongue.

He exited the hut. Anne waited outside for him.

"She isn't here."

I know, because you still are. Luckily for you.

Hydro spat on the ground and turned around. "Who is she? How do you know her?"

She is an enemy of my father's.

"Why didn't you help me with her the first time?"

I did. You escaped with my help.

"And this time?"

Let's go, Hydro Paen. We have jewels to collect.

Feeling the need to erase this part of his life from his memory, Hydro didn't follow Anne right away. His gaze roamed over the hut one last time and then he muttered a single word. "*Palo.*" Orange flame engulfed the thatched hut, burning it down with terrible swiftness.

Screams and shouts from the villagers fell on deaf ears. Though some gathered water and blankets to attempt to snuff out the fire, none dared to approach him. It seemed the lady here had given them her Power, and without her, they were nothing. He reveled in that fact and smirked as flames danced across the thatched building. When he got tired of seeing the smoke rise to the air, he left, not caring if the fire spread.

Hours later, after following a river, a true river that gushed from the forest, Hydro spied a city cut into sections by the very same river. Too large to be anything other than the capital, Kuyan. The abundant greenery of the forest tapered off on the approach to the city, dissipating into a field of brown sand.

"Approaching the Sinking Sea," said the cockpit speakers.

Hydro frowned to himself. *This whole nation is backwards. Seas are blue, not brown. Do they even have a sense of logic?*

The radar bleeped in front of him and the ship flew itself towards the blinking dot, away from the city and across the empty sand. It began its descent when it reached a large hand-like structure protruding from the ground. As it landed itself, Hydro leaned over and peered out past the windshield. He couldn't see much of anything besides the hand and sand. A flicker caught his eye, though, near the base of the stone hand.

There!

The ship touched down and opened its side door for Hydro to exit. As Hydro descended the ramp, though, the ship shook, stumbling almost as if the legs buckled underneath it. Unable to maintain his balance, Hydro was thrown from the ramp to land on the desert floor. He coughed, sand blowing up into his eyes and nostrils.

He pushed himself up. Or tried to. Instead of pushing on the sand, he pushed through. His eyes widened. He yanked them back, feeling a viceroy grip, threatening to suck him under. He had felt something similar only once before. *What is wrong with this nation?*

Thrusters sounded above him. Sand obstructed his vision, suffocating him. He closed his eyes and coughed and spat sand that had managed to infiltrate his mouth. As lightly as he could, he rolled onto his back. The ship now hovered above the sea of sand, humming with the use of anitron. Four large divots where it had tried to land quickly filled in, like a wound healing itself.

Hydro felt his body sink. Forearms first. Then the sand crept into the gaps of his clothing, brushing against his neck soon enough. Using his core strength, he bolted upright, freeing his back from the sinking sand, but pushing his hips farther downward until his whole lap sat beneath the sea.

I don't have time for this. "Maa!"

Hydro focused on first making a solid base beneath him and then pushing that base up like a pillar. It worked. From a little manmade perch of Power, Hydro observed the desert around him.

The ship, oblivious to his predicament, called out. "The jewel."

Yes, yes, yes, the jewel. I know.

Hydro scanned the structure again for the glimmer he had seen previously. Not seeing it, Hydro focused on making a solid earthen bridge to bring him to the base of the giant hand. At a body's length away, he caught a flash of light once more. The jewel sat underneath the shade of the giant's thumb.

There you are. Now, to get to you. Hydro furrowed his brows. *Hmmmm...*

He couldn't dive into the pit of devil's-sand. Instead, Hydro focused on creating a miniature solid hand like the one immediately before him. He formed it below and around the jewel, catching the jewel in its palm while sand sreamed off the edges. Then he brought the small stone hand towards him and grabbed the jewel.

A sapphire.

Hydro twirled the gemstone in his hand, admiring the blue that reminded him so very much of his own planet. Light rippled from its exquisite cuts, like waves rippling in the oceans and seas of Acquava. He closed his eyes. *Aiton.*

He glanced back at the machine. "Are there any more on this planet?"

"Sensors indicate no."

"Good."

He used Power to push himself up to where the machine hovered, ramp extended in midair, waiting for him. Once inside, it closed. With the jewel still in his hand, he sat down at the pilot's seat in the cockpit.

"Call Victor Zigarda."

"Calling Victor Zigarda."

A green light shot out from the panel. Soon enough, the words *connecting* were replaced by a holographic image of Lord Zigarda.

"What is it?" Lord Zigarda seemed hurried and preoccupied.

"I have another one." Hydro didn't waste any time in pleasantries with the man.

"Good. Where to next?"

Hydro glanced at the jewel in his palm, thinking of the blue and of the waves of Acquava. "C-Bot says there are no more on this planet. We will go to Onkh next."

"Onkh? I hope you do not intend to reunite with your brother. The shifter is already there. She will—"

"There is no need to worry. I doubt my brother would want to see me, anyway. Your shifter won't have any reason to do anything."

"Good, that's one less loose end I will need to tie."

"Sure." He didn't entirely understand Zigarda's point.

"When you travel to Onkh, make sure you change the registration on Cere's machine. Guardian Eska is still hunting you. The Hown invaded my Web shortly after you left. They will surely be looking for you while you exit and enter atmospheres."

"Where are they now?"

"I do not have the slightest idea, but you shouldn't be concerned. You have a machine that can hide you, fight for you, and transport you to wherever you need to go."

The words didn't comfort Hydro the way they should have. The Hown, after all, were the best fighters in the universe—after the Guardian of the Core himself. "Sure."

"Listen to me, Hydro Paen. I'm in Rydel, finalizing something, but I will be leaving here shortly. Business calls me elsewhere. It's imperative you do not interrupt me at an inopportune time. I have the scry and your blood. I will track you myself from here on out. There is no need to call. As long as I know you are alive, no harm will come to Aiton."

Hydro's chest flared with anger. He reined in his temper. "It better not."

Zigarda said nothing and the connection ended.

Hydro drummed his fingers on the dashboard in front of him. In the other hand, he spun the sapphire through his fingers for a moment, then placed it in the pouch at his hip.

"We head for Onkh." Hydro called out to the machine. Instantly, it began to fly away from the Sinking Sea.

He had had enough of this nation and its oddities. He had had enough of its starseers and tigers and libertine lords. It was time to return home. It was time to return to Acquava.

CHAPTER TWENTY-ONE

ZARYA

Midday had passed just a few hours before, making it the perfect environment for training as the suns waned. Aiton stepped to the basin of water in anticipation and determination, but also with anxiety and doubt. Half of him loved this part of training, the other half dreaded each time it proved futile.

In his usual manner, Professor Haruko rolled up his sleeves. "Okay, Aiton, are you ready?"

"Yes," Aiton lied. He had worn a blue tunic in hopes that perhaps the color could improve his connection with the water in the basin. It was silly, Aiton knew, but at this point, the want to cast had grown to a need.

"Then say *vesi*."

"*Vesi*."

"Allay your mind with your surroundings. At first, let your senses drift to the distant waves, to the recent rain of this morning, but finally you will want to focus on the basin in front of you."

Aiton first focused on the water, faintly audible to his ears. Then he smelled the rain of the morning, still fresh on his nose. Finally, he observed the water in the basin, water that he would command to obey him. It would do as he pleased: solidify to ice, boil, or even become a mirror.

"*Vesi*," Aiton repeated.

His forearm tightened. His fingers stretched. The water rippled. His eyes widened. The water died with the breeze.

"*Vesi*," Aiton repeated once more.

Nothing.

His shoulder lost strength and his arm fell. *I'm useless. I'm not a Paen.* Aiton crumbled to his knees.

"Aiton! Aiton!" Haruko hoisted the boy up and held him in his arms.

No tears dropped from Aiton's eyes. He stared past Haruko's arm to the stone court. Shock held him stagnant. A sickening realization lurked within him. *Denied. I'm Denied.* If Haruko were speaking, he wouldn't have known. If anyone else had noticed him drop in the courtyard, he wouldn't have known. At that moment, he wouldn't have known much besides the singular, cellular thought: *I'm Denied.*

When Aiton started shaking, he came back from his reverie. He retreated from Haruko's hold and sat on the stone court. He looked up at his mentor. "I'm Denied, aren't I?"

"No. No. No. Aiton. No. *You are not* Denied. The problems you are having everyone has."

"Did my brother have the same problems?"

"By the time your father hired me, Hydro had already cast his first spell."

Aiton's fist tapped the stone court. Curiosity in his eyes, he looked up at his professor once more. "What about my sister?"

"Your sister?" Professor Haruko sat down beside Aiton, hands on his thighs. "What makes you bring up her?"

"I want to know more about her. Is that so wrong?"

Professor Haruko sighed. "No, it is not." Before he answered, he looked around. "Would you like to take a walk?" Professor Haruko offered Aiton his hand.

"Sure." Aiton took it. "Where are we going?"

"Let us wander through the labyrinth." Together they traversed the cobblestone court and walked down the steps to the hedge labyrinth. Professor Haruko entered the concrete walkway, the hedge pressing in on him from both sides. "Your sister, Anya, could cast." Haruko paused. "She could cast very well. So well, in fact, that Finesse, the academy I was headmaster at before your father recruited me, wouldn't have helped her training."

"When did she cast?" Aiton felt so small amongst the hedges towering over him.

"A year after I began here. At the age of five. To be honest, I have never seen anything like it since, nor I suspect shall I ever again. Your brother, from what I have been told, cast his first at the age of seven. Or, perhaps it was eight. I know it was around then."

And here I am. Almost ten... Aiton's shoulders slumped. A part of him didn't want to continue questioning Haruko, but the other part wanted to know more about the family now absent from his life. "What was her first spell?"

"*Salama.* That is why it is so interesting, in part. The lack of natural resources makes it one of the most difficult to cast." Professor Haruko turned another corner of the maze. "And it was blue," he added.

"What does that matter?"

"Remember how I told you, Aiton, that all spellcasters have different levels. *Palo*, for example, can take the form of white, yellow, red, and even blue fire. Those with blue flames are the strongest, and typically, they are casters who lay dormant until they are in their teens. This same concept is consistent with each spell. With electricity, one could cast either a yellow spark or a blue one."

"And she cast blue."

"She did. At five. When I told your mother the news, well, her eyes lit up."

Aiton bit his lip. *Maybe this is why people don't ask questions.* He sighed, heavy enough for Professor Haruko to hear. By this time, they had made it to the center of the labyrinth where a statue of a dolphin arced above a fountain, spouting water from its mouth. The water created a melodic lulling, but it did little to ebb Aiton's anxiety.

"The reason I tell you this, Aiton—"

"Go away."

"Aiton, please, let me help you..."

"You can't. Go away." Aiton kept his eyes locked on the dolphin.

"*Cannot*," Haruko corrected.

"Whatever, just go away." Aiton tried pushing Haruko aside but couldn't.

"Of course, my lord. But, before I go, I want to remind you to look at where all of them are now. They are gone. And you are not, Aiton. You are still here. You are still standing. Every Paen has potential, it is in your blood, and some day you will recognize it." Professor Haruko walked away. "Some day."

Aiton stood below the dolphin, not saying anything. Professor Haruko's footsteps shuffled away, and Aiton was left to listen to the murmur of the fountain. Aiton knew the statue represented the animal bonded to the first Paen ruler of Acquava. After a moment, he climbed onto the lip of the fountain and reached towards the granite statue. He stroked the closest fin.

Lyonell had an animal and Power. Father had Power and leadership. Hydro was strong and confident and had Power. And Anya could have been stronger than all of them. Aiton sighed. *And here I am... useless.* Aiton examined his hands. They were small, barely capable of handling a wooden sword—probably why Korth hadn't sparred with him for a week and a half.

Aiton stepped down off the edge and meandered back to the estate in his own time. Eventually, he wandered out of the labyrinth and let his feet take him to the conference room where they had received Guardian Eska, his apprentice, and the others.

He put his finger on the table shaped to match the borders of Acquava and walked around the circumference. With each province he touched, he thought about the marquises who ruled there. They were his father's people, his grandfather's people, and were meant to be his brother's people. They were never meant to be Aiton's people.

Elbows on the table, hands cradling his chin, Aiton scanned the nation. *How am I supposed to lead without Power? Who will take advice from a Denied nine-year-old?* He sighed and left the room, not wanting to explore the futility of the situation any longer.

Aiton continued farther down the hallway. At the end, a staircase transitioned from placid blue walls to a wide cavern. The staircase led to the secret port that docked the special ships, those set aside for emergency use. Many people didn't think that the castle had a dock at all, for the area was riddled with sea stacks. Normally, it would have been unnavigable, but the captains here were experts at navigation and had to pass a test to earn the job. The other ships, the ones that would go to war, should war ever occur, were docked in the city port where much of the militia lived. Weekly, one of the acqua guards from the castle would conduct regular drills with those that lived in the city to make sure they were prepared.

Two ships made of a thicker variant of seachrome, the same that protected the acqua guards, were tied to the stone dock and bobbed in the waves. It was predictably quiet, as scheduled checks and maintenance were only performed once or twice each week. Aiton maneuvered past the ships, not caring to admire their grandeur. What was there to admire anymore?

He sat at the edge of the pier, shoes off. His legs were long enough to let his feet splash in the water below. Coldness crept into him. It felt foreign, not like water should feel. Not to a Paen, anyway. He looked to the green and blue waters and saw the reflection of a boy who belonged no more to this family than sea lions did to lions on land. Paen was his name, but it was a false one, just like a sea lion. If he truly were a Paen, he would've been able to cast like his father, or brother, or sister. *If I was a true Paen, water could never drown me...*

Something hitched in his throat.

Using the strength of his triceps, he lifted himself off the wood. He leaned over the edge more and more. The waves reflected his image. His lips quivered as he contemplated his next move. All it would take now was a release. A simple release. The water would embrace him and test him.

"A true Paen doesn't fear water. Hydro wouldn't..."

He tilted a little farther. He closed his eyes and tightened his abs, bracing for impact.

Water rippled. A splash against his feet.

He opened his eyes and saw a horse's head slowly rising from the water. It came towards him, first revealing its seaweed-green eyes and snout, then its neck and pale mane. Finally, it surfaced, exposing its large blue body freckled with briny-white spots as if the sea had salted it. The gills on its neck flapped in and out, closing when fully above water. The fins on the backs of its legs retracted. It walked towards him on top of the water like a regular horse on land.

A seahorse? Aiton pushed himself back and stood. He met it at eye-level.

Closer and closer it came, until it was so close Aiton reached out and touched its nose, not giving another thought to the action. It was still wet, but warm and inviting. Aiton moved his hand around the nose to its jaw and closer to its eyes, which focused only on him. Even when Aiton touched its white mane that felt like seaweed, it still kept its gaze only on Aiton, paying no heed to what he did.

"Where did you come from? You're beautiful."

You're not bad looking yourself, Little One.

Aiton stumbled backwards, tripping over his shoes and falling onto the stone pier. "Oh." Aiton rubbed his butt.

The horse neighed and shook its mane. It showed its teeth in a big grin.

"How... how?" Aiton stood again, ignoring the discomfort caused by the fall. He moved closer to the horse. "How did you do that? How can you speak into my mind?"

Because I am yours, if you will have me.

"Have you? I... I... I don't even know your name. How did you find me?"

My name is Zarya... Your distress called to me, Little One.

"You can sense me? Feel me?" Aiton looked at the pier and shook his head. He looked back at the horse. "Understand me?"

We both have seablood. We are meant for one another, if you will have me.

Professor Haruko had spoken of bonding. Of the Power that came with it. The sacrifice. The risk. How each person had an animal they could bond with, but many never found the one meant for them. How each animal had a unique ability they bestowed upon their partner.

Aiton shivered, but not from fear. "What will I gain if I bond with you?"

No animal ever shares its secrets. We bond with the human, not their greed. If you will have me, I will have you.

Aiton contemplated the decision. He looked Zarya in her seaweed eyes; they were a darker green, similar to his brother's eyes. "Zarya, is it?" Aiton leaned in closer.

Yes, Little One.

"Zarya, my name is Aiton Paen. It is nice to meet you." Aiton grabbed her behind the ear and let his fingers run through her white mane.

You as well, Aiton Paen. The horse kneeled on the water, allowing Aiton to scratch her head.

After she returned to all fours, she leaned in and pushed her wet nose into Aiton's forehead. Aiton could feel her warmth, her vitality and vigor, as she breathed into him. But, more importantly, for the first time in weeks, Aiton didn't feel alone. Not any longer.

CHAPTER TWENTY-TWO

VANISHED

"The boy isn't here, my guardian."

"What do you mean, *isn't there*, General?" Arms crossed over his chest, Guardian Eska thrummed his thumbs on his biceps. Alone, he stood in his telecommunicator chamber looking at the holographic images of General Satorus and Captain Chase Arwayn. Chase was third in line to take over for General Satorus upon his retirement.

"After I sent word to you with our plan for the scry, we went to Acquava. We are here at the lord's estate, but..." General Satorus coughed into his hand. "But the boy isn't here."

"Yes. But *where* is he?"

"No one knows. Not even his own council. The boy just vanished."

"Vanished?"

Guardian Eska closed his eyes and massaged his temples. *First Hydro vanishes, then Aiton vanishes. Truly, brothers by blood and whim.* He opened his eyes. "Do you think they've made contact with each other somehow?"

"Doubtful, my guardian."

"Why do you say that?"

"When we arrived at Rhemu, we ordered a scan of the docking history. We found no records of Hydro entering the atmosphere."

"Well, there is that, then. So, what now?"

"We will wait here until the boy's return," Satorus said.

"And if he doesn't?"

"Well, then it most likely means that he's dead and we are back to ground zero in our hunt for his brother."

Guardian Eska sighed.

"It isn't all bad news, my guardian." Satorus coughed into his fist. He tugged at his collar.

Guardian Eska raised an eyebrow. "What do you mean?"

"While examining the docking entries in Rhemu, we found something that is of potential interest to you."

Eska straightened his posture. He arched an eyebrow. "And that is?"

"We believe Doctor Cere's ship was present."

His neck tensed. "Cere? In Acquava? How do you know?"

"Since you gave us a description of the ship, we have also been keeping our eyes peeled for it. You've told us both men are wanted."

Eska nodded. "That is correct."

"Well, Chase here noticed a glitch in the Rhemu docking footage."

"Glitch?" Eska flicked his attention to the man next to General Satorus.

Chase coughed. "Yes, my guardian. As we were examining the docking footage, I noticed a few seconds where lights surrounding the docking zone seemed to flicker, as if something passed in front of it. It happened again a few minutes later."

Without a proper visual, Guardian Eska found the idea difficult to imagine. As if guessing Eska's thoughts, a recorded screen popped up alongside the image of General Satorus and Captain Arwayn. It was a short clip, only a few minutes, and Eska watched it a few times before Chase pointed out the glitch.

"Watch there in the background. Now."

Eska focused. And saw. The lights in the back compound had been covered, as if something had passed in front of them. Yet nothing had moved in front of them.

"The ship is invisible?"

General Satorus inclined his head. "We believe so, my guardian. After noticing this, we ordered a thermal sensor analysis of the image. It showed a bubble-shaped ship fly into the docking port and leave a few moments later."

"Why did it—"

Guardian Eska didn't have a chance to finish his question before General Satorus continued. "One figure disembarked. Cloaked. Invisible to the naked eye, but not to thermal scanners."

Guardian Eska's tried to keep his surprise from showing on his face, but his mind reeled. If Zakk could appear miraculously during the fourth trial, then it made logical sense that Dr. Cere had the capabilities to offer someone else the same sort of invisibility. Who had exited that ship? Where did they fit in the unfolding events? Those were questions that couldn't be answered now. Now, Eska wanted to know how exactly Dr. Cere had constructed a ship that could be invisible. Such a technology was unheard of and warranted caution. Guardian Eska wondered at the limits of the doctor's ingenuity and realized now why Tundra had been so prone to dismiss him as merely a wild imagination bordering on insanity. *Truly, a gifted mind, but lost and corrupt.* Hydro, with all his potential, also now lost. Eska began to wonder how many more lost souls there were in Gladonus right now. How many had he failed as Guardian?

Pushing aside his guilt, he asked. "And the Puwls?"

"No one claimed to have knowledge of this and were just as surprised as we were."

"Do you think the surprise was genuine?"

"It was hard to gauge, my guardian," Captain Arwayn admitted.

"Do we know where the ship went next?"

General Satorus shook his head.

Eska pinched the bridge of his nose. "Thank you, General. This is a start. I will have Conseleigh Iycel take over from here."

"My guardian?"

"She will hunt for Doctor Cere. They have a history and I think she will be up for the task."

"You will send her by herself?"

Guardian Eska shook his head. "No. She will meet you in Acquava and head north with a squad of your soldiers."

"And if the boy returns before she arrives?"

"Stay until she arrives."

"Very well, my guardian."

The connection ended.

Tundra.

Yes, Edwyrd.

Meet me in my chambers. I have an assignment for you.

Inside his chambers, Guardian Eska waited for Tundra. Before she came, he prepped the blood bonding station by placing the golden bowl on top of the pedestal. When she entered, he was waiting for her behind it. If she was curious as to what was happening, her face didn't show it. Like a true and loyal conseleigh to Eska, she approached him, already knowing what was to be expected of her. Standing in front of the golden bowl, she offered her right hand to Eska, grabbing Eska's knife with the other hand. She sliced her palm open and shook his hand.

In unison, they said, "May we bleed, may we bond, may we share thoughts and feelings from this moment on."

Tundra, can you sense me?

Of course, Edwyrd. The connection is perfect.

Eska nodded. "Good. You will be traveling to Onkh."

"Onkh? What is there?"

"A wedding between Marquis Sigurd and Lauren Puwl. I believe it is necessary for you to go."

"You are sending me to a wedding, my guardian? Surely, there are more pressing matters."

Eska nodded. "There are, but you will use the wedding as your cover. I've just received word from General Satorus that they've spotted Doctor Cere's ship entering Rhemu's spaceport." He went on to give the full explanation from Satorus.

"Genus? Do you think he is conspiring with Acquava?"

Eska shook his head. "I am unsure. As are General Satorus and Captain Arwayn. But this is a start. And you will find him for me. I know you have wanted this for some time now."

"And you are finally letting me loose? Why the change of heart? Are you no longer worried about me?"

Eska's heart tightened. That wasn't it at all. He was concerned, but he couldn't show that, so instead of allowing his posture to slump, he straightened his spine and stuck out his chest. "No. On the contrary, I believe you are the perfect person for this job. Your title as my aid will not rouse suspicion. You know the icelands better than anyone else. And the Hown you recruit at the Paen estate will aid in protecting you well enough."

"Sereya? But you mentioned Grime was in Acquava."

"We spotted him in Acquava, but I believe he has made his way to Sereya. He is a Sereyan native after all. And that is the real reason why I send you. While in Sereya, you may have to deal with Lord Grime."

"May? I don't understand."

"Well, if the doctor is colluding with Lord Grime, that will be a serious offense."

"And if I should find information linking Cere to Grime?"

"Depose him. He would be linked to the man who aimed to sabotage my Trials, and thus, this system. That grievance does not go without reprimand."

"That may get messy." If her words implied hesitation, her voice and demeanor did not.

"That is why you will take Hown with you to help enforce the regulation if necessary."

"And then?"

"Find Doctor Cere. And, if possible, bring him back alive. I want to know just how exactly he managed to tamper with the Trials."

"He could be anywhere on Onkh."

"Yes. That I know. Use Captain Arwayn's technique and look at the thermal cameras in the spaceports."

"I will see what I can do. When should I leave?"

"As soon as possible. No one knows where Aiton Paen has gone, and the Hown must remain in place should he return. It'll be best to arrive before he returns as well so that you don't slow down the hunt for Hydro."

"Very well, my guardian." She turned and walked away from him. She paused just before she placed a hand on the door. Pivoting to face him, she raised an eyebrow. "Is that all, Edwyrd?"

Eska maneuvered around the golden bowl. "Is there something more you wish to give?" He folded his arms over his chest.

"I guess not." Tundra opened the door and let it shut behind her.

Eska's bravado failed the moment she exited the room. Out of any mission he had sent her on, this was certainly going to be her most perilous. He had known she expected him to kiss her, to give one last farewell, but to do that would to believe that she wouldn't return. It would be to acknowledge his fear, and he couldn't show her that. For, in turn, what effect would that have on her? Would she be too fearful to complete her mission? Or would she be even more invigorated and perhaps too bold? By leaving her with dry lips, he tasked her with one more mission. An unspoken one, but one that he knew she would realize all the same. She was tasked to return to him. To stay by his side to the end. Whatever end that was.

CHAPTER TWENTY-THREE

A WATER RIDE

S eagulls called overhead, flying above the water and above Aiton. His heart
was fuller than it had ever been, surging with a warmth that even the icy winds
of Katarh couldn't quell. Zarya moved with powerful grace over the vast expanse
of open water. He stayed low over her neck, his face pressed into her seaweed-like
mane. Wisps of water splashed his face, but he didn't care. Not even in the
slightest. Something about Zarya's presence warmed him in a way that he didn't
think possible.

Aiton leaned forward into her ear. "Where are we going?"

Where do you want to go?

Aiton pulled back, tugging the horse's mane as well, bringing her trot to a halt.
He pursed his lips. What did he want? To the west, the suns dipped. Nighttime
would be upon them soon enough. Aiton looked around at the vast expanse of
blue, slowly becoming purple in the fading light. Besides the faint image of his
castle home behind him, only water stretched out on all sides of him. He was
standing on top of water. Water! Well, technically, Zarya was standing on top of
water, but he was on top of her. *If only Hydro could see me now.* Aiton beamed.

The castle in the distance called him back. Duties and obligations called him
back. Aiton sighed. "We should go back."

Is that what you want, Little One?

Aiton's heart pulsed and sang. On top of Zarya, he had never felt so free in his
life. He had never felt so confident in himself or so independent. With her, he
could do anything. He shook his head. "No. Not really. All my life my brother was
trying to escape that castle, and he finally succeeded."

You have a brother? Where is he now?

"Lost," Aiton mumbled. "In truth, I don't know where he is."

Do not be sad, Little One. Every lost person can be found once again.

Aiton wanted to believe her, but after all he had been through, he ignored the
comment. He hadn't seen Hydro in over a month. And the last time still burned in
Aiton's memory, especially at night, burrowing into his sleep. If he went back to

the castle now, he would have to go to bed again. Korth or Darien or Professor Haruko would make him. Here, with Zarya, everything was so much better.

Aiton pursed his lips. "Where are you from, Zarya?"

Seahorses are from many different places, Little One.

"But where are you from?"

I was born near Talyn.

"I have never been there before. Is it beautiful?"

To me, the sea is the most beautiful place. Under the water. But I do not dare dive near Talyn.

"Why?"

The Queen of the Sea—Thalassa.

"She lives there?"

That is what my parents told me, Little One.

"Have you ever seen her?" Aiton gripped her mane tighter and leaned forward.

No. Nor shall I ever want to. To meet her means death.

"Do you think she is there now?"

Zarya neighed. She trotted around in a circle.

"Where is she?"

North near the Hart Isles or Summer Isles. Winter approaches and she will need to feast before she hibernates.

Aiton smiled at his fortune. "Then let's go to Talyn. I want to see your home."

Zarya neighed again. *It is a long journey, Little One. Two days at least. Are you ready?*

Aiton nodded. "Yes. Let's go."

Zarya slowed to a stop once more. She whinnied, waves splashing against her legs. *Then you must be ready to hold on tight. I am faster underwater.*

"I am holding on tight," Aiton said with a smile. "Wait, what—"

The fins on her legs flipped out. Her neck now showed its gills, and she leaped into the air, preparing to dive. Before Aiton could finish his objection, he was already underwater.

Pain. Wetness. An inability to breathe. These were the things Aiton expected, but under the water he found none of that. No salt stung his eyes. His tunic remained loose, not wet and damp. And he could breathe. *How is this—*

We are bonded. You have different abilities now.

This is yours? Aiton thought, seeing if she could truly read his mind.

Every sea animal can grant the ability to see and breathe underwater. But that is not all I will give you.

What will you give me?

You must figure that out, Little One. If you truly want my Power, you must learn everything there is about me.

Aiton smiled. A part of him wanted it now, but his father had always told him, "Good things come to those who wait."

But as Zarya carried him through the ocean, Aiton began to feel disappointment. No eels slithered like snakes in the sea; no starfish spun like acrobats; no schools of fish abandoned each other at any sign of threat. And as nothing upon nothing but blue and green and darkness below passed him by, he asked, *Where are all the animals?*

The ocean is huge.

But where is everything?

Many live closer to shore or farther down in the deeper parts of the sea. Here you will only see sharks, whales, fish, dolphins, and maybe jellyfish. That should be enough.

Slowly, the sea took a toll on his strength. As he drifted off to a gentle sleep atop Zarya's back, who now moved through the water at a smooth and rhythmic gait, Aiton felt warm. Even in this vast emptiness, with no others in sight, he felt warm and safe. Finally, for once, he felt at home.

Two days later, Aiton saw land once more. He could finally see sand sloping away from the waves, and the animals he knew, like starfish and fish and crabs, became more frequent. And, soon enough, Zarya no longer trotted through the water, but put her hooves upon dry land.

He looked up to see the suns, fresh upon his face yet again. It was just after midday.

"We are here?" he asked.

Zarya neighed.

"Can we circle the island? I want to see how large it is."

Zarya did just that, keeping a nice walking gait on the shoreline. The rushing waves, the freedom, the exotic scents, the adventure—he breathed it all in. It made him feel full even though he hadn't had a meal in days. His arms and body grew warm at the thought of having such a privileged experience. This was much better than returning to the castle.

As they made their way around the island, Aiton spotted a larger land mass to the south and east. Aiton pointed. "Is that Talyn?"

Yes.

"Then this is Leviathan Bay!"

Yes, that is where we are, and why I don't prefer to swim in these waters.

Farther inland, trees ripe with fruit swayed in the open breeze. He would need some later, after he finished exploring the outskirts of the island. Much to his surprise, these islands weren't like the Hart Isles, where stones detritus from the trees littered the sand. This sand was white, untouched, and it slowly transitioned to grass and trees away from the water. It seemed pure. A perfect place.

Aiton spent hours on her back, traveling around the island's circumference in peace and solitude. When his stomach growled, he stopped to pluck some indigo fruit that crawled up the sides of the tree. Because of its hardened exterior, he had to squeeze the fruit, collapsing it upon itself to expose its white center. *Mangosteen!* He thought only the Summer Isles had this type of fruit, but he greedily plucked the slippery white pieces out and put it into his mouth, making sure to spit out the pit afterwards. He grabbed a handful and cradled them in his shirt. Only the slushing of the sea and the cry of birds overhead broke any serenity. It lulled him like many things of the sea did, and it refined his senses. He was so at peace with the nature around him that when he heard a distant voice and a soft melody floating through the air, his ears perked.

Is someone here?

Let us check.

Zarya increased her gait and rounded a bend, the view blocked by trees. As the view became less obstructed, the music and voice became softer. Soon it went quiet altogether.

Once past the bend of trees, a woman sitting on a large rock came into Aiton's view. A harp sat in her lap, but she no longer strummed it.

Zarya continued creeping forward and now Aiton saw the woman had the lower body of a fish. *A mermaid.* She hadn't noticed their approach yet, her gaze fixed on a second figure to whom she spoke, a man with black hair who had an oddly familiar build and posture. His back was turned.

Only a few more paces were given to them incognito. Finally, the mermaid saw them, and when she did, she jumped back into the water, harp in hand. The man turned around to face them.

It was Hydro.

CHAPTER TWENTY-FOUR

LEVIATHAN BAY

A tmosphere control had stopped him upon entering Onkh, but as the doctor had instructed him to do, Hydro stood in front of the holographic projector, altering his physical features and voice to those scanning the ship. Before entering the atmosphere, Hydro had pushed a button to rotate the license on the ship to that of one belonging to Acquava. Atmosphere control asked the typical questions and then released him, allowing him to pass.

After docking the large ship in the designated spaceport of Rhemu, he had ejected the left arm of the ship to serve as his transportation while on Acquava. And while he could technically take the extremity to any part of Onkh, he figured that after his initial docking in Rhemu, he would just take the entire ship as airspace control was easier to avoid than atmosphere control stations, which were docked as close to intersystem wormholes as possible. Inside the atmosphere, a ship's location was nearly impossible to locate unless tracked, which had made his acquisition of the first and second jewels simple.

The left arm was a rectangular cube that punched through the air, almost like a hoverbus, but triple its size and much faster. Thrusters attached to its underside fueled it as it sped across the open expanse of water that he called home. Its speed and power caused the waters below it to blast upwards from the thrusters, resulting in a constant deluge of seawater that spattered like rain on the large unobstructed window that allowed him a view.

Rain, even if it was makeshift rain, soothed Hydro. Slowly, a sensation returned to him. One he couldn't quite place, but he felt something stir inside him with each league of blue he traversed. Perhaps it was the seablood coursing into his veins once more after his time away. Perhaps it was simply the sight of the salty sea. But perhaps it was the thought of his brother and how he fared. Aiton's situation weighed on Hydro, and, whether he liked to admit it or not, he didn't know if he was ready to see his brother again. Not with how Hydro had left things.

Hands in his pockets, Hydro stood at the window. He closed his eyes and inhaled deeply. *It's okay. They deserved it. Family loves you no matter what. But...* Hydro opened his eyes and sighed. He tried ignoring the temptation to look to the encroaching landmass to the west, but he failed. There, off in the distance, was the province of Acquis, and on top of the cliff sat the structure that he had called home for all of his life. Hydro bit his lower lip and slumped his shoulders. *But Aiton never deserved what I did.*

You freed him. Along with your father. You are a hero. No goddess controls them anymore. They answer to no one now.

Placing his forearm against the window, Hydro leaned forward, resting his forehead on top of it. Anne took hold of his other arm and rubbed her fingers over his knuckles. It stirred in him a little warmth. In moments like this, where his heart dragged over how he left his brother, her attempts to soothe him were futile, but he smiled, appreciating the effort she exerted nonetheless.

"Here I am, returning home a pawn of Zigarda."

Not forever, Hydro Paen. The sooner the jewels are collected, the sooner you will be freed.

Hydro tore his hand away from her and felt the satchel on his hip. "Those blasted jewels. I want nothing to do with them, but if it keeps Aiton safe..."

He straightened his posture and looked out once more to Acquis; it was closer now. They were passing by the southern tip. Hydro wanted to reach out with his Power to feel Aiton's presence, but didn't. The thought of Aiton was better than feeling Aiton. If he felt his brother, he might also feel his brother's contempt, hopelessness, and loneliness. And Hydro didn't want to feel any guiltier than he already did.

The moment slipped by. Ocean blue now replaced any landmass. And Hydro realized that the left arm of C-Bot was making its way south. *So Eska hid the next jewel in Talyn?*

Talyn meant nothing to him, but everything for his family. More so, his father. When Hydro had found out that his mother hadn't descended from a powerful lineage like theirs, that his father had used Marquis Axyel's forgetfulness and dementia to fake her origin, a part of him felt betrayed. He had spent months questioning why his father had done such a thing, and the only thing that all the elders told him was *love*. A wasted word, in Hydro's opinion.

Once there was a time when Hydro's family had been perfect and whole. Hydro had been excelling at Finesse, and Hydro's sister, to his mother's delight, showed true promise. Promise beyond even Hydro's.

All of that had ended years ago upon a gelid afternoon...

Ice crawled up his fingertips. It froze him in place. His breathing intensified. With sheer will, he clenched his hands and tore away from the window and the cockpit, plopping himself down in a seat in an adjacent chamber. Anne had left him. Alone, Hydro sprawled out over the couch, relaxing as best as he could but never quite finding a comfortable position. He closed his eyes and put a hand to his chest. He had only intended to feel the beats of his heart, but he felt the necklace as well. Even though the black dragon's scales had bit down into his skin, it still radiated warmth. The necklace gave him Power and kept him safe. Both the beating of his heart and the warmth of the necklace helped him forget the inequities of his past failures.

Hydro woke to a slight jostle from the ship and knew it had landed.

He went to the cockpit and peered out the window. They weren't on Talyn. The sandy beaches and copious amount of fruit trees gave that away. Instead, the ship had parked itself on an island in Leviathan Bay, settling on a base of grass and sand within sight of denser forestry. Hydro crossed his arms and let a faint chuckle escape his parted lips. *First Deimos, then devil's-sand, and now this. Eska had chosen his locations well.* Without the help of Dr. Cere's tracking device, they would never have been found. He knew the reputation of Leviathan Bay. The great creature Thalassa supposedly lurked under its waves, large enough to encircle and constrict an island.

Hydro plucked the handheld device out of the empty co-pilot seat and exited the belly of the ship. The air didn't smell normal to him. It wasn't as salty as he would have preferred, being close enough to the trees to smell their scent. The sea slapping against the shore lured him out from the canopy of the ship to bask in the suns' light.

He stood overlooking the Bay that offered nothing but blue and freedom. And home. A few larger rocks that buffeted the brute force of the waves sat on the coast.

"Find the jewel." The machine spoke to him, and as if the mechanical voice hadn't been enough to gain his attention, he felt the handheld contraption vibrate. "Sensors indicate three thousand meters away."

Hydro glanced at the scanner and then into the forest beyond. Contempt crept into his countenance. "Are there tigers or basilisks hiding in this one, too?" he muttered to himself.

No.

Hydro looked down. Anne stood by his side. He turned his head and spat away from her. "Good. I hate snakes."

The only snake here lives beneath the water.

"Thalassa?"

She is one of my sisters.

Hydro frowned. "What do you mean?"

I told you, we are all related in one way or another.

"Yes, but how?"

By blood. Thalassa has First Blood, same as I.

Hydro clicked his tongue and entered the thicket of trees, preferring not to bring up the discussion about blood. His wasn't as pure as he would have liked. Halfway through his journey, he realized the forest was unexpectedly quiet. "Why is no one else here? This island is so peaceful."

It remains that way, Hydro Paen, because of Thalassa.

"Is she really that terrifying?"

No, none of his creations are terrifying. But they are Powerful. Like him. He is my father. Anyone's father.

"Not my father." Hydro scoffed.

No, not your father, Hydro Paen. Any thing's *father.*

The slight word change brought a question to his lip, but he forgot it when he arrived at a clearing. It had been at least an hour. Though the distance wasn't too far, fallen trees and his contemplative gait had slowed him. A pool occupied most of the clearing, with a small bluff rising behind it, jagged and covered in thick vines. Perfect if one had wanted to climb to the top and rise above the trees.

He approached the edge of the pool and looked below. It was deep enough to dive into from above and Hydro thought many a wanderer stumbling upon this place would take the plunge. And more importantly to Hydro, it was clear. He could see the sand below and the small number of fish swimming in the pool.

If Hydro had not been from Acquava, he would have thought this island strange. Untouched in part, but ravaged inland, with trees and debris littering the ground. Hurricanes were mostly to blame. They affected Talyn and the Hart Isles more than most.

While examining the depths of the pool, Hydro noticed a faint glimmer somewhere on the bottom. *The jewel. How to get there?* It was deep. Quite a dive. He wasn't sure if he would be able to hold his breath for that long. He hadn't dived in ages.

Setting the tracking device down on a rock next to him. Hydro tiptoed to the edge of the pool. "Hmm," Hydro hummed, still wondering if there was any other way. He took off part of his belt and set it down beside the tracking device. As he began removing his satchel of jewels, though, Anne stopped him.

Use me. Cast Power.

Without a second thought, Hydro said, "*Vesi.*" The pool rippled. It parted for him, and he followed the sandy carpet with his eyes until he saw what had reflected in the water.

Grab it.

Hydro didn't move forward. He stayed, commanding the water, watching it stay stationary like a wall. It reminded him of the Watery Path. With it, he felt a certain need to experience it. To taste the water, to feel it on his skin.

What are you doing? I told you to grab it.

"I am thinking."

Hydro bit his lips and moved forward, following the sandy carpet downward. The watery walls acted like windows. As he passed fish, he saw some glance his way, but none were as attentive as the sharks were in the Watery Path, those that were made to be loyal servants to Pearl's protection before he sliced off her head. The fish here were aimless, useless, and nothing more than scenery in the sea.

When he reached the jewel, sparkling among a few pebbles, Hydro picked it up and rotated it in front of his eyes.

He clutched it in his hand and then put it in the sack on his belt. "That's three." He beamed.

He started back but then stopped in front of one of the walls of water. He reached out, just like he had the first time he had been taken to the Watery Path and his father showed him the Power and the majesty of water. That same feeling now flowed through his veins.

He touched the water with his fingertips. When he did, he wanted more. Releasing the spell, he let the walls of water crash upon him. Fish swept past him. The water wasn't cold. It was perfect. It awakened something Hydro hadn't felt for what seemed like ages. Since his fight with Pearl. If Anne had tried to talk to him, her words would have been drowned out. This was his home. This was where he was meant to be.

And, as the water gushed in, it floated him up. For the first few seconds, he felt fine, but then his survival instincts kicked in and he realized he needed to swim to the top or drown. No longer could he use Power. To open his mouth was to die.

He began to swim. His clothes, heavy and sodden, dragged at him. A cramp set his calf afire and he began to falter and sink, the distant light of day still far from reach as his lungs began to burn.

He opened his mouth.

And breathed.

He blinked.

He breathed again.

"What is this?" He spoke underwater.

There was no more haste, no more doubt in his survival. He drifted, knowing only that he would be fine. Whatever he chose to do, he would be fine. Here, wrapped in water, he would be fine. Before surfacing, he swam with the fish, trying to see how close he could get before they would dart away. He was not as graceful, but he could breathe like them. The wonder of it kept his lungs strong.

Eventually, when the novelty wore off, he swam back to the shore and pulled himself out of the water. He checked to make sure he had the sack of jewels. After wiping his hands on the long grass to dry them, he picked up the tracking device. Then he reached for the other plastic case Dr. Cere had given him. He didn't strap it to his side right away. Instead, he began to realize what had just happened—he had tried to drown himself. What drove him to do that?

Rotating the pill case in between his thumb and index finger, he shivered as he was reminded of the black pill Dr. Cere had given him. He contemplated leaving it behind, but knew better than that. If what Victor Zigarda said was true, the Hown were after him, and Hydro already knew their prowess. Would he really want to be captured by them and executed by Guardian Eska himself?

What is that?

Hydro roused himself and glanced at Anne. "Nothing." He strapped the pill case back to his side and started his trek back to the ship, Anne by his side.

You could've died, Hydro Paen.

"I never felt more alive."

You know nothing of life and death. Be more careful.

"Did this necklace allow me to breathe?"

No.

His gait hitched. He had expected it to be another gift of Power that he had yet to discover. The fact that it wasn't interested Hydro. He contemplated the meaning of this on his return journey until a soft melody called out to him and pierced his thoughts.

"She ruled the ocean, the lakes, and the sea."

Hydro scanned his immediate surroundings. Only the ship. Nothing else was in sight. The music continued, strangely alluring. He bit his lower lip and strained his ear, trying to discern where the melody came from.

The shoreline.

Hydro maneuvered past his machine and walked out onto the sandy shore. There, on a rock above the water, sat a mermaid. A golden harp rested on her lap and her fingers plucked the strings gently.

"For ages and ages, she ruled as a queen,
Calling herself a First Blood deity.
The Lords came at her calling and bowed to her Power,
And for centuries and centuries she sat and devoured
Hope and freedom. Until one day no longer.

For a mighty man, wielding a mighty blade,
Came along, fought her, and She was slain.
And thus we call him, Hydro Paen, the Freer of Chains,
Hydro Paen, the Freer of Chains."

Hydro moved closer. The sea licked the sand, still not forceful enough to reach his feet.

"Released from our hold, we swim in the seas
Saying the words never said before: Free, free, free.
This would not be possible for most would bend the knee,
But freedom is a gift we will always keep.

Because our lives, now ours, we swim to live longer.
And each day we wait on the day of the foreigner
To return, so we can grace him with tales of how we are stronger
Now that the queen is dead and no longer.

For a mighty man, wielding a mighty blade,
Came along, fought her, and She was slain.
And thus we call him, Hydro Paen, the Freer of Chains,
Hydro Paen, the Freer of Chains."

The fingers stopped, and the melody slowly faded on the wind.

"What was that?"

"Your song, Hydro Paen: The Freer of Chains. The whole sea knows of you now."

"It is lovely."

"Freedom is a lovely thing."

Her daffodil-colored eyes reminded him of the mermaid in Pearl's cave. "Were you the one who kissed me?" Hydro paused and then clarified. "After my fight."

"I was. I wanted to give you something special for what you did."

"A kiss?"

"Not just a kiss..." Her nails strummed the chords of the harp. "Have you not figured it out yet?" She laughed.

"Are you the reason I can breathe underwater?"

The mermaid smiled and nodded. "I am. I wanted to give you the same freedom I had received. Now the sea will never hurt you. You are truly one of us."

Hydro walked closer. *One of you?*

"Come with me?" She extended her hand.

Hydro stepped forward, the water swallowing his shoes and his ankles. He ignored Anne's hand on his shirt. Her daffodil eyes called to him in the same way that Anne had called to him. It enthralled him.

She glanced away, then looked back at Hydro only briefly, put the harp to her chest and leaped off of the rock to dive into the water.

Hydro shook his head and blinked, then turned to see what had diverted her attention.

Sitting upon a blue seahorse freckled in white was his brother.

CHAPTER TWENTY-FIVE

SEARCHING FOR ANSWERS

C ain fidgeted with the emerald owl-shaped ring on his hand in front of the mirror. He took a deep breath and closed his eyes, blocking out thoughts of war and the battle gear of helmets, shields, chainmail, vanguards, and chest plates that lay in disjointed parts around his room. Instead, he thought about the scent of lilies and fire pinks and blue-eyed grass wafting upwards with the lukewarm breeze of a perfect day from the garden courtyard which his bedroom overlooked. Cain smiled. *Peace.*

He opened his eyes and focused. There would not be many more times like this ahead, and depending on how capable the forces of Cresica were, he wouldn't have time to enjoy the nature around him for months, years, or perhaps... No, he wouldn't think like that. There was always another day, but every day was a fight for the next one. *Nothing is given to you. Everything can change in an instant.* Those were two lessons he had learned during the Trials. A lesson that still, to this day, a half year later, stuck with him, slow to go away like the honey sap of a beehive.

Cain reached for his halberd, the only piece of equipment in his repertoire that had actually seen action. The other items he would use in battle were still pristine. With one hand, he dragged his fingers up the spine of the halberd, letting the feel of the weapon calm him like the garden outside. *War and peace. You cannot have one without the other.* Like Cain, all the heroes in the books he read knew that as well. War was necessary to maintain and develop peace, and to survive war, you needed skill, stamina, and strength. When it came to battle, he had all of those things. When it came to things he had less control over, that was when fear and doubt hosted their battlegrounds.

His finger traced the tip of the halberd. The door opened. Cain looked over his shoulder. His father stood at the back of the room. Cain acknowledged his father and smiled, but turned around to face his halberd once more.

"That is a beautiful weapon. You will use it well in the coming months."

A hand touched his shoulder. He tucked his head down and away, hiding the bite to his lower lip as best as he could. Ever since returning home from the Trials,

Cain didn't quite understand who he was. Whenever he looked at his father, a man significantly shorter than Cain, he wondered why his father had been reluctant to give him his hair color, pudgier jaw, and thicker forearms.

"I know, Father."

His father moved around to block Cain's view out the window. He made a fist and rapped his knuckles against his chest. "You and I, Son, we ride into this battle together. You will fight by my side as I fight by yours."

"It will be splendid." Cain continued smiling. "How long until we ride out?"

"A few hours. Please come to the telecommunication chamber before you leave the castle. We are discussing strategy with the others, and I have just been informed that Marquis Sollen has arrived."

"I will be there shortly. I am just finishing up."

His father left, but Cain never heard the door close. He leaned his halberd against the wall next to him. Closing his eyes, he focused his attention on the serenity of the chirping birds and the breeze of the wind that wafted inside. Eyes still closed, he breathed in the flowers' scent once more, envisioning each different flower of the garden in his mind.

He opened his eyes and looked out past the garden. Past the fortifications of the castle walls. Out to the west, where destiny called to him. Hands on the stone wall above his window, he let himself lean forward, halfway through the window. He fixated his concentration and closed his eyes once more, trying to see whatever future that fate beheld. *It will be good once this is—*

"Searching for something?"

Cain opened his eyes and abruptly pulled back through the window. "Mother?" He hadn't even heard her enter. Had he been that lost in his thoughts?

Cain quickly disguised his surprise and went to hug his mother. She wore a green gown with a brown sash that matched her hair tied at her waist. Cain saw more of himself in her, from the countenance to the prominent jawline to the long nose. Even her bad eyesight, which she corrected with glasses.

"Cain, are you okay? You seem..." She looked him up and down. "Lost?"

Cain blushed. She had always been more observant than his father. Pretending, Cain shook his head. "Not lost. Just envisioning the future." He feigned a smile.

"I know you leave soon. Be safe out there."

"Nothing will happen, Mother, I swear."

"Many things happen in war that you cannot predict."

"My training underneath this castle will keep me safe. Father will be right alongside me as well. I guess Marquis Sollen has arrived, so Father wants me in the communication chamber now to discuss strategy." He hugged her once more.

When Cain tried to pull away, she grabbed his forearm. "Cain, you are meant for great things. Remember that. Do not die out there."

She didn't release him, her fingers tight, her face strained. Cain looked into her eyes, seeing an uncertainty there, as if she held some sort of knowledge that he didn't. Before he could truly comprehend her words, she plucked out the necklace from underneath his green tunic. She looked at the feather and then into Cain's eyes.

"And, do not lose this. It will keep you safe." She smiled.

Cain returned the smile. "Of course, Mother. Thank you." He kissed her on the forehead.

"Go. Do what you need to do. I just wanted to come and see you again before you leave."

Cain nodded and left. He walked down one set of stairs and then another. On the ground floor, he took a corridor and then a third set of stairs leading to the telecommunication chamber. Before entering, Cain took a deep breath and composed himself. His entrance garnered much attention from his father and the attendants within. Marquis Sollen stood next to them, all arrayed around a table with an electronic base that emitted a holographic image of the land portion of Agrost.

"Cain, what took you so long?" His father asked. "I told you we were having company."

"Just busy talking with Mother is all. Sorry to keep you waiting, Father." Cain directed his attention to the marquis. "Marquis Sollen." He nodded.

"Save those thoughts for another day. Your mind cannot be cloudy now. Come." Cain's father waved his arm, beckoning his son to join him.

Standing alongside his father, Cain looked at various locations of the map generator, passing over Syf, Kane, and then finally towards his home in Thoth. His attention didn't stay there, however. Either by some polar attraction or simply because it was in the middle of the landmass, Cain fixed his gaze on the independent nation of Kane.

"We will join the forces of Vale at Redding and then move together to Ambit. From there we should restock at Lorian and cut through Kane in order to blindside Cresica with our forces." The captain of the Owl Guards, Castor Leelan, made his way around the south side of the table, drawing out the path while using his finger.

"Why cut through Kane when we can avoid the trouble?" Daven asked.

"Most likely, they will gather at Edgefield. They will be looking for us to advance on them from our territory, not Kanean territory. If it's true all banners of Cresica have been called, then they will outnumber us. We will need every advantage we can get."

"Going through Kane will expose our soldiers to harsher conditions and countless deaths before the war even begins," Cain said. "Going around takes longer, but you cannot put a value on human life."

Cain's father looked at him. "My son speaks true. For now, we ride on the skirts of Kane, refueling at Lorian like you mentioned. Perhaps my mind will change once we send scouts to examine their forces, but let us plan for this."

Castor bowed his head. "Of course, my lord."

"Anything else?"

"I do want to mention that Corke in the north of Cresica may have also been called to support their lady. And, although not a direct threat to us, they could still besiege Seawood and come for the capital from the north, which would divide our forces."

Cain looked at the map and noticed the plan of attack that Castor had drawn from the Cresican side. "If that happens, the division of forces could cost us."

"It most certainly would, Prince Evber. This is why I bring it up." Castor raised an eyebrow to everyone in the room.

The marquis spoke up. "How many of my troops can we afford to not have with us?"

"That is the question, Marquis Sollen." Castor put his arms behind his back.

"I can have a quarter of my men return to Briarwood to help defend Seawood if you wish, my lord."

Cain's father examined the field. "War is like chess. The good leaders know that. And good leaders also know that without the lady, the lord is lost." Cain's father went around the map and scanned parts of Cresica thoroughly. "Christopher, send half of your men back to Seawood."

"Half, my lord?" Marquis Sollen asked.

Cain's father looked towards the marquis. "Yes. Half. Half of that half will board ships and sail towards the Triangle Islands. That is where we will strike first. The land troops will wait at Lorian, there is no need to engage them at Edgefield. If they want to declare war with us, they will fight on our soil, and perhaps we will be able to use Kane as a means to flank them."

"Will that small a force be enough?" Marquis Sollen asked.

"Our ships far outrank those of Cresica, and the Triangle Islands are full of fruit vendors. Taking them should be easy. The other half, Christopher, will tainlwait for Corke in the forest before Briarwood."

"Not at Seawood?"

"No, if we leave the city abandoned, they will think we sent all of our troops to the west. They will approach with less caution than they should, thinking it an easy prize, and we will ambush them in the forest. By taking the Islands and positioning our men on the border of Kane, near Lorian, we can attack the Cresican army as it advances on our front. Surely they will expect our main force to gather at Ambit." His father looked up, satisfied. "Are there any questions?" He looked around the room, his gaze falling on his son last.

Cain knew that look. He had seen it many times over a chess board, or whenever his father solved a puzzle. And it was a look that Cain could never quite imitate, especially since returning from the Core.

When no one said anything, Cain's father continued. "Good. Christopher, spread the word to your men. Castor, make sure the troops are ready. Finnian, stay here and send word to Vale and Ambit." Cain's father strolled over next to Cain and put a hand on his back. "Nathan, join my son and me in the stables as we prepare our things. I need to discuss with you a few things before we leave." Cain's father patted Cain's chest with his gloved hand, then steered him toward the exit. As they walked,

his father spoke to Cain of war, of tactics and decision-making, but Cain hardly heard, though normally such conversation was of interest. Even his praise for Cain's participation during the meeting barely registered. Cain walked without seeing, feeling lost, hardly mustering more than two-word responses. His mind was elsewhere and intent on dragging him along—back to the holographic map and back to the land of Kane.

Outside, Cain scratched the fine blonde mane of the white horse spotted with silver and looked into its large black pupil. It stared back at Cain, never blinking. Cain put his forehead against its own. Closing his eyes, he tuned out his father's final instructions to his advisor.

He shared Sharing one final, deep breath with the steed, he opened his eyes and stepped back to allow a stable hand to saddle his horse.

"A small fraction of my men will stay here to guard the castle should the defenses in the north not hold. The Owl Guard will be in charge of that. Understood, Nathan?" His father glanced at Cain and then back at his advisor.

"Of course, my lord."

His father patted Nathan's shoulder. "Good. You will report to me weekly and stay in touch with the treasurer regarding international trade. Although we are at war, we do not want our people to suffer. Increase trade with Ka'Che or Chaon; they are the next largest food provider. I am certain Lady Clayse will be syphoning our supply here."

"Aye, my lord. My duty." Nathan bowed his head. When he looked back up, his beady grey eyes squinted, leaving all but the flakes of amber in them to disappear. "Anything else?"

"Look after my wife. She has not been herself since this declaration of war."

"My duty and pleasure, my lord." Nathan bobbed his head and turned to leave. But he came to a halt as two lowships approached the stable. "It's Finnian and another gentleman, my lord."

Cain emerged from the shade of the stable and put an arm to his brow to block the glare from his glasses. *What is Senator Numos doing here?* Cain waited alongside his father and Nathan for the two lowships to halt.

The receiver, Finnian Lugas, stopped ten paces from their location. After he exited, he said, "Lord Evber, I am sorry to bother you while you finish preparing, but this man, Sena—"

"Yes, I know who he is, Finnian." Cain's father nodded towards his receiver. "What brings you here, senator?"

"You are preparing for war with Cresica?"

Cain's father crossed his arms over his chest. "What is it to you? They called their banners on us."

"It means nothing to me, I assure you." Senator Numos leaned forward on his cane. "Lady Clayse is doing the same in Cresica right now. I talked with her a few days ago."

Cain's father raised his eyebrow. "What is this about?"

"Part of it concerns your son." Senator Numos looked over at Cain. "Prince Evber, I am glad we could meet again after the Trials, though I could wish for different circumstances."

"What circumstances?" Cain asked.

"In a little under three weeks, nineteen days to be exact, there will be a hearing on Mistral to discuss the ethics and conduct of Guardian Edwyrd Eska."

"Guardian Eska? What has he done?"

"A consolidation of Power. There is a violations of vows. A recent ineptness in his position and his decisions have been…" Senator Numos paused and rolled his eyes upwards as if searching for the right word. Finally, he decided upon,

"Unwise. After all, you should know that he sealed the Twelve. But come to this meeting at find out more."

"How does this concern my son?"

"Well, the meeting will also detail some issues concerning his handling of the Trials."

"Guardian Eska did nothing I consider extreme, Senator. I do not see the legality in this type of meeting. In fact, he has been nothing but supportive since the Trials."

"What do you mean?" Numos eyed him with great curiosity.

"A week ago, his apprentice and Conseleigh Iycel came here to check on me."

"That is right," echoed Cain's father. "Does Guardian Eska, the apprentice, or his conseleigh know of this hearing?"

"No. They do not."

"Then—"

Senator Numos raised his cane. "There are many, though, who have grown too close to the Guardian of the Core. Their role as conseleigh is to advise and serve Guardian Eska, yes. But they must also keep distance from him and be vigilant for any abuse of power." With his cane still raised, Senator Numos pointed it towards Nathan and Finnian. "However, new evidence has come to me recently that draws into question one conseleigh's ability to see that abuse of power for what it clearly is."

"Guardian Eska will not be there to defend his actions?" Cain's father asked.

"No. The families in power must decide if an ethical and moral breach has occurred. Only then would Guardian Eska be informed of the charges against him. Do you not agree?"

"Point taken. It seems bold of you to take actions by yourself, Senator. Especially against the Guardian. I am not sure how much your limited exposure to the Core has allowed you to witness."

"Aye, this I understand. Conseleigh Katore will be speaking on Guardian Eska's abuse of power. I will present on his handling of the contestants at the Trials. *That* I did observe, and I observed quite closely." He played with his eyepiece.

"You mean Mr. Katore. He is no longer conseleigh."

Senator Numos's lips opened a little, then closed. Despite his attempt to hide his surprise, Cain had seen it. Regaining composure, he said, "I assume Conseleigh Iycel told you that, Lord Evber." He smirked. "Yes, Luvan Katore is no longer a conseleigh, but that does not change the fact that he knows a great deal about Guardian Eska's actions. He will be at the meeting."

"Well, although this meeting sounds interesting, my son and I cannot attend. We are going to war, as you noticed earlier."

"Lady Clayse had the same response the day before yesterday. Regardless of what you do, though, the hearing will happen as long as a quorum is present." He pointed to Nathan. "I suggest you send your advisor if you cannot come to the meeting yourself. Have a good day." Senator Numos bowed and left with Finnian.

Nathan turned to both of them. "My lord, I... if you need me to go, I can, but surely you should be there." He fidgeted with the hem of his uniform.

Arms still crossed, Cain's father tapped his fingers on his biceps. He moved his tongue around his cheeks. "No. Leading my men into this folly of a war is more important than some senator's quibble with the Guardian of the Core. You will attend, Nathan, and find out what this evidence truly is so you can report back to me."

"Are you certain? What... what if there is a vote?"

"Then cast one. Try to consult me or my son first, if possible. Senator Numos says Lady Clayse intends to lead her forces personally, so we must do the same and show our valor." His father spared a brief glance for Cain before returning his attention to Nathan. "Is that understood?"

"Yes. Of course." Nathan bowed.

"You will be able to confer with the politicians and senators we have stationed on Mistral. If it comes down to a vote, Nathan, and we are not available, do what is right."

"It will be my greatest pleasure to represent this nation." He bowed again.

Cain's father shook Nathan's hand and then they went their separate ways, Nathan to the castle's living quarters and Cain's father back to the stable. During the meeting, the flux of lowships had dwindled. Now, only a few remained, carrying soldiers past the southern gate of the moat that led to the capital, Thoth, and from there to Redding through the Sage's Valley. Now that the castle grounds were less chaotic, the horses could be mounted without being startled.

Cain's horse's face was now covered with plates of golden steel, matching the mane. The same golden-colored armor covered his horse to just below the ribcage. Underneath the saddle lay a periwinkle blanket, displaying on either side of it the sigil of House Evber: an owl on a branch.

He grabbed the reins, put his foot in the stirrup, and hoisted himself onto his steed's back and then guided it outside, coming alongside his father's mount. "Father, do you really think it wise for Nathan to act as your voice?"

"Do you not trust him, Son?" His father turned around and shouted to the stable boy to inform those still in the barracks that the other horses were ready. The stable boy ran off. His father turned to look at him again. "Well?"

"We have only known him for a few years. And his lack of punctuality could affect others' opinion of you."

"True, but he does give good advice, and that is his role. With nearly three weeks' notice, he should not turn up late to this meeting." His father chuckled.

Cain allowed himself a smile.

"If I could be there, I would," his father went on, growing serious. "My nation needs me in Lorian, though. If they see me gathering around my men, their vigor will increase. That I am sure of. That's setting an example on the battlefield. That is showing courage. It is about finding yourself. All enmity aside, I respect Lady Clayse for doing the same for her people. It will be a shame to have to kill her. But perhaps it won't come to that." Cain's father patted Cain on the back and smiled. "Now, we ride, Son. We ride." He kicked the sides of his horse, urging it forward.

Cain didn't immediately follow. He took one last look at the castle first. *Finding myself. I need to do that now more than ever. Perhaps Father is right.* Cain gripped the reins and squeezed his legs. The horse, eager to stretch its legs, trotted forward at a brisk pace, swiftly leaving the castle and all Cain knew behind.

CHAPTER TWENTY-SIX

BROTHERS

A iton closed his eyes. *It can't be.* He opened his eyes. *Hydro?*
Who is this man? Zarya neighed.

"It's my brother," Aiton said. "Let me down." He patted her neck.

Zarya kneeled, and Aiton pushed himself off her back. Cautiously, he walked towards Hydro. Zarya stayed by his side the whole time, as attentive as an acqua guard.

Hydro kept still. Occasionally, he glanced down to his left, as if something on the sand continually caught his attention.

Silent and unsure, Aiton walked. A million different things vied for attention in his mind. There were so many things to say, to ask, but what were the right first words?

At a loss, Aiton said the only thing he could think of. "Brother? Hydro, is that you?"

Hydro didn't respond, looking again to his left. Only then did he move forward. Even though it was only a few paces, Aiton could tell he looked different, ravaged from his travels. Wet clothes clung to his brother's body. A torn collar exposed the necklace Aiton had espied on his brother after the Trials. It was the necklace that had caused his family so much pain. What Guardian Eska and Cronos had warned Aiton about. *What does it do to you, Brother? Are you still the same?*

Hydro opened his mouth and then closed it. This time, he looked to his right, inland. Aiton followed his gaze and noticed a large ship. He hadn't seen it from the other side of the island.

A tear came to Aiton's cheek as the silence became unbearable. Only twenty paces away from Hydro, Aiton stomped his foot on the sand. "Aren't you going to say anything?" He sniffled. He put his palm to his eyes in order to catch the tears. He sniffled again.

Hydro dashed forward.

Zarya shuffled forward, blocking him from Aiton. She neighed.

Hydro reeled backward. "Aiton. I..."

Aiton patted Zarya on her front left leg. "It's okay."

Are you certain, Little One? His eyes are black.

What does that—

Aiton stopped mid-thought as Hydro spoke again. "Aiton, I'm sorry. For... for everything."

Aiton stepped out from behind Zarya's guard, walking around his bonded animal. Now it was he who didn't know what to say. A simple *sorry* couldn't bring his mother or father back. A simple *sorry* wouldn't fix Acquava. A simple *sorry* wasn't good enough. But what more could Hydro say?

Not knowing what to say or what to do, Aiton looked at the sea. The rock caught his eye and brought a question to his mind. "Who was she?"

"Who?" Hydro's face tightened.

"The one you were talking to." Aiton noticed Hydro look down and to his left again. "Why do you keep doing that?"

Hydro stepped back a pace. A satchel on his belt shifted. "You can see her?"

"She's not here anymore. The mermaid on the rock, who was she?"

Hydro stopped. "Oh. It is one of Pearl's mermaids."

"That's a lie. Don't lie to me, Brother. Please?" Aiton stopped walking forward and looked down at Hydro's feet for a few seconds and then back up to his eyes. They were black. *Why are you acting so strange?* He felt more tears forming.

"What do you mean, Aiton? I'm not lying."

"I know Pearl is dead. I know you killed her. Guardian Eska told me so. I saw it for myself. Her severed head on the floor! Everyone is looking for you. Everyone! Why is it me that has to find you!? Why me!" With each sentence more tears flowed down his face and soon they were heavy enough to bring Aiton to his knees. He put the crook of his elbow to his face and cried. And when he grew tired, he removed it and just cried, not caring any longer if tears hit the sand. *What good is being a Paen anyway when you don't have anything or anyone?*

Something brushed against the back of his head and pulled him closer. His face pressed against wet fabric. Arms wrapped around his neck. After another sniffle, Aiton pushed his head away from his brother's chest. Hydro still held him by the arms, but they looked at each other eye to eye now.

"Why did you do that?"

"I didn't want you to know."

"No." Aiton shook his head. "Why did you just hug me?"

"I... You cannot let your tears touch the ground. I... I was weak once, Aiton, and you were there for me..."

"Don't lie to me. Okay?"

Hydro nodded slowly. "Okay."

"You promise?"

"Yes, I promise." Hydro rubbed Aiton's arms.

Aiton fell back and sat on the beach. He let the sand fall through his fingers. "So, who was she?"

"She *was* one of Pearl's mermaids. She is not anymore, no."

"What did she talk to you about?"

Hydro opened his mouth and then closed it. He cocked his head upward and bit his lip. After a little while he said, "Nothing important."

"That is the truth?" Aiton folded his knees to his chest and clutched his legs. He rocked back and forth.

"The truth." Hydro sat alongside Aiton.

Aiton stopped rocking. "Okay," he sighed. "So, why are you here, then?" Aiton kept focus on Hydro for a moment, but the blackness in Hydro's eyes made him uneasy and soon he looked back at the blue of the sea. He bit his lower lip. *What is wrong with—*

"I needed to gather something from the island."

"Like what?" Cautiously, he turned his attention back to Hydro.

Hydro looked to his left, not saying or doing anything.

Aiton repeated his question.

Hydro shook his head. He reached inside a small sack at his hip and pulled out the blue sapphire. "Here, look."

"A jewel? You came to Acquava for a jewel?" Aiton held out his hand.

Hydro paused, eyeing the hand as if suspicious, then handed over the jewel.

Aiton rotated it in front of him. "What is so special about it?"

"It has a secret Power inside. When I gather enough of them, something magical will happen."

"Like what?" Aiton looked at Hydro.

"I will be able to protect you."

Aiton searched Hydro's eyes. He didn't want to see the black that used to be hazel, but he forced himself to look into them, anyway. "You can protect me already. Come back with me. You do not need this silly thing."

"Aiton, you know I cannot do that. If I go back, I will be killed, and then I will not be able to protect anyone." Hydro took the jewel back and put it in his satchel. "Everything I do, I do for you."

"Bullshit."

Hydro jerked back his head. "What did you say?"

Aiton bit his lip; he hadn't meant to swear. But he was sick of his brother's excuses. "Everything you do is because of that necklace!" Aiton pointed. Immediately, Hydro covered it with his hand. "Professor Haruko says it's a sycophant or something like that. That it's controlling you."

Hydro looked to his left and swung his arm. "Aiton, this necklace is..."

"It's why you aren't you anymore!" Aiton stood up. "Professor Haruko says he can remove it from you. We can go back together. Everything will be okay." Aiton offered his hand. "Do you trust me, Brother?"

Hydro remained sitting, arms draped over his knees. His head was tilted down, shoulders heaving up and down. He sniffled. Then scoffed. "Trust." He looked up. "Of course I trust you, Brother. But I don't trust what would happen if I do not succeed."

Aiton shook his head. "I... I don't understand. What are you talking about?"

"Aiton, my task, collecting these jewels, is for your protection. If I don't do this, if I don't do what is required of me, you will be hurt. This necklace is my burden to bear. I will deal with it. Right now, it gives me the Power to complete my task and keep you alive. If I went back with you, I would still be held accountable for what I've done. I would die. What then?"

"And why shouldn't you be killed?" Aiton inhaled sharply. The question had come out of him on instinct. He hadn't actually meant to ask it. His lips quivered. His fingers trembled, and he tried to remove the sweat from them by wiping them on the sand. He waited for Hydro's response.

Hydro looked at him, unblinking, unwavering. He sighed. "I..."

Silence.

When that silence became too much, something bold seemed to take hold of Aiton. "You killed Pearl. You killed Mother and Father and who knows how many others. Why shouldn't you be punished? Why shouldn't you die?!"

"Aiton..." Hydro stood up and tried to hug Aiton, but Aiton pulled away.

"No. You should be punished for what you did. You left me with a mess. You left me without a home. You left me..." Aiton breathed deeply, trying to hold back the tears. "Alone," he whispered. "Hydro, you left me alone." Tears broke through Aiton's dam. They poured out over his face. Aiton sniffled and dried them with his shoulder and forearm. He waved his arms frantically. "And you didn't even come back to see me, you came back to collect some silly jewels that you think will protect me."

"They will protect you, Aiton. You have to trust me." Hydro took Aiton's hands into his own and squeezed them.

Aiton pried away from Hydro's grip and scoffed. "Trust? You don't even trust me. How can I trust someone who has taken everything from me? All I have is Zarya now." Aiton pointed to the horse behind him.

"Zarya is her name? How is she—"

"We bonded."

"Bonded?" Hydro muttered. His face blanched and Aiton saw the muscles in his neck tighten.

"She came to me when I was at my lowest. She saved me, Hydro, when you couldn't. I cannot cast Power, I am not as strong as you. I am weak, and everyone knows it. I was going to throw myself in the water and see how much of a Paen I really am, and then she came to me." Aiton caught a lone tear on his thumb. Hydro turned away. "Where are you going?"

Hydro never answered. He continued walking inland until he was underneath the belly of the ship. Aiton followed him and paused where the grass and sand met. Zarya stood alongside him. He watched his brother go up into the belly of the ship.

Minutes passed, but eventually Hydro returned, a long object in his hand. Aiton's eyes squinted, trying to see what it was. His pulse quickened. *Father's sword.* Zarya stood in front of Aiton. She neighed and kicked the air, rearing up on her back legs as Hydro unsheathed the sword.

Thump.

The sword landed at Aiton's feet.

"What are you doing?"

"It is only right that you..." Hydro shook his left arm as if he was trying to tear away from something. "I ruined your life, Aiton. You are right. I do not deserve to live. But I would rather have you kill me than anyone else, and with Father's blade. It is only justice."

Aiton walked forward. His brother stood before the sword, motionless. He bent down and picked it up. *Purge.* That is what his father had called it, and his father's father, and who knows how many fathers before him. For such a long sword, almost near Aiton's height, he expected it to be heavy, but it wasn't. It was surprisingly light, but heavy enough that he would have to use both hands to wield it.

"Why did you kill them? Mother? Father? Pearl? Why did you kill them?" Aiton's hands shook and his body quivered, but he made sure to keep hold of the sword. This time, he didn't look away. He forced himself with all the will he had left to look into Hydro's black eyes.

"Aiton..."

"Answer me. Please. I... I need to know... .No matter how painful it will be."

"You want the whole story?"

"I need to hear it. Please?"

"Sit down. This will take a while."

CHAPTER TWENTY-SEVEN

THE LORD OF CHAON

L uvan hadn't stepped foot in the nation of Chaon for almost thirty-two years. Ever since the three-eyed prophetess had read his fortune. He didn't feel right here, not even now, not when that day had so changed his life. He had thought he spoke to Saeluste herself and had even told his wife upon his return about his fortune, but the more he contemplated that day, the more he realized she had never been Saeluste. To this day, Luvan didn't know who she was. And while words were merely water, as the saying went, as the years of his life carried on and on, he found those words of water had started to become ice.

And that ice chilled him.

So, no, Luvan didn't like it here, but business drew him to Kuyan, the capital of Chaon. It sat at the border between life and death, between the greens of the Slaver's Forest to the east and the endless sand to the west. Devil's-sand. Luvan wouldn't need to go there. His business was with Lord Kapache.

Either the city was truly massive or the taxicraft driver had taken the scenic route because it took an hour to get from the port to the gates of Lord Kapache's estate. During that time Luvan had seen a few interesting city views, including one building that boasted on its front lawn a large golden lamp, the one bards said was prison to genies. He had tried to ask his driver about it, but the driver had only replied in broken Common Tongue.

"Power." He motioned with his hands. "Voima."

Luvan sat back, amused at the man's attempt to cast Power, for he kept repeating the spell a few minutes after the sight had disappeared. Another interesting building had been a square temple with pagodas built on top of it. Luvan wanted to ask about this as well, but considering the failure of the first attempt, he just remained silent and admired the building for its unique design. Most likely it was a temple that gave testimony to the Twelve, something no longer possible since Guardian Eska consolidated his power on Mount Volan.

Luvan was dropped off at a cluster of temples on the shore of a lake. Amber-colored roofs and vast grounds of open space made this place more expansive than necessary. The ostentatiously large complex made the men who came out to greet Luvan seem even smaller than they actually were. They yelled to Luvan in a foreign language. He stared at them blankly, hoping someone more versed in Common Tongue would come out to greet him. If he had his golden C, a meeting would not have been an issue. But he didn't; Eska had demanded his pin after the Meeting of the Twelve. All he could do was hope that one of Lord Kapache's higher-ups would come outside and recognize him.

To his fortune, Lord Kapache's receiver, Xin Xián, strolled outside within a few minutes of the yelling. He said something to the guards, who bowed and backed away from their superior. *That is how authority should work,* Luvan mused.

The metal gates to the complex retracted open, and Xin placed his hands together and bowed. "Conseleigh Katore, forgive our guards. They did not recognize you. Conseleigh Rorum usually treats with us. Where is he? Whatever happened to your badge?" He pointed to the clock on his lapel, positioned beside the stitched sigil of Lord Kapache's chameleon on a log.

Luvan offered a weak smile. "Conseleigh Rorum was injured during the Meeting of the Twelve, so I am filling in. The fighting there damaged my badge. Guardian Eska will make me a new one in time."

"Lord Kapache told me what occurred. Truly horrendous. Please, come in, come in." The receiver ushered Luvan forward. "*And* what Guardian Eska did."

Luvan stopped. "What did Guardian Eska do?"

"Seal them and scatter them."

"Who told you this?"

"Guardian Eska, of course. He notified all the lords and ladies about the aftermath."

"Ahh, of course." Luvan feigned a gap in memory. "How could I forget? Sometimes what he does is a mystery even to me."

"Chaon loves mysteries." Xin walked up the steps and through the pretentiously large open doorway, making sure to step over a short barrier at the threshold.

Luvan tried not to frown. *Chaon certainly revels in mystery.* He crossed the small barrier, finding it a nuisance to his continued stride. As they moved through the complex, he learned that every doorway was the same.

"Why are these here?" Luvan asked after a while.

"To deter and slow attackers. Do you not find yourself nearly tripping over them?"

"Yes, that's why I'm asking."

"And that is the reason why. Anyone who attacks us will have a hard time successfully storming the palace. Sometimes the smallest things are the ones that make the biggest difference." Xin crossed another threshold. "Here we are. Lord Kapache will meet you here."

Luvan entered the room. "A library?"

"Yes, he likes meeting everyone here. Just a feeling of his, I suppose. He says you can judge a lot about a person by the way they interact with books." Xin smiled and bowed. "I'll leave you with the literature then." He left.

A globe of Myoli sat on one of the many wooden tables in the library. Luvan strolled over to it, merely glancing at the shelves of literature that lined the perimeter of the room. Out of boredom, he spun the globe, dragging his finger across the uneven, topographical surface, always spying Mount Klaff as it protruded from the globe more than other mountains on the planet. Such a crude and mundane globe couldn't be found on Mistral, but if it had, Luvan wondered how the cartographer would showcase all three nations of Agrost.

The globe stopped spinning and his finger came to rest on a jungle outside of Qotia. A jungle he knew too well. He tsked at the luck.

"Keeping yourself occupied, I see."

Luvan spun around. Zalos Kapache stood in the doorway, two guards at his side. A chameleon sat on his shoulders, licking the air and staring blankly at Luvan.

"Yes, well, Myoli is an interesting planet."

"That it is." Zalos put up his left hand. The guards left. "Have you seen Mount Klaff yet, Conseleigh Katore?"

"It is hard to miss."

Zalos smiled and stepped forward. "Yes, it is. But I mean, have you ever been to Proschi and truly appreciated its size?"

"My travels have not taken me there. No." Luvan extended a hand.

Instead of accepting it, Zalos drew the fingers of his left hand into a fist and covered it with his right, then bowed. Luvan quickly did the same.

"A shame. It's a most beautiful sight."

"Yes. One of the wonders, I'm sure."

Zalos moved around Luvan to the other side of the table. He took the globe in both hands and placed it at the table's end. "Please, sit." He gestured.

Luvan claimed his seat and crossed his legs. Once the lord sat down, Luvan asked, "Why are we meeting here?"

"It's a library. What better place?"

"Typically, I treat with lords in their throne room."

"And *typically* I treat with Conseleigh Rorum, not you."

"I told your receiver that—"

"Yes, Xin told me Conseleigh Rorum suffered an injury during the Meeting of the Twelve."

"Then why are we here?"

"Because this is a room full of knowledge, and I'd like to gain some on what this meeting is about: why you didn't schedule in advance with me, why you came here by taxicraft, and why is it that you don't have that golden C of authority on your chest anymore?" He patted his chameleon's head while arching an eyebrow at Luvan.

Luvan didn't respond right away, drumming his fingers on the wooden table. He needed to choose his next words carefully. "The truth?"

Zalos smirked. "Is that not why we are in a library?"

"There is a lot of fiction in books, Lord Kapache."

"That there is. Sometimes it makes for an even better story than the truth. But what is yours?"

"Guardian Eska dismissed me from his service shortly after the Meeting of the Twelve for not following his commands."

"You disobeyed a superior?"

"He consolidated his Power by imprisoning the Twelve. Do you agree with that?"

The lord didn't respond. He stood up and strolled along the shelves, finger trailing across the spines. "Who's to say if it's right or wrong? We as leaders need to make difficult decisions sometimes for the betterment and continuation of our people."

Luvan remained seated. "And we, as conseleigh, are required to serve him, but we also keep him in check. Advise him. The imprisonment of the Twelve was an abuse of Power. You, as the lords and ladies of the nations, have the combined authority to make him an apprentice, so you also have the ability to strip him of his guardianship."

Zalos stopped, pulled out a book, looked at the cover, and returned it to its spot. "How else has he abused his power?" He gave Luvan a quizzical look.

"There will be a meeting in the Senate on Mistral in two weeks to discuss his breaches in ethics and vows. Come to that if you want to find out."

Zalos took another few paces and stopped in front of more books. He pulled another out, then smiled. "You interest me, Conseleigh Katore."

Luvan chuckled. "I've heard that once or twice."

"Do Eska and the other conseleigh know of this meeting?"

"I do not imagine so. They do not see Eska's faults as I do; they are too close to him."

The lord walked over and laid the book on the table. He tapped it with his fingers. "If you find the time, you should give this a read."

Luvan read the title: *The Arrogance of Authority.* Luvan flipped through the first few pages, then looked up. "Will I see you..." His voice dropped off. The room was empty. *Where did he...*

A moment later, Zalos appeared next to the bookshelf. Luvan blinked.

"It's the Power of my chameleon, Conseleigh Katore." He walked away, blending in with the bookshelves once again. "You may see me there, you may not. You will just have to look closely." The door opened and closed, a faint laughter drifting away behind it.

Luvan sat there, brooding. Bonding had always struck him as abnormal. Eska had bonded to the dragon that killed his sister. And this bond with the chameleon was stranger still. Nowhere near as powerful as the dragon, the chameleon's ability was useful all the same. Never in his life had he found his bond, besides Lucine, and she was already too much to lose.

A memory from the three-eyed prophetess came to mind.

"You have a name given for greatness, Luvan Katore. But every greatness comes at a price."

"What price will I have to pay?"

"You will lose those that are closest to you."

"Is there no other way?"

"Greatness is never given. It is only taken by those who are courageous enough."

Luvan snapped from his reverie. He took the book in his hand and stood up. As hard as he could, he spun the globe once more and left, not caring to see where he would end up.

CHAPTER TWENTY-EIGHT

SWORDPLAY

A s Guardian Eska had instructed, Eirek waited outside on the stone court in the crimson and gold that reflected Eska's sigil of a dragon breathing fire, wings outstretched. In solitude, he walked along the circumference of the stone court, kicking the ground with his feet, wondering if there was anything else he should be doing. *Is this a test?* He didn't know, but if it was, he didn't want to fail. While he had heard Guardian Eska's praise of him at the end of the crystal scry conversation, he hadn't been in any mood to react, and only hours after, before sleeping, had he felt a fire in his heart and swelling of his confidence. He had slept soundly that night.

Since then, though, there hadn't been much interaction with the Guardian of the Core. Seemingly preoccupied with other matters, he had assigned Eirek to the habitat arena to hone his combat skills with past conseleigh and to the library to sharpen his mind. Two days after the blood scry problem, Eirek noted Tundra's absence from the estate, as did Ethen, who was almost back to full strength, yet still hobbled here and there.

A shadow passed in front of the sun, bringing a moment of welcome shade. Eirek cocked his head to the sky. Vesel flew north, towards the mountains. Eirek stopped pacing and shielded his eyes with his forearm. The dragon flapped its wings across the expanse of silver sky. His new knowledge of the history between Eska and Vesel gave Eirek a newfound respect for his mentor. *To constantly have a connection with the animal that—*

"Eirek."

Startled, Eirek jumped around to see Eska strolling toward him. Behind him were two of his staff, Colin and Dimitry, cradling various weapons. What interested Eirek more, though, was the farrago of items that Eska carried through levitation: a few large stones, a wooden shield and a steel one, an assortment of dinner plates, and, above him, a large marble pillar.

The servants laid the assortment of weapons on a bench at the edge of the court and left. Eska moved his arms and pushed the other objects floating around him to various parts of the stone court, keeping the plates by his side at his feet.

"You train with me today."

Eirek felt a prickle of anticipation. "You?"

Eska nodded. "Yes. Ethen is still recovering, and now that I have squared away the assignment with Tundra, I am ready to focus my attention on picking up where Ethen left off. Do you remember his last lesson?"

"Be proactive."

Eska smiled. "Good. Yes, but what was the mantra he told you. Do you remember that?"

"Warriors still..." Eirek thought for a moment. "Warriors still standing, don't stand still?"

"You have a good memory. Today's lesson is a continuation of that. While it's true that footwork and constant cognizance of our surroundings are pivotal to our survival, it is also important to understand the difference between weapons, for not all weapons are created equally. There are advantages and disadvantages to all weapons, from the grip, the mobility, and even the quality of steel. Take a look at these." Eska walked over to the bench of weapons and waved for Eirek to join him. "Take each one and swing it in front of me."

Eirek bent down and grabbed an axe first. Taking it by the wooden throat, he swung it in front of Eska like he would a sword. Instantly, he realized it swung slower than a blade, that it was top heavy, and that the weight wasn't evenly distributed. All three things together threw Eirek off-balance immediately.

"You feel the axe pulling you, don't you?"

Eirek nodded.

"Good. It is one of the axe's drawbacks. You can circumvent this by holding it higher on the shaft, Eirek."

Eirek moved his hands up the wooden handle. Upon Eska's instruction, he repeated the swing.

"Now, what do you notice?"

"I was faster and maintained my balance. And the movement was easier on my shoulder, which means it will take more to fatigue it."

"What does this do to the overall capability of an axe?"

Before answering, he took some time to swing the axe using both methods. "The axe is quicker when I adjust my grip, but it doesn't have as much power."

"Good. Although you may lack finesse with the weapon, that is something we can fix. I am happy to see you are observant, at least."

"I have a sword, though. I won't use an axe."

"That isn't necessarily true. A good fighter, like Zain, knows how to use all weapons. Even Hydro, I imagine, has had some rudimentary training in all weapons. In fact, I would say it's safe to bet that all the Trials participants could use any weapon to some degree of skill even if it isn't the weapon they specialize in. That is what—"

"Except me." Eirek sighed.

Guardian Eska let out a slight chuckle. "And yet, here you are as my apprentice. For that is another lesson that you will learn some day. Not all battles are fought by steel. Some battles require intellect to win, and I think you already know that deep down inside of you.

"But, anyway, my purpose in our next weeks of training is to get you to a rudimentary understanding of how these weapons function, so that should you come across it in battle, you are that much more prepared. Here."

Eska moved. A flash of white lanced toward Eirek, striking him. Eirek stumbled back, grabbing his stomach. A plate shattered on the ground. An instant later, Eirek brought up his axe in time to block another incoming plate.

Eska readied another plate. "Swing this time. Don't just block. Focus on your timing."

Eirek adjusted his grip lower on the handle, where it felt more natural. For the next hour, he batted plates out of the air with his axe while he maneuvered around the stone court. Eska varied the pace of each projectile, causing Eirek problems. As he began to adjust, Eska sent plates two at a time, sometimes from different angles so Eirek was forced to rotate and combat multiple threats at once. On these throws, more often than not the top-heavy head of the axe would slow Eirek, exposing his side for the second plate to hit him after he successfully swiped down the first.

Eska did not let Eirek rest. After brief instructions on movement to avoid the second plate, training resumed, this time with volleys of three plates even though Eirek hadn't mastered two. Despite his mythril armor, his ribs began to hurt from the steady stream of impacts. *How can I—*

Two plates slammed into his stomach, bending him over and making him drop the axe.

Then another plate came to his side.

And another.

"Hey!" Eirek covered his head and picked up his axe with one hand to swipe away the relentless barrage. In his haste, he gripped it higher on the handle.

Focusing again, he batted the plates out of the air with much greater ease. By holding it higher up, he experienced less drag, allowing him to pivot as necessary.

The plates stopped.

"I was waiting for you to learn to switch your grip. Good. Do you see why you must learn the intricacies of different weapons?"

Eirek nodded.

Eska extended his arms outward. He moved his lips, causing his eyes to glow. *He's using Power.* The shields on the ground levitated to Eska, the wooden shield on the right and the steel shield on the left.

Eska held out his left hand. "Attack the shield using the axe."

Eirek swung. The shield pushed the axe away, a reverberating clang the only aftermath.

"Now, the other arm." Eska held up his right.

Thump. Eirek pulled back the axe.

"Again."

Eirek swung. Eska raised his shield. The combined force resulted in the axe sticking in the shield. Eska pulled away, dragging Eirek a little off balance before he let go.

"You would be powerless if this were to happen. Axes can easily damage wood and other materials." Eska raised his right arm. "But they can also cost a soldier his life."

"Is that only an issue with an axe?"

"No. Weapons get stuck in wood, or even in bodies, all the time, Eirek. That is what I want you to notice."

"But... but, well, mine didn't."

"What do you mean?"

"During the first trial, I... well, I killed a man in the labyrinth. It didn't get stuck at all. Sure, I had to pull it out of him, but when I did, it was easy."

Eska cleared his throat. "*That* trial was rather an unfortunate one. I am sorry you had to experience your first there."

Eirek nodded. He paused for a moment and then continued. "What was your first?"

Eska slumped his shoulders. The shields slid off his arms. "My first..." He tilted his head down, hiding his eyes. "That is a story for another day. We should continue practicing."

Eirek raised an eyebrow, intrigued by his mentor's unusual state. He had never seen Eska exhibit nostalgia or remorse before, at least not like this. Before he could ask any questions, Eska continued.

"To get back to our topic, your sword is special, and I will demonstrate that to you later." Eska picked up a sword and handed it to Eirek pommel first. "Here, take this weapon."

The first thing Eirek noticed was the handle of cold steel, except for a small part that was leather. He moved his hand to the leather section as best as he could.

"No. Grab it by the steel, Eirek. Do not let your skin touch the leather."

Eirek adjusted his grip. Although it wasn't uncomfortable or hard to hold on to, he could imagine it being difficult to maintain his grip during a prolonged battle when his hand would be sweatier. The second thing he noticed was the weight. Compared to his own blade, it was slightly lighter. That intrigued him quite a bit because he knew his blade was already fairly light. Finally, the last thing he noticed was the coloring; it was a lighter color of silver than the other weapons on the bench. The coloring reminded him of something, but he couldn't quite remember what.

"What you have their, Eirek, is a zircha blade. This one has been uploaded with every weapon possible."

Zircha. His eyes lit up. "I received one of these as a Coronation gift from Lady Scule."

"And I believe some zircha armor from Lord Requart, if I'm not mistaken?"

Eirek beamed and nodded. Then his shoulders slumped. "I've never used them."

"And that is because you've never really had a chance. Today is a new day, though."

With newfound interest, Eirek examined the weapon again. He put his fingers to the blade and traced them along the flat. Just like a regular sword, the thickness tapered off towards the top.

"By holding the sword with the grip that you have now, all you need to do is merely think of the weapon you want to hold, and it will change for you. Try it now."

"Aahh..." Eirek fumbled. "Axe." He chose the first thing that came to mind.

Almost instantaneously, the sword transformed into an axe. The part he held did not change, but the blade and the pommel disappeared completely, leaving Eirek holding an axe by its throat.

"What do you notice?"

"How... how..." Eirek stared.

"I will have you read on that later. What do you notice about the weapon now, though?"

"It feels the same."

"Good." Eska put his hands behind his back. "The weight of a zircha weapon will never change. You can purchase different weighted zircha weapons, of course, but once the initial weight has been calibrated, it will form into whatever you request, using the resources available." Eska removed the axe from the wooden shield and then held the shield in front of him, hands on its sides, in a rather unconventional method. "Now strike the shield using that axe."

Eirek did so. Just like the other axe, it got stuck in the wood.

"Now think about changing it to a short sword."

Short sword. The weapon grew in his hands, going through the shield, even managing to crack it slightly at the bottom. Eirek let go and stepped around the shield. The blade had stopped about a hand's length away from Eska's face.

Still holding the shield in front of him, Eska turned his head to Eirek. "Interesting weapon, is it not?" He lowered the shield. "Zircha steel has existed for less time than I have been Guardian. They are weapons but also status symbols for those with wealth or rank on the battlefield. That is how Hydro had one during the Trials."

"I saw Cadmar's weapon change as well, though."

"I assume the weapon may have been his father's. He is second in command to Lady Aprah. And, from what I hear, still in the throes of the Passage." Eska took the blade out of the shield.

"Cadmar told me about that during the Trials."

"Yes, it is quite difficult."

"You've done it?"

Eska shook his head. "No. When I was apprentice, the nation of Gar didn't exist yet. There was no such thing as the Passage. In my state now, I don't think it'd be as difficult, but from what I know of it, it is grueling. That is why it takes almost fourth months to complete in most cases."

Eirek's mind wandered a little, trying to determine where Cadmar might actually be. It hadn't been four months since the Trials finished. It had only been two and a half or so. He had lost count of the days, but somewhere in the frozen tundra of Sereya, Cadmar was traveling, doing another trial since failing at the Core. Eirek wondered if it would finally get him the respect he craved from his father.

Eska's voice brought him out of his thoughts.

"During your time living abroad and getting to know the other nations, I would encourage you to complete the Passage yourself and really understand what it is like to be an elite. Why Garian elites hold themselves so proudly." Eska walked to stand beside Eirek. "Do you see this slit here?" He pointed.

Eirek nodded.

"This is where you insert chips of data about a weapon you would want uploaded. A warrior who uses zircha steel protects this above all else because if that is damaged, then the weapon will not function. The more uploads, the deadlier the weapon—but also the more skilled a wielder has to be. To give you some sort of benchmark for what that is like, Eirek, consider the fact that each of the Hown can wield two zircha weapons at once."

Eirek's eyes widened. "Two?" His voice quivered.

"Yes. Two. To become a Hown, one first has to prove he or she is ambidextrous with their weapon of choice. They also have to know how to use a zircha weapon, which most weapons academies will teach. And then they learn to wield two while on Hown as part of their training." Eska smirked. "Now, change this one to whatever you want." Eska handed the weapon back to Eirek.

Eirek spent thirty minutes switching it to every weapon he could think of, from mace, to lance, to halberd. The sword could even change into a particularly heavy throwing knife. The weapon that surprised him the most, however, was the shield. He had never thought of a shield as a weapon.

"Is there any weapon it can't change into?"

"*That* is a good question, Eirek. And I was wondering if you would ask it. Good. Yes, there is. Only one. Can you figure out which weapon?"

Eirek thought back on all the weapons he had just transformed the zircha into, trying to recall what he might have missed. His brows arched. He held out his arm and triumphantly said, "Bow." The weapon didn't change.

"Very good, Eirek. Why do you think this weapon cannot change into a bow?"

"Bows require arrows."

Eska nodded but waited for his apprentice to continue.

"And arrows leave the bow. It would... It would alter the weight."

"That is correct. Because the arrows are designed to leave the bows, if the weapon were to be transformed into a bow, then the arrows would have to be separate. And while this could certainly happen, why may that not be a smart thing to do?"

"Extra weight on the back. Awkward movement."

Eska's eyes beamed. "You catch on quick. Exactly. I hear from Lady Scule that they are trying to overcome this predicament, but her family has been mentioning that to me for years now, so who knows if there will ever be a zircha bow, but that certainly would be something to see." Eska padded Eirek's shoulder.

Eirek looked up to Eska. "So, you want me to become skilled with this weapon?"

Eska shook his head. "No. I want you to be good at *recognizing* that type of weapon. And the easiest way to do that is by viewing the person's hand. If it's skin-to-steel contact, it most likely is a zircha weapon, as they need the touch in order to change the weapon."

"Is there another way?"

"You may or may not have noticed the weapon's lighter color. And most zircha steel carries a forging mark. Look at the fuller." Eska drew his finger across the middle part of the weapon where it was the thickest.

Eirek noticed a black streak that grew from the guard of the blade until the mid-point. "What is that?"

"It's called the sword's vertebrae. It is what holds the zircha steel in place, and what allows it to mold so quickly. Just like our vertebrae, it can bend and contort, and that is why it can take the shape of any weapon. It is an interesting piece of technology, I must admit."

"Who invented it?"

"The Scule family."

Eirek scanned the blade once more. "Why don't you want me to train with this one? Surely it is the best."

"The word *best* is subjective. Certainly it requires the most skill to use effectively, but it still does have its drawbacks."

"Like?"

"Go to the marble pillar that I placed over there in the stone court."

Eirek turned to look at it and then looked back at Eska. "The pillar, sir?"

"Yes. Come on." Eska pushed Eirek forward to the pillar. He stood alongside it and swung his arm towards it. "Now swing."

Eirek frowned. "What?"

"Swing."

Eirek looked at the pillar. And then to Eska. "Are you sure?"

"Swing, Eirek."

This is crazy. He took a step back to gain momentum and swung forward. The impact sent vibrations up Eirek's arm, almost causing him to release the weapon.

"Again."

"I already—"

"Again. With a different weapon this time."

Eirek obeyed, and again, the same result happened. Eska made him use every single weapon upon the marble pillar. The only result was an increased soreness in Eirek's shoulder and forearm. When he got tired of the games, Eirek asked, "Why are you making me do this?"

"Because I want to make sure you understand, Eirek, that even this sword, as wondrous as it is, is still just a blade. Just like any of these other weapons."

"But no weapon could swing through a pillar like this."

Eska laughed. "I will take that as a challenge." Eska reached around his back and drew his own weapon. "Please stand back."

Eirek stood a few paces behind Eska.

With a single, fluid motion, Eska swung across his body from high to low. If Eirek hadn't been standing there with Eska, he wouldn't have believed it, but the sword went straight through the marble, which didn't appear to impede Eska's follow through or stroke at all. The pillar crashed to the stone court, crumbling into more pieces upon contact.

"How—"

Before Eirek could finish his question, Eska finished it for him. "This, Eirek, is an Ether Weapon. One of only eleven. You have one on your person now. Draw it."

Eirek pulled out the blade at his hip. It was shorter than Eska's blade, and the pommel was a fancy display of the Core, seemingly attached by nothing but its own energy, whereas Eska's blade had a simple, round pommel. Unlike Eska's blade, his didn't have a leather handle, so Eirek maintained direct contact with the weapon at all times.

"I noticed this during the third trial. I was rather shocked to see another one. Now that I know that Galan gave you this weapon, I believe Ancient Lyoen may have handed it down herself." Eska put a gloved hand on Eirek's shoulder and turned him to one of the boulders of the stone court. "Go, use it on that rock. Thrust, do not swing."

A little wary, it wasn't until Eska encouraged Eirek again that he finally thrust forward. When he did, he found that the sword entered the boulder with only a slight amount of resistance. He pulled it back and swung again, and then a third time, plunging through the rock effortlessly. Before he managed to use it a fourth time, Eska halted his fun.

"That is enough, Eirek. This is the blade that you will be using."

"Can anything stop it?"

"Only another Ether Weapon. That is what makes it so dangerous. I assume you had little resistance with the stone?"

Eirek nodded.

"Imagine what it would do to an opponent." Eska walked to Eirek's side. "How does it feel in your hands?"

"It is heavier than the zircha steel."

"Good observation. What else?"

"I assume it can't transform."

"Assume?" Eska's brows arched.

"Well, the grip is steel-to-skin, like a zircha weapon. Yours is traditional."

Eska examined the two hilts. "Interesting," he muttered under his breath. He narrowed his focus on the slight deviation, then flicked his gaze to Eirek. "Try to change it."

"Mace," Eirek said.

Nothing.

"Lance," he tried.

Still nothing.

"Hmmm." Eska sighed. "Well, I suppose that answers your assumption. It can't switch, and that may be its only downfall when compared to the zircha weapon. Many times, though, people only excel in one weapon anyway, so needing more than one is not so paramount. The zircha steel, I find, appeals to fighters who want to appear flashy."

"Who else has one??"

"After Pirini Lilapa, we consolidated a bunch of the weapons that the Twelve were using here, but I gave one to Riagan before sending him away. Besides him, I know Cronos has an Ether Staff. Hydro has his father's Ether Blade, Purge. Four are still unaccounted for."

"Is there anything stronger than an Ether Weapon?"

"It depends on how you define strong. Each of the Ancients supposedly had a weapon of their own design and make, made from the materials that their pyramids were built around. The Smiths, when they created the Ether Weapons, copied those designs, surely, but the material unlikely. I have never seen such a weapon, and I most likely never will."

"Why is that? Have you not seen it through the reimaje?"

Eska shook his head. "The reimaje only grants me the previous Guardian's memories, and so I only know of those weapons through a conversation Guardian Raule had with the Twelve when they gave him Adonis and explained to him its strength." Eska raised his sword and then sheathed it. "To view an Ancient's weapon, Eirek, would mean that I have died."

"Why is that?"

"Because Gladima will have been reopened, and I would die before I allow that to happen."

"How can someone reopen Gladima?"

"Blood."

"Blood?"

"The *right* blood. Ancient blood. As it was the Ancients who sealed Gladima in the first place."

"My blood?" Eirek asked, his voice quiet.

Eska crossed one arm over his chest and put the other hand under his chin. "That I am unsure of. Although you are likely to have a trace of Ancient Blood, I do not know if you have the necessary amount in your veins."

Eirek followed Eska's lead and sheathed his own blade. "Who would?"

"Galan would have. Or Naydeia does, certainly."

Eirek traced the veins of his forearms. "Do you think Zigarda will reopen Gladima with my blood?"

"What makes you think he has your blood?"

Eirek swallowed. "Well, if he had Gabrielle's blood, maybe he has mine as well. Maybe he even has all of the Trials participants."

"I..." Hands clasped behind his back, Eska tore away from Eirek, pacing the stone court. He came to a halt in front of Eirek and leaned close, one hand coming to rest on Eirek's shoulder. "Was there ever a moment in the Trials where your blood was taken from you, Eirek? I need to know."

Eirek bit his lip and thought back. He blinked. "Yeah. Actually, there was."

Eska's eyebrows arched. "When?"

"After I won the second trial. I had an interview with Senator Numos. He needed my blood for identity verification."

"Numos." Eska breathed, straightening to his full height. "Numos. What would..." Eska's voice tapered off. He put a hand to his head and closed his eyes. It was only for a minute or two, but Eirek hadn't seen Eska so deep in thought for some time. "If Senator Numos has colluded with Victor Zigarda to steal blood and tamper with the Trials or its participants, both will be punished accordingly. But even if Zigarda has your blood, Eirek, I don't see him using it to reopen Gladima. There is no incentive for him to do so. I suspect Zigarda may just be a pawn to other forces in play."

"Like what?"

"The resurgence of the necklace is my greatest concern. Galan dying. It makes me feel the Third One is making his move and perhaps has sway over Zigarda in some fashion."

"You think Zigarda is working for the Third One?"

"It is speculation, but Zain has confirmed Zigarda has shapeshifters in his employ. Shapeshifters, Eirek, were the Third One's first attempt at creating life, like his brother and sister, but he failed. Or, at least, he didn't make them as beautiful as his siblings' creations, so he chose to create animals instead. And it started with Desmós. If the Third One is guiding Zigarda in some way, it makes him more lethal than he already is."

"But you are so strong. You have Adonis and Vesel, and you can levitate things... how can you levitate things?"

Eska chuckled. "Perhaps I will explain it to you someday." Eska bent low, coming to eye-level with his apprentice. "To be clear, Eirek, I am not afraid of a fight. I have the understanding and training to win, but what I am afraid of is what someone like Victor Zigarda represents."

Eirek looked into Eska's eyes. "And what is that?"

"Change, Eirek. Change moves people. And when people move, they can do many things."

CHAPTER TWENTY-NINE

ASSIGNMENT

Eska didn't think it possible to be elated, considering the position that he was in. Victor Zigarda, Senator Numos, and Dr. Cere were all suspects in tampering with the Trials, possibly even conspiring to overthrow him. There seems little doubt it would come to that sooner or later. He knew Victor Zigarda dreamed of usurping him, maybe even challenging him again after their encounter during the last Trials, but he couldn't charge anyone based upon grudges and suspicion. There had to be solid evidence that tampering had occurred, otherwise any judgment Eska cast would be seen as an abuse of his power, and he knew after the Meeting of the Twelve, he didn't want to step over that boundary more than others already presumed he had.

He had no idea if the three worked in tandem or if each had their own separate agendas, but he understood them. And understanding someone was pivotal thwarting them. Victor had a clear motive and was probably the most justified out of the three. Dr. Cere, Eska assumed, was working with Zigarda the same way Tundra worked with Eska. But how had Senator Numos become mixed up in it? What was his endgame?

Eska didn't need to understand Numos yet, but he did need to attempt to back him into a corner. After Eirek admitted that Numos took his blood, Eska knew he needed to act. Although he wasn't sure where Gabrielle had gone after the Trials, if Victor Zigarda had her blood, then either someone must have given it to him or she would have had contact with him. His discussion with Zain and Carla Sonetta made the former more plausible. Given how he had collected Eirek's, Numos likely also had vials of blood from Hydro Paen and Cadmar Briggs. Maybe even Prince Evber and Zain Berrese, but he wasn't sure if Numos had interviewed anyone who hadn't won an event.

From solving the crystal scry problem to being the impetus for Eska's recent epiphany about Senator Numos, Eirek was no longer a budding apprentice. To Eska's surprise, with each passing day, he grew more and more impressed with his young apprentice's mind, and his sword and Power skills were improving steadily as well. He would be able to handle situations by himself soon enough. But time was a factor now, and Eska knew he needed to expedite his apprentice's training personally. Ethen was a fine weapons instructor, talented in battle surely, but Eska needed him elsewhere, which was why Eska was headed to his apothecary.

"Guardian Eska, what a pleasant surprise. What may I do—"

"My guardian." Ethen's voice cut off the adored.

"Ethen, how do you fare?" Eska looked to Adored Amiti. "How does he fare?"

Amiti walked back to where Ethen lay on a bed with one leg suspended in mid-air with a cast on it. When Eska came closer, Ethen relaxed his shoulder blades, letting his head fall to the bed again. Amiti pushed some buttons on the monitor next to the vials of maro nectar that lay waiting for Ethen every four hours.

"Ninety-five percent. Three more doses of maro nectar and proper rest and he will be good to go. He should be ready to leave here by night tomorrow."

"This is good. Adored Amiti, you may leave us now."

"Of course, my guardian. Please let me know if you need anything."

Eska nodded and then switched his focus to Ethen. "I have an assignment for you."

"Eirek's training will be expedited. Trust me, my guardian. I will—"

"I will handle Eirek's training from here. I have a different task for you."

Ethen's head cocked to the side. "What is tat?"

"It's been brought to my attention that Senator Numos may have had some part in sabotaging the Trials. I need you to go to Mistral. You are to conduct a follow-up investigation with the senator. I want to know if he has had any dealings with Zigarda as of late, and I want to know his purpose for drawing contestant blood during the interviews."

"He drew blood?"

"That is what Eirek just brought to my attention not an hour ago. If this is true, those blood samples could be invaluable, especially if Zain Berrese is to be believed and Zigarda is employing shapeshifters."

"And do you believe 'im?"

Eska nodded. "I have no reason not to." Eska crossed his arms over his chest. "When you question Numos, be coy. Remember, the Mistralian people are silver tongues. They can talk their way in to, out of, and around just about anything, especially those groomed in the field of politics."

Ethen nodded but there was a twitch of nerves in his jaw. "Perhaps..." He sighed. "Perhaps I overstep my boundary 'ere, my guardian, but Luvan would be much better suited for tis task ten me."

"He is no longer a conseleigh."

"I know tis, but perhaps while in Mistral, I should implore 'is 'elp. 'e knows the nation better tan I do."

Eska mulled over his conseleigh's words. In truth, a part of him had wanted to extend an invitation for Luvan to return to the Core, now knowing what he knew. The other half, however, didn't want to be so forgiving. That half still couldn't come to grips that Luvan had disobeyed a direct order and was partially responsible for the current state of things.

"If it pleases you, you may send word to him, but only to reconnect briefly. I do not want him engaged in our activities."

"But—"

"But nothing. He disobeyed direct orders. You may reconnect with him for sentimental purposes, but I do not believe we need him reaffliated here." Eska sliced his hand through the air, ending the dispute.

"Aye, my guardian." Ethen's shoulders slumped.

"I apologize. I... I shouldn't have shouted like that. All of this puts me a little on edge. I do not know where I went wrong when it comes to Luvan, but somewhere along the line I did." He pillared his arms on the side of Ethen's bed and looked down. "And now I am losing all of you."

"You haven't lost us. We choose tese missions because we believe in you. Tat is why Riagan accepted his assignment. And tat is why Tundra will come back when she is finished in Onkh."

Eska closed his eyes and thought about her. He reached out and felt her pulse. He smiled, then opened his eyes and straightened his posture. Looking down to Ethen, he said, "I needed to hear that. Thank you."

"I may become a silver tongue yet."

Eska guffawed. "That you may. Spend enough time in Mistral and you will."

"How long should I spend seeking out Senator Numos?"

"I don't suspect it will require more than a few days. Take notes on who comes in and out of his home. We know where he lives. Luvan picked him up to bring him to the Core, so you can use that ship to easily retrace the route to his home."

Ethen nodded. "Will do, my guardian. Tell me, 'ow does Eirek fare?"

"Good. Today, we focused on understanding the advantages and disadvantages of weapons. He constantly surprises me."

"You mean regarding Senator Numos?"

"No. Nor the crystal scry." Eska shook his head. "He pointed out something today that I failed to realize." Eska pulled Adonis free and gingerly held the weapon out for Ethen. "What do you notice about that weapon?"

"It is an Eter Weapon, of course."

"Yes. But is there anything unusual about it?"

"Besides tat it can cut trough anything? I would say no."

Eska laughed again. "I believe you will do fine on Mistral." Eska took back the weapon. "No. He noticed that my weapon has a leather hilt."

"Well, as it should. Only zircha weapons 'ave steel—"

"His Ether Weapon doesn't have leather."

Ethen tried adjusting his posture, but with his leg in the swing, he wasn't successful. "Does tat mean someting? Maybe it is very worn? It is centuries old."

"I thought of that, too. He is, after all, a descendent of Galan, but Galan never fought in the Great War. He left before it started. At least, that is what legends say."

"What does tat matter?"

"It matters because I am unsure how worn that weapon could actually be, especially if he has spent most of his life hiding himself from the Third One."

"What are you suggesting? Tat 'is weapon could... could change?"

Eska laughed. "I have no idea what I am suggesting. I am still processing the information myself, but wouldn't it be something if these Ether Weapons could do even more?"

"Tey are already te strongest weapons. An extra function would make tem..." Ethen never finished his sentence. "I don't even know what tat would make tem."

"I am not sure either, but it is an amusing thought all the same. It gives me something to research now."

"I tought tat was to be your apprentice?"

"Yes. And I am going to use him to help me test some theories and conduct some research when he's not training. But when you return, I am giving him back to you."

"You are not continuing 'is training after I return?"

"You *are* his training after you return. I am arranging only sparring matches between you two. And once he is able to best you in battle, he will face me."

"Does 'e know tis?"

Eska shook his head. "He doesn't need to know. This will be a lesson in adaptability."

Ethen gave a subtle smirk and stroked his conical beard. "It would be my pleasure."

Eska swiped the bottle of maro nectar and tossed it to Ethen. He caught it in the air. "Then I suggest you drink up and recover faster."

Ethen popped the cap off the vial and took a swig.

CHAPTER THIRTY

ANYA PAEN

Hydro stalled, his heartbeat a dull thud in his stomach. He didn't want to talk, but he knew that Aiton deserved it. With everything Hydro had put him through, Aiton deserved the truth—no matter how painful that was for Hydro or his brother. He looked once to his left, expecting Anne, who had been nothing but a nuisance since he had met his brother, but she wasn't there. Hydro looked back to Aiton, who had put down the sword and taken a spot in front of him, the seahorse curled behind him so he could rest comfortably.

Aiton finding his bonded animal warmed Hydro in ways he didn't think imaginable. And it chilled him just as deeply. The feeling of warmth and cold at the same time placed Hydro's body in a state of confusion, prickling his skin in some moments and then relaxing only seconds later. An ebb of confusion and clarity, his mind inundated him with thoughts. *How did Aiton meet his bonded animal? What was the process like? Was Ritam my own? Did I...* Hydro couldn't stomach finishing that last thought. *Surely, it couldn't have been my bonded animal. Why would it have lived on a completely different planet?* Yet, in the aftermath of the encounter, a warmth had left him. And Anne had refused to speak further on the matter. Hydro flexed his fingers, examining them.

"What are you waiting for?"

Although he still looked at his hands, Aiton's voice brought him back to reality. Coldness overtook his fingers and spread throughout his body. Hydro straightened and turned to his brother.

"I think it is best, Aiton, if I tell you the reason Mother and I were so estranged. It all happened because of your sister."

"Anya?"

"Yes."

"Professor Haruko mentioned that she was one of the most talented spell casters he had ever seen."

"He talked about her?"

"Only briefly. I demanded it, but then quickly regretted it."

"Are you sure you want to hear?"

Aiton nodded his head.

Hydro took another deep breath. "What Professor Haruko told you was true. Anya could cast Power like no other. When she was your age..." Hydro shook his head. "No, even younger, she never saw nine. At thirteen, I still studied at the Finesse Academy in Symeria. Even though I was four years her elder, Anya surpassed me. Mother couldn't stop boasting about her whenever I returned home. And, Father, well, by her eighth year she was almost at Father's level. That's when he decided to employ Professor Haruko privately because no ordinary academy, no matter how prestigious, would be able to benefit her."

"What happened?" Aiton asked. "Where did things go wrong?"

"The year before you were born a winter came that had been unlike any other."

"What do you mean?"

"It had snow, Aiton."

"Our winters have snow. I've seen it before."

Hydro shook his head. "Not like this. It snowed here as much as if it were Katarh." Aiton's eyes lit up. "Yes. It snowed so much we called it a blizzard. Father said it only happened once every twenty years or so. Because of the rarity, Anya wanted to go outside. She wanted to walk upon the snow, and I did as well. As Father had business and meetings to attend to, Mother took us out with some of her servants and a few guards to play in the forest. Mother had missed the snow, so she wanted to see it and feel it again."

"Does it snow in Talyn?"

"No."

"Then how could she have missed it?"

Hydro's heart heaved. "Father never told you, did he?"

"Tell me what?" Aiton crossed his legs on the sand and leaned forward.

"Mother is not from Talyn. She is from Crake, a small town in the Roil province." Hydro expected more shock, but Aiton sat with a blank face. "I found out when Anya cast her first spell of Power at age five. Electricity."

Aiton nodded. "Professor Haruko told me that."

"In passing, Father said to me how shocked he was and how much of a miracle it had been to have such a Powerful family. I said to him, 'Why? Mother is from the Axyel line. Surely she can cast Power as well?' Then he told me that she wasn't, that in fact, she was nobody... a..." Hydro hesitated, "a commoner. Charismatic and intelligent enough to catch Father's eye, but it made me question everything about us and our family. It made me question myself. I remember not speaking to either of them for weeks, and since that day, I held a grudge against her."

"Why? Crake or Talyn, does it matter?"

Hydro sighed. "More than you know, Aiton. Discovery of her lie would bring weakness to our name. And it decreased the possibility that her children could cast, or certainly cast with any strength and skill. Maybe that is..." Hydro stopped speaking when Aiton examined his hands. "You still have not cast yet, have you?"

Aiton shook his head again. "No," he whimpered. "It is because of her?"

Hydro bit his lip. "Yes."

It is not his mother that makes him that way.

Hydro looked to his left. Anne stood next to him, peering down at his brother. "What are you doing here?" Hydro asked.

It was Ancient Lyoen who never wanted equality. And Ancient Bane did so in the wrong way. My master's voice was never heard.

"Who are you talking to?" Aiton interrupted.

Hydro took a breath and sought composure. "I... I only meant to say that if you have not cast yet, then what are you doing here? You should be with Professor Haruko."

"He cannot help me. No one can."

Hydro grabbed his brother's forearm. "I will."

Aiton glanced from Hydro's hand to his eyes. "Finish the story."

"So all of us went out to the lake in the forest. Mother told us how the people where she is from would skate on the water. That it was solid ice, and it was fantastic because you could feel so powerful on top of the ice, gliding effortlessly like birds in air. She had told us of this activity many times during the winter, and when we went out that day, she finally let us do it. She had even had the blacksmith fashion skates for Anya and me.

"We watched her first, gliding like a swan on the lake. She even managed to gracefully jump from one foot to the other. Next, Anya and I tried. Anya learned quickly. She learned many things quickly, to be honest, and Mother was pleased about that. I... well, I did not. Skating was not for me. In fighting, we move our feet and our body, but in skating, you simply glide. A half an hour later, an hour, I no longer remember by this point, I was more exhausted than I should have been because my technique was rigid. However, Anya kept on skating and even hoping like Mother had. And on one of the hops, the ice broke."

Aiton's jaw lowered, and his eyes widened.

"Cold water took her. Horribly cold water. I scrambled to reach her but fell a few times before I was able to skate to her. Mother was already there, screaming and crying, telling me to help. I pulled her out. It took me a while, but I did. I... I still remember how cold it was." Hydro flexed his hands. "I... I have never felt anything like it. My hands, my forearms, they were soaked in a sickening cold, the same cold that held Anya in a vice-like grip. The guards blundered their way onto the ice. Mother kept crying, 'Do something. Do something. Cast fire. Make her warm.' I tried. I did. I said *Palo.* I said it many times. Anya watched, teeth chattering, too cold to speak the word herself. The guards that had accompanied us did not know Power. Mother did not know. She just kept yelling at me. 'Are you Denied? Do something!' And I kept saying *Palo*, but the fire never came..." Hydro exhaled. "It never came."

"Why not?"

"I... I am not sure. If I had to guess, it was because my body was too cold to cast that sort of spell. My hands could not tap into my Power because they could not feel it. Mother made me remove my tunic and coat to try to keep Anya warm as they road back to the palace. She did not even allow me or the servants to ride in the hovercraft, insisting that they would get their faster without us. When I got back to the castle, Anya had passed and mother was a wreck. Len and Darien tried consoling Father, but he never spoke. Elias comforted Mother. And Korth, Korth searched for me and the two others with me. I would have frozen as well, I think, if the guards had not let me borrow some of their clothes. We swapped cloaks back and forth as we walked. And since that day, Mother never looked at me the same. A year after, she gave birth to you and gave you more attention than she had ever given me, hoping, I assume, that you would fill the greatness of Anya's shoes. Mother even told me one night, 'If my first child cannot even cast Power, and my second child was the greatest caster of them all, my third child is meant to do extraordinary things.' "

"Mother said that?"

Hydro nodded. "She put her faith in you. Everything, really, after Anya died."

"But why did you kill her?"

Hydro still didn't remember all of what he had done that night. His body had acted, yes, but it was as if he had watched from outside himself. It was as if some sort of higher transcendent Power had commandeered his body that night. How to explain that to Aiton? He couldn't. Instead, he said, "That night, Aiton, when you found me in Anya's room. Mother had found me first. She told me I should not have been in there, that I am the last person she would have ever wanted to see. And then..." Hydro sighed. His skin prickled as he wrestled with the memories of that night.

"What?" Aiton had completely rotated to keep his eyes locked on Hydro.

"She said she wished I was never born. And she kicked and hit me. And all of it was enough to cause a change in me. I... I am unsure of what it was... but I went to that room that night to kill her, to make her pay for all the things she had put me through." Fire burst from Hydro's hands. He hadn't even said *palo*, but it circulated his fingertips. He quickly snuffed it out by clenching his fist. "I... I never wanted to kill Father, but he wanted me to pay for what I did to Mother, so it became a matter of survival for me. And when I took Purge, it felt right to me. Like I had to take it. And then I went to Pearl and sliced off her head."

"But why Pearl?"

"Because she is the only thing that rules our family. The sharks that guard the Watery Path are the past lords of Acquava. They are always in service to her. I... I decided to save Father from that service so he could swim anywhere, not just among those islands. That is why I did it."

Aiton sat silently for a long time. Hydro expected as much after all that he divulged.

We need to go, Hydro Pean. Other jewels are waiting. Anne tugged on his shirt.

He felt the need to look at her, but he didn't. Instead, he continued watching Aiton. His brother was deep in contemplation. Once more, Hydro tried to put his hand on his brother's head. Aiton didn't brush him off. He rubbed it a little, and then he stood.

"I... I need to go, Aiton. I hope you can maybe one day forgive me for all I have done."

Aiton stood as well. He picked up Purge in his hand and pointed it at Hydro. "I cannot forgive you, Brother. Not yet. But I do understand, or at least, I think I do." Aiton looked down at the blade and then back at Hydro. "You are sure you cannot come back with me? I can tell everyone what you told me. It will make a difference, I know it will."

Hydro crouched on his feet. "I cannot. But I will tell you that when everything is over, I will come and find you. You will see me again, Aiton, but first I need to leave so that I can protect you." He stood up.

"Then... then you need this." Aiton handed Purge to Hydro. "Take it. It... it belongs to you. You will need it to protect yourself."

Hydro had forgotten he actually did need the blade to complete his task. Luckily, Aiton handed it over willingly, unaware or uncaring that rightfully it belonged to him. Hydro no longer deserved it, but nonetheless, he took the sword and sheathed it. He crouched down one last time, arms opening wide.

Aiton just stood there. "I... I cannot hug you. Not yet. Maybe not ever. But I will wish you a safe journey."

Hydro's smile dropped. He swallowed hard. His shoulders tensed, and he let his arms fall slack to his sides. His throat tightened. "Thank you," he choked out. Hydro stood up and began to walk away. "Aiton..."

"Yes, Brother?"

Hydro looked over his shoulder. "You *are* a Paen, remember that. Will you? For me?"

"Of course." Aiton nodded.

Hydro turned to face him completely. "Even if you have more of Mother's blood in you, you still have Father's, too. And he was a great man. I did not agree with Mother on many things, but I do think she was right when she said you will accomplish great things. It is in our name. We are all meant for great things; do not let anyone tell you otherwise." Hydro raised his arm and pointed towards the forest. "Farther inland there is a pool with a rocky bluff as its backdrop. It is perfect for climbing. Maybe it will be good practice for you, before you climb Mount Klaff."

Hydro let a smile come to his lips, but he turned around, ready to retreat. It pained him enough when Aiton didn't hug him; he didn't want to face the realization that his actions had ended any of Aiton's dreams.

CHAPTER THIRTY-ONE

SHOWING

Aiton grasped Zarya's seaweed mane as she trotted over the water. Even though it had been two days, Aiton could still feel the soreness and the calluses in his hands from climbing the bluff as Hydro had suggested. He had been right; the vines had made it easy, and there had been several jutting edges along the way large enough to rest on. At the very top Aiton had seen the whole ocean, blue over blue and the suns dipping below. As Aiton sat there, watching the red sun and the blue sun sink below, he watched the sky and wondered where his brother had gone. Would he see his brother again? When? Where? The uncertainty made him long for that answer in the sky. Even now atop Zarya's back, he looked to the horizon, wondering.

You have been thinking of your brother much, Little One.

"How did you—" Aiton shook his head and chuckled. "Of course. Yes, I was. I am unsure if I will get to see him again."

Zarya didn't respond for a little while. Then, she said, *Only time will tell.*

Aiton thought about that for a moment, then asked, "Why did my brother have black eyes?"

It means your brother is bonded.

"What do you mean? I saw no animal with him."

Because he has no animal. Not yet.

"Then what do you mean?"

Desmós calls to him and wants to be with his master again. Your brother could awaken him.

"Well, where is this Desmós? Who is Desmós?"

We call him the Great One. The First One. He was the first animal ever created. He was perfection.

"And now?"

Now he is dead. Or, at least, that is what I was told. But it seems as though he lives through your brother now. The black eyes gave it away. Only Desmós ever had black eyes.

"How do you know all of this?"

Do you not think we are spoken to by our mothers and fathers as well, Little One? Even animals have history. Some more than you care to know. Zarya neighed.

"What happens if Desmós awakens?"

Zarya shook her head. *Nobody knows. It has been such a long time without him and his master. It is uncertain what will happen if they are reunited.*

Aiton bit his lip. "Master?"

"Yes. His creator."

"Was it one of the Twelve?"

Zarya neighed. "One of the Ancients, Little One."

Aiton reserved himself to silence for a time, until asking the question that had been nagging him. "Will it be something bad? I mean, if they are reunited?"

Maybe not something bad. But surely something incredible. The Power that Desmós had with his master was one unrivaled.

"That's what Hydro meant when he said the necklace gave him the Power necessary to accomplish what he needed to do. Whatever that is."

Most likely, yes. It is clear that Hydro hasn't lost himself to Desmós yet.

"How can you tell?"

I don't believe we would be riding back to the castle right now if Hydro didn't have control of himself. And whatever would have happened, I would have lain down my life for you, Little One.

"And I for you, Zarya." A smile came to his lips and a rush of warmth filled his heart.

Fifty leagues away, the province of Acquis came into view. In a few hours, he would go back to his life as Lord of Acquava. But this time he wouldn't have to do it alone. That made the smile on Aiton's lips grow even wider. And he knew his brother was alive. Safe? Aiton still couldn't really say. But Hydro was alive, and that is what mattered.

"Can we go any faster?"

The horse slowed to a stop. *We must go underwater to do so.*

"Let's do it." Aiton raised a fist in the air.

Hold on tight, Little One.

Under the sea they went, Aiton closed his eyes. He hoped in his dreams to see his brother again, and this time give him the hug he had been reluctant to give.

When next Aiton woke, it was to the splashing of waves on rocky sea stacks. Zarya maneuvered in between these to the stony pier. She kneeled and let Aiton off her back. Balancing on the tips of his toes, he reached behind Zarya's ear and scratched it and put his nose against hers.

"When do I get to see you again?"

Whenever you want, Little One.

"How do I call you?"

Say my name, and I will be at your side as fast as possible.

Aiton patted her mane. "Then goodbye."

Goodbye, Little One. Zarya neighed and disappeared under the water.

Aiton climbed the steep steps, slick with slime from the early advances of winter. He gripped the limestone walls with his hands for balance. Without any incidents, he made it to the lowest part of the castle. He bypassed the basement and walked up to the first floor, greeted by nothing other than dead silence.

Where did everyone go? There were no servants in sight. No sounds of preparation drifted from the kitchen. No guards sparred in the courtyard. *That's strange.*

Aiton shrugged and went to the staircase that led to his room. When he reached the foot of the steps, however, a shriek came from on high. Aiton jumped back and noticed the red-haired maid, Salina. Without a second glance, she dashed up the stairs as fast as she could. Aiton followed her with his eyes as far as he could. *Where is she going?*

He climbed the stairs, keeping his eyes up ahead. Within moments, a hustle of footsteps and a chorus of shouts halted his advance on the second floor. Salina had returned with Darien and one of the other acqua guards, Holden. Elias hobbled on his cane down the steps after them.

"Aiton, you're here. You're alive." Darien rushed down the steps and hugged Aiton. "Holden, contact Korth and Professor Haruko to return to the estate. The search is over."

"Of course." Holden nodded and darted up the steps, taking them two at a time.

"Why wouldn't I be? Where is everyone?"

"You have been gone for five days. No one knew where you went. Korth and Professor Haruko led a search party for you. We... we thought you were taken... or worse."

Aiton's fingers tapped his legs. Unsure of what to say, he smiled weakly. "Well, I'm back now, and I'm fine."

Elias glanced from Darien to Aiton. "Where did you go?"

"Uhmm..." Hands behind his back, Aiton rocked back and forth from his toes to his heels. "I went to Talyn."

If Aiton could have captured a portrait of the bulging eyes on Elias and Darien at that exact moment, it may have given him happiness on end for a few months. In truth, he didn't know how their heads contained such exaggerated expressions. Aiton laughed at them all.

"This is no laughing matter!" Elias pounded his cane on the ground. "How in Abaddon did you get out to Talyn?"

"Uhmm..." Aiton bit his lip and titled his head upwards. "A seahorse?"

"A seahorse? A seahorse?" Darien muttered and massaged his temples. "The Prince has mindloss. I am sure of it. Salina, take him to the apothecary to have him treated."

Salina nodded and bowed. She went to take Aiton's arm, but he pulled away and stepped back. "I don't have mindloss. It's true. I met a seahorse, and she took me there." He looked at the three of them. A flurry of steps came from above.

Holden reappeared. "Korth will be here in a few minutes. As will the others."

Others?

"Good. Can you please take Aiton to the apothecary, he seems not to want to go with Salina."

"What is wrong with the little one?"

"I am here. You can ask me." Aiton said, having enough with being talked down to. "I am not sick. I am telling the truth. I went to Talyn."

Holden raised one of his non-existent eyebrows. "How did you get to Talyn?"

"A seahorse!"

"And how did you manage to ride a seahorse?"

Aiton shrugged. "She let me."

"She?"

"Her name is Zarya."

"Zarya, eh?" Holden looked back at the others. Then he switched his focus to Aiton again. "Where is this Zarya now?"

"In the sea, probably. She lives there."

Holden chuckled, and it became contagious to the other three. "Yes, I am sure she does. She is a seahorse after all."

"Take him." Darien waved his hand.

"I am not lying. I can show you her if you want." Aiton tensed. He wasn't exactly sure if he should show her off, or if she would prefer not to be seen, but he hoped it would be okay.

More commotion, this time from behind Aiton. Professor Haruko, Korth, and the rest of the acqua guards now blocked his escape to the first floor. Behind them strolled two men he didn't recognize at all, but who wore black suits with a golden H pinned to their chest. Conseleigh Iycel stood in between them, wristlace coiled around her forearm like usual, her blue eyes focused on Aiton, chilling him.

"Aiton!" Korth took the steps three at a time until he reached Aiton. He dropped to one knee and hugged him. "Where have you been?"

"I would like to know the same thing." Professor Haruko put one foot on the bottom step.

Holden answered for Aiton. "He claims to have gotten a ride to Talyn from a seahorse."

Korth grabbed Aiton's arms. "Aiton is this—"

"Why is she here? Who are the other two?" Aiton never looked away from the men in black and from Conseleigh Iycel.

Korth maneuvered his body in front of Aiton. "They don't matter now. What matters is that you're safe. Is what Holden said true?"

Gaze still fixed on the two men in black staring Aiton down, he remained silent. He didn't like them.

Korth shook Aiton a little bit. "Aiton, is this true?"

The two men in black turned to whisper something private to Conseleigh Iycel. Aiton turned to Korth. "Mmhmm. I can show you."

"I think we all want to see this seahorse," Darien scoffed.

"Agreed," echoed Professor Haruko.

"Follow me."

"Where is he going?" one of the men in black asked.

"To show us his seahorse."

"We have business," the other said.

Darien waved him off. "Let the little lord have his fun first. He wants to show us his *seahorse*." Darien pinched the air with two fingers on the last word.

Aiton gulped and hurried out of the room and down the steps. *Who are those men? What do they want?* He continued forward and walked down another set of steps, down to the corridor that held the private meeting rooms. The pitter-patter of the footsteps behind him didn't allow him to contemplate more. Cold, now more than ever, he called out to his horse. He needed her warmth. Her confidence. *Zarya, can you hear me?*

Silence.

Zar—

Yes, Little One?

Aiton's eyes widened. *I want you to meet some people who look after me. Are you near?*

I can be with you soon.

I'm sorry if I am not supposed to show you off. I never got your permission.

Don't you worry, Little One. I will see you soon.

A warmth stuck with him as he walked. Every time Zarya and he communicated, he felt more alive. He felt whole. She invigorated him, while the others behind him simply motivated him. He opened the door to the last set of steps that were carved out of the face of the cliff. The realization gave Aiton pause at the threshold. *Should I show her? Will they like her? What if they don't? What will they say?*

"Is something wrong, Aiton?" Korth asked.

Aiton turned around. "Who are those men? Will they hurt her?"

Korth ignored his first question. "They aren't here for her, Aiton. They are here for you."

"Me?" Aiton's lips trembled. He looked down to the stony steps, now looking more like a plank that led to the Locker. *Me?* "What do they want with me?"

Korth pushed Aiton a little to make him continue down the steps. Using the limestone wall as his guide, he descended. One step. Two steps. Three. His heart beat. He paused again. *By showing her, will I open up myself to questions about my brother?* He thought. *Well, I don't have to tell them I met him. But maybe I should? Would it truly help him? Or hurt him? What can I do?*

"Aiton?"

"Uhhh, I'm fine. Follow me. Sorry."

Aiton descended the steps to the stony pier. The ships swayed with the slight sea breeze that filtered in from the mouth of the cave. Zarya wasn't here yet. He walked to where he first met her and waited. The others waited behind him.

After a few minutes, Darien spoke. "Well?"

"She is coming."

"What were you doing down here anyway, Aiton?" Professor Haruko asked.

"I..." He didn't want to admit the truth. "I..."

I'm here, Little One.

Thank you. We are on the pier. He spun back around on his toes. "She's here!"

Just like before, a slight ripple spread out across the blue. With the appearance of her face, murmurs came from behind him. Whispers became chatter as her body came up out of the water and she walked across the sea to stand beside Aiton. She neighed and shook her white mane, bowing afterwards as if she was truly a palace-bred horse.

Aiton turned around. He plopped his arms at his side and exhaled. "Everyone, this is Zarya."

Professor Haruko's jaw dropped, like all the others. He stumbled for words. "Ai... Ai... Aiton, is this, is this?"

"She's mine. We bonded."

"Bonded?" Haruko coughed.

Darien echoed the sentiment as well.

"Mmhmm," Aiton hummed.

"Aiton, this is beautiful. Simply beautiful." Darien's eyes lit up as if he had just found a treasure chest from a sunken ship. "Holden, Haruko, Korth, Elias, a word if I may." He pulled the others aside and walked back. They formed a circle, excluding him.

Salina put herself in front of Aiton, prying away his attention. "Can I pet her, my lord?"

Aiton smiled. *Zarya, she wants to pet you, is that okay?*

Of course, Little One.

"She said yes."

Salina stepped forward and put her hand to Zarya's nose. "She is beautiful."

"I think so, too."

"May I as well, mi lord?" another servant asked.

"Mmhmm."

Aiton lost interest in the group conversation about Zarya and delighted in seeing others admiring his horse.

Zarya neighed and shuffled back and forth, keeping her position on top of the water. *Do the others like me?* She tilted her head at the group.

Aiton glanced back at the group. They had stopped now, and all collectively looked at Zarya. *Could you not hear them? They love you.*

I only recognize your voice, Aiton Paen.

Yes, they love you, Zarya. Everyone does.

She neighed and the servants who had been touching her retreated a few steps. Zarya rose on her hind legs and kicked the air. Afterwards, she ran around the pier, trampling over the waves as if they were grass. Enthralled, Aiton watched her.

A tap to his shoulder blade pulled Aiton away from the majesty of the moment. Behind him were the two men in black and Conseleigh Iycel.

"Lord Paen." Conseleigh Iycel bobbed her head. "Truly a wonderful day for you. Congratulations on your bonding with Zarya. Guardian Eska would be pleased to know that you've undergone an experience like he did." She tried smiling, but the scar on her face made it crooked. "With me are General Satorus and Captain Chase Arwayn—"

"Aiton!"

Aiton looked behind the two figures to see Korth calling for him.

The older man, the general, coughed into his hand and turned to face Korth. Korth and the others stayed huddled together and advanced no farther.

General Satorus. Where have I heard that name before?

In the background, Zarya neighed and trotted to stand on the water alongside Aiton's position on the pier. Hands still behind his back, the younger man straightened his shoulders and stepped a little towards the horse, putting himself slightly in between Aiton and Zarya.

Everyone else was silent now. Even the waves had hushed in deference.

"Who are they?" Aiton nodded his head towards both men, who had remained silent up until this point.

"They are—"

"Aiton Paen, as Conseleigh Iycel mentioned before, my name is General Satorus. I lead the militia based on Hown," the general spoke, the authority in his voice made even more substantial by the echo of the cavern. Not once did he ever look away from Aiton. "We've been searching for you. I believe it's time for us to have a talk."

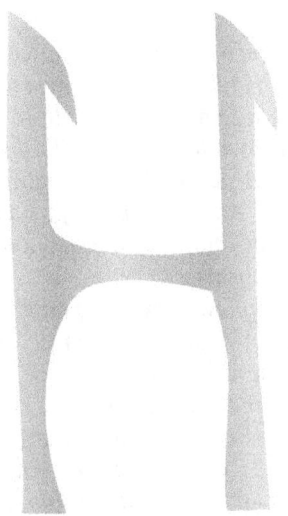

INTERLUDE - CAPTAIN'S LOG

While initially confused by the sudden disappearance of Aiton Paen, a quick survey of the people in his charge told similar stories of shock. They were not hiding him from us. He truly had disappeared. It mattered little in the end, though, for he came back five days later and provided us with what we needed—a blood sample.

The draw was painless. He didn't fight. I suspect he had no realization of what we were actually going to do with it once we finished the draw. Nor his handlers, who did not offer any protest or advise him against complying. This was fortunate considering his bonded animal was nearby. I am certainly glad I didn't have to tear her up; it would have left him broken and scarred in ways I do not think he would have been able to survive. And then this plan with the crystal scry may not have worked. As it was, the horse didn't try to fight or impede on the general as he took an adequate amount of blood, more than enough needed to hunt down Hydro Paen.

The first drop of the blood did nothing much, though, besides showing us that Hydro is in possession of some sort of ship. How that ship got through atmospheric controls in the first place, I cannot begin to know, and is something worth examining should our trail for Hydro go cold or if the scry should stop functioning. Based upon the position of the suns and what we could see from below, Hydro was headed west and passing over Acquava. The altitude was too high to make it plausible he would touch down on the Hart Isles, and surely he wouldn't be so dumb as to try and visit his brother, so the province of Acquis is out of the question. That leaves Gar as the only possibility. It has to be, and that is where we are placing our bets.

However, this information means nothing if we can't pinpoint where in Gar. A description of his ship would be nice, but there is no record of him passing through atmospheric control, making it nearly impossible to hunt him. We could try and scour the spaceports logs for anything unusual like we did in Rhemu, but I contend our best bet is using the crystal scry and coordinating with the two Hown soldiers who have stayed behind with Aiton. Conseleigh Iycel selected ten more of our troops, second-ranked Captain Oliver Thane among them, to help her in other affairs related with Guardian business.

Regardless of that fact, though, we are still a mighty force. More than enough to handle Hydro, even with this slight illness most of us have been struck with recently. Only rarely does one of us ever go into fits of coughing, but they are severe when they do happen and draw attention. I, myself, have never personally had such a fit yet, but I have felt an irritation in my throat every once in a while, making it harder to breathe. To counteract the coughing, we have started taking vitamins from the apothecary kits on board the spaceships. They provide adequate relief for at least a few hours.

There is nothing more to this chase now than sitting and waiting. Aiton's blood is all we needed. Hydro will lead us to himself.

For the honor and glory of the Guardian of the Core, Edwyrd Eska, this is Chase Arwayn signing off.

PART III - FOUND

CHAPTER THIRTY-TWO

THE RESISTANCE

"We're here."

Gabrielle arched an eyebrow and tilted her chin to Zain's voice. "How do you know?"

"Because there is nowhere else to go."

Already? Gabrielle extended her arm, her fingers brushing against a dirt wall. To her side, someone shifted. Vibrations on the ground.

"We can't be here already." Perrine huffed. "Judging from the food we still have, I'd say we're only halfway. This could be a resting point."

That made more sense to Gabrielle. While she hadn't seen sunshine since her incident with Zakk, she still could faintly keep track of time, even if it were just her sense of fatigue guiding her.

"What do we do?" Carla Sonetta asked.

"Hey!" Zain yelled. "Let us through."

"Shouting won't do anyzing, Zain." Gabrielle felt for his arm and found it raised up and pounding on the wall in front of them. She lowered it. "Let me try somezing." She cleared her throat. "I want to speak to Guy Parsons."

Almost immediately, a voice from a speaker infiltrated the underground tunnel. "State your name."

"Gabrielle Ravwey. I've come on behalf of Gracie's Academy."

"That name means nothing to us."

"Cabal Sendel sent us here. Rune gave us access to zis passage. Is zis Soeco?"

The man ignored her question. "Do you have proof?"

Gabrielle fidgeted in a pouch she kept at her side. She felt around for the coin with the embossed scorpion on it and pulled it out. She held it up above her. Shadows turned into light. The ground rumbled. Mini tremors under her gave way to large tremors before her.

"The wall is opening," Zain said.

Gabrielle's lips parted. *We're here. We are actually here.*

A chorus of whispers from the others in the cavern echoed, nearly matching the sound of the wall slowly opening before them. Gabrielle didn't have time to smile or think about how they had arrived so quickly. Carla Sonetta locked elbows with her and shuffled forward. "Come on."

Her cheeks grew hot. She hoped it was in reaction to the white light now shining upon them, but she suspected that wasn't all. She hadn't seen Guy for a few years, and while she would never look upon him again, a talk with him was coming. And that conversation was long overdue.

Minutes passed, and all she heard were slight drips of moisture counting her steps and the sea of footsteps behind her. Damp and slightly cold, she held onto Carla Sonetta's elbow for warmth. The sound of gushing water became clearer and clearer as she continued walking, as did the earthy smell tingling in her nostrils. A slight incline at one point caused her to lean her body forward to continue a synchronous pace with Carla Sonetta. Eventually, that incline plateaued and the sound of water dominated the room, so much so that she could hardly hear the voice that spoke.

Carla Sonetta tugged her elbow and leaned into her ear. "They have us surrounded."

"What do you want?"

"Guy?" Gabrielle searched for a voice she hadn't heard for years.

"No. He's no longer with us."

"Where is he?" Gabrielle tilted her head to the new voice. It was stronger and more authoritative than the other man's.

"He's dead."

Gabrielle sagged against Carla. "Dead?" She had meant to only think it, but the word escaped her mouth all the same. "How? When?" Gabrielle took a breath and tried to steady herself. "I need to speak wiz whoever is in charge."

"There is no one in charge," the weaker voice said.

"We can take her to Cleaver."

"All of them?"

"The rest can stay here. Gabrielle and I can go," Carla Sonetta spoke before Gabrielle had the chance to say anything.

"Me too," Zain said.

A rustle at her side announced his arrival, and her other arm was taken.

"Relinquish your weapons and follow us. The others stay here."

"We'll be back," said Carla Sonetta.

Gabrielle reached to her side and pulled out her sword, extending it blindly in front of her. It was taken, and that was that. They didn't even ask her if she had any other weapons on her, but even if they had, she would have said *no*. Would they really check a woman's leg? Her dagger still concealed, she walked forward, sandwiched between Zain and Carla Sonetta.

Guy is dead? Did Cabal know this when he handed her the coin? How recent was his death? What did that mean for the rebellion? Gabrielle tried processing all of these things, but ended giving in to thinking about nothing. What would happen would happen if it was the will of the Ancients. She thought silently in her head: *Ancients, give me the words I need to face this unknown.* She squeezed Zain's hand, hoping to attract his attention. She mouthed, "Ancients, to zis I pray." And she hoped Zain saw.

The clatter of footsteps on cement faded away, as did the dripping water, then she heard doors slide open. Motors hummed. Artificial heat soon replaced the coolness of the chamber they had just come from. Two levels of stairs later, Gabrielle heard a rapping on a door. Three raps.

Before the call was answered, Gabrielle asked, "Who will we be speaking to?"

"The Cleaver. He's not from around these parts, but he was second to Guy."

"Why do you call him za Cleaver?"

The man chuckled. "You'll see."

Doubtful. A pair of heavy feet approached from the other side of the door, and then she heard a creak of hinges.

"Yes." Then. "Who are they?"

"Women claiming to have ties to Guy."

"Guy's dead."

"I understand, sir," Gabrielle spoke. "We've come from Rydel. Cabal Sendel sent us. He gave me this." Gabrielle flicked the coin forward.

When she didn't hear it clatter on the floor, she assumed the man caught it. *Good reflexes.* She stepped forward. "You are za Scorprions, correct?"

"*Were* the Scorpions," the man corrected her. "Brady, you can leave us." The voice was as heavy as his steps. She couldn't place the accent, but he certainly wasn't from Mendeck.

Shuffled footsteps. The door closed behind.

The coin clinked on a surface.

"Come closer. This certainly is a rebellion coin. You got this from Cabal in Rydel?"

"We did." Gabrielle nodded.

"He's been a benefactor to Gracie's for a long time," Carla Sonetta added. "Victor Zigarda is after our party."

"Why is that?"

"Because of me," Zain stated.

The man scoffed. "And who in Abaddon are you?"

"Zain Berrese."

"And what is that supposed to tell me?"

"He escaped from Victor Zigarda's Web," Gabrielle said. "He has crucial information for za rebellion."

"The rebellion is finished, like I said, lady. Without Guy we don't have a tactician."

"I'm a tactician." Zain brushed up against Gabrielle's left arm.

She could tell he had straightened his posture and puffed out his chest. "What happened?" she asked, steering the conversation back. "When did Guy die?"

"A week and a half ago or so. We were in Aeston, gathering supplies from our usual vendors. Usually, ain't nothing much going on in that city." The man let out a rough bark of laughter. "But that day just happened to be one of those days where everything goes wrong. You ever have those?"

If you only knew.

"Marquis Stronghand just happened to be preparing for war. Soldiers were gathered and boarding ships.

"Guy thought it would be a good idea to engage them as they were busy organizing themselves. We burned a few of their ships along with some of their crew, but we took casualties and had to retreat. Guy died in the fighting. He tried to kill the marquis, himself. Damn fool," he muttered the last words.

"Did you hear of where they were headed?"

"Mox."

"Mox, but that doesn't make sense..."

"What does make sense in this world? Why would Aeston be gathering their army?"

"Zere're going to war wiz Ka'Che. Victor Zigarda must have put a warning out to all za marquises to be on high alert after our party escaped. We just barely managed to avoid getting captured in Rydel."

"Zigarda's moved his forces from the capital, then? Where is he now?"

"I don't know."

"Then what is your business here? Your information is useless."

"How so?"

"Zigarda is the lord, without him, the rebellion would win."

"And za rebellion can win. We are here to gazer men to fight za battle in Pelopon."

"I just told you they are going to Mox."

Zain spoke up. "Mox is just a diversion to draw troops away to the south. They want to take Castle Semson in Pelopon."

"Yeah, and what makes you so certain?"

"It's exactly what I would do. I told you, I'm a tactician for Gazo's."

"And we are Gracie's Academy!" Carla Sonetta moved forward. "The women who are here with us are highly skilled and capable."

"Sure. Yeah. I've heard the names, but the force you got ain't nothing but a ragtag, slapdash crew. You're talking about goin' to war."

"We are more than that," Carla Sonetta said, an edge in her voice.

The Cleaver scoffed. "Yeah. Yeah. I've heard that before."

"How long does it take to get from za Brew Frontiere to here?"

"Two weeks, give or take."

"We got here in one. Maybe a little more. But it certainly wasn't two."

"And how am I supposed to believe that?"

"Check our rations," Gabrielle countered.

"You could have had more food than a two-week journey required."

"More food means more weight. It would only slow us down. We brought wiz us exactly what we zought we would need. Za fact we arrived days ahead of schedule demonstrates our endurance."

The Cleaver didn't respond for a little while. Gabrielle felt him push breath out. "And how did you know you were even going to get here?"

"Faiz."

The Cleaver grumbled at that. "Faith. We all need some of that, don't we?"

"And I can get Gazo's soldiers to fight if we can get to Ka'Che," Zain said, "but we need your help in securing a ship and we need your soldiers. I saw how many there are of you."

"Not many compared to an army. You didn't see the force I saw at Aeston. If Zigarda called all his banners, then it'll take more than just us to beat them."

"We don't need to beat them all, we just need to beat Zigarda."

"And you don't know where he is!"

Startled, Gabrielle jumped back at the pounding of a fist on a surface. Recoiling, she shook it off and stepped forward a few paces until her legs ran into a table. She put her hands on the tabletop and waited.

"Listen, all of you, we cannot handle another defeat."

"We won't be defeated."

"The numbers are not in our—"

"Who said it will just be us?"

"Sure. It may be the Scorpions, a group of girls—"

"Gracie's Academy," Carla Sonetta corrected.

"*Gracie's* Academy. Gazo's, too. Sure. We are still outnumbered."

"We will have my uncle's forces," Zain said.

"Who is your uncle? The Lord of Ka'Che?" Cleaver scoffed.

"Actually, he is."

"Well, ain't that *convenient*. You just seem to be everything, don't you? An escape artist. A tactician. And now part of the royalty in Ka'Che. By the Twelve, I've—"

"All of it is true."

"It is," Gabrielle affirmed.

"Then surely he already knows about what's coming."

"We've tried. The call never got through."

"So, then it's already too late?"

"Not if we go to Aeston and steal a ship. We can help the soldiers at Mox, recruit Gazo's, and then secure Pelopon."

"Idealistic plan, kid. But the fact of the matter is, Zigarda won't be there. He is the head. Zigarda is connected with Acquava, with Chaon, and who knows what other nations. As long as he is alive, reinforcements can come and destroy whatever changes are made. A *proper* tactician would know that." After a few moments of silence, the Cleaver continued. "Now leave."

"Let's go, Gabrielle. It is clear this is a useless battle. This brute doesn't want to hear anything us *girls* have to say." Carla Sonetta tugged at her arm.

Gabrielle didn't budge. "You said you want Zigarda, correct?"

"Yeah."

"I know how to find him."

Chair swiveled. Elbows thumped on the table. "I'm listening."

"Zigarda may or may not be at Pelopon. No one knows. But find a man named Zakk Shiren and you will find Zigarda."

Gabrielle shrugged off Zain's hand.

"Is that name supposed to mean something?"

"He is Zigarda's confidant and personal guard."

"That isn't what we have reported."

"Zen your information is wrong. He was sent after Zain during za Trials, and again when Zain escaped za Web. Za two have history togezer."

"He seems more like a dog. How do you know he is Zigarda's personal guard?"

"Because he did zis to me." One arm as her pillar on the table, Gabrielle leaned forward and removed her glasses, showing her eyes, raw and punctured and blind. She couldn't see his face, but she could hear his sharp inhale. The slight rumble on the table signaled retreating hands as if he leaned back just a little. "I'm blind now because of Zakk. If he wasn't Zigarda's top guard, zis would not be a possibility."

"And what gives you that confidence?"

"Because I have never been beaten. Ever. I have defeated boz of Gazo's premier students, Zain here and even Zakk. I have beaten princes. I have even beaten za apprentice to za Guardian of the Core in a weapons tournament."

"Is that so? The apprentice to Guardian of the Core?"

"Yes." Gabrielle smirked. She had baited him with the title, but in truth it had been her easiest match in the Trials.

"How do I know you ain't just making all of that up?"

Gabrielle's smirk flattened. She set down her glasses. Based upon everything that she had felt so far—the man's breathing, his voice, the table movement—she snatched the dagger from her garter and snaked it under the man's chin, pushing up with the blade just enough to make sure she hadn't misjudged. She hadn't.

The man made a strained noise of surprise. "How did you get that—"

"Because we *girls* at Gracie's are more capable zan you zink. If you don't believe zat we made zis journey in half za time as ozers, zen believe zis—I have never been beaten, and even zis blind woman could have taken your life."

The Cleaver coughed. "Can you still see shadows with those eyes of yours?"

"Shadows sometimes. But mostly darkness. Even after Zakk did zis to me, I put a knife to his zroat, just like I'm doing to you now. I made him forfeit. Zat is how all za women at Gracie's are still alive."

"So then Zakk is dead?"

"No." Her point made, Gabrielle removed the dagger from underneath Cleaver's chin. She kept it out on the table within reach. "But, he is a man. A Gazo's man. And a sense of duty binds him. Zat is why Zain is adamant about recruiting zose men overseas. Zat is what calls him to fight in zis war. Zat duty lives in him just as a sense of duty and protectiveness lives in me. He is a student of Gazo's, just like Zain, and zey share a special bond together, even past zat."

"What kind of bond?"

"Zey are brozers."

"Brothers?"

Zain coughed.

Gabrielle ignored the slight pressure on her left arm. "Yes..." It was a lie, but sometimes one had to weave deceit with decency to be formidable.

"Does he know they are brothers?"

"We are."

Zain's voice could have been more confident, but hopefully Cleaver wouldn't be able to hear the hesitation. Her wish went unanswered.

"Yeah, and I'm as blind as your friend. You aren't brothers."

"We are. I mean—"

"Pull up an image of him. Surely if you know Zigarda, zen you know zis man," Gabrielle cut into Zain's babbling.

Gabrielle heard movement, and then Cleaver said, "Brady..."

"Yes, sir." The response came from a speaker.

"Run a calculated scan of the food supplies the newcomers have with them. Then pull up an image of a man named Zakk Shiren and give it to me. I need a word with you."

Perhaps a half hour later, a door opened. Footsteps. Based upon the voice that followed, Brady had come to stand beside Gabrielle.

"Sir, I have—"

"You want to tell me what this is doing here? I thought you checked them?"

Gabrielle raised an eyebrow and smiled to herself.

"Sir, I... I did. How—"

"Carelessness gets people killed."

A thud came to the table, and the dagger hit Gabrielle's hand. She picked it up and put it behind her back.

"Now, what do you have for me?"

"Seems like enough food is left for another week or so. And here is the image. Well, best we could find, anyway."

After the sound of rumpled paper, the chair swiveled again. "Well, Abaddon take me now, there is a resemblance. You *are* full of surprises, ain't you?"

"That is right before we escaped. Then he followed us to Gracie's."

"And now you're here."

"And now we're here."

"Zrough Zain, we can find Zakk and zus, Zigarda."

Cleaver scoffed. "So use that bond of yours and tell us where he is."

"You give us what we want. We give you what you want," Gabrielle spoke for Zain, not wanting him to ruin her story. "You may have lost a tactician with Guy, but Zain can fill zat void. At Gazo's, zere will be dozens of men you can choose from if he isn't good enough. Men zat can surpass Guy's caliber."

Silence.

"After we help you, we find Zigarda?"

"Yes," Zain said.

"Absolutely," Gabrielle said at the same time.

The Cleaver grunted. "Very well, Zain Berrese, Ms. Ravwey, you have my resistance. We will join the fight."

CHAPTER THIRTY-THREE

PAINTING A PICTURE

C ross-legged, Guardian Eska sat on the stone bench at the edge of the training
court. His gaze darted between the two combatants. "Begin."

Eirek leaped forward.

So it is Eirek to start the offensive. Interesting.

Ethen batted the attempt away with a simple flick of his wrist. He let the
apprentice have his fun for a handful more strokes before parrying and countering
with a punch to Eirek's face.

It connected.

Eirek tumbled backwards, but rolled to a crouching position. Ethen hadn't been
able to capitalize on the move, for a barrier of earth had blocked him from
advancing. The conseleigh quickly overcame it and again the two of them traded
blows back and forth. For safety precautions, they still only used ordinary weapons
instead of the Ether Weapons, but this challenge would let Eska see how far he had
taken his apprentice while Ethen was away on his duty in Mistral.

Surprisingly, he was holding his own against Ethen. Either that or the former
Gazo's instructor was taking it easy on him, but Eska had told Ethen not to. He
needed to see Eirek's performance, for it was in this aspect and this aspect alone
that his apprentice was truly lacking.

During Ethen's absence, Eska had trained Eirek's Power endurance, had worked
with him on using his left and right side equally, and had made him get more
acquainted with various weapons. No matter the situation, Eska wanted Eirek
ready.

Eirek ducked. He swung upward, forcing Ethen backwards. Again, they went
into a series of strikes and counters. Both were hardly using any Power in this
duel. That concerned Eska.

Ethen.

Yes, my guardian. Ethen held his lance upwards, blocking a sword slice from
above. He shoved his elbow forward, swinging the butt of his weapon into Eirek's
ribcage, sending him back a step.

Why aren't you using Power?

You said you wanted a thorough evaluation.

I've seen enough.

Very well. "Maa."

"*Maa,*" Eirek countered.

The two wills battled for control of the earth magic. Ethen built a spire trying to skewer Eirek, and Eirek held it back.

"*Vesi.*"

A fist of water came at Eirek from the stream that flowed to the court. Eirek raised a hand, countering it with a shield of his own water.

Eirek moved his hand down to the ring on his finger. "*Salama.*"

Electricity tore through Ethen's water spell, eradicating it, then shot like a boomerang out towards Ethen. The conseleigh swiped up with his hand, diverting his earth Power to knock it easily away. Eirek closed the gap on the conseleigh. At least, he tried to, and he would have succeeded if Ethen hadn't successfully split his earthen energy to knock away the electric boomerang and shackling Eirek to the stone court at the same time. As it was, Eirek had already committed to an overhead strike, and when he had tried to jump, he fell immediately to his face. His elbow hit the earth hard. The sword went flying from his grip. Ethen stomped a boot on Eirek's back. Eirek collapsed.

Eska's shoulders slumped slightly, but he reminded himself not to be disappointed. Eirek didn't need to be better than Ethen just yet, he only needed to be good enough. And since the Trials conclusion, Eirek's transformation had been astonishing. The young man had successfully cast three spells of Power simultaneously, and while that ultimately led to his downfall, it was still a feat. For the most part, he had matched Ethen blow for blow in weapons. It was only the combination of all of those things together that still showed his inexperience. And that would take time and practice.

Eska stood and walked over to the court grounds. "Good performance today. Both of you."

Ethen extended a hand down to Eirek, who took it and got to his feet. "Warriors —"

"Still standing, don't stand still," Eirek finished with a huffed breath. He brushed off his clothes.

"True, but tat wasn't what I was going to say."

Eirek straightened to attention.

"Warriors at Gazo's know tat you should *see each brushstroke of battle, for it determines ta war's portrait.*"

Eirek didn't respond. He waited, as if he expected Ethen to continue.

"When you moved your hand to tat ring of yours, I knew you would use electricity. While you readied your spell, I split mine, keeping one half ready to counter and ta oter locking your feet in place."

"You knew what I was going to do?"

Ethen laughed. "Most people are quite predictable. And when you can predict your enemies' movements, battles and wars become tat much easier."

Eirek's eyes glimmered for a second. He bit down on his lower lip and flicked his gaze to Eska. "May I be excused? I need to check on something."

"Is everything okay, Eirek?"

"Yes. Well. No. Maybe. I don't know. It's about Cresica."

Eska nodded slightly. "You want to see how it is going?"

Eirek blushed.

"If you feel as though you must, I am not one to stop you, but it may be better not knowing."

Eirek darted off, leaving Eska and Ethen on the court alone.

Eska crossed his arms over his chest. "He still has yet to let go of his past and embrace his present."

"It will come in time, my guardian. Not all of us are fireborn."

Eska sighed. "No. Not all of us are. That reminds me, I have to check in with Riagan later." Eska strolled back to the estate, Ethen at his side. "His performance today, what did you think?"

"He fought well. Compared to 'ow 'e was in ta Trials, it is ta difference between ta Krine Sea and the Long Ocean."

Eska smiled at the comparison. "Yes. He still cannot use everything in unison, but I suppose practice will help in that."

"It will."

"And now that you're back from Mistral, it'll be your continued duty to see that he progresses up to my standards." He paused on a stone step and turned to Ethen. "I must say, you have done better work than the sages."

"Tank you, my guardian." Ethen bobbed his head. "I will continue to work wit 'im."

Eska clasped Ethen on the shoulder. "Good. At least there is that." He continued walking.

"I am sorry I couldn't bring good tidings from Mistral."

"It can't be helped. I do wish we had a location on Senator Numos, though. But the Hown are spread too thin right now as it is." Eska paused, reminding himself to speak with General Satorus as well later.

"Why not just issue a mandate for 'is capture?"

"Because I have no solid evidence to go on yet, only the words of my apprentice and Zain. Even then, who is to say that he gave the blood samples to Zigarda? There is too much speculation. As Luvan would say, I would be abusing my authority."

Eska rounded the corner of the estate and began walking up the steps.

"Perhaps it would be wise to reach out to him."

Eska stopped halfway up the steps. "Why do you say that?"

"He is missing as well."

Eska walked down the steps. "Missing? You made contact with him?"

"Tried, and you never said I couldn't. I only met Lucine."

"And?"

"And she told me in passing that Luvan and Numos 'ad been spending time together recently."

"Is that so?"

Ethen bobbed his head. "For a few weeks now, 'e 'as been out on other business."

Eska clicked his lips together. "That is certainly interesting news. Something I'm not quite sure how to digest yet, either." Eska continued up the steps. "Do you think they are working together?"

"Doubtful." Ethen hurried ahead and opened the door for Guardian Eska.

"Why do you say that? They are both from Mistral, after all."

"Luvan disliked 'im in ta Trials. I don't tink he would lower himself."

Eska bit his lower lip. "I am going to my chambers now. Good job today, Ethen. I especially liked the message at the end. It was poetic."

"It wasn't my message, my guardian. Just another saying from Gazo's."

"Truly a..." Eska closed his lips. "Never mind. I will see you later." Eska gestured to the button at the back of the staircase. "If you could."

Ethen pushed the button. The center of the lobby lifted away from the rest of the floor and carried Eska towards his chambers on the third floor.

Inside his chambers, he walked over to the desk and plopped himself into the chair. He sat there for a while, massaging his temples. Normally, what he had witnessed between Ethen and Eirek would have made him happy, and it had, but this unfinished business with Senator Numos, and now potentially Luvan, took his mind in other directions.

I will deal with that later. Eska sighed.

Putting his thumb on the metal surface of a drawer handle, it read his fingerprint, and the locking mechanisms clicked open. The drawer contained the crystal scry, another device that looked like a small mirror, and the jewel he kept hidden. The drawer was no vault, but the jewel was hidden enough to keep it away from unwanted eyes. Besides, there were the other security measures in place.

Access to the Core was limited. Any intruder would first have to figure out how to bypass that. Should they somehow manage that, Vesel and Eska and any of his conseleigh present would be there to greet them. And should the individual manage to survive the confrontation, it would still require an extensive search of the entire estate, and most likely that individual *would* be looking for a high-security vault, not a simple desk drawer. The drawer itself required Eska's thumb scan, and the doors to his chambers sensed his presence, only opening to someone else if he was already inside. Or, of course, an Ether Weapon, if someone preferred the harder way.

Ethen and Eirek's demonstration earlier had brought Eska a measure of reassurance, and now he would touch base with the other operations in play and hopefully receive more good news. Hopefully.

He withdrew the hand-held mirror and stood it on his desk. Letting it power on, he searched for Riagan's name in his telecommunicator. Once selected, he moved his wrist under the mirror-like device, syncing them together. The words *Riagan Inferno* appeared before him.

One beep.

Two beeps.

Connecting.

Moments later, the face of his youngest conseleigh appeared on the screen. At the top of the mirror's frame, a bright circle captured Eska's image and transmitted it to Riagan.

"Riagan, how are things going for you? Where are you now?"

"You know I cannot tell you that, Guardian Eska."

"Good. I am just making sure." Eska laughed. "But do tell me how things are going for you."

"Things are good here. It is nice to be back away from the Core."

Eska pursed his lips slightly. Although it was nothing that should concern him, he noticed the slight slip of tongue by his youngest conseleigh. By saying the word *back*, it implied that he had returned to his home planet of Pyre. Eska would have assumed as much, as Riagan's bonded animal, wife, and son were on Pyre, but even such a minor mistake could be disastrous. Eska let it go. There were more difficult things ahead.

"Listen, Riagan…"

"Yes, my guardian?"

Eska explained to Riagan how he had uncovered a plot to hunt for the jewels and how the search might eventually lead to Riagan, putting him and those he loved in danger.

"Die by fire, die with honor. Living in Pyre, nothing is higher."

Eska forced a smile when he heard the Pyrean proverb, knowing his conseleigh didn't understand Eska's history and why he no longer quoted it. "Your words speak volumes to me, Riagan."

"Until death I will carry out my duty to you and your position as you command."

"I appreciate your resolve." Eska waited a brief second to see the smile on his conseleigh's face. "If you see any suspicious activity, notify me immediately."

"Of course, my guardian."

"Goodbye."

The connection ended and Eska sat for a moment, deciding what to do next. A breeze fluttered in through the open window. It reminded him of Zeph. Did she know someone was hunting them as well? Of course she did. There had always been an air of prescience about her, one she most likely had gained by her intimacy with Ancient Bane and through her First Blood. He thought about reaching out to her but decided against it. Any attempt to take the jewel from her would be faced with a challenge. She was safe. She had the Power of the wind with her, a Power only he shared, and only thanks to her gift during his first encounter with Pirini Lilapa.

Thinking of her, though, brought to mind her words: *fit for fate. Hmmmm.* It seemed too much like coincidence for the jewels Zigarda gave Eirek to be the ones chosen to seal the Twelve. In fact, the notion that there were even twelve jewels to begin with ate at Eska's mind. Had Zigarda planned all of this? Had he somehow known in advance that there would be a fight during the Meeting of the Twelve? No. It couldn't have been him alone. Surely this was evidence that Zigarda was under the instruction of the Third One. Only an Ancient could have foreseen an event of such magnitude. Perhaps the Third One had even *planned* it? Who was he to question the limits of an Ancient?

Leaning back in his chair, Eska drummed his fingers on the table. *If the Ancient really is on the playing field, there is only one way we can stop him.* Sitting up straight again, he scrolled through the call log on the mirror in front of him until he found General Satorus.

One beep.

Two.

Three.

Nothing.

That's odd. Eska tried calling again. This time, on the second beep, General Satorus answered.

"Guardian Eska."

"General." Eska nodded. "Why the delay in answering? Is everything okay?"

"We were busy coordinating a scrying session." The general coughed. He itched at his throat.

"And?"

"Nothing this session, my guardian."

"Nothing? What does that mean?"

"It means Hydro is most likely sleeping or resting."

"But it should be well into the afternoon there."

"It is."

"Then—"

"Then this information is just as valuable. Either Hydro operates mostly at evening and sleeps during the day, or he is outside the comfort of his ship."

Eska cocked his head at the detail. "What would make you think that?"

"To be honest, I believe it's the former. The first time we..." The general paused to cough into his fist and then unbutton the top of his collar. "The first time we used the scry, he was flying off into Gar with the suns behind him. But today is also an unusually hot day. He very well may be needing a rest or a slight reprieve from the heat, which means—"

"He is outside his ship," Eska finished the sentence.

"Correct, my guardian."

Eska beamed at the astuteness of his Hown. Hydro couldn't outrun them forever, and if they could deliver Hydro to him, then he could bring the man to the past Guardians in the Crypt and ask for advice on how to deal with the damned necklace he wore.

"Very good, general. Your cough. Has the apothecary medicine not been effective?"

"It seems to be providing us temporal relief, but nothing..." General Satorus coughed again. "But nothing permanent."

"And everyone has this?"

"All have shown some signs."

"What are the other symptoms?"

"Some are experiencing a loss of appetite as well."

"Where are you now?"

"Eastbarrow."

"How many of you are left?"

"Two remain with Aiton. Ten with Conseleigh Iycel. And the rest—"

"Tundra only took ten?"

The general coughed. "Yes, my guardian. Conseleigh Iycel took ten. Don't worry. All highly capable. Captain Oliver Thane is leading her party."

Eska bit his lip. He had slipped, and General Satorus had noticed. Or had he? Besides, why couldn't Eska use Tundra's first name? Professionalism. That was why. Eska swatted away the thought and the others that dared to creep up alongside it.

"Use the rest of the day. Admit yourself to the best apothecary you can find. See if the adored can diagnosis you properly."

"Will do, my guardian." General Satorus nodded.

Eska nodded and ended the connection. Once again, he massaged his temples. He took a long, deep breath in and then slowly exhaled. Opening his eyes, he stood up and made his way around the chamber, catching sight of the wall opposite the veranda. Four paintings hung on the way, each representing a piece of home for the conseleigh who served him. Today, they caught his attention more than other days. Perhaps the unconscious byproduct of Ethen's advice.

Eska had seen many paintings come and go over his years as Guardian of the Core. When a new conseleigh was inducted, he removed the old conseleigh's painting and stored it in a room adjacent to his own chambers. Occasionally, he would go stand among them and reminisce over the drawings, remembering the conseleigh to whom they had belonged.

Luvan's painting was still up. Why hadn't he removed it yet? Had he been so distracted with Eirek's training? Perhaps it was merely because he hadn't initiated the process of finding a replacement yet. Regardless of the reason, Eska surveyed the painting that showed the floating province of Halo. The Talia Mountains stretched up into the sky and out from the mountain range flowed the Stream of Heaven. The painting showed a rainbow sweeping across the waterfall, almost as if it were a gate to the majestic scene.

The second was a quaint painting of the small town of Proschi and the magnificent backdrop of Mount Klaff behind it. In the painting, the tall, obelisk-like mountain had a blue-ish hue and aura Eska hadn't noticed when he had climbed it. Or, rather, when he had soared to the first level on Vesel. The mountain seemed to reach forever upwards, and he hadn't known how high Vesel could fly, so they had gone no farther. But he had stood there at the threshold of the passage that led into the mountain. What one would find inside Mount Klaff, though, well, no one knew that.

The third painting showed a field of volcanoes known as Abaddon's Towers. Located in the north of Pyre, Guardian Eska had never actually seen it in person until he had spent a year in Pyre as part of his apprenticeship to Matthau Crevon. The site was certainly awe-inspiring, but it left a scent of sulfur that wouldn't wash away for a week. This may have been typical in most places in Pyre, or Therus, but in Nova there weren't any volcanoes, only hot springs and dragons and mountains.

The last painting showed Crestal's Palace, a tall and ominous structure at the north pole of Onkh. Tundra had told him the palace was made of holy water. With its affinity came great Power. Eska had never been inside, but Tundra had. She had told him how it reflected how she handled the loss of her husband, and how she had appeared weak and meager. It had reflected her soul.

It was that day Eska remembered as he stared into the painting. As was customary with all of his conseleigh, he always asked them why they chose that specific image to be drawn. Over the years, he had received all sorts of answers. Many overlapped. But Tundra's had been different. Open. Unadulterated. Raw. It showed him a strength and reaffirmed why he had chosen her to be his conseleigh. And although it may have been wrong, he had taken her hand that day, as though to hold her in the present and keep her from being drawn into the past. To his surprise, she didn't let go. Looking at the painting again, he wondered if he would ever have the strength to see the innards of that palace and truly know himself as well.

Guardian Eska closed his eyes and allayed his mind.

Tundra.

Yes, Edwyrd?

Where are you?

In Symeria, Edwyrd. It is the night before the wedding.

How do things fare?

With me, the mission, or the boy?

Eska chuckled slightly at her icy tone. *Everything.*

I am fine, but I cannot say the same for Aiton or the Hown. The boy is less cooperative now that he's learned what the Hown are doing.

Surely they can manage a boy of nine.

They can. It is the horse that is the problem. It intercedes on Aiton's behalf when they try to apply pressure to him.

The bonded animal's loyalty is no surprise.

I never said it was. It is just merely inconvenient. After the horse was taken away to the stables today, they resorted to blindfolding the lord in his room. I heard the whinnying of his horse not even seconds after.

Yes. General Satorus notified me they coordinated something today.

You spoke with him?

Yes. Eska paused.

What is it, Edwyrd?

He sighed. *Why did you take so few Hown with you?*

More men will only slow us in our search for Doctor Cere. More should be used to deal with Hydro.

Yes, but even a handful more could ensure your safety in the north.

So you do worry about me?

Eska broke his connection for a second. When he realized his jaw had slackened, he closed it and focused on her again. *You...*

I? She played innocent.

You are putting yourself in jeopardy by not taking more.

I was already in jeopardy when you sent me away without a kiss.

Eska coughed. *I did that to give you a reward for coming back to me.*

And I did this to make sure you still truly appreciate me. Does that make either of us less vindicated? She toyed.

Well played. After the wedding, what will you do?

Go to Lady Aprah as we discussed

Good. While you are there, tell Lady Aprah to lend you some of her elites.

I am unsure how willing Lady Aprah will be to comply.

Tell her it's an order.

An order?

Yes. It is. Safety for my conseleigh comes first.

Nothing may even transpire. I will need reason to deal with Lord Grime, and I may not even be able to locate Doctor Cere.

It is better to have them and not need them than to need them and not have them. Plus, the elites will have knowledge of the north more than the Hown with you.

This is true. And from Acquava?

No need to bother Acquava. They already are dealing with enough.

Understood, Edwyrd.

A long moment passed before Eska communicated with her again. *I...* Guardian Eska sighed. *I was looking at your painting again today.*

And?

Stay safe out there.

I will return, Edwyrd. As sure as the snow falls.

Eska smiled. *I await your arrival.*

He ended the connection with her. Remaining where he stood, he continued looking at the painting of Crestal's Palace. It caused a slight twitch in his hand. He flexed his fingers. Before everything was over, he hoped that he could hold her hand once more.

Chapter Thirty-Four

THE WEDDING

Much like the funeral for Aiton's mother and father, the wedding was held inside the garden area of an estate. Winter grapes of blue and purple hung on the trees in the courtyard. Water trickled down manmade mountain decorations and flowed into manmade streams on the floor that cut their way to a fountain in the center of a courtyard. Before the center fountain, rows of white chairs faced an archway and a bethel behind it.

The walls were high enough to block any wind, but a light snow fell on the grounds and dusted a blue carpet that led to the raised stage draped in white. Aiton sat upon this raised stage at the request of Marquis Sigurd and his wife. Conseleigh Iycel did as well, to Aiton's right.

This was what a wedding was supposed to look like. But it didn't feel like one to Aiton. The presence of the Hown and their unwavering stoicism cast a shadow over the sense of joy that should have accompanied such an event. Instead, the air was thick with tension and the attention of the guests kept wandering the dais to the uninvited guests.

Aiton shifted in the chair more than once whenever the Hown looked upon him. Even if it was a casual glance in his direction, he felt it. And right now, he didn't need that. He had a speech to prepare, but Aiton knew something wasn't right. The Hown had been relentless, always asking that he close his eyes while they monitored something. Aiton didn't know what they were doing, but he was sure it was related to finding his brother. Only after they had taken blood from him did he realize what he had done and how he had betrayed his brother. Since then, he had been doing his best to thwart their efforts to locate him, refusing blindly any more of their requests. That's when they had started using blindfolds on him, but Aiton found a way around this, too, opening his eyes after the blindfold was placed on his head and closing them again only moments before they took it off. Hopefully Hydro could make it off the planet before they found him. He looked down at his forearm, still seeing the spot where General Satorus had extracted a vial of his blood. He rubbed it. *Hydro...*

Tundra put a hand over his fingers, steadying his. She smiled.

She had told him they weren't going to kill Hydro, but that he was to be taken to Guardian Eska to fix him. That calmed Aiton slightly, and he had almost revealed to her the rendezvous with his brother at Leviathan Bay, but a part of him didn't trust her. At the end of the day, the conseleigh and the Hown were still loyal to only one individual, the Guardian of the Core, and would the Guardian really allow Aiton's brother to go unpunished for what he had done to the family? To Pearl? Aiton didn't think so, so he feigned a smile for her, pulled his hands away and set them on his lap. Then he looked over to Korth, Haruko, and Darien, who sat in the front row as well. Those were people he could trust.

Then he filtered his senses to connect with Zarya, who stood amongst the winter grape trees in the back, lapping up the fountain water. Marquis Sigurd had wanted her to stay behind in the stables as horses should, but Darien had argued that a bonded pair should not be separated, just as in a marriage, saying, "What better way to bring two people together than by two already brought together?"

With Aiton atop the dais stood the chaplain, a man dressed in white with metallic blue letters designating the number *twelve*. To his left sat Marquis Sigurd, a man built like a warrior. While in his mid-thirties, his hair had grown longer than Aiton thought a man's hair should grow; it was tied back. His eyebrows were rather well-groomed, and he had a thin mustache under a hooked nose.

Marquis Sigurd leaned into Aiton's ear. "Your horse is a beauty. For how long have you had her now?"

Aiton turned to look at the man. "Less than a week."

"Ahh, newly bonded, then? Just like my wife and I are going to be."

Aiton nodded.

"Thank you so much for agreeing to say something on our behalf. So many people are anxious to hear your words as the new lord." He shifted his gaze. "You as well, Conseleigh Iycel. It is an honor that you made time for us. You and your, uhmm, guests, shall I say?"

Aiton opened his mouth to begin, but Conseleigh Iycel spoke first. "My pleasure, Hekter. We are happy to be present. Bonds are truly beautiful things."

"That they are. And my wife is truly beautiful." Hekter shifted his gaze to Aiton. "I apologize, by the way, for the loss of your family. Your father was a great man." Marquis Sigurd placed a large hand over Aiton's two tiny hands already clasped together on his lap.

What are you two talking about? Why is he holding your hand?

My father. I'm... I'm remembering his funeral.

I can sense your joy. Why are you smiling?

Normally, I wouldn't. But this marquis said my father was a great man.

And what of it?

Well, he was. I can tell that now. His funeral was better attended than this wedding. Aiton could see Zarya moving her head and calculating. *Not in number, Zarya. In quality. Guardian Eska, his apprentice, even his other conseleigh. None of them are here. Only Conseleigh Iycel, and that's because she has to be here. She told me. It may look impressive with the amount of people here, but it is nothing like my father's funeral.*

Perhaps they are busy?

They were busy in the time of my family's pain as well. Pirini Lilapa was close, and the apprentice had a meeting with the Twelve to attend.

Then it certainly seems your family is truly of higher caliber than those stable-stuffers. Zarya shook her mane.

Aiton laughed.

"What is so funny, my lord?" Marquis Sigurd moved his hand on Aiton's shoulder.

"Only my horse." Aiton giggled again. "You are right, though, Marquis Sigurd, my father was a great man." Aiton beamed.

The chaplain bent over. "Shall we begin, Marquis Sigurd?"

The marquis offered a quick smile to Aiton, then to the chaplain. "Yes, let us begin."

The chaplain adjusted his blue vestment with an overlay of black. A blue sash tied at his waist kept the bottom half of his robe from touching the floor. "All, we are gathered here today to witness the union of two single souls to be bonded together as one. After, they will share one heart, one mind, and one purpose." The chaplain turned away from the audience and extended his hand. "Marquis Hekter Sigurd, come forth."

The marquis walked over to the chaplain and stood underneath the gazebo. Silence and stillness.

"Are you ready to recite your vows and accept your duties?"

"I am," he nodded.

"Are you ready to be the captain of the ship as you and your wife to-be sail into a new life together?"

"I am ready for the position."

"And are you ready to stay steadfast to her, your love unending like the sea? Are you ready to say more than watery words, but to make these words ice?"

"I am ready for the responsibility."

"Then let the bride come forth and behold the words for herself." The chaplain extended his arm and directed the audience's attention to the back of the garden.

Lauren Puwl wore a deep blue layered dress and a matching pearl necklace. Silky sleeves of royal blue hung past her elbows. Her hair had been brushed forward into a poof so that it hung to the sides of her face and covered her ears. She looked nothing like the Lauren Puwl Aiton had met at dinner the night before. Her dress hid her girth, the sleeves hid the flab on her arms, and the hair did well to conceal rosy and plump cheeks. The distance and makeup hid any blemishes Aiton had noticed before, and she radiated elegance.

She strolled down the blue carpet, dress dragging along the light snow that had fallen since morning. Her mother and father walked side by side with her, their arms interlocked with hers. All walked in sync with one another down the carpet, though Lauren paused and looked directly at Zarya for a moment. When she continued, Aiton heard Zarya in his head.

Little One.

Zarya, what is it?

That one looked at me.

I saw that. What was it about?

Her eyes. They wanted me.

What do you mean?
They wanted me.
Her sigil is a seahorse. She probably has just never seen one so close before.
If you say so, Little One.

Aiton squirmed slightly in his chair as the bride ascended the steps to meet Marquis Sigurd under the gazebo. Her parents settled into vacant spots in the front row.

"Lauren Puwl from Rhemu, I now ask you the same questions as I did the man before you."

Aiton listened as the chaplain repeated the questions and she gave similar answers.

"Before we proceed to the Plunge, is there anything you would like to say to one another?"

When he heard the words, *the Plunge,* the guests shifted slightly in their chairs. Even Tundra moved to glance toward the pool behind the gazebo. A small stone bridge extended from one side of the stone court to the other side. It looked similar to the one in his own estate, except smaller. Aiton had heard of the Plunge, but he couldn't recall the exact details.

"...no matter the time we receive, I will do those things forever. Take this ring as a symbol of our eternity, no matter what the sea says." Lauren Puwl finished and put the ring onto Hekter's finger.

"Let this day be one that not only forever changes our lives, but the lives of our people. I will be the sea in your blood. I will take the salt from your tears, and never let the sun set on your dreams and desires. No matter the time we receive, I will do those things forever. Take this ring as a symbol of our eternity, no matter how the water weighs in." Hekter Sigurd slid a ring onto Lauren's finger.

They turned away from Aiton and the audience to face the bethel behind them. They stepped out from the shelter of the gazebo and walked with the chaplain to the edge of the water. Tundra stood. Aiton followed suit, but atop his chair in order to match her height.

"What's going to happen?" he asked in a hushed tone.

Tundra shifted her head slightly to Aiton. "They are about to tie their marriage. However long they can remain underwater determines the length of their marriage."

Aiton saw the chaplain place his hands on their backs. Then he pushed them forward, and they fell face-first into the water. Five seconds. Ten seconds. The ripples began to subside. Twenty.

What are they doing? Zarya asked.
They are in the water.
Why?

Aiton didn't respond to Zarya, for the two resurfaced, gasping for air.

The chaplain pulled them out, Lauren first, and Marquis Sigurd after. He snapped his fingers and two men who had been standing in the shadows at the end of the walls came forth carrying robes. Once both were cloaked, he brought them forward again, raising their arms as if they had just finished a marvelous fight. After clearing his throat, he announced, "The sea has spoken. These two shall have a marriage full of happiness and bliss for thirty-four long years."

The crowd cheered. Marquis Sigurd came to stand before Aiton and Conseleigh Iycel. "It would honor us greatly if both of you could say a word."

"Of course." Conseleigh Iycel nodded. She stepped forward to the podium and grabbed it with both hands, not wasting a second to go into her speech.

Aiton took the moment to sit down and start thinking of his own speech. He caught some of Conseleigh Iycel's words, but he also took the time to ask Zarya for help.

Zarya, what do I say?

Something beautiful, Little One. Something from the heart.

"...bond is nothing to be taken lightly. Neither is the Plunge. I know of the heartache a broken bond can bring, but I hope that neither of you experiences it so unexpectedly as I did. Be reminded to always cherish each other. Cherish the small things. Praise your partner's goodness. Forgive flaws. Never take for granted one another and always recognize that person for who they truly are. Your soulmate. Your bond. And now your family."

Family. Aiton bit his lip. *What would Hydro say?* Aiton recalled one of his brother's last words to him. *He would tell me that I'm a Paen. And that is what I will tell them.*

Conseleigh Iycel tapped his leg. "Lord Paen, I have finished. It is your turn now."

Aiton hopped off his chair and approached the podium, lowered now to compensate for his height. He gripped the sides of the podium and cleared his mind and his throat. "All of my life I have grown up with people I respect: my father, my mother, and even my brother." Aiton's gaze drifted for a split second to the three in the front row. Darien shifted under his words. "I am standing here with the confidence they have instilled in me since their lives were cut much too short." A knot formed in his throat. He regretted using the word *cut.* "Nonetheless, it pleases me to see such a long future ahead for both Marquis Sigurd and his bride. As the saying goes in Roil, 'the sun never sets' and now it truly stands as a testament to their newly formed union. I know from what I saw between my father and my mother that the love they shared was strong. I felt the same way about my brother. Even now, after everything that has happened, a part of me feels that way." Aiton scanned the crowd. The Hown betrayed no reaction to those words. "The other half of my heart belongs to my horse, Zarya, who saved me when I was at my lowest." Aiton turned his attention to Marquis Sigurd and his wife. "I hope that both of you get to experience the love that my parents' experienced and the love that I have found now."

Aiton nodded at the newlyweds. Darien sat comfortably now. Korth stood and clapped his hands. Professor Haruko followed. Soon, more and more stood. In the back, Zarya neighed and went up on her hind legs, kicking the air. Aiton blushed under the immensity of the applause. Tundra clapped fervently behind him. The marquis and his wife stood and clapped as well, whispering to one another all the while.

Aiton turned around—but somehow he still saw the scene that had been spread before him. He faltered and turned back to the podium. *What was that? What is going on?*

My gift to you, Little One.

This is your ability?

It is. Near-perfect vision, the perfect wedding gift, isn't it?

Things couldn't be clearer. Aiton beamed. *I'm a Paen. And no one can take that away from me, no matter how hard they try. Brother, you were right.*

Tundra came up from behind him. Before she even placed a hand on his shoulder, Aiton turned around to meet her. "Beautiful speech, Lord Paen. Short and sweet. Your father would be proud."

"Thank you, Conseleigh Iycel."

"Can I steal you away for a moment?"

"Now?"

"Yes, the ceremony is finished. My time is limited, but I have things I need to discuss with you."

"Okay."

As the attendees came forward to offer their individual congratulations to the newlyweds, Aiton followed Conseleigh Iycel to where Zarya was tied to a tree by the center fountain. It was just the two of them, and Aiton had noticed the looks of concern on the faces of his retainers when he left the dais with her.

"I wanted to offer you and your horse congratulations as well, Lord Paen. Can I touch her?"

Aiton beamed. "Of course."

"Her name is Zarya, correct?" Aiton bobbed his head, and Conseleigh Iycel ran a finger through her white mane. "A fitting name during these troubling times."

"What do you mean?"

Conseleigh Iycel shook her head. "Forgive me. It's nothing. Her name means protector of warriors. Perhaps you will be a mighty one someday? How is your Power faring?"

For the first time that day, Aiton's shoulders slumped.

"Oh. I'm sorry to hear it is not better, Lord Paen. Don't worry, you will get there. It just—"

"Takes time," Aiton finished her sentence half-heartedly. "I know. I've heard it before."

Tundra scratched Zarya behind her ear. "Do you know that the apprentice to Guardian Eska didn't cast Power until after Coronation?"

Aiton's eyes opened. "What?"

"It's true. I was there the night he first cast. It did not come easily to him."

"What changed?"

"I'm unsure. I suppose he found it within himself. Maybe you will, too."

"I hope so." Aiton smiled again. Things weren't so bad. The apprentice was much older than him and he cast Power late. Thoughts about the apprentice and Guardian Eska soon made Aiton bite his lip. He noticed some of the Hown watching him and the conseleigh. To avoid their gaze, he turned his head down. Kicking his feet on the ground, he asked. "Are you here because of my brother as well?"

"No. Your brother doesn't bring me to Acquava. The Hown are dealing directly with him, as you've come to find out. If anyone can find him and detain him, it will be them."

Aiton looked at her again. "What would happen if they found him?"

"He would be brought before Guardian Eska. He has something quite valuable."

"The necklace?"

"How did you—" Tundra stopped. "Never mind. You were there with us when we first learned about Hydro. Yes, the necklace he wears is very important. We need it."

"But he needs it!" The words tumbled out of Aiton's mouth. Immediately, he pressed his lips together, not wanting to betray more.

Conseleigh Iycel cocked her head. "The only thing he needs is to be rid of it. If the Hown find him, that will be an easy fix. We can just use Edwyrd's Ether Weapon to slice it off of him."

Aiton swallowed hard. He looked down at his hands. Not wanting to say anything more, he was glad when she continued speaking.

"I am here because of other Guardian matters."

"We were wondering why all of those Hown were with you, Conseleigh Iycel." Hekter Sigurd entered the conversation with his wife attached to his arm.

"Yes. They are helping with an ongoing investigation."

"Investigation? Sounds exciting, doesn't it, Hekter." His wife nudged him.

"Yes. It does, dear. But it's none of our business." He stamped his foot. "Anyway, forgive my wife and I for our intrusion, but we just wanted to take a moment to offer a token of our gratitude to Lord Paen." Marquis Sigurd shifted his gaze to Aiton. "It means a lot to us that you have come all the way from Aquis to join us." He lifted his arm, signaling for his wife to speak.

"The chaplain said Hekter and I will have thirty-four happy years. I wanted to give you one of our servants for every ten years." Behind her were three other individuals: two women and one man. The two women wore the seahorse badge of Rhemu, and the man wore the setting sun of Roil. "The two women are Medea and Penelope. And then there is Saxon. We hope they find places in your estate, my lord. They are our gift to you."

"We won't need any more servants around the castle grounds." Hands behind his back, Korth now entered the conversation, along with Professor Haruko and Darien on either side of him.

"Surely you must since..." Hekter's wife paused. She sighed. Then she whispered. "Since the incident."

"No need to bring that up here, Marchioness Sigurd," Conseleigh Iycel immediately said. "Let's not sour a good day with bad memories, shall we?"

"Of course. My apologies. Let us also not sour it by not accepting our token of appreciation."

"It is customary not to refuse a gift, Lord Paen." Conseleigh Iycel nodded.

Hekter's wife beamed. "See!"

Before Aiton could say anything, Korth spoke. "Aye. Of course. My apologies in refusing the help in the first place. Thank you so much; they will be made welcome. They can ride back with us tomorrow."

One by one, at the marchioness's instruction, the servants bowed to Aiton and introduced themselves. Medea, he noticed, had interesting eyes, grey with yellow flakes in them. But other than that, all of them said the same thing, giving him thanks for accepting him into his servitude. What was more interesting to Aiton was seeing the intense inspection of all three of them by Korth, who stood near him, legs apart, arms crossed. After they finished, they stood by Hekter's wife again.

"We will see you all again later at dinner tonight."

"Not me," Conseleigh Iycel said.

"You are leaving so soon?"

"Yes, Marquis Sigurd. I'm sorry. Business calls me elsewhere. Can you arrange for transport to the spaceport? My ship is docked there."

"I will set everything up for you and your men." Hekter Sigurd bowed. "Come dear, let us go. We have many guests to talk to. Conseleigh Iycel, if you will follow me." He gestured away from the crowd of guests, but one of the Hown strode forward, halting him.

"Conseleigh Iycel."

"Yes, Oliver?"

"While we are to accompany you after this wedding, we should conduct one more scrying session with the men still here. It will be much easier given the..." The man coughed into his fist. He scratched his neck. "Given the circumstances." The Hown's eyes flicked to Zarya.

Tundra lifted her eyebrows and rubbed her elbows. Before saying anything, she turned to the marquis and his wife. "I will meet you in a little while after this concludes. Please leave us now." She turned her gaze to Aiton's council. "That goes for you as well."

Aiton was left alone. He shivered as one of the Hown encroached upon him, a black blindfold in hand. *This again. Well, this isn't so bad. After this, they will leave with Conseleigh Iycel, and I'll be free of them. Good. Just one more—*

"Are you ready, Lord Paen?"

"Just like the last times?"

"Yes." The man crouched down in front of Aiton. "Now close your eyes."

"Of course."

Aiton went through the motion again. He smiled and closed his eyes. Zarya's presence warmed him. Footsteps. Hands rubbed Aiton's shoulder. His hair rustled. *Just like last—*

The blindfold pressurized around his face, squeezing his head and keeping his eyes shut. Hands squeezed the top of his arms. His heart quickened.

He struggled and wobbled. "Hey. This is..."

"Do it now," the Hown ordered.

Another man said. "Scan now."

Zarya whinnied, but the rope tying her to the tree held her fast. The hands behind him held him in place. Zarya's feet trampled the ground, but Aiton couldn't see what she was doing. He couldn't see anything.

"Done. We got him."

The blindfold decompressed and fell down around his neck. The Hown pulled the hateful thing away. Aiton stood shivering, as if he had just taken the Plunge himself. *Got him?*

A hand came to his shoulder. "Aiton..."

Aiton blinked, only then realizing it was Conseleigh Iycel, stooped over in front of him.

"The Guardian of the Core will take care of your brother. Don't worry." She stood upright again. "Hown, let's go." She left, ten Hown surrounding her.

Two remained with Aiton, hands on their weapons as they glanced between Aiton and Zarya, who now nuzzled Aiton's cheek. Normally, that would have been enough to warm him, but not then. *Got him?*

Conseleigh Iycel could say all the kind words she wanted, but at the end of the day, Aiton knew words were only water. And Hydro wouldn't allow himself to be taken easily, not when Aiton's safety depended upon it. His Paen pride wouldn't let him. Aiton knew enough about his brother to know that. His heart plummeted to his stomach, tying it in knots, and he fell to his knees. His teeth chattered in a futile attempt to keep him warm. Alone in his thoughts, all the possible outcomes surged through his mind, playing over and over again, keeping him frozen like ice. A single thought formed: had this been the cold Hydro had felt once upon a time?

CHAPTER THIRTY-FIVE

PROPRIETY

Outside of the docking station in Visis, the smell of winter came to Tundra's nose through the mix of rain and snowflakes as the temperature hung at a point of indecision. To some in the south, this would be considered cold, but never for Tundra. She lived for this. For more than half of her life, she had lived in cold far greater than this.

From the skyscrapers and the buzz of hovercrafts that was Visis, she turned her eye to the south, to an expanse of open terrain, save for a few suburbs of the metropolis. Mountains rose as its backdrop, but Mount Volan dwarfed all, turning them to mere hills. Even with the suns at full force and at their zenith, the moon still hung about as well, almost full, but much closer now since the aftermath of Pirini Lilapa. She pursed her lips. *Blasted suns and moon. Because of you, I am here and not with Edwyrd.*

"Where to, Conseleigh Iycel?"

She turned to acknowledge Captain Oliver Thane, a man with broad shoulders and a thick neck. At least, that is how he should have looked. Now, he looked rather worse for wear, although he still had a full head of brown hair. His eyes lacked luster, and bags underneath them spoke of his inability to get a proper night's rest. His shoulders looked meager now; his black uniform didn't fit him the way it always had while in service to Eska.

"We go to the heart of the city. That is where Lady Aprah is. Tell the others to get the hovercrafts from the cargo."

Thane turned around and left her for a few moments. She breathed in the deep smell of winter. Wind blew her hair across her face and lifted her blue dress speckled with white roses. It had laced sleeves down to her wrists. Below the left cuff was her wristlace, which she had restored after her confrontation with Hydro. The fact that he had managed to avoid Hown scouting parties thus far worried her as much as what worried her in Sereya. She would deal with one thing at a time, though; that was all she could do.

When she heard the humming of the hovercrafts behind her, she tucked blue strands of hair behind her one ear and put the other hand on the scimitar at her hip. Thane sat in the driver's seat with a few others from the Hown in the back. She boarded the hovercraft and sat beside Thane. The hovercraft sped off, two others following behind.

"Thane, are you well?" Tundra spoke against the wind. In truth, she knew the answer already, but she wanted to hear it from his lips.

"Truth be told, Conseleigh Iycel, almost all of us Hown have been besieged as of late in some way."

"Have you notified Guardian Eska of this yet?"

"We have." Thane shifted his body and pulled a container from his belt. He rattled the contents inside. "We have medicine on the ships and on our persons, but they haven't done much other than give temporary relief."

"Perhaps we should go get you checked out at a proper apothecary. I'm sure Lady Aprah will have one." Tundra crossed her arms.

"Nothing more than a lack of appetite here and a cough there. I don't believe it is a cause for concern. We will still be able to keep you safe."

"Yes, well, I'm evaluating you and your men. The manhunt for Hydro Paen is the first time Edwyrd has called upon Hown since I became conseleigh."

"And he is running out of room to run."

"Yes. I know. The Sacred Passage. That is quite the precarious situation for your men. Sacred beasts are numerous in that area as well."

"That's why the general is waiting for Paen to come back out."

"That could be weeks. Or months. Maybe even years. What if he is ascending to the top?"

Captain Oliver Thane coughed and laughed into his fist at the same time. "Then it'd be foolish to try to follow him. We let him come out on his own terms. We can determine why he was there in the first place. It's all a game of cat and mouse."

"And that is the game we are about to play with Doctor Cere."

"There is no one better to have on your team, then. Well, maybe Chase."

"He is the tracker, yes?"

Thane nodded. "Our best tracker. That's why he went with the general and I am with you."

"And your expertise, captain?"

"Enforcer." Thane chuckled. "And I hear our work in the north might get a little messy."

"I am quite capable myself, Captain." Tundra shifted in her seat. She had her hands crossed over her chest, her thumbs drumming her arms.

"So, I've heard. But there is no harm in preparing."

"Yes, I suppose you are right." She grabbed ahold of Thane's shoulder. "Go to that hill." She pointed forward.

Thane nodded.

As she rode deeper into the heart of the city, nostalgia took hold of Tundra. In the time of her late husband's rule, Visis had been a town with only a steady population and scant structures. A far cry from the metropolis that swallowed them now. Servant robots pulled their owners on the sidewalks. Hovercrafts rushed around them and above them on the low and high airroads. The city thrived with a vivacious heartbeat.

Visis's prosperity brought a slight smile to Tundra's lips. *At least when one ruler fails, another one succeeds. If only Grime knew that ruling was more than politics and Power, then I wouldn't have to waste my precious breath on him.* Tundra sighed.

She knew the real key to ruling was propriety. If something wasn't done in the proper way, then it marked incompetence, and when incompetence started to show its head, pores would start to show on that hideous face, until finally, that head needed to be cut off. And that is what she was about to do.

After they reached the base of the hill, a guard came out to speak to them. "Conseleigh Iycel, Lady Aprah is awaiting you inside and her receiver is at the top of the hill. There is an electronic ramp for you and your men to the east." He pointed.

"Last time I was here there were stairs."

"Aahh, yes. You can use the stairs instead if you want. I'll have the ramp disabled. Same direction, please." The guard raised his arm, pointing them in the same direction as before.

Thane drove the hovercraft into the compound and parked it at the bottom of the hill. They exited and without another glance at the hill, Tundra began climbing the steps.

"Conseleigh Iycel, are you sure you want to climb them? There are a lot."

Tundra turned around and saw Thane and the other Hown hadn't even begun climbing yet. She laughed. "Of course. I prefer to exercise these old bones before the real action begins. Don't let an old woman like me outperform you now. Let's go." She turned around and began climbing again.

At the top of the staircase stood Gøti Lanam, a man as old as Tundra but nowhere near as physically active as she. Skin drooped around his neck and ears. A clock on his left lapel signified his duty as receiver.

"Conseleigh Iycel, this is certainly a pleasant surprise."

She could tell by his voice he spoke true. "Receiver Lanam, I wish it was under better circumstances that my men and I come here." She strolled to his side and turned around, watching the Hown summit the hill.

Gøti's eyes widened as he saw them. "Hown have come as well?"

"Yes. The task at hand is too large and important for just me. Take me to Olivia."

Gøti gave a quick, nervous nod. "Of course. Lady Aprah is this way." He walked away and then stopped. "Oh, I should mention." He turned around. "You will have to let us scan your body for viruses. Everyone. Sorry, it is only protocol."

Tundra narrowed her eyes. "Of course, no worries." She stepped up onto the metallic circle. A beam went around her. Seconds later, a beep sounded, and a virtual screen appeared in front of her with the word *clear*. She exited and joined Gøti on the other side in front of the double-steel doors. *That is no surprise, but what about them? If they really are carrying a sickness, it might jeopardize things with gathering elites.* She pursed her lips. *How to...*

"Your men, Conseleigh Iycel."

Yes, I know. "Thane," she called out.

He walked forward until he was at the edge of the circular platform. "Yes, Conseleigh Iycel."

"You and your men wait outside."

"Outside, Conseleigh Iycel?"

"Yes. There is no threat here. Our threat is north."

Thane nodded. "As you command, Conseleigh Iycel."

Inside, Gøti led her up a winding staircase to the second floor and then down more corridors. The hallways were wide enough for three people, and electric sconces illuminated certain sections in red light and others in yellow. At last they came to a halt in front of two guards barring access to the room beyond by crossing their halberds.

"Conseleigh Iycel."

Tundra turned around as the click clack of heels came to her. Lady Aprah approached, overshadowed by a giant of a man next to her. Trotting in her wake was her advisor, Jööurr Eldredge, similar in age to Gøti.

"Olivia, you look well." Tundra nodded.

"And I feel well. Forgive me for my tardiness. I just finished a conversation with some of our excavation team in the south. I heard of your arrival and sent Gøti to meet you. I hope he kept you company."

"He did." Tundra smiled.

"Where are your others?"

"I told my men to wait outside." Tundra moved back towards the wall, making space for Lady Aprah.

"How strange." Lady Aprah moved past her towards the guards. "They would have been more than welcome."

"Yes, I'm sure. But it's better to begin acclimating them to the cold now; it's only going to get worse the farther north we go."

"Interesting. You have a few things to discuss with me, correct?"

"A few things, yes."

"Very well."

Tundra followed Lady Aprah into her chambers. Lady Aprah sat on a couch large enough for her advisor and receiver to join her, while Tundra settled into a comfy white leather chair. The large man stood behind them, arms crossed.

"Tea?" Lady Aprah asked.

"I am fine with a glass of ice water, thank you."

She stood and walked over to a waist-high console behind the couch. Tundra could now clearly see the ink on her lean back, made visible by the low back of her dress. Silver, and shaped like curved blades rising along her shoulderblades to meet in an arch at the base of her neck.

"If I may ask, what is the ink on your back?"

Lady Aprah put down the pitcher of water and came back to the sitting area with a full glass in her hand. She gave it to Tundra and then sat down. "Those are the tanfas my mother used while in the rebellion. I wear it as a reminder of her."

"Are you a fighter like she was?"

"Hmm, I am not sure. Horm, what do you believe?" She turned to the large man behind her.

"Quick and lethal is how I be describing you."

"You train with your elites?" Tundra sipped her water.

"Why, of course. Never ask someone to do something that you would never do yourself. That is part of being a good leader."

"I agree. Tell me, have you done the Passage then?"

"No. My advisor and Horm here will not let me. I have *obligations* as Lady."

Tundra feigned a smile. "Of course. How is Cadmar Briggs? I hear from Edwyrd you have given him another chance at being an elite."

"I *have.*" Lady Aprah nodded. "I couldn't deny the Guardian of the Core's request. Cadmar is not with us at the moment. He is still in the process of doing the Passage, actually."

"And where is he at now?"

"Horm?"

"Seventy-two."

Tundra's gaze shifted to Horm. "And how much longer does he have?"

"If he be alive, be at least another three weeks. Maybe more."

"Most likely more," Lady Aprah added. "Horm is using his own record as a gauge. And no one has beaten that yet."

Tundra took a sip of her water, trying to contemplate the brutality of such a test.

Lady Aprah shifted her left leg on top of her right. "Now, why are you here, Conseleigh Iycel?"

Tundra put down her water. "I'll be quick. One reason is actually to discuss Cadmar Briggs with you."

"Oh?" Lady Aprah cocked her head.

"He won one of the Trials while on the Core. A vial of his blood may have been taken from him and that same vial may have fallen into the hands of shapeshifters."

Lady Aprah moved back slightly. "Shapeshifters?" Her voice rose.

"Yes. Edwyrd has reason to believe they are populating our system again."

"I thought they all died with the Conquest," Gøti said.

"It seems now they may have only gone into hiding since then."

"How did you stumble upon this information?"

"One of the other trial contestants saw a shapeshifter himself."

Lady Aprah poked her cheek with her tongue. "Interesting. I will keep that in mind. Thank you. And the other reason?"

"The north."

"What is in the north?"

"An incompetent leader that I have to dismiss, and a man named Doctor Genus Cere who needs permanent removal from his position."

Lady Aprah furrowed her brows. "And how do either of these things concern Gar?"

"I would like to request the aid of your troops."

"Of my troops or of my elites?"

"Elites, forgive me."

Lady Aprah stiffened slightly. "That is a significant request."

"Yes, and my business up north is even more significant. This *doctor*, if you can even call him that, and I have never seen eye to eye on certain issues."

"I thought you brought with you Hown? Surely, they are more suitable than my men here?"

"They are better warriors, yes. But only a few are native to this planet and acclimated to the weather in the north. Your men," Tundra motioned to the man behind her, "have passed the trial to become an elite, correct?"

Lady Aprah narrowed her vision on Tundra. "They have. But why mine and not any of the Paen acqua guards?"

"Yes, well, I just came from the wedding between Marquis Hekter Sigurd and Lauren Puwl. It does not seem right for me to request troops from Acquava at such a joyous and busy time. Now, will you help?"

Lady Aprah leaned back. "Do I have a choice?"

"No, these are direct orders from Guardian Eska. I was just being courteous."

"And how many do you require?"

"Twenty-five should suffice."

Lady Aprah fumbled with the drink in her hand. "That is half of my elites."

"If it makes you feel more content, you can choose which soldiers you give me. I don't need your best. Any of them should be suitable."

"Horm?"

"Yes, my lady."

"Pick twenty-five of our elites to ride north with Conseleigh Iycel."

"My honor, my lady." He banged his shield three times and left the room.

"You will have your men in a couple of days."

"Thank you, Olivia."

"My pleasure, Conseleigh Iycel."

Tundra observed no gritting of the teeth, but she could still sense Lady Aprah's reluctance to obey. Fortunately, she knew her place and her rank. And she knew how to command authority when needed and give respect when asked. That is what made her a leader: propriety. Which was why Tundra had told Eirek to observe Lady Aprah when he had visited. And in her travels with him after the events of Pirini Lilapa, she could sense that he had; and some day, to a new group of conseleigh, to a new set of lords and ladies, that would make a difference.

CHAPTER THIRTY-SIX

QUESTIONS

S ince reuniting with Aiton, a week and a half had passed. During that time, Hydro flew over the seas of the Summer Ocean and into Garian territory. There, the machine flew towards a large mountain that Hydro could only assume was Mount Volan, for it dwarfed all others in comparison. Sensors indicated that another jewel was there, and while Hydro wanted to simply fly the machine directly to the jewel, Anne advised him against it, saying that the Sacred Passage only allowed those with Power to traverse its territory. Anyone or anything without Power would be subject to the onslaught of creatures roaming there, and that included Dr. Cere's ship. So, against his better judgment, he left the ship outside of the Sacred Passage and entered, ready as he could be to navigate its wide expanse and massive chasm he saw from above. And, if legends were true, the beasts that roamed within the Passage itself. .

Before entering the Passage, he called Victor Zigarda and notified him of the next jewel's location. He made sure to mention the expected delay in contact due to the travel requirements. Lord Zigarda had suggested he take the ship directly there and not waste time, but Hydro ignored him. Anne, Hydro felt, offered better information, and so he would find the jewel on foot. By himself. No machines except for the small handheld radar that could hone in on the location more accurately.

While traversing through the Sacred Passage, he met a variety of creatures such as centaurs, golems, and even trees that held leaves with the faces of human beings. On an unusually hot day, he rested for a bit in the shadow of a boulder, only to awake as the boulder rose to its feet. Hydro scrambled away to avoid being trampled by the golem. With Anne's help, Hydro bypassed a centaur's riddle, though he believed that he could have done it by himself, and the other creatures had left him alone. Still, even with that good fortune, it took him a week to stand before the feet of giants. True giants. Giants that would have likely crushed his ship with their massive earthen clubs if he had tried to fly C-Bot within the perimeter.

These mountains had stepped out from the face of the mountain, causing it to shake and bringing Hydro to his knees. With their presence came an earthy smell that seemed to pour from their cracked skin. When all four giants had stepped out of the mountainside, the rocks stopped falling down around him.

And as the first giant spoke in a loud, low voice that reminded Hydro of the seahorn at home, he could do nothing but stare. But while the seahorn signaled an advancing enemy, he had no idea what any of the sound that came through the giant's lips meant. Hydro could only cover his ears and cower as his skull rattled.

You need to cast the Power of earth, Hydro Paen.

Hydro blinked at Anne's appearance next to him. "How do you know?" he shouted.

I am older than the giants, Hydro Paen. I know more languages than they do.

"Do giants not have First Blood?"

These giants were not born in Gladima, but they are loyal servants to my master all the same.

"Your father controls giants?"

He controls all creatures and animals, Hydro Paen. Now, cast earth.

Hydro frowned. Who exactly was her father? Could Zas really be such a powerful magician that he could control animals?

Cast earth. Anne's eyes glowed a dark black.

Instinctively, Hydro said. *"Maa."*

He raised the spire of earth to the height of the giant's knees. The giant responded, offering more words that Hydro couldn't understand, and then lowered his hand.

Board his hand, Hydro Paen, you have passed his test.

Hydro didn't move. He scanned the giant up and down and took a deep breath—that he immediately regretted. The sharp, overwhelming smell of pure earth flooded his lungs, and he turned to the side, trying to retch. When the sensation subsided slightly, he brought his shirt up to cover his nose and mouth, preferring the stench of sweat and unwashed clothing to what had just hit him.

It gets better the higher we get.

Hydro straightened and turned back around. Not needing any more encouragement, Hydro stepped onto the palm that could crush him at any moment. The giant lifted him up, and Hydro took the opportunity to inhale some pure air as it rushed past him. When the giant's hand stopped moving, a second giant spoke.

Anne translated. *"Vesi."*

Hydro called forth a geyser that he pushed upwards to the giant's knee. Just like before, the giant offered his hand for Hydro to step upon and then raised him up to the feet of the next giant. This time, as he cast the necessary spells of fire and electricity with ease, he couldn't help but think about someone else standing in his place. *Did the commoner climb Mount Volan successfully? He must have; I saw him in Mendeck. But how did he make it up the mountain? Did he do it alone? Could he understand the giants?*

At the top, Hydro stepped out onto a ledge. And on the ledge, he found only destruction: remnants of a palace that could have been beautiful if fully intact. Half shattered walls bore scorch marks. Pillars of gold and silver and copper lay broken and strewn over the mountaintop. Some pillars were still intact, valiantly holding up portions of a second floor and a mostly destroyed third-floor balcony. Above the third floor, a gable still had one glass window fully intact, but two others were broken. The remains of those windows were now shards on the mountaintop, sparkling in the suns' light.

With heavy breaths and heavy steps, he walked forward, getting a closer look at the aftermath of whatever chaos had been unleashed. As he drew closer, he could clearly make out the image on the unbroken window—an unknown man in a suit of armor with a great sword by his side and wings behind him. Words were written underneath of his figure, but the suns' glare made them impossible to read. Hydro stopped. A sparkle reflected from the balcony. He pulled out his radar and noticed he was practically standing on top of the bleep. *That has to be the jewel.*

Determined to get to the third floor, he walked to the entrance of the mansion. "Who lived here?"

Each of the Twelve called this their home.

"Is this Axiumé?"

No. This is only halfway to Axiumé.

"Only halfway," Hydro muttered. He looked up at the part of the mountain the palace was built into. It extended even farther above, clouds obscuring its supposed peak from view. "What is at the top?"

Even I do not know that.

Something tightened in Hydro's chest as he realized the true immensity of such a mountain. Mount Klaff had been enormous, yes, but Hydro had already traveled so far and he had only managed to make it halfway up Mount Volan. How much more difficult would the rest of the journey be if he wanted to reach the summit?

The jewel, Hydro Paen. Find it.

Hydro shook himself free of such thoughts. He bypassed one fallen pillar and then climbed over another one, which blocked him from opening one side of the double doors. With a grunt, he pulled open the other door just enough to peek his head inside. Sunlight infiltrated the vestibule where statues upon statues had collapsed upon one another.

Hydro clicked his tongue and pulled his head back. *I'll have to find another way up.* Hydro climbed back over the pillars, understanding now that he would need to climb the slabs of earth and boulders that looked like a broken avalanche in order to reach the third level.

As he traced a probable route with his gaze, he asked, "What happened here?" He began his ascent on an inclined slab of earth. His eyes flicked to the moon; he reached out with his arm, wanting to touch it. "Why is the moon so close?"

Pirini Lilapa.

"The Curse happened here?"

I only imagine it must have for such a beautiful place to be ruined.

Hydro jumped to another slab. "It looks like the Twelve fought here. Was it their fighting that moved the moon closer?"

Yes.

"Are they really so strong to move objects so large at their whim?"

That Power is nothing compared to the power to create and to destroy. To bond and to grant wishes.

Hydro hoisted himself up onto another slab of stone. "Only the Ancients Lyoen and Bane have those abilities, yes?"

All of the Ancients have those abilities, Hydro Paen.

With one hand on another slab of earth, ready to pull himself up, he paused. "What do you mean, *all?*"

You ask too many questions, Hydro Paen. Get the jewel so we can leave.

Hydro clambered up to another level and traversed the rocky landslide until he could go no farther. He was eye-level with the third floor. A purple jewel sat on the veranda, sparkling in the sunlight. He would have to jump to it. Giving himself room to accelerate, he backed up and then sprinted and jumped, fingers reaching for the railing. It crumbled, giving way under his weight. Hydro scrambled for something to hold on to. From this height, if he fell, it wouldn't kill him, but broken bones would be likely. Using the strength in his shoulders and triceps, he pushed himself up and over the ledge, then collapsing onto his stomach.

He smiled, then laughed, through his heavy breathing. *I did it.* After briefly reveling in his accomplishment, he pushed himself to his feet and walked over to the amethyst, which lay amongst shards of stained glass from the gable above. After he placed the jewel in his satchel, he bent down and picked up a few of the shards, then tried to piece them together like a puzzle. He gave up after a few minutes, but his efforts showed him they had also been portraits of people in great suits of armor, like the one that remained, and he wondered who they had been.

Arms across his chest, he looked up at the last stained-glass portrait. The face wasn't familiar. Now he could see the writing clearly. *"Ajid Volintasey Fuan."* *What language is that?* Hydro tried pronouncing the words.

May we find each other again.

"What?"

Anne stared up at the image. *That is what the words mean.* She looked at Hydro and smiled and then returned her gaze to the gable. *It is beautiful, is it not?*

"I don't understand. I don't know who that is."

You will soon enough, Hydro Paen. Soon enough, everyone will remember.

CHAPTER THIRTY-SEVEN

LOST IN LORE

A fter the initial bout with Ethen, Eirek's days had passed in quick succession, one after the other. He had messaged both Linn and Cain after that training session to see how they fared, and also to glean how much longer before their two armies collided. Linn was almost at Edgefield, and Cain was approaching Ambit. In a week, the only thing that would stand between them would be the firelands of Kane, but Eirek presumed that both would want to avoid those and would choose to skirt around it to the north. While he had never actually been to the firelands, he had heard countless stories of the savagery of the people of Kane while growing up. Even his uncle had woven a few stories about them as well, although his were always much lighter in nature. The Song of Fire was an entire ballad sung in celebration of Syf's victory over the Kane riders every New Year's Festival. In a month's time, the forces would collide.

To his surprise, though, both of his friends seemed more interested in his well-being and time with Eska rather than the upcoming battle. Both had asked him how he fared and more questions than Eirek had anticipated about Eska's training regimen. And if Eska had been fair. Eirek told them his thoughts, mentioning briefly the missions Eska had given the conseleigh without informing Eirek. He spoke also of the hunt for Hydro and the blood scrying. Out of all the things Eska had done recently, forcing Aiton to allow his blood to be used against his brother was the one Eirek thought most cruel, though he understood the necessity. Cain and Linn had both seemed rather disheartened by the end of the telecommunication, and Eirek assumed it was because of his lackluster stories. Cain, Eirek knew, lived for stories of heroes and monsters and dreamed of becoming worthy of a story of his own, so it was no surprise that by the time Eirek had finished, he seemed distant, as if Eirek had lacked the storytelling skill to motivate Cain and fire him up for what was to come. Or perhaps it was just Cain sinking back into the reality of the situation. The same had happened with Linn.

Both conversations gave him the impetus he needed to train harder than ever, wanting nothing more than to best Ethen in battle. If he did so, perhaps it would show Guardian Eska that he was competent enough to be on his own and that he could start his twelve years of apprenticeship training in the other nations. Then, under his influence, he could stop the war from happening and the unnecessary bloodshed that came with it.

This new goal gave him a sense of purpose and identity. When not practicing against Ethen, he practiced against other holograms in the habitat arena, and when his body needed a break, he would refuel it with ard leaves and train more. Each night, he would collapse on his bed, ready to begin the monotony again the next day.

It was within one of these days that Eirek found himself standing over Ethen, sword angled down, pointing at the other man's chest. He had caught Ethen off-guard with a show of Power first, creating a fissure where Ethen had been standing. As expected, Ethen had hopped to the side to avoid being swallowed, but landed in a small puddle Eirek had created. This tactic had taxed his strength, but it had allowed him to create it without drawing attention to the puddle, for he didn't pull it from the stream next to the court, but from his own body.

When Ethen splashed into the water, Eirek activated his ring and said, *"Salama."* Electricity flowed up Ethen's body, shocking him, the conductivity increased by the lance in his hand. It fell out of his grasp. Eirek lunged forward and swept the lance away with his foot, and then brought a knee into Ethen's bent over body, which sent him sprawling backwards. And that was that. It was the quickest victory Eirek had ever won, and it was in no doubt due to the incalculable training sessions against holograms in the habitat arena where he had seen how past conseleigh used Power in the most interesting of manners. One conseleigh rode the earth like a wave of water, using it as a transportation construct rather than a combative move, maneuvering through the city streets arena effortlessly. While engaging another on Pyre-like conditions, Eirek had been surprised when he was quickly drowned in a pool of water. He had evaluated that match over and over in his mind, until finally coming to the conclusion that the hologram had drawn upon its own virtual sweat to cast such a spell when the source for the Power was otherwise nonexistent. And this had given Eirek the idea of testing similar limitations with Power.

Eirek extended a hand down to Ethen and pulled him up. Ethen blinked a few times at the hand before finally accepting it.

Eska strolled over to the court, clapping his hands. "Very good, Eirek. Very good. You have improved dramatically over the past week."

Eirek beamed.

"It's time Ethen trains you in zircha weapons now."

Eirek deflated. "Am I not ready to go live in the twelve nations?"

"You believe because you beat Ethen once that you are ready to leave here and live abroad?"

Eirek nodded. "I do. That was our fastest fight yet. I've learned to utilize Power efficiently. I've learned to combine it with sword techniques. My footwork is improved. I'm not predictable. I've—"

Eska swiped the air. "Point taken, Apprentice Mourse. But do you think you are ready?"

"I already told you that I am."

"Do you believe that truly?"

Eirek puffed out his chest. "Yes."

"Answer a few questions, then. Where is the Academy of Power located?" Eska paused, raising his eyebrow at Eirek's silence. "What is devil's-sand and how do you avoid its snare?" Eska paused again, waiting for Eirek to reply, but he had no answer. "How do individuals in Lurid travel? Still nothing?" Eska raised an eyebrow. "How about one from your own planet, then. How did the land of Kane come into existence?"

Eirek blushed. He should know how Kane had come into existence, but he had only ever learned what Kane was and who populated it, not its origin. Eirek cleared his throat. "What does any of that matter?"

"It matters, Eirek, because you may come into situations that aren't battles. You may encounter enemies that aren't humans. You will encounter nature. You will encounter culture. You will encounter *life* when you leave here. And you will have to live, travel, and work alongside the citizens of the nation you live in each and every year. Not everything in life is a battle, and in some battles swords, are useless." Eska had been pacing around Eirek this whole time, but then stopped in front of him. "Tell me, have you ever heard this expression? '*The pen is mightier than the sword.*'"

Eirek shook his head. Instinctively, he looked down at his own sword, wondering how a pen could ever outmatch it.

Eska laughed. "It's a Mistralian saying. It means that sometimes the best weapon we have is our words."

"But words are water?"

Eska chuckled at that. "The Acquavans surely think so. And that is why the pen is mightier, for it implies you have to write down your intent, and by doing so, you are held accountable. You have to commit to it. Or, at least, you should. And that is why books can be so powerful. Because they are full of written words. I suggest you read more about the other nations so that you have a foundational understanding of the life in each before stepping foot in them. This way you can focus on building rapport with the general citizens and the powerful alike, touring the entirety of the nation, and truly understanding its identity—the good and the bad—instead of asking a constant barrage of questions based upon each nuance you find. Once you have a basic understanding of each nation, Eirek, then I think you will be ready for the next step." Eska turned his attention to Ethen. "You and Eirek will begin practicing with zircha weapons come tomorrow. I want his reflexes as sharp as his mind is going to become."

Ethen bowed his head. "It will be my pleasure, my guardian."

That day had humbled Eirek. For all of his advancement in combat, he had neglected other aspects of his training. Of course, he should have rudimentary understandings of the various nations before stepping foot in them. It made sense. But in another way, Eirek wondered if Eska was denying his request merely to deny—to remind Eirek who was in charge. Would he do that? Eirek didn't like to think so, so instead he got lost in the lore of the other nations, replacing his long hours in the habitat arena with long hours in the library. After an initial scanning of the copious volumes of literature in the library, it was obvious to Eirek that this would take longer than a month. Despite what he felt, he would have to find some way to help Cain and Linn from the Core.

Knowing he had already given Linn advice, and that advice had led her to declare war with Epoch, Eirek decided it best to focus his efforts first on Epoch. He didn't want to appear contradictory and weak to Linn, and growing up in Cresica had given him a decent understanding of life there. Nor did he think there was anything he might say that would sway her from her course.

Like Cresica, Epoch was rich with history. Eirek immersed himself with the lore of the Sage's Valley and how the Zas Labyrinth came to be. He read about the nation's wood trade and how the most sacred tree in Epoch was the lone Yggdrasil tree in Ambit. There had been another one in Lorian, but legends claimed that it had been set aflame and cut off at the trunk, toppling over to the land of Kane. That widened Eirek's eyes. *Of course.*

He was ashamed he hadn't thought of it before, but if Cresica and Epoch were going to go to war, they would have to cross the lands of Kane, or, most likely, skirt around to the north. Still, perhaps there was a hint somewhere in the nature and myths of Kane. How did it, in fact, come to be? Answering that question would give him another shot at impressing Eska. The only thing he knew about Kane, though, was the song he had always heard during the New Day Parade in Syf.

That is where he would start. He dashed back to the computer mainframe and searched for the keywords: *Cresica New Day Parade.* Within seconds, a handful of book titles came up with selected pieces of text that fit his search request displayed as well. He scanned each, finally deciding to go with a book called: *Cultural Traditions of the Planets: Agrost Edition.* That is, after all, what Eska wanted him to learn. After he selected his choice, a small lightbeam emanated from the device and he followed it to the appropriate shelf and book.

He settled into a comfortable chair and skimmed the table of contents until he found the section he wanted.

The New Day Parade is a celebration that occurs at the turning of the year in Syf. While other nations simply recognize this day as the beginning of a new year, the citizens of Syf see it as a chance to pay homage to the founder of their city, Syf, who, with the strength of Tomahawke, defeated the raiders of Kane who were stretching their influence wide upon the plains of Cresica, after having mysteriously appeared there not even a decade before.

Eirek continued reading, trying to glean information that he didn't already know from his history classes in school. Everyone knew the reason Cresicans celebrated the New Day Parade, but that wasn't what Eirek was searching for. He wanted to know more about the battles leading to the celebration. Who exactly were the people of Kane? How did the people come to be?

After another hour of reading the boring text, Eirek gave up and tried a different search. This time, he entered: *Kane Cresica Syf War.* New results showed, along with some of the previous results. One title interested him, a title he had passed over previously due to its lack of relevance: *One Hundred Tales.*

Eirek shifted his weight to his left hip. "Where have I seen that title before?"

"Stuck on something, dear?"

Eirek turned his head. Dina, the librarian, polished one of the tables with a cloth.

"No. No. I'm okay." He waved.

"I find nothing better than immersing myself in a good story whenever I'm feeling lost. A good story makes us forget about this world and transports us to a whole different one."

"Yeah." Eirek nodded. He knew that already.

"Lots of good heroes in those stories. Mmmhmmm." She hummed.

Heroes. Hmmm... Eirek selected the title and followed the tracing line to the book. As soon as he plucked it out of the shelf, he recognized the cover. *Cain's book.* He had remembered Cain briefly flashing it to him while they were on their way to the Core.

Feeling a little more hopeful, he plopped down, opened the book, scanned the contents and finally turned to a story called *The Song of Fire.*

The first thing Eirek saw was the picture of a tall man with fiery red hair. In one hand, he held a lance in his hands, raised to the sky. In the other hand, he gripped the reins of a horse but that had a mane of fire.

The story itself spun a tale about how a nation of fire grew from the ashes of an Yggdrasil tree that mysteriously caught flames one day. Wind blew the ashes westward. Soon the tree had burned so severely that it couldn't support itself anymore and toppled over to the west. Wherever the ashes and embers touched, the earth turned to charred and burnt land, and the animals became animals of fire. The tree sank into the ground, causing that area to have the same burnt coloring that the tree had. It was in the aftermath of this chaos that a group of people rose up, like a phoenix from the ashes, and they came to be known as the Kaneans. Brains afire, and with fire in their hearts, a man named Andrej led them. With the confidence of a True King and a spear that could slice through anything, he proceeded to conquer more and more land, marking their territory in ash. Plains that were once green soon became barren.

"True King?" Eirek muttered to himself. He put a finger on the page to not lose his place and flipped back to the start of the story. He stared at the image for a while and noticed a few little details: a feather necklace of burnt orange hues and a spear made not of wood, but of something metallic and, most curious of all, depicted with a faint amethyst sheen. Eirek's eyes widened. *An Ether Weapon? Is that?* Eirek shifted in his chair, immediately wanting to find Eska and show him his discovery, but he didn't have the complete picture yet, so he continued reading.

Wishing to stop this pestilence, a man called Syf had asked members of the Twelve for strength and valor in battle. And he received it. His forces halted the momentum of the Kaneans, and he chased them all the way back to a city called Edgefield. There, in his home territory, Andrej's spirit revitalized. He challenged the man called Syf to a champion's battle. The winner would decide the loser's fate.

The two men, Andrej and Syf, fought one another unaided. The story, told from Andrej's point of view, showed him clearly winning against Syf now that he was back on his own terrain. However, things changed when Syf cast a great spell of earth to blanket the felsic floor, transforming it into mere earth, multiplying his strength and syphoning Andrej's. The battle ended with Andrej's forfeit when he was kicked to the ground and his lance was ripped away from his grasp by Syf's axe.

Andrej's feather necklace now exposed, Syf hesitated over it. He then showed his own necklace, a brown feather with barbs of green spotted throughout the vane. The two talked, then, and Syf let the man live and returned his weapon to him under the condition that they would never again try to take Cresican lands, otherwise Syf or his descendants would make sure their lineage ceased to exist. Andrej returned to Kane defeated but with his life still intact.

Eirek flipped back to the front of the story once more. Transfixed by the image on the left-hand page, Eirek traced his fingers over it. He squinted at the drawing, trying to dissect as much detail as he could. A few things were clear from the story. First, the man Andrej had an Ether Weapon, and if Syf could match him in battle, it meant that he, too, had one. He had most likely received it from the Twelve when he asked for their Power. Next, the story noted that Andrej only grew more powerful in his homeland, the firelands of Kane. There he fought like a True King, whatever that was. But Syf had been able to match him, and both had feather necklaces. Did that make them both True Kings?

Eirek slumped again in his chair, ruminating about everything he had learned. But as he turned the story over and over in his mind, he knew what he needed to do. Without a second thought, he picked up the book, making sure to keep one finger on the page he needed, and took it from the library. In the lobby, he rode the lift to the third floor and marched towards Guardian Eska's chambers. He knocked on the door and Guardian Eska opened it.

"Eirek, what can I do for—"

Eirek bypassed Guardian Eska and put the book on the table. He pointed to the story he had just read, turned, and said, "I want to know more about True Kings."

CHAPTER THIRTY-EIGHT

THE STUMP

Ambit was a city of rare, antique beauty stemming from the large Yggdrasil tree that stood as the unique city's backdrop and was the sole tree on the lands of the estate of Marquis Edym Langol. Since leaving Castle Thoth, his father's forces had cut through the forest and through the Sage's Valley to meet up with Marquis Soren Mesh at Redding, and in total it had taken them two weeks to get to Ambit. Marquis Mesh brought his army from the Vale, and now, at nearly full capacity, they were a force of ten thousand. Lorian, once they arrived in another few days, would add perhaps another thousand or more. While the soldiers finished gathering supplies from the city, Cain and his father sat underneath the shade of the Yggdrasil tree on Marquis Langol's estate.

"Certainly an impressive sight, is it not?"

Cain got caught looking up at the massive boughs that held vibrant green leaves and were home to a menagerie of birds. Keeping focused on the tree, he replied, "Yes, there is certainly nothing like it in Thoth."

"It is one of a kind, Prince Evber. I mean that quite literally now. The other in Lorian is just a stump."

Cain knew that quite well, even though he had only been there once. But he would never forget. He looked at Marquis Langol. "I have heard."

"You did more than just hear, Son. That is where you killed your first man."

"Is that so?"

Cain shifted in his seat underneath the intense scrutiny of Marquis Langol.

"Yes. When Lorian was having its problems years ago, I took Cain along with me to clear up the mess. Surely you remember the raids?"

"I do." Marquis Langol nodded.

"Well, I wanted Cain to see what happens when you let something such as that go unanswered, so we took the Kanean captives to the stump and sliced off their heads then and there."

"What poetic justice, destroying them on the tree they themselves destroyed," the marquis said.

"How did they destroy it?" Cain asked.

"They set fire to it, of course, and while it burned, they chopped it down. It's said the tree fell on their land and thus turned it to what it is today, the firelands."

The story seemed highly unlikely, but Cain wouldn't say that; his father needed Marquis Langol's support, his city, his supplies, and, most importantly, his men if they were to win against the large Cresican numbers. But if he could ask, he would have wanted to know how it was possible to even chop down such a gigantic tree like the Yggdrasil tree, much less do so while it was on fire.

"Are the roots of the Yggdrasil trees really intertwined?"

"What gives you the idea?"

"Your sigil, Marquis Langol."

The older man adjusted his glasses and patted his flabby chest as if he had forgotten about the sigil he had adopted for the seventy years of his life. He looked down his hooked nose at his blue tunic and saw the brown trees with intertwining roots. "It seems that they are." He laughed and looked at Cain. "I do highly doubt that to be accurate, though. They are big, but I do not believe they are so big. But, two trees look much better than one tree and a stump." He chortled this time, as if this was the funniest thing he had said in years.

"It certainly does, Edym." Cain's father echoed the laughter.

Cain didn't know if his father truly believed that Marquis Langol was funny or he laughed out of respect for the old man. Trying to help his father, Cain offered up a small smile.

"How does this one stay alive?" Cain looked up again. A bird flew out from under its cover. In its position now, the tree shaded all of Marquis Langol's estate, and even minor parts of the city, though most citizens still dwelled under the suns' rays.

"Father," a voice called out, "the preparations for the city and for the army are now finished."

Cain readjusted his position and looked out into the shadows of the estate. From behind a sliding glass door strolled a man of perhaps forty years. He had wavy, short hair like Marquis Langol that bounced with each step of his aggressive pace towards them. The air he cut through blew back his cape, though the Yggdrasil brooch at his neck kept it secure. He wore a long-sleeved brown shirt with cuffs of the same electric blue as the sigil on his chest.

"Joshua, it is good to see things are ready." Marquis Langol stood up and brushed off the imaginary leaves on his knees, then looked at Cain. "That is a story for another day. It will have to wait. Your army is ready."

Cain stood alongside his father. When he did so, he felt like a giant. He towered over everyone present by at least half a foot. He walked with the others around the castle's walls until they reached the front of the estate. A turnabout with a water fountain, a large road wide enough for two hovercrafts, and a line of trees with purple leaves marked the elegance and extravagance of the Langol family.

Marquis Langol shook each of their hands. "Thank you for being such good company. Daven, I am saddened that I cannot ride into war with you this time, but I will keep Ambit free from the clutches of those Cresicans. *That* I will guarantee you. I may not have much strength in these bones to hold a sword, but I can conjure Power as well as Guardian Eska."

Cain bit his lip. He never had spent so much time with Marquis Langol before, but with every passing minute, he noticed that the stories kept getting grander and grander. The last one had almost caused him to laugh at its absurdity. Cain looked at Joshua, who blushed over his father's remarks.

"Your company was grand as well," Cain's father said, easily maintaining his composure.

"I am glad you think that." Marquis Langol nodded. "Joshua will accompany you to Lorian and into battle. Although not as excellent a companion as I, he will prove more capable in fighting, won't you, Son?" The old man shook his son's shoulders.

"My duty is your duty," Joshua replied, bowing. "If you are ready, let us be off." He turned and walked towards the hovercraft parked on the roundabout. He hopped in the driver's seat and waited for Cain and his father to board.

Cain shuffled to the back, letting his father sit in the co-pilot's seat. The hovercraft started. Dust flew up around them. By the time it settled, they were already one hundred paces down the road that led to the estate. While they drove, he never looked forward, preferring to continue to stare at the Yggdrasil tree behind him.

The day after, while en route to Lorian, Cain's father had received word from their advisor, Nathan Alaois, that he was on his way to Mistral for Senator Numos's meeting. Cain's father related to Nathan some of the information Cain had gleaned from a call with the apprentice while on their way to Ambit. Cain didn't know if sharing the information with his father would be beneficial or not, or how doing so might affect Eirek or Guardian Eska, but he had found himself questioning the Guardian of late, after everything he had heard.

Two days later, they arrived in Lorian, a town about half of Ambit's size overseen by Baron Roger Yung, a tall, thin man who had been born in Chaon but grew up in Epoch. That fact was made clear by the shape of his eyes, along with the absence of facial hair—except for the thin beginnings of a mustache—and a skin tone that wasn't quite Epochian. The baron's father had been of the Chaon descent, but he had married an Epochian baron's daughter who had been studying the Adored arts in Qotia. She had two younger brothers, and when it was discovered that neither of them could cast, and that her son could, the new family had moved to Epoch to begin grooming the boy who would take his grandfather's place. Due to this history, Baron Yung knew much about the adored arts, he could cast Power, and his superior privilege in being raised lavishly made him seem rather overqualified for such a position as Baron despite his true nationality.

And it was this air of privilege, Cain believed, that was the cause of Joshua's increased angst and authoritativeness since arriving in Lorian the day before. The heir to the marquisship in Ambit constantly reminded Baron Yung of his place and made sure to use the baron's surname whenever possible, as if the baron had forgotten his own skin color and accent, to ostracize him. Such reminders, Cain thought, were petty.

"My forces here in Lorian can scout the northern passage outside of Kane's borders. There are plenty of able scouts in my command, as we use them constantly for Kane," Baron Yung said.

"Any force has capable scouts, Yung, but you should send your own."

It was the evening war session, and now that they had all of their forces assembled, it was crucial they meet and discuss the next part of the strategy. Through it all, Baron Yung had proved rather thoughtful and capable, and his suggestions had sat well with Cain's father and the other marquises and generals in the room.

"Of course. My apologies, Marquis Langol. I will send out ten of my scouts on the morrow, but I feel compelled to add that, after our conversation last night, I feel as though our plan is missing something."

"What is that?" Cain's father asked.

"Our strategy revolves around the Cresicans thinking that we will join forces at Ambit, and not here due to the size of the city. This is a rather faulty fallacy."

"Why do you believe that?"

"Any company has scouts, and if theirs do not see a large force at Ambit or outside of Ambit, then I believe they will look elsewhere and find our troops down in Lorian."

"Go on." Cain's father nodded and narrowed his brows.

"So far, we've received word that Lady Clayse's army is at Edgefield. Chances are they are going to go around Kane to the north, so it may be better to have a distraction force at the fork between Lorian and Ambit. A large enough force to make it appear to be our full strength. Once this force is spotted by our enemy, they will report back. It is my belief that they may rush to attack. At this time, the distraction force can go north to Ambit and lead the Cresicans in that direction, and then the bulk of our forces in Lorian can surround them from behind. With such chaos, the war would not last longer than perhaps a few weeks."

Cain's father examined the sprawled map. Cain knew exactly what his father thought about: chess. His father had told Cain once that he had won a chess tournament in Epoch at the age of ten, and he believed it had parallels to warfare. Cain liked the game and was good at it, but he liked books and the stories they contained more.

"Joshua, how many of your father's troops still remain at Ambit?"

"A little more than a third of our force remains stationed there."

Cain's father traced the map with his fingers. "If we maintain our strategy in seizing the Triangle Islands with our ships currently en route from Seawood, then Ambit would make finer sense in the restocking of supplies and could provide vital reinforcements if needed. I believe the bait would work..." Cain's father looked at Joshua. "Joshua, you will take a third of our total force and set up camp outside Ambit."

"So, we will be the bait?" Joshua looked at Cain's father sternly, the black wavy hair falling down in front of his face.

"Being from Ambit, you know its terrain better than anyone. Also, you will have the most open line of communication with your father as you retreat to Ambit once you see the bulk of the Cresican forces."

Joshua's frown grew. "You are asking us to lead them to a nearly defenseless city."

"That is why our timing must be perfect. We will wait and provide back up, assuming that you do what you are supposed to. We will initiate the assault from the rear before your city is in danger."

Joshua glared at Baron Yung, who did not return any of the sentiment. When unsatisfied with this, Joshua said, "With such a large force I believe it necessary to not be the sole commander of the troop."

"Of course. The barons from the surrounding cities of Dadger, Redding, and here can accompany you as well. That should be enough to be convincing." Cain's father looked at the barons, who gave an acknowledging nod. "Roger, I believe it is necessary for you to stay here, so send someone in your stead."

The heads of the other barons turned to his father's words. Joshua whipped around when he heard the disparity.

In a gentle, inquisitive voice, Baron Yung said, "My lord?"

"You have contact with the scouts that you will be sending from Lorian. We will need that information if we are to time this strategy effectively."

"Should those reports not come to my camp, my lord?" Joshua asked.

"Your main goal is to be a decoy force. Your intel is not as crucial as the ones that we need to gather."

"But to be blind is to die in a situation such as this."

"Then you can send scouts from Ambit. You said yourself that everyone has their own, correct?"

"I..." Joshua sighed and looked down. "Yes, my lord." He nodded and gave Baron Yung one last glare before wiping the disdain from his face and pushing it down into a closed stance with arms crossed against his chest.

"Good. Then it is settled. Sleep well tonight, for we begin tomorrow."

When Cain stepped outside after the meeting had finished, he stepped out into a gust of hot air. Even though the suns were descending, they would still be out for another few hours. Cain took this opportunity to stroll around the encampment stationed on the northern edge of the city. While in the midst of this stroll, he cocked his head and raised an eyebrow when the telecommunicator on his wrist vibrated. *Eirek?*

Cain immediately accepted the call. "Eirek, what may I—"

"Where are you?" Eirek burst in. "I need to speak with you."

Cain's glanced around. "Perhaps it is best if I talk somewhere a little more private. Can you excuse me for a moment?"

"Sure."

Cain maneuvered his way to the outskirts of the camp. He wiped his sweaty hands on the sides of his pants, wondering if Eirek had found out about the meeting on Mistral. Did he know Cain had supplied information against Eska? Would Eirek hold that against him? Cain forced himself to take a deep breath. Making sure no one else was around, Cain held the watch back up to his face. "We are in Lorian right now. What is it?"

"Do you know anything about True Kings?"

Cain shook his head. "What are you talking about? True Kings?"

"That necklace you wear. Where did you get it?"

Instinctively, Cain tugged at the collar of his shirt, pulling out the feather necklace. Its fiery hues were exaggerated by the suns. "My mother gave this to me when I was really young."

"Your... your mother? Has she ever been to Kane before?"

Cain shook his head. "Not that I am aware of. The closest any of us has ever been is Lorian. Why are you asking?"

"I..." Eirek fumbled over his words. "It's stupid. Never mind."

"Eirek, tell me. You seem confused. What is this all about?"

Eirek sighed. "I read something the other day in the library and thought of you. It was called the Song of Fire. It was a story in that book you brought with you to the Trials."

"*One Hundred Tales*?"

"Yeah," Eirek admitted. "The man on the front cover looks like you and has a necklace just like yours."

"I do not remember that."

"Andrej. He was tall. He used a spear. And he had fiery hair and a fiery necklace. Just like you. He... he was from Kane."

"Are you suggesting that—"

Eirek put his hands up, calming Cain's rising voice. "I know. I know. It's stupid. Just, ever since that day in the lobby after the Trials, you seemed lost. Like you didn't know who you were. I... well the man just reminded me of you. I thought..."

"That I was a Kanean?" Cain scoffed. "My family is of the purest blood. My family has been ruling for over six-hundred..."

"Yes. I know. I know. Sorry. Anyway, I have to go. I have zircha weapon training. Goodbye, Cain."

Cain ended the communication. "Pah." Bristling, Cain clasped his hands behind his back and continued walking, trying to blow off the steam stemming from Eirek's infernal implication. "I couldn't possibly be." Cain shook his head and laughed at how ridiculous that would be.

Thoughts in constant flux, he let his feet take him and his mind follow aimlessly as if it were the shadow on the ground being dragged along. He meandered without a destination in mind, or thought he did, but his feet, it seemed, had an intent of their own, bringing him to the only other place he had been in Lorian—the stump.

Cain fought the urge to turn back, for to do so would be to admit that what he had done the last time he was there was wrong, and as the saying went, "*A guilty man is his own executioner.*" So, instead of turning around, Cain walked up a slight incline towards the stump.

Being nearly one hundred meters wide, the stump occupied the vast majority of the whole cliff. It looked just as dilapidated to his eyes now as it had at the age of twelve. It wasn't a clean-cut stump. It was jagged, with the tallest portions reaching Cain's waist. It was like an alcove of smaller stumps attached to the large base, and some of those smaller stumps were clean cut and some were rather conical or jagged. But the one he remembered, the one that Cain walked to in between the other jutting parts, that one was clean cut.

To his fortune, no memories resurfaced of that day twelve years ago. He didn't feel his father's axe in his hands as he imagined he would have. He didn't see the man's head on the stump or hear the voice pleading. And there was no feeling of blood spraying across his face with each of the three blows it had required to sever the man's head. He didn't want to test his luck, however, and avoided going too close. Instead, he approached the edge of the cliff. After the executions, they had tied ropes between jagged pieces of wood and the headless bodies, then thrown the bodies over the cliff, leaving them to dangle. No trace of the ropes remained.

Cain took a seat at the edge of the trunk and looked out over the land of Kane. In the dying light, it was nearly a land of total blackness, as if the soil was made of charcoal. Cain wondered if it had always been like that or, like Marquis Langol had said, if the burning tree had fallen that way and some sort of magic in the tree had caused the land to stay charred.

When another warm breeze hit Cain, it compelled him to sing. He sang a song he didn't know he knew, and the breeze carried it to strangers and animals he couldn't see.

Centuries have passed
But our flame still glows
Will it last?
Oh, time only knows

As long as we bleed fire,
We will always remember him
And we'll bleed fire
While we wait for his kin
To bleed fire
And drink from the flames
And feel that fire
While remembering his name

Gone is the king
But long live his reign
A tribute to him
We sing the song of flames

As long as we bleed fire,
We will always remember him
And we'll bleed fire
While we wait for his kin
To bleed fire
And drink from the flames
And—

Footsteps.
Cain stopped. He kept his head forward, but listened closely.
The footsteps drew nearer.
He resisted the urge to turn around. Instead, he hummed the melody, pretending as if he didn't notice. While humming, he moved his hand to the two batons on his hip that, when put together, made his halberd. He opened the latch to his baton's carrier. Showing the deftness of his training, in a single fluid motion, he rose to his

feet, whirling around while pushing the buttons on the batons to form two separate halberds. The blades came to rest against the flesh of a man's throat.

The man's eyes bulged. "Please, don't."

Cain looked around. The man was alone. His hands in the air, the man tried to move back, but Cain moved with him, keeping the blades of his axes in place. He noticed the slight freckles on the cheeks, the bushy eyebrows, and finally the hair, even redder than Cain's.

Cain frowned and pushed the blades deeper into the man's neck. "Who are you? What do you want?"

"Stannon. My name is Stannon." The man moved back again, and this time, Cain held his distance. "I've come to take you home, brother."

CHAPTER THIRTY-NINE

COMMANDS OF A CONSELEIGH

U nlike the first time she had come to Sereya in the days and weeks before Pirini Lilapa, this time Tundra had decided to lead her company around Ice Horn Sea instead of using Peril's Pass. She made the choice because she wanted to do a thorough scout of each city before coming to Iberene. She still needed something to link Lord Grime to Dr. Cere, and so far, she had nothing. Well, not quite nothing, but not enough to go on yet.

The major city of Eurador had provided the most information. While surveying the docking records and the video footage, one of the Hown noticed a slight bend in the shadows over the course of a few minutes. It seemed that Dr. Cere had been there. She had never hated a man's genius so much. *Invisibility to humans and invisibility to ships. Who else has access to this technology?* She shuddered at that thought. How he managed to create such technology, she didn't know, but she would definitely ask him once she had him in her custody. Assuming she didn't kill him first.

A scout thirty miles around Eurador revealed nothing. North Cliff Village was just as useless. But Tundra appreciated visiting the minor cities more than the major cities, for the people were less suspicious and more likely to talk. She hoped to receive the same respect and trust from those in Soya, but only time would tell. Its proximity to Iberene made it much more susceptible to influence from the capital, but it still was a small town of only six thousand.

She stationed the hovercrafts outside of the city. Before she spoke to the men, she took a chance to admire Crestal's Tower in the south, a half day's voyage away.

"What is that structure?" Captain Thane asked.

"Crestal's Tower." She turned to the man. His cheeks looked more guant than before. *Is it from the cold or something else? Perhaps bringing the Hown this far north was a mistake.* She bit her lip and stepped sideways. The move went unnoticed.

"What is it made out of?"

"Pure ice."

"The whole thing is made of ice?" He coughed.

"*Pure Ice.* There is a difference."

"Ice is ice."

She smiled. "No, there are different varieties. Just like you have dirty water and clean water and holy water that the churches use, there is ice and then *pure ice.* The latter is formed with holy water."

"I don't understand."

"The story goes that when Crestal's Tower was created, *vesi* was said, and the water rose. The sculptor then formed its shape under Crestal's direction."

"I still don't understand the difference."

"The difference, Captain Thane, is that the sculptor was pure of heart. Free of sin. And so when he built it for Crestal, it was built with a special ability."

"What does it do?"

"It shows you who you truly are. At the top, inside, her palace is like a giant mirror. If you look closely, it is like you are looking into your own soul. It is the kind of thing that either breaks you or strengthens you."

"You have been up there?" Captain Thane pointed upward with a gloved finger.

"Once upon a time, when I was Lady of Sereya, yes."

Her voice got lost in memories. Her first meeting with the goddess chilled even her Sereyan blood. Crestal was warm and welcoming and affectionate, but her palace was a different beast altogether, and Tundra had wondered afterward how such a woman could spend her days in a place such as that. Tundra had been summoned there a few days after her husband had passed away, and as she walked through the circular room that sat atop the tower, she couldn't help but see herself in the reflective, crystalline walls. But it wasn't her; it was a version of her, much like how Captain Thane appeared now, gaunt and weak and barely alive. What frightened her most, though, is how accurately it had described her at that point.

She looked back at the Tower for another moment, wondering how she would appear now amongst the crystalline walls of truth.

"Conseleigh Iycel, your order?"

Thane's voice pulled her back from her reverie. "Let's search the city for clues."

Scouring Soya for information wouldn't take long, and they had arrived before noon. With any luck, they could make it to Iberene before nightfall if they wanted to, but Tundra was unsure that was a wise course. She wanted to enter and leave Iberene on the same day. Staying longer would open her to attack or retaliation from Grime for what was to come.

While she spoke with Baron Connor Ertich, her men took time to survey the city. Baron Ertich was a younger man, with a full head of blue hair and eyes of blue and specks of snowflakes. His rosy cheeks spoke to his jolly demeanor, and in Conseleigh Iycel's opinion, he represented one of the more delightful families of Power in Sereya.

"Conseleigh Iycel, what a pleasant surprise. It's been so long."

"Aye, it has been much too long, Connor. How is Soya? Have you come to fill the same snowshoes as your father?"

"My father left big ones for me to fill, as did his father before him."

Conseleigh Iycel knew that as well. Their family's last name came from the sea the city stood watch over. His father and his father before him were whalers, and as such, they had a sigil of a whale blowing air from its blowhole. This also explained the whale blubber jacket he wore. The jacket's smell wafted to Tundra's nose, and although she didn't have much of an appetite for such things, she didn't let on, not wanting to offend him.

"Yes, but I believe you will honor them and your people with your rule. Crystalis and Leonteis rely on your shipping trade and skilled crews to carry supplies from the capital to trading posts." Tundra nodded. She removed a white glove from her left hand and adjusted the wristlace on her right.

"I noticed you brought Hown here with you. Is..." He looked around, leaned forward, and whispered. "Is that true?"

"Yes. Hown are here."

"And the others? From Acquava, I suppose?"

Tundra shook her head. "None from Acquava. The others are elites from Lady Aprah. They know these winterlands as well as us Sereyans."

"Such a force. There must be something important that calls you here then."

"There is, actually. Guardian business. Do you remember the name Genus Cere?"

"Genus Cere. Genus Cere..."

"Perhaps it was before your time. He was employed by my husband and worked for him on armor and battle designs for the Sereyan troops. I retained him under my reign until I banished him for activities unbefitting of my rule. I have reason to believe he is still in Sereya."

"Battle designs? Of what kind? Lord Grime just bestowed upon us a passel of new equipment."

Tundra raised her eyebrow. "Like what?"

"Like this."

Baron Ertich took off his right glove and held up his hand. On his index finger was a blue ring, but not the blue of the Kafir flower; this was an icy-blue, a blue beyond the cold.

She held out her hand. "Can I see it?"

"Certainly." He handed over the ring. "Is this what he was designing?"

"Did Astor tell you what exactly this ring does, Connor?"

"The ring is just an activator. He also provided a fitted device to strap on our bodies."

Tundra turned her head sharply to face him. "Where is that?"

The man flinched at the sudden movement. "Back in my compound."

"How many have it?"

"Lord Grime provided us with twenty, I believe."

"Can I see it?"

"Sure, follow me."

Tundra held onto the ring and followed the man back to his chalet. Inside the compound, she was led to the armory and introduced to his captain of the guard, Noel Cypress.

"Noel, where are those devices that Lord Grime shipped to us recently? Go get one."

Noel glanced from Baron Ertich to Conseleigh Iycel and then to the C on her blouse. He nodded. "Of course, Baron Ertich."

A moment later, he returned with a metal device that looked like an X. It locked in over the shoulders and strapped around the back. In the center of the device was a large blue circle, the same icy blue as the ring.

"Have you been shown how it works yet?"

"Supposed to give us an ice shield of some sort." Noel handed it to Tundra.

Tundra passed her hands over all of it, nostalgia slowly returning to her. *This is it.* "But he never showed you?"

"No." Noel shook his head.

"No, no, he did." Baron Ertich slapped his captain of guard on the arm. "One of Lord Grime's Ice Guards came out and demonstrated it to us. It covers us in ice. It gives us wings. It makes us immune to attacks."

Tundra shuddered. Sure, it did all of those things, but it also... She breathed deeply. "Thank you very much for your time. May I have this?"

"Of course." Baron Ertich nodded.

Tundra noticed the grimace on the other man's face. *Hmmm...* "Thank you."

"Has Astor Grime not been able to aid your search for Doctor Cere?" the baron asked.

Noel's head jerked at the name. Tundra noted the movement but didn't react. She didn't want to betray herself. It was clear to her now that he was most likely more loyal to Grime than to his own Baron. She would have to take this conversation elsewhere.

"Searching for him has been like searching for a whale in the Ertich Ocean." Tundra laughed. "Speaking of, it's been a while since I've seen it. Do you mind accompanying me there?"

"With pleasure." Baron Ertich smiled.

Once outside the chalet's estate, they walked towards the snow beach that lay on the south side of town.

"Connor, do you trust your men?"

"My men. Why not? They have served me for a good while."

Tundra gave a faint nod. *He is certainly idealistic. He has no idea of the snowstorm that may be coming. How much to tell him?* Tundra toyed with the idea, but in the end decided to tell him only what he needed to know, for even Tundra did not know what would happen in Iberene.

"Just take care of yourself. You have a good heart. Keep those who are loyal to you closest."

"Did you sense something from Noel?"

"Where was he born?"

"Iberene."

That explains it, then. "Interesting. Perhaps consider someone here in Soya to be your captain of guard. Next to family ties, geographical ties are the strongest."

"Thank you for your concern, Conseleigh Iycel, but I assure you everything will be fine."

Tundra feigned a smile. "Sure." She sighed. "In truth, Connor, we have not visited Iberene yet. We will head there tomorrow, but we have confirmed that

Doctor Cere's ship landed and departed in Eurador two-and-a-half weeks ago. It left the following day."

"What does the ship look like?"

"A purple bubble, as strange as it may seem."

Baron Ertich bit down on his lower lip as he thought. "I think I would have noticed something like that."

"Yes, I figured as much. Hmmm." Tundra crossed her arms over her chest. *Cere isn't a fool; he wouldn't be caught using his device unless it was absolutely necessary. How to find—*

"When did you say he left Eurador?"

"Two-and-a-half weeks ago." Tundra adjusted her wristlace and put a strand of blue hair behind her ear.

"Well, I didn't see anything, mind you, but I did *hear* something."

"You *heard* something?"

"I did. I was down at the dock, overseeing a set of shipments from Leonteis and then the sky seemed to rip apart."

"Rip apart?" Tundra raised her eyebrows.

"I'm not good at my words. Sorry. I mean, something screeched across the sky. It sounded like a jet engine, but there was nothing to see." Connor stopped. "Here we are, Snow Beach."

Tundra looked upon Snow Beach, a small depression that led into the Ertich Sea.

"It's beautiful. I forgot how much I liked the serenity of this spot." She turned to face him. "You don't think it was ships coming into Iberene's docking station?"

"It couldn't be. You know as well as I do, that's a day's ride by hovercraft. That sound wouldn't carry. And I barely heard it."

"But, I thought—"

"I meant to say that the people on the whaling ship heard it as if it passed right over them. They talked about it when they came into port, and I overheard their talk."

Tundra evaluated the information. "Are some of these people still in town?"

"Yeah, they are staying at The Icy Dream. It's near here." Connor pointed to a place farther down the beach.

"Thank you. Connor, I'd like to keep both of these items." She turned the ring between her fingers.

"Of course. We have more than plenty for my best soldiers here."

"Please think twice before using them. They are protective, yes, but there is only so much cold even our Sereyan bodies can tolerate." She patted the baron's shoulder and left.

The Icy Dream was a modest-sized wooden building with its name carved in ice below the gable. Tundra entered, drawing the attention of the patrons, and found Boras, the man in charge of the elites Lady Aprah had given her, talking to a few individuals.

"Conseleigh Iycel, I have information."

"So do I, Boras." She joined him.

He glanced down at what she carried. "What is that?"

"Our reason to visit Lord Grime tomorrow. Now, which one of you heard the strange noise at the dock the other day?"

A flaccid-looking man dressed in plaid and a whale blubber jacket raised his hand. "I am one of them. We all heard it." He pointed around at his group of people.

"Tell me what you know."

"The sound came from overhead, yah. It almost blew me straight over. Look at me, I ain't that heavy." The man turned his hands on himself and indicated his chest. "I heard it come from the east and disappear into the west, to the mountains, yah."

"And it sounded like engines from a spaceship?"

"I reckon that's how they sound, yah. Although I have never traveled in one."

"Hmm," Tundra looked at all the men. "All of you are in agreement?"

The group of five looked at each other and nodded.

"Good. Thank you for your information. Boras, let's leave." She stood and left the inn, walking towards the pier in the distance. Looking across the sea, she saw the mountains that divided Sereya and Acquava.

"You reckon he be there?"

"I do. We have to at least check it out."

"What makes you be so certain?"

"Lady's intuition."

At dawn, they left Soya and rode for Iberene. The travel, tense and full of anticipation and silence, made Tundra's breathing heavier. So many things could happen at Grime's chalet; she hoped for the less violent option. If she was lucky, she would revoke his title formally and that would be the end of it. And, if she wasn't, well, then the snow might turn red as the dawn.

A little after midday, the hovercrafts arrived in Iberene. Tundra told Thane to accelerate and lead the men through the city. They wouldn't park their hovercrafts on the outskirts like they had in Soya or the other cities. Iberene was much too large for that, and the situation much too volatile.

As Tundra directed him, she also began talking with the man. "Are you ready, Thane?"

"I am." He coughed.

"You look worse for wear, if I am being honest. Turn left and go straight."

"No need to worry about me, Conseleigh Iycel. I have been pushed through trials much tougher than these."

"Has the cold gotten to you yet?"

"No. Not yet. This suit keeps me quite warm, actually."

Tundra looked at the black leather he wore. She had never asked Eska to explain the material, but now she was curious.

"At the roundabout, continue straight. You will see a large chalet at the end of the road."

Ten minutes later, all of her men were parked outside the chalet. Guards on the wooden parapets of the walls looked down at her. Within moments, the wooden doors opened and Tundra walked forward with Boras and Thane directly behind her. The others followed in rows of four, two elites and two Hown together.

Per his duty, Lord Grime's receiver, Jel Paron, met them first. She saw his nostrils flare as he recognized her and took in the presence of the thirty-five guards behind her. "Conseleigh Iy—"

"Lord Grime. Now."

His head bobbed in a hasty nod, and he retreated inside the chalet. While Tundra waited, she took a look around at the men on the parapets. All of their attention was on them. From the back of the chalet, men also approached, dressed in wolf fur and the stitching of Lord Grime's white dune sigil on the right side of their cloaks. Though Tundra wanted to rest her hand on the hilt of her ice scimitar, she resisted. Her job as a conseleigh was to do things as efficiently and peacefully as possible.

When Lord Grime at last emerged from within, there were men behind him as well. Some Conseleigh Iycel knew as her husband's ice guard, the men sworn to protect the lord and train others. Their visors were raised, but they had come fully armed with longswords and shields. *This might be interesting.*

"Conseleigh Iycel, what a pleasant surprise. You must really adore me if you visit me—"

"Save your words, Astor. They are water anyway."

The man stopped mid-stride. He stood upright and put both hands on the crystal cane in front of him. "Then, by all means, do not waste time. Tell me what you need to tell me."

Before she spoke, she looked around. No signs of distress yet. She cleared her throat and then said, "Lord Astor Grime, acting in my power as the conseleigh to Onkh, and under the authority of Guardian Edwyrd Eska, I hereby remove you from the position of Lord of Sereya."

Lord Grime spat on the ground. "For what? Ludicrous. This is an—"

"Thane!" She snapped her finger.

The Hown captain moved to stand next to her, the device she had procured from Baron Ertich the day before in his hands. Tundra took off her left glove, exposing her wristlace to Lord Grime, which he immediately took note of. She removed the ring Baron Ertich had given her and held it in front of her.

"I have knowledge that you have supplied these crystallizers to all of your citizens."

Lord Grime scoffed and raised his arms. "So what? Regenerating that idea is my prerogative, Conseleigh Iycel. It doesn't concern you."

"No, but it does mean a few things, Astor. First, it means that you lied to me when I came here last. Second, it means that Doctor Cere and you are in collusion and that he is here on Sereya. Third, all of that means that you failed in your duty to exile him fully when I was Lady of Sereya." Tundra walked closer. With each step she took towards Astor Grime, his Ice Guard advanced as well. She stopped an arm's length away from him. "You are hereby removed from your position." Tundra turned around and began walking away.

"You are making a mistake."

Tundra stopped. She turned halfway and put her hand on the hilt of her scimitar. "Is that a threat, Astor?" She glanced at the men around the premises and looked back to her own. All of them stood observant, ready, hands on their hilts as well. She glared at him, keeping her hand on her hilt. "Well?"

Tundra didn't need to observe Grime's men to understand that some would fight for him and others would not. She didn't know the exact number, but she did notice that the Ice Guards had removed their hands from their hilts. *If they don't engage, then the others probably will not join as well.*

Grime's bushy blue eyebrows drew together. "No."

"I did not think so." She took her hand off of her hilt. "Once I finish my business with Doctor Cere, I will begin making arrangements for finding someone to replace your incompetence." She turned around and began walking away again.

"To Abaddon with you and Guardian Eska."

Tundra stopped but did not turn. She chuckled to herself, seeing her own breath in the shadow she cast. "You," she unwound one piece of her wristlace, "do not listen," another layer, "very well," another piece, "old man." She pinched the crystal beads on the wristlace as she removed another layer. "Do you." She undid the final strand and kept the handle in her hand. She let the coils fall to whisper in the snow. And then she turned, lashing out with her whip. It found its mark, snapping around Astor Grime's wrist. She yanked, pulling him to the snowy floor.

The sound of steel surged throughout the compound. Boras and Thane came to her side, shields raised. The others had gathered in a circular formation, weapons out, shields ready. Astor Grime scrambled to regain his footing, but he couldn't break the hold of Tundra's whip. While he was on all fours, she kicked him in the stomach, flipping him over onto his back.

He coughed up blood, staining the snow red, and snarled at his men. "What are you all doing? Attack!"

"You stupid man." Tundra snapped her wrist and launched her whip at his neck. It coiled around him, cutting off his air. Not thinking about repercussions, she dragged him forward. "You will never threaten Edwyrd or me ever again." With one clean swoop, she brought her ice scimitar across his neck, decapitating him.

His head rolled to the feet of the nearest ice guard. A pool of red now marred the pristine snow. Tundra looked around and tugged the whip free. She called out to the tense faces.

"Does anyone else feel like losing their head?"

No one spoke. But they didn't have to; their actions spoke for them. Each person in the compound took their hands off of their hilts.

"Good." Tundra rolled her wristlace onto her arm. One eyebrow arched, she yelled to the stoic Ice Guards in front of her. "Clean this mess up. Receiver Paron?"

The receiver whimpered and came out from behind one of the ice guards. "You... you..."

"Go get Grime's advisor."

The man turned around, tripping over himself, and then scurried away back to the chalet. While she waited for the advisor to come out, she took careful note of the guards on the parapets and the Ice Guards before her. All the Hown and the elites had their weapons drawn. The time passed like ice melting, but eventually Advisor Katarh came forward.

When he saw Grime's body, he jumped back with a shriek. "You... you actually killed him."

"For the time being, you're in charge." His jaw dropped. She turned around. "Men, let's go."

Ignoring the barrage of questions that came from the advisor behind her, she walked through the crowd of her men. She spoke to no one, only focused on the exit in front of her. An ice controlled her now, an ice so cold that even the fires of Abaddon would do little to melt her.

CHAPTER FORTY

PURPOSE

Z ain had never been to Aeston, but he had heard of it. It was synonymous with
dreamers. Those who wanted to live beyond their means traveled to Aeston to
experience luxury if their fortune saw fit or poverty and ruin if they couldn't make
things work. The latter part in the stark dichotomy of the city was the only thing
that Zain could say mimicked the other parts of Empora because unlike the other
cities farther north in Empora, the southern city of Aeston retained more of its
greenery, not succumbing to the industrialization that had fueled Rydel at one point
and Mendeck in the present epoch. The vibe made Aeston a city that lived up to its
reputation, welcoming Zain in ways he couldn't imagine in other parts of Empora.
To some extent, it didn't even feel as if it were part of Empora at all.

Flying into the city on a hovercraft two days before, Zain had noted a large
banner on a hill spelling out its name, A-E-S-T-O-N, a beacon for anyone traveling
north from Chaon or south after the Great Bridge. Furthermore, the second night
that Zain had stayed there, he had been walking around with Nyrin, checking out
the city and helping to gather supplies for the voyage, when they came across a
forest of lights. They had passed the square earlier, but now, with the lights on,
they stopped to admire the unique sight. Palm trees outlined in lights formed the
shape of a square. The streetlights were just as tall, making the trees glow
vibrantly, scaring away any darkness threatening to overtake the surrounding area.

After a ten minute walk, he and Nyrin reached the inn they were staying at.
Unlike Rydel and unlike Terran, Aeston wasn't dangerous. At least, not right now
—the soldiers had already sailed away. They were about to disrupt Ka'Che; there
wasn't anyone left to hunt Zain's party. Not here, anyway.

At first, Zain didn't say anything while packing the clothes he had purchased in
the city with the silver spells given to him by Carla Sonetta. Everyone in the group
had received a stipend from her. Zain and Carla's group was responsible for
gathering the supplies needed for the journey, and the Cleaver's Scorpions were
responsible for securing the transport through connections they had in the city. The
next day they would be leaving, but it would be too cumbersome to try to load the
ships and leave on the same day, so their task was to pack their things and leave

them outside their doors. The Scorpions would come around and take them to the procured ships during the grave of night, making departure the next day swift and easy.

When Zain finished packing one bag, he asked, "What were you thinking about back there?"

"Back where?"

"By the palm trees."

"Oh…" Nyrin folded a piece of clothing and put it in a bag. "It's strange something so beautiful lives in a nation so notorious, isn't it?"

"I was thinking about that too, actually. Aeston doesn't seem like a part of Empora."

"Perhaps that's why it's sectioned off?"

"Yeah, maybe…" Zain picked up another bag and began filling it with more clothes. He stopped halfway through. "You remember when we crossed Krine Sea the first time?"

"Which day?" Nyrin chuckled. "It was a long voyage."

Zain laughed as well. "Did you ever see the light lilies at night?"

"Is that what they were called?"

"Bern Denardi told me about them. The light forest tonight reminded me of those."

"How so?"

"Because every darkness needs light."

"That's its purpose? To dispel the darkness?"

"Maybe. Bern would say that it's nothing special, though. That square only lit up because it got dark. If it learned to be bright all the time, then it truly would be a sign. The words he said reminded me that even though this city looks beautiful and welcoming, it still bites. It's not all good. Remember what I told you about the Scorpions on the way here?"

"Yeah…" Nyrin finished his bag and went to get another bag. "They launched a failed attack."

"That's what I was told." Zain sighed.

Nyrin echoed Zain's sentiment. "After you told me that, I began thinking about all the possibilities that could happen. My family lives in the south of Ka'Che."

"Callumbra?"

Nyrin nodded.

"What do you parents do there?"

"My mum's an instructor and my pa works for the marquis in Callumbra."

"Is that how you got into the guard in Pelopon?"

"Yeah, my father reached out to Lord Vangle when recruiting occurred. I guess my pa saw something in me or maybe wanted something better for me than our small town."

"Callumbra isn't small."

"My pa works there, but we live outside it. Not much to do in the south besides herding cattle. But I'm not complaining. I'm thankful for what I have, and I have faith that I'll see them again. Someday, when all this is over."

There it was again. The word. *Faith.* "What kind of faith? Which do you believe in?"

"The Twelve, of course. That's one of the reasons I accepted the position at Castle Semson."

"I don't understand." Zain stopped packing for a moment.

"Well, I figured that maybe I would get to hear Lord Vangle talk about meeting them some time. I hear only the lords get to meet them. Well, and the conseleigh and of course Guardian Eska. Has your uncle said anything to you about them?"

Zain shook his head. He wasn't sure if that was a lie or not. He never saw his uncle much, and it's not like he was raised in the castle walls, but from what he could remember, his uncle never mentioned anything about the Twelve.

"I heard that the new apprentice got the chance to meet them. I bet that was a spectacle."

"So you don't believe in the Ancients?"

"Never have seen them."

"But you've never seen the Twelve either."

"Right. Well, I guess it's not that I don't believe in the Ancients. They existed at one point, I'm sure. But now it's the Twelve that look over us. They are the ones that keep us safe. I pray to the Twelve every night to keep Callumbra safe."

Zain chuckled. *If only...*

"What are you laughing at?"

"It's nothing." Zain shook his head.

"Do you believe?"

Zain tensed. He looked down at the cremain ring on his hand. He resisted fingering it. "I'm not sure. I guess I don't see things the way you see it."

"We're here right now. We are about to go home tomorrow. Isn't that proof enough?"

Zain opened his mouth to respond, but then closed it. He clenched his fist. Nyrin knew his father was dead. Didn't that mean anything? "Anyway, I think Callumbra will be safe," Zain said, ignoring the question. "Mox is the port-side city. It wouldn't make sense for Zigarda to invade Mox and then Callumbra and then Pelopon. My guess is he is hoping to use Mox as a distraction to move soldiers away from the capital."

"Yeah. Maybe you're right." Nyrin finished putting the last piece of clothing in his bag and started placing rations of food on top. "What do you think will happen to Pelopon?"

Zain stopped mid-movement. He kept his hand on a tunic inside his bag longer than he needed to before setting it down with the others. He withdrew his hand and looked at Nyrin. "I don't like to think about those things."

"Your mom is there still, isn't she?"

Zain's heart ached. Not trusting himself to speak, he began packing food on top of his clothing as well.

"Zain?"

"Yeah, she is."

"I... I shouldn't have brought things up. I'm sorry. I get like this when I start thinking of possibilities. My mind goes to places it shouldn't."

Zain didn't know what to say. His name had been Nimble Nyrin on the ship, not Nervous Nyrin, and Zain wished it had stayed that way. If it had, he wouldn't have brought Zain such discomfort now.

Shaking his head, Zain picked up his bags. "You ready with yours?"

"Yeah." Nyrin grabbed his things.

"Let's go."

Zain and Nyrin put their bags outside at the designated location, then decided it was time to sleep.

Nyrin crawled into his bed and shifted around for a moment until he was comfortable. "Zain?"

"Yeah?" Zain sat on his bed, leaning forward, fingers interlocked as he twisted the cremain ring.

"I'm sorry about your father."

Zain jerked his head up, no longer fidgeting with his ring.

"And thank you for being our light." Nyrin smiled and then rolled over and went to sleep.

Zain blinked. He didn't know how to respond to such a sentiment. A light? Did a light attract darkness or repel it? If he was a light, when would things start to shine? Or by being a light, was his only purpose to be surrounded by darkness? If it was, Zain was certain he didn't want to be a light at all, not if it meant more darkness was on the way.

A little after dawn the next day, Zain's party had set sail. The Scorpions had managed to procure two separate vessels from the scanty fleet that remained in the harbor. Behind them, the city of Aeston faded into the distance, the ostentatious sign and the Great Bridge beyond it slowly losing prominence on the horizon. Before them lay the Krine Sea.

Zain had finished arranging the things in the cabin that he shared with his men. With only two ships and over one thousand people, all the rooms were crammed with at least four individuals, even if they didn't have the beds to match. Zain's room was better than many, for it had two beds, meaning that he and his troops would rotate each night who would sleep on the floor.

Making his way above deck, Zain saw Gabrielle over by the bow of the ship. Her friend, Perrine, was by her side. Since the conversation with Nyrin the night before, he had wanted a moment to talk to Gabrielle alone, so he took this opportunity to approach her.

Before he even stepped up beside her, Gabrielle had turned her head and smiled. "Zain?"

"How did you know?"

"Your footsteps are heavier than Carla's or Emilia's and Perrine is already here."

Zain smiled at Perrine. "Can I join you both?"

"Sure." Gabrielle tapped the wooden railing next to her.

"Alone?"

Gabrielle turned to Perrine.

"It's okay, Gabe. I'll let you two talk." Perrine walked away.

Zain stepped forward and leaned his arms on the railing. He didn't say anything for an awkwardly long time.

"What's wrong? What do you want to say?"

Zain sighed. "I want to start believing."

Gabrielle turned her head. Just briefly. Just for a moment. Then turned it back to the sea. "What's stopping you?"

"A question."

"Go on."

"How does faith explain all the horrible death and cruelty we see? If there is some entity keeping me safe, why not everyone?"

"Everyone? Like your father?"

Zain sighed. He fidgeted with his ring once more. "Yes. Like him. Like Gerald. Like Guy. Like anyone who has died for a cause. The crew that came with me. They were all good people."

Gabrielle didn't respond for a little while. Instead, she tucked a strand of hair behind her ear. After a quick muttering under her lips, she spoke. "Zat is certainly a good question. What you need to remember, Zain, is zat every life is significant. No one is born into zis world without a purpose. I believe zat when a person dies, it's to fulfill somezing or because zey have already fulfilled zeir purpose."

"So my father's purpose is already finished? How is that fair?" Zain hadn't meant to raise his voice, and he tried to rein himself in. The quick outburst had caused Gabrielle to flinch. "I'm sorry for yelling."

"It's okay. It happens." She reached out, feeling for his hand. When she found it, she squeezed. "Zain, faiz isn't fair. Only Ancient Lyoen knowns everyone's purpose. It's created at birz. But Ancient Bane is the one who determines when zat purpose is complete."

"But..."

"You will never know what someone's purpose is. You may never even know what your own is, but know zat you have one." She looked at him. "And if you have good faiz, zen you may realize it one day."

"If someone doesn't believe, do they still have a purpose?"

"Of course. Every life has a purpose. Believing, truly believing, is za only way you can realize your own zough." Gabrielle drew her hand upwards, first grabbing hold of his shoulder, and then tracing down his chest to his heart.

"What was my father's purpose then?"

Gabrielle turned away and shook her head. "I cannot begin to say. Zat is only somezing za Ancients know."

"Guy's?"

Gabrielle continued shaking her head.

"How many people need to die for a purpose to be complete?"

"As many as necessary."

"How cruel is that? How can you worship such... such..." Zain didn't know how to finish his thoughts.

"Zain, za Ancients test us. Zey test us to see how strong we are."

Zain took hold of her face. He removed her glasses. "So this is a test?"

Gabrielle's dead eyes revealed nothing, but Zain heard the tremor in her inhale . "I zink so."

"You give yourself for them and do you ever hear them?"

Gabrielle shook her head. "Zat isn't what faiz is about. Faiz is knowing somezing is right even when you cannot see it."

"And what does faith ever get us?"

"Faiz allowed Grace Sabore to walk over za Krine Sea."

"What?"

"It is anozer part of za story you have never heard. Carla will tell you za whole zing someday. Zey guided her life, Zain. And zey guided her daughter's life. And zey guide all of our lives if we let zem. But you have to let zem. You have to believe. You have to have faiz. Without it, any trial you are tested wiz won't make sense to you."

Zain gave Gabrielle her glasses. "I'm sorry for my outburst."

She put on her glasses and then rubbed his arm. "It's okay. We all have moments of weakness. You're worried about your mozer. Maybe even Zakk. I understand."

"How did you know?"

"Because it's only natural to feel somezing for zose closest to you."

"Will they be a part of my test?"

Gabrielle shook her head. "It isn't for me to say. But whatever happens, keep faiz. If you do, za Ancients will reward you in zeir own time."

"And what time is that?"

"Whenever zey have decided zat your purpose is complete, zat your trials are finished."

"And what happens if I don't pass their trials?"

"Let's not zink on zat." Gabrielle smiled. She grabbed hold of Zain's chin, went up on her tiptoes, and kissed his cheek. "Let's look at za Krine Sea." She came in close to him, wrapping one arm around his waist.

"But you can't see."

"Just because I can't see, doesn't mean I don't know where I'm going. Za Ancients usually guide us in such a way. We can't begin to fazom zeir purpose, Zain, but we can be assured it will be beautiful once it's complete." She leaned her head against his shoulder.

Zain wrapped one arm around her and rested his head on hers, looking out into the Krine Sea. It seemed important to absorb the calm and the serenity of the moment because he was certain they weren't going to last, and if he truly was a light, then darkness would find him soon enough, for that was its purpose.

CHAPTER FORTY-ONE

THE CRYSTALLIZER PROJECT

White-capped mountains encompassed her, even though she could barely see now that night had fallen. The peaks formed the Northern Pass and were natural boundaries between Sereya and the Katarh province of Acquava. Snow clung to evergreen trees at the base of the mountains. Polar bears and Clydesdales and even a family of mammoths had added to the natural scenery during the day. It augmented the normality of the situation. And that is something Tundra didn't like because if things were normal, then it would be that much harder to find Dr. Cere and to protect Edwyrd. She itched for something to happen.

With the last bit of light from Lugh, she noticed the path ahead narrowed and grew steeper. "Stop here."

"Here, Conseleigh Iycel?"

Behind her, Boras stood up, examining the terrain. "We be out in the open. There be nothing around us."

"Precisely. There is nothing around us, so you two shouldn't be so worried. Now, stop."

Thane pulled over the hovercraft. When he did so, the others followed him. Just like they had during the previous stops, they formed a large circle and then began setting up camp in the middle. They were a day from Iberene and at the mouth of the Northern Passage.

"Conseleigh Iycel, are you sure we are going the right way?"

She exhaled. "Yes," she lied and walked away. "Now, set up camp."

In truth, it wasn't as much of a lie as it was unconfirmed. Cere certainly could be in the area, but there were a plethora of other passes through the mountains or places to hide. Time would tell if she could draw the doctor out of hibernation. For now, she walked towards the silhouettes of the mountains in front of her.

The warmth from within the circle of hovercrafts quickly dissipated, and when she took her last step from light to dark, a coldness enveloped her. The snow rose above her snow shoes, reaching past her ankles. A williwaw pulled and pushed her dress and her mythril shawl to and fro. The environment tried to bite her, but it couldn't pierce her skin, so even though she stood there as a bystander to the wind and the snow and the cold, she wasn't a victim. She caught herself looking up at the stars in the night sky. She wondered if Edwyrd looked up at the same night sky as she did, like she often caught him doing when she woke during the middle of the night. She always asked what he looked at, or what he looked for, and he always told her the same thing: memories.

But what memories did he dream of? Were they unpleasant memories of his own Trials? Of Deimos? Or the death of his sister? Or did he remember pleasant things like his parents, his successes as Guardian, or her and the transformation of their relationship from colleagues to lovers?

She closed her eyes and took a deep breath, inhaling the cold, the snow, and the mountain air. When she opened them again, she saw a bright blue flash across the night sky. *A falling star.* She smiled. Then her smile curved inward. The flash lasted much longer than it should have; in fact, it was still continuing and getting larger. Her eyes followed it. A buzzing resonated behind it and a gust of wind came after. She turned and watched in horror as the flash of blue impacted a portion of the camp. *What is that?*

Commotion. Cacophony. Confusion. All of these things filled her ears as she ran back to the encampment as fast as she could. Continued blue flashes bombarded the camp, sending up a chorus of screams, shouts, and the sound of shattering ice. When she moved into the light, she saw movement above, bird-like, swarming over them and shooting blue flashes down from the sky.

One of the soldiers ran towards her. "Conseleigh Iycel, we are—" A flash of blue struck him, and he stopped moving. Ice ran up his body. In a matter of seconds, he was frozen in place, a block of ice. A swoosh cut through the air in the form of a large bird, or perhaps a man with wings. It spiraled into the ice, shattering it and splattering the man's body across the snow. Tundra followed the flying shape upward, her heart beating faster as she recognized the icy wings on its back, the black device that hugged its chest, the blue crystal embedded where the heart should be, and the crystalline skin.

The crystallizers.

A quick survey of their encampment showed a handful of their hovercrafts had taken damage, and icy shards of body parts lay like pieces of hail about the ground. She ran towards the middle; Boras and Thane were still alive and barking orders at their men.

"*Vesi.*" Tundra waved her hand and an arch of snow covered them, blocking a blast from above. The snow turned to ice. "Thane, have you gotten a good look at these things yet?"

"No, Conseleigh Iycel. They took us by surprise. I suspect five to ten of them, considering the damage they've done. *Vesi.*" He shot a pile of snow up at the sky, hitting the incoming blue light, not stopping it, but instead turning it into a ball of ice. It collided with a hovercraft, pushing it up into the air and flipping it over.

This has to stop. "They're the crystallizers I was telling you about. They're harnessing the Power of ice. Thane, you and two others come with me. Boras, continue guarding the area with the other elites. Keep us and yourself safe from the blue lights."

Both men nodded their understanding. Tundra went to the outskirts of their perimeter of hovercrafts. Thane and two of his men followed. She kicked the snow until she found the ground underneath. She faced the men. "Kick the snow out from under you until you see dirt. We need a circle. One person takes the north, one the east, one the west and one the south. We kick out a line of dirt until we see the other person's starting point. Understood?"

Confusion fell upon their faces as clear as snow on the ground, but none questioned her. Thane directed them to their posts, and they began kicking with their snow boots until finding earth. During this time, Boras and a fraction of his men launched an assault on the crystallizers in the sky, using Power to raise pillars to skewer them. But the Power was too slow. Others focused on forcing snow to mix with the flashes of blue light, hoping that the balls of ice that came after wouldn't be lethal.

Perhaps ten minutes later, Tundra finished her portion of the circle. She went to the center to help the elite ward off the attackers while the others finished. When she noticed one Hown had to maneuver his line past a flipped hovercraft, she ran to help him. As she reached him, a flash of blue came from her left. She saw it and dove out of the way. But he didn't. It hit him and within seconds the screams of being frozen solid cut through the campsite.

She knew what came next.

And she was ready for it.

She searched for the buzz with her ears. *To the left.* She drew her scimitar. She saw the spiral form, and she swung upwards at the incoming foe. It connected. The ice shattered, deluging the ground in a hail of death. Instead of flying away, the crystallizer spiraled downward, crashing into another hovercraft and sliding across the snow towards the center of the camp. She sheathed her scimitar. The others moved to attack the fallen foe.

She ran towards the landing point. "Stop!"

The intruder on the ground raised an arm, which now looked more like a cannon. Not taking her time to undo her whip, she yanked it off by the bottom, the hard crystals biting her forearm. She lashed out towards the cannon and yanked it backwards. The shot of blue meant for her men sailed harmlessly into the distance. She stepped onto the enemy's forearm and saw that she had damaged one of his crystal wings with her scimitar.

"*Maa.*" She waved her free hand over her head and instantly a shield of earth rose over Tundra and her surviving men. Attacks continued to rain down, but the earthen dome merely vibrated.

The man underneath her yelled and screamed and cursed to any of the Twelve he could think of. She smirked. *It worked.* He writhed, and it took her whole strength to keep the man's arm in place. She commanded two soldiers to take control of the captive, then

turned to her officers. "Boras, take tally of your men. Thane, do the same with yours."

As she waited for the count, she looked at the captured man. His armor was a suit of ice. Wings fluttered, but by their own control or the man's she wasn't sure. Not yet, anyway. Instead of a helm of armor, ice encrusted the back of the man's neck to where hair would typically begin, and this crystalline armor extended over the man's entire skin. While one arm had a cannon for its hand, the other had a large lance, like those a knight would use when jousting. And below the suit of ice was what troubled her most. It was the same type of device given to her by Baron Ertich.

"Elites now be at ten, Conseleigh Iycel."

"Including you?"

"Eleven, including me."

"Okay." Tundra pursed her lips. *Less than half of what I started with. Hopefully, Olivia won't mind. These things happen in war and retribution.* "Thane?"

"Seven, including me, Conseleigh Iycel."

The elites definitely had suffered more from the barrage, but that was to be expected. She was glad that the fragility of the Hown had not become an issue yet. She only hoped it could stay that way until they left Sereya and returned to the Central Core.

The captive spat. Anger seethed out of him as he breathed heavily, keeping an intense fixation on her. "Are you Conseleigh Iycel?"

"I am."

He smirked. "Doctor Cere is expecting you."

"Is he now?" Tundra crouched on the balls of her feet in front of the man. She pinched the ice-like blade of her scimitar and drew her fingers up from the heftier part to the tip. "Good. I figured he might be. Where is he?"

The man laughed. "You think I would tell you that."

Tundra's smile flattened. "No. But you don't need to. I already know."

"You have no idea."

"Oh, but I do."

"Impossible."

"I think not." Tundra smirked. "Do you hear that? Nothing. Your friends realize that it's futile to try to save you."

Everyone listened to the silence.

"That doesn't matter."

"Oh, but it does." Her blue eyes looked into his. "They are on their way back to report to Doctor Cere right now. To tell him the casualties like the good little soldiers they are. They want the praise for their sneak attack." Tundra harrumphed. "But the thing is, I was expecting this."

The man's eyes widened.

"Watch. And watch closely." Tundra released her hold on the earth. Vacant night air rushed in to meet them, but there was no chaos, no confusion, and no death. Tundra looked at the fire her men had built. "*Palo.*" It came towards her, engulfing her.

She split it into four parts and pushed her arms outward. The balls of fire shot out from her position into the night sky, soaring west, north, east, and south. Four miniature suns now lit up the sky. She scanned the expanse above, waiting, hoping. There, to the northeast, dark silhouettes betrayed by the flare of light. She reached down inside of her, pulling on her Power, and combined all the fire in the sky to that one location. A barrage of blue lashed out to meet the impeding red but failed to stop it. Tundra focused her mind, then brought her outstretched arms together and clapped the air. A cloud of red burst overhead, swallowing the night sky whole.

"Your friends already told me where Doctor Cere is." She turned her attention back to the man who lay on the ground in front of her. "Tomorrow morning, we will drive that way and find the bodies of your fallen comrades. And when we do, we will find the doctor's base. So, you see, I don't need your information."

He writhed harder, but the soldiers kept him stationary. Once he realized it was futile, he said, "Kill me. It won't matter."

Tundra unsheathed her scimitar. As the steel screeched against its scabbard, his eyes followed the blade. "You would like me to kill you?"

"Go ahead, kill me like you killed our lord."

Word certainly travels fast. "No."

"What?"

"I'm not going to kill you. I'm going to let the fire kill you because a quick death with my blade here would be too good for you." She addressed the men holding him. "Bring him in front of the fire."

The two elites dragged the man to his feet and sat him down next to the fire. Slowly and painfully, the ice suit melted. Screams rang out. Tundra listened in bliss. She watched as the man's hardened body shriveled and melted as if he didn't have any bones, until he was a puddle of skin on the floor.

She heard retching from among both the elites and the Hown at this demonstration.

"What was that man?" Thane asked.

"A lab experiment."

"Did you know we were going to be attacked?"

Tundra pinched a puddle of skin and rubbed it against her fingertips. She wiped her fingers in the snow and stood up. "I had a feeling Doctor Cere would try to ambush us."

"How did you know?"

"He has never been patient. When I told him his crystallizer project would have to wait, he cursed me. I found out he had been working on it without my approval. Now I see that he has succeeded in his plans."

"But how—"

"When I mentioned Doctor Cere to Astor Grime yesterday, I expected Grime would send warning to Cere as soon as he could. Obviously, he did. Well, someone did. And now we know where he's hiding." She tilted her head northeast.

"Our men..." Boras's voice tapered off, more disturbed by the melted man than Thane.

"Our men did what they were trained to do. They fought. They served. And some survived. They died for a greater cause. They died for Guardian Eska. That is who you serve, correct?"

Boras gave her nothing but an empty, lost stare.

"You are correct, Conseleigh Iycel," Captain Thane said.

"Good." She ignored Boras. "Take all the bodies or parts of bodies you can find and burn them. It will be good for the afterlife if they leave with a little fire in them."

Thane left her. He staggered a little, put a hand to his side, and leaned on a hovercraft, just for a moment, then pushed himself upright and barked orders to his men.

She bit her bottom lip and turned to the other elites. They stood around the fire, looking at the carnage. "How are all of you?"

"You led us into a trap," Boras said.

Tundra snapped her gaze to him. "What was that?"

"You be hearing me. You led us into a trap. Half of the elites died because of—"

She calmed her breathing. She narrowed her gaze. Not giving an inch, she stalked forward, stopping in front of him, chin jutting out, unblinking. "They died because of that monster in the mountains." She cut him off and pointed outwards toward the darkness. "Do you Garians think that Sereya accepts your sovereignty? That they revel in the nation that you've become?" She looked towards the other elite now. "They don't. They openly hate you, like Victor Zigarda openly condemns the Guardian of the Core. We are here to stop that man from making more of these things." She pointed to the pool of skin on the ground. She held up her hand to an incoming Hown. "Rest now. Save your strength. I have a feeling you will need it tomorrow. There are sure to be more of these."

"What be they?" A different elite asked.

Tundra loosened her stance. She moved away from Boras and bent down to the pile of skin once more. She grabbed the device that had sat over the man's chest and held it to the inquisitive elite. "This is what we picked up in Soya. It is fueled by crystals that pump cold into the wearer's bloodstream. It takes over. Makes you ice." She showed it to the other elite. "It hardens your body to the point where you have no need of a shield. This was Doctor Cere's original plan. But the cannon and the lance suggest he has made some upgrades. We will need to take precautions tomorrow."

"We need to be facing more of them?" another elite asked.

"Aye. Lots more. So get some rest and enjoy the night we have left."

She stood up again. Boras had already left. A Hown came over to talk to her, but she brushed him aside, not wanting to deal with anything else. Her plan to lure the doctor out of hiding had worked, although it had cost them. She felt a morsel of regret, but such things were necessary. And, after all, it was for the greater good. Tomorrow, she would meet the doctor yet again, and she would end his plot against Guardian Eska. Her itch had been scratched. And as her gaze drifted up to the night sky, she wished that it would turn to daylight because she didn't want to keep the doctor waiting. No, not at all.

CHAPTER FORTY-TWO

LAST RESORT

Hydro's journey back through the Sacred Passage was less adventurous than the way in, probably because return trips always seemed shorter. There was no more anticipation in the air. It had dissipated when he secured the jewel, the fourth, and put it in the satchel at his side. As he glanced at the small collection, their sharp edges and smooth faces, he couldn't help but wonder what trouble they would cause. Eska obviously had not wanted them found, and without Anne and his necklace, Hydro assumed they would have remained hidden, for it was her Power that had led him up Mount Volan successfully.

He would need to notify Lord Zigarda immediately after returning to his ship. He didn't want the paranoid and overly anxious lord to think that Hydro had abandoned his purpose. He knew what he needed to do to keep his brother safe, and he would do so. At all costs. Hydro wondered, as he approached C-Bot, what Aiton was doing in that moment.

He was two hundred meters away when the hovercrafts converged. Six of them. Surrounding him.

"Hydro Paen, stop where you are!"

Hydro tensed and his hand went to the hilt of his sword as his gaze darted from ship to ship, assessing his options.

The speaker was a large man with a helmet and visor that covered his eyes but not the scars on his face. He pushed a button near his ear, bringing a scanning device over the visor. Dressed in a black suit with red stripes and golden lapels, he strolled forward, hands clasped behind his back, making no effort to hide the golden H pinned to his left chest pocket.

Hydro swallowed hard and shifted his feet. *Hown. How did they find me?*

"I am General Satorus of the Hown. You are wanted for the murder of Lord Hydro and Lady Atesia Paen. You are wanted for the murder of the goddess Pearl. Under orders of Guardian Eska, I am to place you under arrest to stand trial before him. If you come willingly, there will be no need for violence." The man moved his hand to his hilt.

Hydro remained silent, his tongue pushing into his cheek. *Bare hands.* Hydro looked around. *All of them have bare hands.* It was a small thing, but to Hydro it meant a great deal—every one of the eighteen Hown that now surrounded him carried zircha steel. And because they were in Guardian Eska's service, those weapons would be fully calibrated and the men highly skilled. No doubt they could all use Power. Hydro's hand still rested on his hilt.

They moved in closer.

You must not let them take you, Hydro Paen. We have work to do. Anne stood by his side, hand over his.

"You will help me?"

Always.

Hydro closed his eyes. He inhaled deeply. Hydro let the Hown see his Ether Weapon. "You think zircha steel can outmatch Ether?"

"One on one, of course not. But there are more of us and only one of you." Satorus raised both of his arms, gesturing to the surrounding men.

"I have Power on my side."

"No... you don't have anything, I'm afraid. Chase." General Satorus looked up and nodded.

Boom.

Hydro hit the ground, flung down by something heavy and thick. The sudden jolt tore his sword away from him. Darkness.

"*Maa.*"

Nothing.

"*Salama.*"

Nothing.

"*Palo!*"

Still nothing.

"Why is my Power not working?" He pushed on whatever restrained him, realizing it was a net that had hooked into the ground. Hydro struggled and struggled but to no avail; he stopped when he heard a second man speak into a communicator.

"Guardian Eska..." The man coughed. "we have successfully managed to locate and capture Hydro Paen. We are bringing him back to you now. See you soon." Another fit of coughing occurred. "What in the name of—"

Blasts, shouts, chaos, and cacophony cut him off. Struggling under his net, Hydro tried prying the net from the terrain, but he couldn't get his fingers under the black mesh. He started kicking, hoping it would give if he applied enough force. Wails and sirens and blasts and shouts erupted around him.

"Immobilize that—"

"Take cover."

What is going on? Hydro kicked furiously at his net. It started to give way. He kicked again, but then changed tactics. Using what little room he had to maneuver, he turned himself around and began kicking the other side. *If I can get to my sword, then I can slice this open.* Hip open, leg at ninety degrees, he pushed with all his might and kept doing so until his leg got tired. Then he beat the same spot with his opposite leg. Slowly but surely, the net was failing.

"Fire! Bring it down!"

"Hit!"

Light filtered in from outside. Chest to the ground, Hydro peeped out of the crevice with one eye. Purge lay just within reach. Positioning himself on one shoulder and with one arm as support, he reached forward.

A loud thud shook him off kilter, the force like a seismic earthquake, so strong, in fact, that his sword jumped in the air a few inches.

Hydro restabalized himself and reached forward. His fingers inched their way closer to the hilt. *Come on now, just a little...*

"Bag him up. Let's take him back before that machine starts up again."

Before he could grab hold, he was yanked away, the sword sliding out from his fingertips. *No!*

The net closed in again around him. Hydro was locked in darkness once more. "Anne?"

No response came.

"Anne! I need you."

She didn't answer.

Panic creased Hydro's brow. *"Palo. Vesi. Salama. Maa."* No Power obeyed him here. Even air seemed a finite commodity. It was like he was adrift in space, captured in infinite black.

"He's still moving in there."

Another man laughed. "He'll pass out eventually, Chase. Good shot."

"That machine, are we going..." Chase coughed. "Are we just going to leave it?"

"The others are examining it." The other man coughed. "Let's just get him on the hovercraft and to the ship."

Hydro couldn't focus on their conversation any longer. As it was, it was hard enough to breathe. To maintain consciousness, he cycled his breaths, allaying his mind as best as he could under the duress. Even then, he knew he couldn't change the inevitable. Soon he would succumb to whatever this device was, fall unconscious, and then it was only a matter of time before Guardian Eska would decide his fate. That fate would then be declared across the planets, from nation to nation, and his family's name would be tarnished even further. He couldn't allow that to happen. Not to Aiton. Not to his father's legacy. He would decide how this would end. No one else.

There was only one thing he could do. Using the little space allowed to him in this vacuous bag, he pushed himself to one hip and reached to his other side satchel.

Before he could open it, he landed hard and the impact shuddered through him.

Hydro sucked in a deep breath, taking as much air as he could. It would be one of his last before he would lose consciousness. Something jolted underneath him, sending him flying upward. When he hit the ground again, the jolt forced his breath from his lungs. A wasted breath. Again, he inhaled. He felt dizzy. His vision was weakening. His fingers twitched as his blood vessels fought for what little oxygen remained in his bloodstream.

Hydro pried apart the satchel on his left side. He felt the plastic container that Dr. Cere had given him. He didn't need to see it to know what was inside.

Hydro released the last of his air. Felt it pass between his teeth and lips. He wouldn't need it anymore.

He held the black pill up before his face with his thumb and index finger. He closed his eyes. *Father, I am sorry for how things ended, but I freed you. I hope you roam the oceans now. Brother, I failed you, just like I failed our sister. But now the Paen name won't need to suffer any longer because of me.*

He popped the pill in his mouth and bit down.

CHAPTER FORTY-THREE

FAREWELLS

E ven two-and-a-half weeks didn't alleviate the tension and suspicion that threatened to overrun Castle Semson's walls. After discovering that the communication chamber had been sabotaged, an investigation followed, leading to the discovery that any attempt to make calls outside the Ka'Chean territory had been blocked. And then Erie, Lord Vangle's advisor, had deduced that communication had been reduced to calls within their nation.

When he proposed this, Brisine had immediately rebuked it, saying, "What about Zain and Laron? They communicated with us before they left Empora."

Erie already had a counter argument. "When is the last time they contacted us?"

Brisine had bit down on her lower lip. Erie had been right.

What troubled everyone even more is that they still had not solved the issue. They recognized the problem, but they could not begin to figure out a solution to whatever was jamming their signal. They had looked at the codes on the telecommunicator's mainframe; they had rescripted algorithms, recoded data; they had even reset the entire system, but still the problem persisted. All in all, it suggested two things: the perpetrator was still in the castle sabotaging the system, or the virus that plagued their system was extremely intuitive and resilient. Given their many attempts at undermining the sabotage, Brisine and the others close to the lord thought it was the former.

Even that, though, had led to dead ends. Surveillance footage showed no one except those authorized to be in the chamber. DNA testing and fingerprint collections all matched with who each one claimed to be. Some of those questioned thought it to be a massive breach in ethics to conduct such invasive testing, but no one failed the test, and while the protests might be suspicious, suspicion and hunches couldn't get them the evidence needed.

All of this, coupled with recent news from Callumbra that they had been overtaken and forced back to Mox, wrenched Brisine's blood dry. She only imagined what her brothers were going through. Lukas still lived and was now leading the army since Marquis Ropis had fallen in the battle to defend the city. No matter how many falcons they had, the enemy had that many more sparrows, and the sheer number of them was what overwhelmed Callumbra, not skill, Brisine presumed. It could never be skill. She didn't have to imagine how it weighed on Abraham. She could see the toll it took on him in the bags underneath his eyes, his somber and pensive attitude as of late, and even now, he isolated himself on his throne, fist holding his chin, deep in thought at the recent news.

"How long before the party can reach Mox?"

"With a force so large, it'll take a week. The good news is that Chaon forces will need a month to make the journey, and there won't be as many, that I can assure you."

"How can you assure me of that?" Lord Vangle gritted his teeth and turned his head towards the guard who had taken over in Lukas's absence.

"Some will stay back to defend Callumbra. It may be best to call on other—" The man stopped, realizing his faux pas.

It was too late.

Lord Vangle seethed in the form of an abrupt chuckle. "I can't call for reinforcements!" He waved his hand at the man.

"I know, my lord. Sorry, my lord." The man bowed low.

Lord Vangle took a deep breath in. "Leave," he said.

The man turned on his heel and scurried out of the chambers. Brisine flinched as the door closed loudly behind him. There was too much tension in the room. She cast a nervous glance to Shayna, whose uncertainty was clear in her expression.

When no one said anything, Erie stepped in to offer his opinion. "My lord, as incompetent as that man may seem, he does bring up a good point."

"Callumbra is lost, Erie." Abraham stopped massaging his temples and looked at his advisor. "Is there truly good in any of this?"

"I never meant to suggest that there is good, just that there is..." Erie rolled his eyes upwards. "Well, there is always a lighter shade to the water, as they say." He laughed slightly. "Mox and Callumbra together, along with the other minor cities there, they can hold Chaon. They won't have the element of surprise as they did when they first attacked, and the Crossing will certainly halt any of their progress farther north. We can bottleneck and stop their advance.

"And it will be months before Pelopon is in any real danger from the south. By then, this meeting concerning Eska will have occurred, and we can resolve this discrepancy with Chaon peacefully, face-to-face without further bloodshed. Regardless, during this time, I would recommend sending word to the surrounding northern cities and requesting aid. That will allow us to bolster the troops in the south even more."

Abraham took a deep inhale, held it, and then exhaled. "Aye. There is that. The meeting in Mistral is at the end of the week. If we go there now, we may be able to hold the necessary conversations sooner rather than later. It may be that Lord Kapache is already there."

Erie nodded. "It is certainly not out of the realm of possibility."

Abraham sat up straight again. "Thank you, Erie. I truly do appreciate your advice."

"My honor, my lord." The man bowed.

Abraham hoisted himself off the throne. "I'll put a message through to Ramsey to bring his forces to the capital."

"Wait, my lord." Erie held up a finger. "Why don't we send this message personally? Have a team of four split up and deliver the messages in person to the northern cities. This will keep our actions here private. I... While we have no proof of corruption within our ranks, I do not trust the telecommunication chamber anymore. And I know you feel the same way."

Abraham nodded. "Another good idea. See that it is done and that only those directly involved are informed. After, pack your things. You're to come with me to Mistral. I could use your advice and words there as well."

"As you wish, my lord." Erie bowed and ducked out of the room.

"Shayna, bring our daughters along. Kylan, you will come to the meeting, too. It'll be good for you to see what a senate meeting is like."

"Yes, father."

"Bri, you can come along as well if you wish."

With a heavy sigh, Brisine shook her head. "I can't. Zain and Laron are supposed to arrive home soon."

"We haven't had any communication from them in weeks."

"I know, but I've been counting the days. It'll be any day now."

Abraham smiled. "All right." He nodded. "We will be back before anything further escalates."

Brisine returned the smile. "I know."

In her room, Brisine went to the dresser next to her bed and pulled open a drawer. Inside, underneath her clothes, was a drawstring velvet sack. She opened it, just as she always did when waiting for her husband's return. The vanishing sand inside had been Laron's last gift for her, something that could get her out of a hard place in times of need. Hopefully, she wouldn't have to use it, but this war encroaching from the south did anything but ease her fears. Her fingers felt the grainy sand and the stones inside. *Please come back, Laron. Please.* She sniffled.

A knock came to the door, jolting her. She put the bag back, closed the drawer, and went to the door. "Shayna?"

"Can I come in, Brisine?"

"Of course. Yes."

Shayna entered the room and sat down on Brisine's bed. After closing the door, Brisine joined her.

"Brisine, dear, why don't you come with us?" Before Brisine could refute, Shayna grabbed her hands. "I know that you miss Laron and Zain. I understand. But what is a few more days? Won't it be therapeutic to be outside of these walls for once?" She took one hand away and waved it about the castle. "You could see Jamaal. You can be safe."

"The Twelve will protect me."

Shayna opened her mouth and closed it. She exhaled through her nose. "I will say a prayer for you as well. Maybe they will arrive before we leave. If they do, would you come with us?"

"Of course. But my family comes first, Shay."

"We are family." She shook Brisine's hands.

Brisine smiled and nodded. "I know. But I can't wait to see Laron again."

"Of course. What is the first thing you're going to do when you see them?"

"I'm going to greet them with open arms and hug them. I want to grab Laron right by the shoulders, look him in his eyes, and tell him how much I love him."

Shayna giggled. "And then?" She arched her eyebrows.

Brisine laughed. "And then I'll show him where he'll be spending his nights at the castle."

"And then? Will you examine the *jewels* he brought for you?"

Brisine gasped and slapped Shayna's arm. "Shay!" She chortled and then righted herself. "I will definitely be inspecting for quality." She gave a quick head nod and then burst into giggles. "And polishing as needed." She giggled again.

"Bri!" Shayna squeezed Brisine's hands. "Aahh, how I miss this. You and your family should spend more time here in the castle. I do get lonely within these walls. That's why I'm looking forward to leaving for a time. Are you sure you don't want to come?"

"I don't need to go there to do that."

Shayna guffawed and slapped Brisine's thigh. "You are naughty, Brisine Berrese." Shayna stood. "I will send up some prayers tonight as well. Take care, Bri."

"Thank you, Shayna."

"Of course." Shayna exited the room.

Brisine remained on the bed. Her gaze wandered to the nightstand. She leaned over and grabbed a picture off the little table. It was their last family photo. She pressed her fingers to her lips and then brushed them against the faces. She would see her husband soon, and her wait would be over.

The day before her brother's family left with the advisor, another portion of their army went south to bolster the forces. This would leave them only momentarily weakened at the castle until the northern cities sent aid. Pelopon was now left with only fifteen hundred men, and most of them lived outside the castle walls in the city.

Brisine noticed Hector had been chosen to stay behind, as well as a few of the other comrades he talked to while in the dining hall. The only reason she remembered him was because of his missing fingers. He had been one of the first people to come back from Rydel, and now that Zain and Laron's ship was soon to dock, she supposed that he was here to greet the others who had chosen to stay behind in Mendeck with Zain.

Before leaving, Abraham had asked her one final time if she wanted to come, but her resolve hadn't wavered. Zain and Laron weren't back yet, but she felt they must be close. A woman's intuition told her so. And that intuition was right.

It was the day after Abraham had left that while strolling through Pelopon, catching a nice sea breeze and enjoying the sweetness of spring, that she spotted a flag on the horizon. Immediately, she stopped what she was doing and ran back towards the castle.

In the castle, she scurried through the halls, coming across Hector, who had been playing dice with fellow soldiers. "Mrs. Berrese, you seem winded. What's wrong?"

"Oh, Hector. Good. You'll want to know this, too. My son is finally back!"

He stood immediately. "You're certain?"

"I just saw the ship from the city docks. They will arrive soon." Brisine scampered off, heading to a stairwell that could lead her down the serpentine steps.

At the port built into the castle cliffs, she paced up and down the stone pier where the lord's ships docked, her hands behind her back, envisioning the meeting in her mind, wanting everything to be perfect, when both Aeneas Khréos and his first captain, Bern Denardi, stopped her.

"What brings you to the docks, Mrs. Berrese?"

"My husband. My son. They're coming. They're back." She turned on her heel and looked out to the sea. Sure enough, the ship would be docking within half an hour.

Bern Denardi hobbled up to her on his wooden peg of a leg. "Well, that's strange."

Brisine arched her eyebrows. "Strange?" She turned to the man, who had a cigar hanging loosely between his lips.

Aeneas came along on her other side. "I'd say so. They aren't supposed to be docking here. What makes you think that?"

"It's my son. My husband."

Bern plucked the cigar out of his mouth and waved his hand, quieting her. "I understand that, Mrs. Berrese, but that still is an Emporian ship. It should be docking by the city pier."

"Oh," escaped Brisine. In all the excitement of seeing her loved ones again, she had forgotten that they were, indeed, supposed to dock at the city's piers. "Maybe they are just as anxious to see me as I am them." Brisine giggled.

"Sure." Bern hummed. "That son of yours got a thick skull."

Brisine tried to laugh off the senile man's comments, but they did hold more than water's weight. Her lips pursed to the side. She heard footsteps. From the left, from the steps leading up to the castle's lower grounds, came Hector and a half dozen or so men.

Aeneas turned to look at them. "What are you doing here?"

"We were told that the ship has arrived." Hector moved forward, his group following him.

"Who told you?"

"I did. Sorry." Brisine blushed. "When I saw the sails, I had to run back to the castle."

Aeneas looked down at her, but then glanced at Hector. "Yes, but still, what are you doing *here*?"

"I can't be here to see the men I voyaged with return?" Hector crossed his arms.

"They're supposed to be at the other dock." Aeneas raised his shoulder, signaling his eagle to fly up into the air. It did, screeching before it did so. The eagle took one lap above the ship and then darted out of the bluff to the open sky beyond, vanishing from view.

The ship had reached the dock now. She could hear footsteps on the deck. Soldiers she didn't know threw ropes out to dock the ship. Other men threw the plank to the pier. It bounced a few times upon impact, pumping like Brisine's heart. She clasped her hands together. Her toes tingled. *Where are—*

Two heads appeared at the top of the plank. Laron and Zain.

"Mom!" Zain shouted.

Brisine's heart fluttered.

"Brisine," Laron said, smiling.

Brisine covered her mouth and nose with her hands, closed her eyes, and inhaled deeply. *Thank you, Twelve, for bringing them back to me.* Grinning wildly, she opened her eyes and spread out her arms, ready to receive Zain and Laron's warm embrace. They were finally home.

CHAPTER FORTY-FOUR

THE DOCTOR'S APPOINTMENT

An hour past dawn, Tundra and the other survivors left the ravaged campsite. It was another hour and a half in hovercraft until they saw the pile of corpses that had gone up in flares the night before. Although they had never had a total count of how many crystallizers attacked, she found seven lying in the snow. Like the man they had interrogated, nothing remained of them but pools of skin, void of any bones in their bodies. With each pool was one of the devices they had worn strapped to their chests.

"Thane, you and your men, check the remains," Tundra said, and then added. "We are searching for anything related to a Doctor Genus Cere, understood?" The men before her nodded. "Good. Elites scout the perimeter. Get to it."

She surveyed the men as they picked up the flabs of skin, handling them as if their condition was contagious, only plucking at them with their fingertips. Not wanting to see the investigation herself, she looked around. She scanned for hidden areas or narrow paths that would make approach difficult, anything that might make a perfect home for a coward such as Dr. Cere. At the same time, she kept surveillance on the sky as well, not wanting a repeat of the night before.

"Conseleigh Iycel."

She turned on her heels.

"I found this."

A Hown coughed and then handed her a keycard. She flipped it over. Scorch marks marred the other side, and the flames had melted some of the rounded corners.

She held onto it. "What else?"

"Conseleigh Iycel."

A second man drew her attention and she turned and saw an elite farther out, waving her over. When he called her name again, she thanked the Hown for his find and walked to the other soldier. "Yes?"

"There be a body. Up there." He pointed up towards a northern valley. "There be something you ought to see."

"Thank you. Let's go." She followed the elite two kilometers to the entry to a valley in the pass.

The snow came up to the knees of her white snowsuit. She still wore her mythril shawl for extra protection on her upper body, but the suit was composed of durable microfibers that would make glancing blows negligible. The only thing she needed to worry about now were direct stabs and thrusts.

In similar fashion, the Hown had changed their suits to white with a push of the H on their chests. The transformed suits kept them warm and camouflaged them with the snow. Just as zircha weapons could change according to the situation, these suits were composed of zircha and synthetic fibers that altered the elasticity and the durability of the suit depending on the environment and needs.

The elite, as was their custom, had not changed outfits, relying instead on the skins of mammoths or polar bears and their shields.

"Is this what you wanted to show me?" She crossed her arms and looked down at the pile of skin that had begun sinking into the snowy plain.

"No, Conseleigh Iycel. Up here. Look there." He pointed down the length of the valley.

She followed his instructions. "And?"

"Now look there." He pointed to the other side of the valley. "There be no snow."

She furrowed her brows and looked from one side of the valley to the other. There was snow farther up the bare shoulder, but nothing at the base. If the man hadn't pointed it out to her, she may not have noticed it. *Well, well, well.* With a smirk, she turned to the man. "Tell the others to join us. We have an appointment with a doctor, and we would not want to keep him waiting."

The man left. She watched him go. *The doctor certainly is clever.* The valley obstructed any wandering eyes, and while the terrain made it difficult for hovercrafts and people on foot, the crystallizers had plenty of room to fly.

She spun the keycard around in her hand while continuing to observe the location of the supposed base. *Let's hope you can get us inside.* She knew being inside was paramount to their survival; a fight out in the open would turn into another massacre.

The hum of hovercrafts stopped as the men arrived. She waited until Boras and Thane approached.

"This be it?" Boras asked, gaze flinty.

"Yes, it appears that way. Thane." She looked to her left.

"Yes, Conseleigh Iycel?"

"Your thoughts here. The best plan of attack?"

Thane coughed once and then was overtaken by a fit of coughing long enough to give Tundra pause.

"Thane?" Other soldiers of Hown were also caught in a fit of phlegmy coughs.

"Conseleigh Iycel, please forgive me." He coughed. "Something must have been caught in my throat. *Vesi.*" He pointed to the snow on the ground and lifted some into the air, changing it to water. He tilted his head back and dropped it into his mouth. The redness in his face lifted as the water brought a measure of relief. "We have to get inside. There is no alternative. A group of us should scout the perimeter and try to find some sort of opening."

"What about the crystallizers?"

"We are fighting on a different field now. It's more cramped here, but at least it's daylight. We won't be ambushed again. They don't fly low unless they are about to go for a kill, so Davis and Harold here can shoot them out of the sky. We will need to bring the fight to them."

"How do you reckon we do that?" Boras asked.

"All of your elites can cast Power, correct?" Thane waited for Boras's confirmation. "We go in pairs then. One will cast Power and lift their partner on a mound of snow to the height of the crystallizers, the other will be ready to engage them in weapons combat or with Power. All Hown soldiers have fully uploaded zircha weapons. The closer we are, the more successful our attacks will be."

This was the type of plan she expected from Thane, who General Satorus had trained as his eventual replacement. Tundra now added to the plan. "Go in groups of three. One Hown with every two elite. Boras, Thane, and Harold, stay here with me. If this be a trap, I won't risk all of our men being exposed at once."

Thane and Boras split their men into five groups. The first group trekked across the land as if they were using the Northern Passage to get to Acquava; their objective was skirt around the side in search of an opening hidden from their current vantage point. The second group went towards the specified area by following the ridge of the mountain as best they could as to avoid an open, direct approach. *That* was left to the last group. Tundra and the men with her stayed behind, observing the battlefield as the pieces on the board moved into place.

Come on, Doctor, make your move. I've made mine.

Halfway to their destinations, a low rumbling sounded. She scanned the mountaintops, searching for the origin, and caught sight of two windows opening higher in the mountain. Crystallizers emerged. One. Two. Three. Soon there were enough in the sky that she couldn't count them on her fingers. "There." She pointed to the opening, the soldiers still around her. Harold strung his bow. "Wait. The first arrow will give away our position. Let's get closer to."

"But our men—"

"Have a competent plan, thanks to you, Thane. Now, follow me."

She hurried to the opposite side of the mountain, looking towards her troops, who were now out in the open, exposed. Flashes of blue barraged the land. After the first blast came from the opposite side, they pivoted their focus to their attackers. As flares of blue spiked down into the valley, mounds of snow carried soldiers into the sky.

They were holding their own as Tundra reached her destination, but she knew it couldn't last forever. Her hand brushed against snow, revealing not mountain stone but metal painted to mimic the mountainside. *This should open!* Her fingers traced the area up and down, looking for something. Eventually, she noticed a groove in the center. She dug her finger in and followed it, making a flat line in the wall.

"Look for a switch or keypad. It has to be somewhere. Once it begins to open, be ready to take fire. Thane, you will come with me inside. Boras and Harold, give us cover." Everyone nodded. "Okay, let's go."

She and the men ran their hands over the metal wall they had found. In a matter of a few minutes, Harold called her over. She hurried to the man's position and saw a keypad. Taking the keycard out from where she had stowed it underneath her wristlace, she swiped the card and waited as the pad read *processing.*

Come on, come on.

A mechanical voice spoke. "Key card accepted."

A loud, low humming started. Gears turned. The mountain shook, showering them with the real snow above the fake facade. A doorway yawned open in front of them.

Yellow light filtered out from inside. Shadows of movement flickered in the dim interior. *Hurry. Come on.* She unwound the wristlace, readying her whip. She unsheathed her ice scimitar. Next to her, Thane removed his black gloves and tucked both inside his belt loop. Then he unsheathed the zircha swords on his right and left hip. He changed his left to a shield and kept his right one as a sword.

The hole was bigger now. She looked back. Boras and Harold loosed arrows at crystallizers as pillars of snow, then ice, constantly changed the landscape on which the others fought.

"How many left?"

"Six."

"Signal to your men to get inside."

The mouth was now open completely. Twenty soldiers equipped with axes, swords, or lances waited for them inside. Two ice guards stood on a platform above the others, behind a railing. Tundra looked up to see an array of archers on a second level, bows strung, arrows aimed down at them.

"Stand down. I am Conseleigh Tundra Iycel. I am only here for Doctor Genus Cere. If you try to interfere, I will be forced to take action," she yelled, imbuing her voice with confidence and authority, hoping some would value their lives more than their supposed duty. "Where is he?" she muttered.

"Lady Iycel, you disappoint me. Do you not recognize me anymore?"

Where is that voice coming from? She looked around, flicking her gaze up once more to the archers. Focusing on the first floor again, she now noticed an older man standing in between the two ice guards on the raised platform. She blinked and shook her head. *Was he there before?*

Dressed in a black lab coat, glasses sitting atop the bridge of his nose, an air of power and arrogance hung about the man as heavy as the maniacal grin he displayed. "It's nice to see you again, Tundra."

"Genus Cere, you are under arrest for the attempted plot to overthrow the Guardian of the Core, Edwyrd Eska."

"Oh, is that so?"

"Yes. Order your men to stand down. None of their blood needs to be shed today."

Dr. Cere frowned. "I don't believe you're telling the truth."

"What do you mean?"

"To be honest, I don't care if the Guardian lives or dies, but my employer is very much interested in his demise, and I'm not one to fail on projects. You should know that, Lady Iycel. I mean, look at my crystallizers." Dr. Cere laughed. "So, it won't be an attempted plot, it will be a *finished* plot. Guardian Eska *will* be overthrown. Unfortunately, you will not be alive to see it. Kill them." Dr. Cere turned; the two ice guards followed him.

A barrage of arrows rained down.

"Fall back," Tundra yelled.

Harold unleashed two arrows before stepping back to join Tundra under cover just inside the entrance. Two bodies fell, slowing some of the soldiers advancing on them. It gave Tundra a split second to assess the progress behind her. Twelve of her fifteen soldiers ran towards her position, wading through the snow as fast as possible. Only four of the crystallizers remained flying, but each one took advantage of her soldiers' undefended movement, turning a few of them into statues of ice.

"*Salama.*" Tundra extended her one arm across the hangar, halting the advance of Dr. Cere's men with a wall of electricity. While keeping part of her mind focused on the wall and their attempts to destroy it, she spoke to the four with her. "Harold, give them cover as they make their way to us. Boras, once they make it through the door, use Power to close the opening with ice."

"That'll trap us," Thane said.

"Yes, but we won't have to worry about getting shot at from behind."

She directed her attention to the enemies in front. One writhed on the ground in shock. He had gotten too close to Tundra's spell. The battle was now at a standstill as Dr. Cere's forces watched and waited, not daring to go closer to the electric field.

"Status of our troops?"

"Here."

"Count?"

"Eleven."

"Close the opening."

"*Vesi.*"

Good. Now for—

The lights went out. Her spell died. Darkness surrounded her small party. Hordes of footsteps advanced. *They're charging blind.*

"Men, form up. Ready your weapons."

The unified sound of the unsheathing of steel sung as loud and as sweet to her as a church bell. The lights went on. The attackers were two steps away. Arrows flew. Bodies fell. The Hown and the elites swung upwards to meet the incoming rain of steel from their adversaries. And soon the room erupted in a chorus of screams and grunts and clashing and slashing. An all-out cacophony of noise became the only constant.

The battle had begun.

I need to get to Doctor Cere before he finds some way to escape. Tundra lashed out with her whip, slashing open a man's thigh. He tripped, but another behind him jumped over him and jabbed a long lance in Tundra's direction. She dodged it by rolling out of the way. She sprang up, lashed out with her ice scimitar, and exchanged a few rounds with the man in front of her. When he raised his sword, she leashed her whip around the man's arm and dragged him forward onto his belly. She kicked the sword out of his hand and plunged her scimitar through his back.

She looked around for her Hown men. "Thane!" The man was dueling two others. He swatted one sword down and shoved a boot into the man's stomach. He stepped back and stumbled over another body. Instead of slowing, he used the momentum of the fall to roll backwards and directed his attention behind him, hitting a man's face with his shield, sending him skidding across the floor. Thane ran after him, not letting the man establish his bearings. The man managed to lift his sword, but Thane switched his shield and sword to two lances and skewered the man through the ribs.

Thane turned to her, his face set with grim determination. "Conseleigh Iycel, what may I do for you?"

"Stay alive and follow me."

They turned to face more of the onslaught. The battle was going their way. Tundra looked back and noticed Boras still concentrating on the ice wall. An attacker was coming for him. *No!* Tundra ran towards the enemy soldier and flipped her whip, but she knew she was too late. She wouldn't get there in time. As she made one last, desperate sprint, an arrow lodged in the man's shoulder, disorienting him. Another arrow flew, this time skewering his leg. The man stumbled and fell. Tundra slid to a halt and turned to see Harold, bow in hand. He nodded at her—and then a flash of blue hit him. *No!* Ice surged up his body.

More flashes of blue forced Tundra to take cover. Four more of her men, and even more of Dr. Cere's own men, became crystalline statues, only to shatter moments after.

"From above!" Another archer came back to her position underneath the lip of the mountain cave. The others continued to fight, both parties now looking out for flashes of blue from above while maintaining their focus on their adversary in front of them.

"Conseleigh Iycel."

"How many arrows you have left?"

The man quickly counted. "Eight."

"Good. We are going to attempt to bring those crystallizers down. You fire and I'll lace your arrow with electric Power, understood?"

"Yes, Conseleigh."

"Thane, tell Boras to shield us with some of the ice cover when I raise my arm."

Thane nodded and slipped away.

"Are you ready?" The archer nodded. Tundra looked back to Boras and Thane. They nodded as well. "Let's begin."

Tundra followed after the archer. When he loosed an arrow up in the air, she quickly coated it with electricity she pulled from the lights still in the room. It found its mark. The crystallizer faltered in the air, its wing paralyzed, and fell, twisting and spinning—until it leveled out, unharmed, the wing regaining functionality.

Damnit.

"How accurate are you?"

"As accurate as I need to be."

"Aim for the black devices on their chest."

The crystallizers fired at them. Tundra raised her arm and Boras's ice shield formed and swallowed the impacts. Tundra watched the flying men, their forms disfigured through the shield of ice. She returned her attention to the battle on the ground. Enemies closed in.

"Thane."

"On it."

Thane sprinted to their position and engaged the incoming adversary in a quick bout, ending in Thane bashing the man's skull in with his zircha shield after swiping out the man's balance with his lance.

"Let's go to the left."

They moved out from under the shield of ice. The archer released another arrow. It hit, but not the device. Again, the man fell halfway and then recovered.

This is too slow. I need to be with Doctor Cere. She turned around. "Boras. Ignore the wall. The fight is in here now. Hurry."

The wall died and with it a gust of cool mountain air filtered in through the hangar that had begun smelling of death and sweat.

"Continue shooting down those crystallizers. Thane, you and I will find Doctor Cere. Provide us cover."

The two elites nodded. Tundra and Thane raced from behind their shelter of ice. Paying no attention to the others still fighting around them, they sprinted through a door at the back of the hangar to enter a series of hallways.

"Where do we go?"

"Up."

They found a staircase and took the steps two at a time. On the fifth and last level, they emerged in another hangar, this one smaller and with a sharply sloping ceiling. The peak of the mountain, Tundra realized. Cool air filtered in from vents she couldn't see. As silently as possible, she and Thane darted from hiding place to hiding place to avoid the handful of men loading the ships, all while making their way toward the strange purple ship at the far end.

Good, it's still here. Perhaps we can use the information inside to find out who else may be involved.

Carts large enough to hold human cadavers were being maneuvered onto a different, larger ship. Alongside them were bags of red liquid. *What in the Abaddon's name...* Dr. Cere talked to a man with a furunculous face, pointing from another area to the ship. Her eyes followed his gestures, and he pointed to another room with a glass wall. She could make out what appeared to be a series of water-locked chambers.

Cere turned her way. Tundra didn't hide. He frowned, his mouth twisting in annoyance. He patted the man on the arm, said something, and the other man glanced her way as well. He darted off into the room without further hesitation.

"Lady Iycel, so you still live. How... disappointing," Dr. Cere said.

All around, men stopped working. The two ice guards with Dr. Cere moved alongside the old man.

"I feel the same. I thought the men you received from Astor Grime and Marquis Desmier would have been more challenging."

Dr. Cere walked towards her, the Ice Guards at his side. Ten more men from around the perimeter soon joined them.

"Well, perhaps you'll find these men a little more difficult. Kill them."

The ten men charged Tundra and Thane, weapons drawn. Tundra wasted no time in launching an assault, knowing Thane would do the same. With him, she rushed one group of five. He launched one of his zircha lances through the air, piercing a soldier's chest, crumpling him. Tundra lashed out with her whip, wrapping it around a man's forearm and dragging him to collide with one of his comrades. The man stumbled and fell to his feet, and she quickly decapitated him before exchanging blows with another man beside him. Thane retrieved his lance, crouched, and swung the lance into a new opponent, forcing the man off balance. Thane finished him, punching his shield into the man's face while jabbing forward with his lance through another man's throat with deft precision.

In short, they made quick work of the first five men and did the same with the next, but before they had a chance to rest, the two ice guards entered the fray. Both were more muscular than the ones before and in true Sereyan fashion had ice for eyes. They unsheathed scimitars similar to Tundra's. They each pushed a button on a metallic armband and shields formed in their hands. She twisted her lips. *That man needs to be put down.*

She and Thane exchanged blows with the ice guards. To her surprise, Thane's condition didn't seem to be having much of an effect on his ability to keep up with his new opponent. She knew from being Lady of Sereya that these men were strong warriors, and at her age, she needed to be alert and ready. She lashed out with her whip, trying to wrap it around the man's leg. He swiped it out of the way with his scimitar.

From her peripherals, she noticed Dr. Cere. He carried a black chest plate, a glass screen, and a bag. And he was boarding the ship. Others followed, rolling stretchers with bodies up into the ship's cargo hold. *He's leav—*

Pain erupted in her face. She shot back across the floor, landing on one of the dead bodies. Her whip and scimitar fell from her hands. Her vision blurred and a roar sounded in her ears as she tried to right herself. Lights flashed. She blinked. Her opponent towered over her. Defenseless, she looked around.

Nothing.

He swung down. She rolled out of the way. He swung again. Using her mythril shawl to catch the blade, she then pulled, trying it yank it away from him, but he overpowered her and ripped the shawl away from her. It floated to the ground behind him. Eyes wide, she kicked at the back of his leg, where there wasn't any ice armor, but it did nothing to his muscular hamstrings. He swung his sword again. Tundra pushed herself backwards. But not far enough. The blade cut through her cheek and she felt blood gush down her jaw. Before the man could finish her, a lance erupted through his back, then another through his head. She ducked, but there was no avoiding the shower of blood.

Thane stood behind the man, shoulders outstretched in his follow through. He pulled back, and the man crumpled to the floor alongside her. Thane offered the end of his lance to help her up onto her feet.

"Thank you."

"My pleasure, Conseleigh Iy..." Thane coughed.

And then that coughing erupted into a fit that brought him to his knees.

"Thane!" Tundra knelt beside him. He held her back with one arm, while the other hand tore at his collar. She torqued her head to Dr. Cere, who stood there in a sickening awe. He muttered something under his breath. "What is happening? What are you doing to him?"

She turned back to Thane. Blood gushed out from his mouth, painting the metallic blue floor red. He tried to stand, but collapsed. His weapons fell from his grasp, reverberating throughout the hangar. Tundra flinched at each cough. Thane clawed at his neck with the fervor of a mad man. And even when he got it loose and unbuttoned half of his shirt, he fell onto his back his entire body spasming.

Foam fizzled from his mouth. Blood spilled from his eyes and slid down his cheeks to meet the foam. He blinked. When he opened his eyes again, they were wide. And they never shut.

"Thane!" On her knees, Tundra shook the man. "Thane!" She pivoted on her knees to face Dr. Cere who laughed and clapped his hands together in glee. "You monster what is... What did you do?"

"*I* did nothing."

The way he corrected her sickened her. She grabbed her scimitar, whip, and mythril shaw and readied herself. "What did you do?" She pointed the scimitar at him and stepped closer.

"I already told you, Conseleigh Iycel. *I* did nothing. I have been over here all along. But I do wonder how the remaining Hown are faring." He chuckled to himself.

"How... what..."

"Oh, Conseleigh Iycel. This is where we differ so much. You only saw the present. You never saw the future. You never saw what Sereya could become, only ever what it was. And that is a shame."

"What are you talking about?" She lashed out with her whip.

He disappeared and then reappeared to the right as the whip snapped at empty air. "Like I said to you before, Lady Iycel, I always follow through on my endeavors. *Always.* When I learned that you had abdicated your throne to Astor Grime in order to work for Guardian Eska, I returned to Sereya, hoping he would see a vision you failed to appreciate. Unlike you, he *had* visions for the future. I met with people in his circle and learned of Victor Zigarda's loathing for Guardian Eska. It just so happened that I hated you for not funding my projects, not seeing my intelligence, not seeing my potential. All I wanted was the recognition I deserved. Victor Zigarda gave me that. He gave me everything I asked for. And we worked together and devised a plan. With him, my projects flourished, and I told him I would help him achieve his desire: vengeance. Edwyrd Eska stole from him everything, just like you did to me when you banished me from Sereya."

Tundra snarled. "Edwyrd stole nothing. He won it. He and Victor faced the Trials. Victor merely couldn't compete with him."

"Perhaps. But that's another story... This task that Victor wanted to accomplish was so ambitious that we needed a plan. The right plan and the right time. So we waited and prepared and waited some more. And eventually the Trials came, and then it was time to put our plan into action."

"How does this relate to Hown?"

"Well, Hown defends the Central Core, does it not? If we wanted a chance at usurping Guardian Eska, we needed to get rid of them first. And, that is what I have just done. Well, not me per se, but I did plant the seed." Dr. Cere chortled to himself. "Oh my, it does certainly amuse me to see you this upset."

Tundra seethed through her teeth. "How?"

"Do you think it was by accident that our Emporian ship met you at the same time as the apprentice came out from the Central Core? No, we needed you to find us there, so that we could get access, even just for a second, to Hown."

Tundra recalled the ship landing. It had been right before the funeral on Acquava. She narrowed her eyes and stepped closer to Dr. Cere.

"When your young apprentice opened that case, a bug flew out, just like a few others that had been in a small box in our ship. Their mission was to bite and implant little metallic eggs in the bloodstream of all the men there. This would eventually dissolve through the acidic nature of the human organs and intestines, or it could be triggered."

Tundra's eyes widened. "Why didn't you kill them sooner?"

"I told you. *I* didn't kill them at all. Although I was ready." Dr. Cere shook a device in his hand, smirked, and set it down on the table. "It turns out that your men are too good at what they do. I guess that is why they are the most renowned soldiers in all of Gladonus, after all? Well, should I say *were*." He cackled.

Tundra felt her bottom lip tremble and bit down to stop it. "What are you talking about, you crazy…"

"Come now, Lady Iycel. That's not nice. I've been nothing but…," Dr. Cere thought for a moment, "*crystal clear* in what's been done." He chuckled.

She lashed out with her whip.

Dr. Cere turned invisible. When he reappeared again, he was beside the purple bubble-shaped ship.

"How did you do that? You were behind Zakk Shiren? How did he get mixed up into this whole thing?"

"Oh, that boy. Well, we actually wanted Zain. We watched him for months and planned on capturing him before the Trials even began. Zakk and he had begun fighting, however, and so I watched the scene play out from the forest."

"You needed Zain for his father?"

"Correct."

"Then why Zakk?"

"Well, Zakk was like Zain's brother. And we used his loathing of Zain and Zain's betrayal to our greater goal. Anger is a very strong motivator."

"No."

"I am wrong, am I? Tell me what is motivating you now to come here and try to capture me?"

"My duty."

"Duty? No, you are here because of your hatred. You want to get revenge for everything that has happened and will happen." Dr. Cere looked at the chest plate on the table and strapped it on, keeping his eyes fixed on Tundra all along.

"You are planning on overthrowing Guardian Eska, and I vow to stop it."

"Even if you stop me, Lady Iycel, there will be others."

"What do you mean?"

Dr. Cere shook his head at her and clicked his tongue against his teeth. He chuckled. "Do you think Victor is the only one who wants Guardian Eska overthrown?" He finished strapping the sides of his chestpiece together.

She lashed out with her whip. "Talk."

He turned invisible again, and this time appeared in front of the table, no more than ten feet in front of her. "No. There has been enough of that. This is the point where you die." He donned a pair of goggles. "I'm sure you remember this machine, yes? Well, now it's been upgraded, as you likely noticed." He pushed the black button on his chest and ice grew out from it, overtaking his body like a parasite. Unlike the others, though, he grew along with the ice, his body becoming thrice his actual size. Tundra's mouth hung slack as she witnessed the transformation. *How is that...*

Behind his goggles, his icy eyes turned dark blue. Within moments, crystalline armor covered the rest of his body. Wings like a butterfly's sprouted from his back. His left arm became a cannon, like the others, but his right remained a hand.. He reached behind him and withdrew a large blade of ice, similar to Tundra's, albeit much larger. When the process finished, Dr. Cere had grown to the height of a spaceship.

Looking at the crystalline monster the doctor had now become, she curled her lips. *He has to be put down.*

He swung at her. She ducked and rolled out of the way. He blasted her with his cannon, and she barely avoided the maneuver.

"*Salama.*" She called on the electricity from the room. She swirled her hand around her, and it formed a dome. She backed away from him, gauging his movements. He hadn't taken to flight yet, and for that she was thankful. *How to defeat—*

"Conseleigh Iycel!"

She looked behind her. Boras and four other elites made their way towards her. No Hown.

A flash of blue streaked toward her, encasing her, but she didn't freeze. Instead, the surrounding electricity was frozen. On instinct, she ducked. The cannon boomed and half of her frozen electric shell vanished. Dr. Cere towered over her.

"*Salama.*" She struck out with her whip towards the crystallizer's heart, but it bounced harmlessly off of Dr. Cere's icy sword.

She sprinted to Boras.

"The others be—"

"We will talk later. First, we need to kill *that.*"

Wings flapped. Dr. Cere pounced over to their location, shooting a blast of ice while in midair. Everyone scattered to safety, though one Garian was caught in the blast. It froze him, and Dr. Cere severed him in two soon after.

Tundra clenched her fist and regrouped with Boras.

"And how do you reckon we do that?" the Garian asked.

"You Garians know how to climb, right?"

"What we best at."

"Good. Go to that ship over there and climb up behind it. I will lead Dr. Cere to it. Take out his wings."

Boras nodded and signaled for one elite to join him. The other two battled against Dr. Cere's large sword, keeping him at bay.

"*Salama.*" Tundra swung her whip, now sparking with electricity, towards the crystallizer. When the whip cracked the air, the electricity flew from it like darts and found its mark on Dr. Cere's body. The attack did nothing but draw his attention. *His ice is too thick.*

He raised his cannon and fired, then flew towards her and swung his sword.

Tundra rolled out of the way. She steadied herself and lashed out with her whip, tying it around his cannon arm. As he began to fly away, she tugged and tried to keep him in place. "Help!" The two Garians pulled on the whip with her and used his own momentum against him to fling him back towards the ship.

Dr. Cere crashed into it but quickly got up. When he did, Boras and the other elite were there to jump onto his back. Both elites began hacking off each wing. Using this distraction to her advantage, Tundra ran forward.

"Follow me," she called to the remaining elites.

Dr. Cere swung his sword blindly over his shoulder, slicing Boras's partner in half. Boras jumped off before the same fate could befall him. Dr. Cere turned and fired the cannon at the floor, sending Boras flying into a hangar wall, crumpling to the floor upon impact.

Still not cognizant of Tundra's position, Dr. Cere checked his wings. He tried flying, but could only hop. The damage to the wings had already been done. Tundra lashed out with her whip and wrapped it around one of the large crystal legs. Receiving help from the others, she pulled and Dr. Cere fell onto his back; the sword slipped out of his hand and shattered into shards of ice.

"Now's our chance. Follow my lead."

Tundra and the two others climbed onto his body. The doctor raised his cannon arm. Tundra dropped and hugged the crystalline armor. The shot went right over her and into one of the elites behind her. Before he could charge it for another attack, she took her icy scimitar and plunged it down into the black heart on his chest. "*Salama.*" Electricity flowed from the wall of the hangar to her sword. The elite did the same with his axe.

Dr. Cere's body shook in violent fits, threatening to throw them off, but they held on. His arms and feet twitched and flicked and flailed. He moaned. Then he went limp. The ice began to melt and Dr. Cere's body began to shrink.

"That be it?" asked the elite alongside her through panting breaths.

"I think that's it," she breathed back.

She retrieved her sword and sheathed it. Not wanting to stand on the melting body, she hopped down to the floor. The elite next to her ran to his superior while she waited, arms crossed, feet tapping, watching the scene.

"Boras!"

Boras had struggled to a seated position and waved his arm. "I... I be fine... Sir Horm hits harder than that," he joked.

Tundra tried to smile. *Well, at least two of them are alive still? Twenty-three elites and ten Hown...* She shivered. *What will Edwyrd think of this?*

Ice water ran between her feet. The doctor lay in a pool of it, but he didn't move. Was he still alive? She went over to his body and crouched down. "Speak, you fool."

Nothing.

She put her fingers to his neck. No pulse. The man was as cold as death. "A shame." She put her hands on her knees, stood up, and walked back over to the two remaining elite.

"What kind of man is that?"

"A dead man, unfortunately. And dead men tell no secrets. I would have liked to learn some things before killing him." Tundra folded her arms across her chest. "Are there any more of you downstairs?"

Boras shook his head. "We be what's left."

Tundra chewed on her lower lip. *Lady Aprah certainly won't be happy with me.* "Well, at least the threat is gone now." Tundra feigned a smile, hoping her annoyance at the situation wouldn't show. "Before heading back, let's do a full scan of this facility and see what we can find." She turned on her heels.

"Conseleigh Iycel, those others be..."

She looked back. "Gone." She sighed. "I know."

"They just be... be coughing and coughing and..."

"I know, Boras. I saw Thane die before my eyes."

"Why?"

Tundra shook her head. "I don't know, but it's something I hope to find out."

"What about the bodies?"

"Collect the Hown weapons for Lady Aprah. It'll be my gift to her for allowing me to use her elites. The bodies we will burn before we leave. For now, let's scour this facility for clues. Anything that may link Doctor Cere to other conspirators or give away a next move."

"A next move?" the other elite asked.

Tundra nodded. "Men like Doctor Cere always have a next move."

She turned around and went towards the doctor's bubble ship, hoping to examine travel logs first. That would give her the most reliable information. From there, perhaps something else would come out of scouring the hangar, but she doubted it. The other, larger ship and its cargo had gotten away during the fight. Had there been others before that one? Why were bodies being rolled onto it?

The uncertainty of everything muddied Tundra's mind, not allowing her to think clearly. She scanned the travel logs as diligently and efficiently as her unsteady breaths, wandering mind, and shaky fingers allowed. To her dismay, the travel logs had been erased. *Curse that man.* She slammed her fist down on the control panel.

She tried steadying her breathing but couldn't. Instead, her attempt at peace only ended up becoming a war of questions in her mind. How was Dr. Cere able to stay so many steps ahead of them? How did the Hown actually die? And who else wanted Edwyrd dead?

CHAPTER FORTY-FIVE

OUT OF TIME

H ydro lurched sideways. Then forward. Next thing he knew, he flew through the air and landed hard on his back, rolling until he succumbed to friction. In all the jostling, the bag enclosing him had loosened. He could see a faint light flutter through. Hydro blinked, trying to comprehend what had just occurred. The ringing in his ears and throbbing in his skull threatened to overwhelm him, but Hydro tried as best he could to pry apart the small gap in the bag. Inch by inch, he pulled it apart, loosening it like a stubborn knot.

His hand exited first and then his head. Supporting himself with one arm, he raised the other to shield his eyes from the light that flooded his vision. Everything was so light now. So bright. Hydro twisted saw half his body still was in the bag. He crawled out. What had that bag been? It had syphoned all of his Power. He looked around. Where was he?

Before focusing on that, he took a moment to massage his temples. With a groan, he asked himself. "What just happened?"

I'd like to know that, too.

Hydro looked to his right. Anne stood alongside him. Hydro huffed, ignoring her for once. He got to his feet and looked around. The hovercraft had crashed and toppled into the dirt nose first and now lay on its back, part of it crushing a man's arm underneath. A second body lay outside the range of the hovercraft, face down in the dirt.

"Did you do this?"

No.

Hydro walked towards the body. He kicked it over, revealing the Hown who had introduced himself as General Satorus. The man's face was wet with blood. The ground where his face had rested was a pool of crimson, almost as if he had drowned in it. Hydro kicked the man again.

Nothing.

Hydro flicked his gaze to the other Hown, the one crushed by the hovercraft, and walked toward it. The corpse looked up at the sky with blank eyes. An open mouth filled with red told Hydro that he had choked on his own blood.

Hydro's stomach churned. *What happened here? Was it the...*

Hydro's eyes widened. But how? The pill had been to kill Hydro, not them. Unless… Unless Zigarda had wanted to keep that a secret. But why? Did Dr. Cere or Zigarda know that he had used it? What did that mean? His eyebrows arched.

Taking a moment to count the jewels in his pouch, he then retraced the way back to the entrance of the Sacred Passage. All around, Hydro saw bodies with gaping holes or limbs torn from their sockets. Some of the Hown were merely squished, so flat they were hardly recognizable as once human. The ones who weren't dismembered in some way lay motionless in pools of their own blood. There was nothing *sacred* about this area anymore.

Hydro shuddered at the massacre.

He noted his sword still lay on the ground, although a Hown had seemingly tried to grab it and now lay dead in a coating of blood that had originated from the orifices of his face. Standing over the dead man who held Purge, Hydro tapped his foot and bit his lower lip, surveying once more the field of cadavers that lay like weeds across the ground. Truly, what had happened here?

He pried Purge out of the man's cold, dead grasp. Seeing his sword stained with blood, Hydro wiped it on the Hown's black tunic and then walked over to C-Bot. The machine stood behind a set of two large boulders, cannons on its shoulders, ready to fire, but completely immobilized. A black tarp hung over its face, similar to the material that had ensnared Hydro, except this was meshed and not whole.

"Maa."

A pillar of earth drew him face level with the machine, and then, carefully, using the tip of the blade as if he were etching out his name in a tree, he cut loose the black mesh on the ship's face, noticing a slight crack beneath the windshield. The machine jolted back to life in front of Hydro and flapped its wings. Well, it tried to, but they sputtered and stopped.

Hydro frowned. The Hown had definitely immobilized Cere's weapon. But did it still function? If it couldn't fight anymore, or at least to the same capacity, could it at least still hunt down the jewels? Hydro entered the ship and strapped himself into the pilot's seat. This would be the moment of truth.

He held his breath and pushed the button to transform the machine back into a ship.

It worked.

Hydro exhaled.

While the polymorphous machine took its time forming itself back into the spaceship, Hydro looked out over the field of dead Hown, thankful that the machine had come to his rescue, or at least had tried. *How would I have done alone?* Hydro regretted that thought as he counted twenty-three bodies on the ground. And then he remembered the other two farther away. Twenty-five Hown had been hunting him. Were there more? Had the other Hown succumbed to the same twisted fate?

One thing remained certain in Hydro's mind: He would have died if he had tried to fight them. Even now, he should be dead. Why wasn't he?

He gritted his teeth and punched his tongue into his cheek. There was no aftertaste from the pill. After biting down, he had felt a tingle briefly flood his mouth and then the substance had dissolved, leaving not even a taste of a trace.

The whole scenario brought questions to his mind that normally he wouldn't like to think about, but given the alternative—facing the reality of what he had tried to do—he welcomed the questions openly, making space for them in his thoughts.

What had the doctor actually given him? What other secrets were he and Zigarda hiding from him? Why wasn't he dead? How did the Hown find him? What would have happened if he hadn't escaped? Did Zigarda know what had just occurred? Regardless, he needed to let the old man know he was still alive and still accomplishing his mission.

The ship finished transforming.

Without wasting any more time, he placed a hand on the glass panel on the control board, waiting for it to scan his identification and give him access to call Zigarda. It took longer than usual. Hydro pressed harder. *Why aren't you working?* He lifted his hand and realized the glass was cracked. Hydro pounded his leg with one fist.

"Connect me with Lord Zigarda!" Hydro yelled.

"Connecting with Lord Zigarda." the mechanical voice called back.

Hydro's heart fluttered.

"Connection failed. System damaged."

Hydro's shoulders slumped. He sighed. He tapped his fingers on the control board, contemplating what the aftermath of this unexpected development would be.

"Where is the next jewel?"

Blink. Blop. Blip.

The three sounds repeated and reverberated on the dashboard in front of him.

"Sensors indicate there is one jewel left in the north."

"Let's go."

From his leather seat, Hydro felt the anitron kick in. Around the ship, dead bodies floated in the air briefly under the spell of anitron before falling back to the earth as the ship took off towards its new destination. As C-Bot flew north, Hydro looked to the east and saw the Summer Ocean, beyond lay the Summer Isles and then Acquis. There, his brother was learning to fill their father's shoes. And he would, if given the time to grow into that duty. But Hydro feared that was the one thing his brother now lacked even more than he did.

Hydro stood upon a crystal glass plateau. How many hours had passed since taking off in C-Bot, he couldn't be sure. Time seemed to conspire with the whirlwind of thoughts in his mind to disorient him. Here, out in the open wind, it was gelid enough to make Hydro's seablood shiver. His hands lingered on the handles of two silver doors painted in brumal blues and whites. Dr. Cere's machine hovered behind him, waiting for him to enter the crystalline palace and collect the jewel. Given his previous experiences, though, Hydro was anything but anxious to see what lay beyond those double doors. In improper attire and completely exposed on this plateau of ice, an unexpected williwaw forced his hand to pull back and opened the doors before him.

Inside, everything was crystal, from the floors to the walls to the crystal chandelier that hung above a throne stationed in the center and carved of ice. A thousand Hydros were reflected back at him by the countless facets and angles. Unlit sconces hung around the circular room. The whole place looked pristine, holy, as if it had been untouched for years.

After his eyes adjusted to the reflective brightness of the place, Hydro spotted a jewel, striped black and white like a zebra, atop the crystal throne. The streaks of black here made it stand out starkly against the expanse of crystal. Hydro smirked. *Well, this one was much easier than the rest.* He climbed the stairs, picked it up, sat down in its place, and opened up his satchel.

When he touched the armrest of the crystal chair, he immediately pulled back. *Everything is so cold.* His rear was quickly growing cold, despite the layers of protection. His fingers shook. His teeth chattered, speaking a language all their own.

A breeze wafted toward Hydro from a large glassless window that faced towards the west. He moved towards the opening and looked out over the snow dunes and the large lake below and the narrow bridge of ice that connected the southern half of the continent to the northern half.

He shivered as he stared out. Wind slapped him again, and he pulled away. Slowly, he walked around the circular room, breathing warm air onto his hands. He didn't like this feeling. He had only felt cold like this once before in his life...

If you are cold, Hydro Paen, cast fire and make yourself warm.

Not taking his hands away from his mouth, he looked down and to the left and found Anne. "It is too cold. It is impossible."

Nothing is impossible now that we are bonded, Hydro Paen. Go ahead, cast fire.

Hydro took his hands away from his mouth and held them out in front of him. "*Palo.*" Fire sprouted from his hands and climbed over his palms and forearms. *Fire. It's fire.*

Feel its warmth.

How—

Don't you wish you had the Power you have now, then? When it mattered more than ever.

Hydro clenched his hands, eclipsing the fire and pushing it out around his knuckles. *Anya...* The cold tried its hardest to seep back into Hydro's veins, but the fire around him wouldn't allow it. He wouldn't feel cold again. He wouldn't be helpless again. And as long as he had the necklace, he would never be Powerless again. "Things would have been different."

They most certainly would have, Hydro Paen. History would have been different if you had been able to cast that spell and save your sister.

His mind began fantasizing about things that would have been. *How far could Anya's skill have grown? Would our family ever have been fractured? How would Aiton and Anya have gotten along?*

The thoughts carried him across the crystal room until he stopped in front of a mirror. It hung directly in front of the icy throne. He had been too fixated on the jewel to see it when he first had entered, and then the breeze had called to him. But now, the pearl-white frame sparkled, reflecting the radiance from the icy chandelier above the large, circular chamber. It didn't look like a glass mirror, though. Like everything else in the chamber, it seemed to be composed of crystal. Crystal so pure, he could see himself reflected perfectly in it.

He looked.

Black.

He saw black.

He closed his eyes and stepped back. He shook his head. *What is that?* His heart racing, he opened his eyes yet again and went close to the mirror.

Black.

"Why are my eyes black?"

They aren't black, Hydro Paen.

"I can see them. Yes, they are. They are black. Black as shadows." He looked at Anne at his side. "You lied to me. What are you? Who are you?" Hydro looked at the mirror, but to where Anne should have been, not at his own reflection this time

The mirror shattered upon Anne's shouts and screams and shrieks. Hydro shielded his face with his arms. Pain lanced through his arms as the shards cut into him. The room's temperature plummeted, becoming colder than anything Hydro had ever experienced.

"Palo."

Fire spun its way around him, keeping him from the cold. Underneath him, a large, black snake slid across the floor—no, not across, under the ice. He took an involuntary step back as he noticed wings on its back. And limbs the length of his body that protruded from it in places where the black scales seemed to stop.

"What... what is this?"

Hydro pivoted, his torso twisting constantly, trying to keep track of the black presence underneath the ice as it snaked up the walls and across the crystal ceiling. The chamber seemed to press in around him, constricting him. Even though the fire kept him warm, it didn't help his discomfort, and he staggered to the icy steps and collapsed. As he choked and coughed, the flames sprouted higher, until Hydro illuminated the room by himself. But now he was too warm; the Power was quickly overtaking his body. Despite his efforts to control it, he couldn't. So he let it die completely, and then he slumped on the steps, exhausted and panting.

A black face looked down on him from the crystal ceiling above. Its red tongue took the form of the chandelier, and it spoke to him in a voice that Hydro did not know. It was a deep voice, an old voice, a tormented voice that knew pain and agony. A voice similar to how he felt.

"Who... who are you?" Hydro rubbed his eyes, hoping it was a conjuration of his troubled mind. "Where is Anne?"

Anne was never with you. Just me, Hydro Paen. Desmós.

Where had he heard that name before? He no longer stared into the eyes of an innocent little girl, but the black eyes of a dragon the likes of which he had never seen. Hydro's mind raced. *Beware the girl with black hair. Is this what that monster meant?*

Hydro tried to swallow down his fear. "Why? Why are my eyes black?"

Do you not think that being able to cast any spell should demand sacrifice?

"My eyes?"

Since you can cast any spell at any time, you have the Power of all spells: earth, wind, fire, and lightning. All four flow through you at once. Black is the

combination of everything, is it not? Black is everything that you have done and everything that you will do.

"Black is my soul?"

It will not stay black. Do not worry, Hydro Paen. My master will clear your eyes and allay your worries.

"Why? Why do you show yourself to me like this now?"

I didn't choose this. This room chose this. That cursed mirror chose this.

Hydro tried to find the shards of crystal glass on the floor, but in this overwhelming abyss of darkness, he couldn't. Did he dare another question? Moreover, did he dare another answer? "Why were you a little girl? Who is she?"

Would you trust me if you had met me like this?

Hydro thought about his answer in silence.

"Should I trust you now?"

Yes. The word was drawled out, shaking the chandelier as the tongue moved back and forth. *I will never lie to you, Hydro Paen, unlike them, out there. I told you I would give you Power beyond your wildest imagination, and now you have it, an ancient Power. That is how bonds work. Until your very last breath, my strength is your strength.* The chandelier swung again.

He couldn't see it, but he could hear the crystal chimes call to him, though whether they moved at the command of the wind or this creature that was and yet was not there, he couldn't say. Hydro looked around. The whole room had turned black, and if Hydro hadn't known he was in a room with crystal floors and ceilings and walls, he would have thought he was in deep space, where stars didn't shine and hope was forever lost.

CHAPTER FORTY-SIX

THE STEM-WINDER

"Lords, ladies, senators, politicians, and representatives of the individual nations, I hereby call this meeting to order." Neil Raiden lowered his hands. "Before this meeting can truly begin, roll call will be taken."

After the Speaker of the Senate established that a quorum was present, Senator Numos would begin the verbal assault on Eska. Like a true Mistralian, Numos didn't have notecards. Luvan assumed the man had practiced his speech enough, had strong enough conviction, and knew his goals well enough that notecards would only impede his state of flow. He sat next to Luvan, both hands on top of his cane, waiting for Speaker Raiden to finish his duty.

From what Luvan saw, quorum wouldn't be an issue. He had already counted at least nine of the twelve families in power. Those missing were Lady Clayse and Lord Evber. And while Lord Astor Grime didn't make an appearance, his sons, both of them, Whittiker and Canice, filled his absence. Lord Zigarda's presence only reaffirmed in Luvan's mind that Senator Numos had secret dealings with the man, for how else would he have known about the meeting? Luvan had gone to his Web only to find it completely vacant, save for one man who helped him gain access to the telecommunication chamber. He would deal with that later.

After notifying Pyre, Luvan had busied himself with drafting a speech. But not just any speech, a stem-winder. One that would sway any supporters for the Guardian over to his cause. The toughest opposition would be Lord Garrett Omyon, who he knew to have been Guardian Eska's mentor before Eska competed in his own Trials. Luvan had a plan for him, but even if he didn't obtain the lord's vote, he assumed there would be enough support to at least bring Guardian Eska before the assembly and hold him accountable for his recent actions. The only other nation that he foresaw problems with was Cresica, and only because the apprentice was from there. But Luvan had planned for that as well. Regardless of how either of those two nations voted, if Senator Numos could withhold his end of the bargain, then the two-thirds majority would be met, and their plan would advance to the impeachment.

"Finally, Lord Evber of Epoch. Are you present?"

From the audience, a voice called, "I, Nathan Alaois, have been granted permission by Lord Daven Evber to assume his voice and duties while he remains occupied elsewhere. The voice of Epoch is present."

"Very well. Quorum has been met. I leave you in the hands of the organizer of this meeting, Senator Nyom Numos of Mistral." Senate Speaker Raiden bowed and returned to an empty chair at the back. Before he sat down, Senator Numos hoisted himself up with a grunt, shook the man's hand, and proceeded to the podium.

Numos looked around the chamber before speaking. His goal was simply to make opening remarks and demonstrate the potential abuse of contestants in the Trials. This would only amount to circumstantial reasoning, however, it would be Luvan's testimony that would win the crowd.

"Lords and ladies, and those granted authority by those absent, I would like to say thank you for coming here today. I know your duties are great and your responsibilities endless, so I do not take lightly your decision to be here, nor will I waste your time." A pause. "There is a threat we must stand against.

"Yes, there is a threat here unlike any other. It runs like a wolf on the plains of Cresica, unchecked, wild, and unafraid. It stalks into the villages and cities of every nation with the ability to either protect or demolish. That threat that I speak of today is the Guardian of the Core, Edwyrd Eska.

"None of you elected him to be Guardian of the Core, but Guardian he is. Some of you may have had forefathers or foremothers who played some role in his election." Numos paused. "Some of you did not. But, *none of you* elected this man. This man was not given any of your votes. Well, besides you, of course, Lord Omyon." Numos extended a hand and bowed to the only lord with First Blood in the room. He cleared his throat and continued. "Still, we remain under his jurisdiction because of a vote almost two centuries past. Why should we allow ourselves to be manacled to this man any longer?" He paused and let the words seep in.

"Let me tell you a story from my time at the Trials. I won the great pleasure of being Guardian Eska's sole observer during the Trials. And I watched as six contestants vied for the position that Eirek Mourse now holds. As I observed the contestants, I did not see much that should earn them the authority of Guardian. During the first trial, they were tested on partnership, yet two of the three teams exited the trial with one partner in need of serious medical attention. I ask, where was the partnership? Surely they should have sustained fewer injuries if it truly was an event that tested such a trait.

"The next trial aimed to test intelligence. Each contestant was given a riddle, the answer to which would lead them to the hiding place for a secret orb. It was a well-designed task, and it did test critical thinking, but during that task, two more individuals ended up sustaining grave injuries. Your nephew, Lord Vangle, and the son of Lord Evber both succumbed to the strength of Hydro Paen. The very same man who Guardian Eska decreed is now the target of an inter-system manhunt. I will get to that point later, though." Numos paused and looked up towards where those of Onkh sat.

"The third trial gave perhaps the only real glimpse of what a Guardian should do —protect. But even this weapons tournament failed in providing accurate data, for we all know that a Guardian's might not only comes from the ability to wield a blade, but also the might of Power the Guardian wields. *Palo.*"

Luvan sucked in a sharp breath when he saw a blue flame wrap around Numos's hand. *The man can cast?* He had hidden the ability well. All this time, Luvan thought Numos had been merely skilled with words—and perhaps a fork. Luvan bit his lower lip. *He's a powerful sage as well. Interesting.* Luvan closed his eyes and continued honing his speech as Numos concluded his account of the fourth Trial.

"All of these may have been well-intentioned, but they have led to serious grievances besetting us now, and I believe those heartaches started with the Trials. The Trials, meant to find an adequate apprentice, did much more than that. They became a catalyst that has caused the fiber of those contestants to change and morph into derelicts and delinquents." Numos quickly put up his hand, holding one finger up with it. "By no fault of their own, mind you, but by the fault of the Trials and Guardian Eska." He paused. "Where is the proof, you may ask? How do we know that it was indeed the Trials that changed them? Well, that is why I have gathered you all here today. You are the proof, as in many cases they have affected you the most. I would like to call on the voice of Empora, first. Lord Zigarda, please stand and state what you have observed."

Luvan knew why Numos had chosen Empora to go first. With Lord Zigarda at the helm, Empora would be boisterous and vocal about the transgressions. Luvan also assumed Numos would juxtapose the events of the Trials with other complaints that preceded them, of which Zigarda no doubt had many. Both things would encourage other nations to speak up.

Gears rolled and Luvan heard the telltale humming that signaled the appearance of the projector screen at the rear of the chamber. The lights dimmed further. Luvan looked towards Neil Raiden; the old man squinted now at the projector screen being utilized. Neither spoke, but twisted in their seats to see the footage clearly.

The video showed Zain and Gabrielle on the streets of Mendeck. A crash had just occurred and civilians ran to and fro in the streets. Emporian guards were trying to make their way up the mound of wreckage to get to Zain, but together they killed them. Luvan felt his mouth drop open and hurried to shut it. *Is... is this real?* He turned back to the audience for a brief moment, trying to gauge their reaction. All sat in stupefied silence, engrossed in the footage, which ended as Zain and Gabrielle drove away from the wreckage.

The lights came up.

"Empora takes great shame in showing this video. One of our own, Gabrielle Ravwey, a universe-renowned fighter, killing her own kind. Zain, a reputed fighter as well, helping."

From a different part of the same row, Lord Vangle stood up. "When was that footage taken? My nephew could never have done a thing like that. I thought you sent him home on Emporian vessels, along with his father."

"It most certainly did happen, as you can see, Abraham." Lord Zigarda spoke. "What pains me even more is that it happened only after the day in which we spoke." Lord Zigarda turned to the others. "For those of you unfamiliar with the situation, Zain had traveled to Empora to be reunited with his father, who had been doing work for us. Although not completely finished with the work, we graciously let him go when Apprentice Mourse barged into our estate with Conseleigh Iycel, demanding Zain and his father's release. Empora is a good nation. Who are we to question the authority of the apprentice and conseleigh? That is when we made the call to you, Lord Vangle. Do you remember?"

Lord Vangle nodded.

"After that call, as they were being driven out of the city, your nephew slew one of our soldiers and took the hovercraft himself. He and his group of ruffians that had been sent as *envoys*, mind you, and nothing more. I do not know why such an attack even occurred, but it is blatantly apparent from the video that after doing so, there was a chase that ended in this crash."

From the politician's section of the crowd that Luvan couldn't see, a voice emerged. "I find it hard to believe that my brother would just kill someone for no good reason. He is not like that."

"You knew him before the Trials. But, tell me, did you ever see him after?"

"No, but I saw him during."

"Yes, I heard that Guardian Eska had allowed you entry for some unknown reason. And what was his condition there?"

"He... he was in the apothecary."

"For what?"

"A fractured hand and... a fractured jaw."

"A fractured jaw, yes? That means he must have received a blow to the head, a serious blow at that. Perhaps something changed within him that day." Numos now directed his attention to Lord Vangle. "Tell us, before you sent Zain on this trip to Empora, what was his condition like?"

"He..." Lord Vangle looked down at, Luvan assumed, Zain's brother, and then continued. "He was brash and talking nonsense."

"Nonsense? Explain." Numos encouraged.

"He mentioned that his mother and he had been hunted by shapeshifters."

"Shapeshifters?" Numos guffawed. "They have not been seen for centuries. Has anyone here seen a shapeshifter?"

Luvan looked around the room. Everyone was looking around at everyone else in Numos's prolonged silence. Everyone besides Lady Aprah, who shifted in her seat and bit her lip as if she wanted to say something, but chose not to. *Hmmmm...*

Senator Numos turned his focus back to Lord Vangle. "It seems your nephew and his mother are the only ones, Lord Vangle. How *convenient, hmm?*"

"My brother wouldn't lie!" Jamaal Berrese stood up.

Numos shifted his gaze back to Jamaal. "Everyone lies, Mr. Berrese." The words cut across the room. He let the statement sit for a little before turning to Lord Vangle. "Now, getting back to the question I asked earlier, why would you let him leave in such a condition?"

"I didn't want to let him leave, but his mother convinced me. I did so under the stipulation that he would use a ship. I hoped that whatever had been bothering him would fade with the days out on the Krine Sea."

"Well, it didn't, and now many of our soldiers and even some civilians are dead and gone, thanks to Zain and Gabrielle," Lord Zigarda said.

A man stood up next to Lord Vangle. "Excuse me for my impudence, Lord Zigarda, but it seems rather contrived that Zain and Gabrielle were at the same spot at the same time."

"Aahh, certainly. I understand your concerns. That is how fate can be, unexpected and, in this case, fatal. As contrived as it may seem, it is as simple as serendipity. Before we received our instructions from Apprentice Mourse to send Zain and his father back home, we had already made a call to Gabrielle Ravwey. As you know, she was a Trials contestant from Empora, and we had wanted to do an interview with her in hopes of inspiring the people of Mendeck and countless other cities, that they, too, could one day achieve an opportunity or recognition as great as hers. She happened to be coming into the city for her interview as Zain was exiting."

"Do you have proof of that call?"

"Certainly, we do." Lord Zigarda nodded towards Senator Numos.

The lights dimmed again and Senator Numos pushed a button on a remote to bring up an image overtop the video on the projection screen. It was a call log showing a call made from Lord Zigarda's telecommunication chamber to the chamber located in Gracie's Academy. The timestamp and date were a few days before Zigarda would have released Zain. While the call had only lasted for five minutes and thirty-four seconds, it still showed that Zigarda had indeed talked with someone at the Academy.

"From what I have heard Senator Numos say, all I can say is that these Trials were handled in a negligent manner compared to the Trials I underwent."

"And what was so different in your Trials, Victor?" Garrett Omyon of Nova stood. "I see this meeting for nothing more than what it really is, a vindictive attempt to ruin the position and stature of a man who beat you two-hundred-years ago."

Hair on Luvan's forearms prickled. The two elders in the room were locked in a glaring contest. After a long moment, Lord Victor Zigarda responded.

"You were not at the previous Trials, Garrett. You merely sponsored Edwyrd's participation. First, it is important to note that the Guardian of the Core at that time, Matthau Crevon, took an important interest in all of his participants. Inter-system transportation was at its inception, so far in the primitive stages that anyone here today would call it truly functional. But that didn't matter because the Guardian himself picked us up at specific locations and transported us back through the Power of the reimaje. Even this initial act created a bond of trust and security with all the Trial participants, much more than arranging large cargo ships to pick them up.

"Next, my own Trials only took place on the Core. That meant the environment was highly controlled. It did not throw contestants perilously into labyrinths or ask them to scale treacherous volcanoes in an attempt to escape death.

"Finally, it only tested skills of relevance."

"Such as?" Lord Omyon asked.

"Intelligence. Power. Combative skill. The things that would keep Gladonus safe, not partnership and fortitude."

"And these things, like partnership and fortitude, do not matter?" Lord Garrett Omyon crossed his arms over his chest.

Lord Zigarda chuckled a little. "You try to put words in my mouth. Of course, partnership and fortitude matter, but the individuals chosen should already have those qualities—they cannot be formed from a mere trial, as Edwyrd thought to do. It is clear then that the quality of Edwyrd's choices was already lower than Matthau Crevon's."

"There is even preemptive evidence that supports Lord Zigarda's claim, Lord Omyon." Senator Numos interjected. He clicked something in his hand and another image popped up on the screen. "This is one of Guardian Eska's letters. One sentence may stick out to you in particular: *The Trials you face will be extremely difficult, designed to push you past your maximum potential.* I fear as though the necessity of Guardian Eska's Trials to be overly difficult may be a result of improper candidate selection. With improper candidates, it makes sense that the Trials, then, may have broken the psyche of the contestants. Tell me, I ask, are there others here who have similar stories? Pray tell, we need to know."

The representative of Epoch rose. "My name is Nathan Alaois, and I am here on behalf of Lord Daven Evber. I can comment on a few things. First, Lord Evber's son, Cain, has always been a knowledgeable lad with a sensitive yet fierce nature about him. The weeks following the Trials, I noticed he seemed unsure of himself. He lacked his usual disposition and preferred to spend more time with books than he did practicing his combat skills or attending meetings with his father. It was almost as if he didn't know who he was, like he had lost himself. Second, I was in the telecommunication chamber with Lord Evber when Guardian Eska's apprentice and Conseleigh Iycel were present."

"Present? For what? Why were they there?" Numos asked.

"From what I gathered, Guardian Eska had sent them there to check on the contestants involved in the Trials."

"Why?"

"I cannot say. I speculate, however, that perhaps even Guardian Eska knew that he had perhaps pushed his contestants too hard and wanted to see if others had experienced symptoms like Berrese's."

"Go on."

"During the discussion, Apprentice Mourse unleashed an outburst at Lord Daven. He accused us of starting a war with Cresica!"

A man bolted from his seat. "You did start a war with us! That *thing* came over and burned our whole city to the ground. It killed Lady Clayse and countless others."

Luvan knew from his time as a conseleigh for Agrost that the man's name was Aeryn Shirewood, Lady Clayse's advisor. Luvan remained in his seat and watched as bickering descended on the assembly, spreading from the Clayse and Eyber representatives to other nations. Ka'Che longed for answers from Chaon. Sereya began yelling at Gar. It engulfed them like the raging wind surely did outside.

Luvan wondered how much longer Senator Numos would let this continue. They had an agenda, after all. Although sowing discord amongst the nations was one of their goals, Luvan did not figure it would be so easy. His interest, however, remained locked on Garrett Omyon. He had asked a question, but besides that, had remained silent in his place on the seventh level. If Luvan could manage to get his support, then impeaching Eska would be easy.

"Enough. Enough." Numos put up his hands. "Nations will be able to handle their individual disputes later. Let us not meander through the jungle of suspicion, but instead forge ahead down the mighty stream of justice." Numos waited for those standing to take a seat. "Acquava... do you have a story to tell?"

Luvan knew that Numos had strategically planned for Acquava to speak last. Not only because it would be the strongest emotional testimony coming from a lord so young, but also because the situation with Hydro Paen was well-known. They had been told to be on the watch for him and that Hown would be hunting him down, as Guardian Eska had considered him extremely dangerous since the incident involving his family. If Acquava didn't speak, they would lose face. At a time like this, they could not afford to. But recalling the details of that night could be too much for little Aiton Paen to bear.

Aiton consulted with the group of individuals around him, and then he stood. "I... I want to say that my brother is a good man. He made mistakes, yes, but he is good." He looked back at his supporters and then continued. "I want to tell you all something, something I have not told anyone here yet. Not even those sitting behind me."

Luvan frowned and leaned over in his seat. *What could this be?*

"I saw my brother recently."

He had seen Hydro? Where? When? Luvan jolted to his feet to get a better view of the boy who now had all eyes on him.

"I saw him while I was on the island in Leviathan Bay. I did not expect to see him. I suppose, like Zain and Gabrielle, as Lord Zigarda pointed out earlier, it was simply serendipity. But I did see him. After he killed our parents, I began questioning many things. I... well, I didn't even know who he was anymore because the man that I used to know would never have done any of those things. He is proud of his heritage. To be Paen means something, just like to be an Evber or a Clayse or a Voux. It means that we are leaders, and that is all Hydro ever wanted. That is why he participated in the Trials.

"I saw him, and this time was much different from the last time. When I met Hydro after the Trials, he seemed like himself, though not entirely. It seemed strange to me that he had run away at the end and that my father's acqua guard had found him on Chaon. It seemed strange to me that he had wandered into my sister's room, a room that had been closed for years. And when I saw him plunge a sword through my father and heard the screams that I now know were my mother burning alive, I... well, I refused to believe that it was him. Even though I saw it with my own eyes, I tried to refute the evidence.

"When I saw him again on the island, his eyes were black, the very same color they were the night he killed our parents. I could never forget eyes like that. But more than this, what really shocked me was that it seemed as though there was another person with him. He kept looking to his left, but I could not see anything there. I... it was discussed when Guardian Eska came to give his condolences that Hydro had been under the influence of a necklace. Apprentice Mourse made it clear to us then that this necklace had been taken by Hydro during the first trial. Even if this testimony does not directly show that it is the Trials themselves that broke my brother and caused him to kill his family, I believe that Guardian Eska should be held accountable for allowing such a devastating item to be found during his Trials. As Lord Zigarda mentioned earlier, holding the Trials on planets outside of the Core brought in factors that were not originally meant to be included."

Garrett Omyon rose to his feet. "I want to clarify to everyone here that the Trials are not made by the Guardian of the Core. They are made by the conseleigh. This was your own experience, was it not, Victor?"

After Lord Zigarda acquiesced and admitted that it was true, Luvan came forward, towards center stage. Upon noticing Luvan, Senator Numos made room for them to stand side by side.

"Yes, they are made by conseleigh," Luvan said, letting his voice carry. "And I will admit that I developed that specific trial, Lord Paen. It was not my intent to have such an item present, and I blame my own carelessness in not acknowledging the stories and myths about that place. But it is also my duty to obey the commands of the Guardian of the Core. He wanted a trial to push them past their breaking point, and I gave him that. He never stipulated that the Trials should only take place on the Central Core, for Guardian Eska believes the Trials of the Core are meant to test their person, their being, their core…," Luvan pointed to his heart, "not that they should be literally held on the Central Core. Guardian Eska accepted that choice, knowing full well the ominous nature of that place. He and I are both culpable for that, but now there is a larger question we must answer. What more can we allow Guardian Eska to oversee? It is clear his own viewpoint is skewed and disjointed from that of past Guardians. Lord Paen, since Pirini Lilapa, how has Acquava fared?"

Aiton shivered. "Horrible."

"Expand upon that please, Lord Paen."

"With his decision to seal the Twelve and the problems caused by the fight on Mount Volan, countless areas of Acquava are being swallowed by our seas and oceans. People complain to me, yet I do not have the power to change the tide. If Guardian Eska has the Power of the Twelve, then why doesn't he put the moon back in place? Why hasn't he?"

In an effort to not be biased, Luvan was going to defend Eska, making an appeal for him due to his lack of First Blood, but he decided against it. This would fit well with their argument, however tangential to the truth.

"And then he sends the Hown after my brother?" Aiton continued. "Using my blood to find him. And then, just before I came to this meeting, the two Hown with me convulsed right in front of me. They died in spams of blood and pain, and I had to watch that. I have gone through—"

Luvan cocked his head. "Excuse me, Lord Paen. You said the Hown died right in front of you?"

Another man stood up alongside Aiton. "It was a gruesome scene. The lord should not have had to watch it."

Lady Aprah stood. "The two remaining elites that went north with Conseleigh Iycel told me of the same thing. They just dropped dead in violent convulsions."

Luvan grew hot. *The Hown are gone?* He resisted the temptation to scratch his neck. As furtively as possible, he glanced at Numos and Zigarda, trying to gauge their reaction. Neither seemed to care. The confusion and lapse in dialog allowed the jeers of the Grime brothers to fill the hall.

"Two more came back than should have."

"Serves them right. They helped take off my father's head."

"You'll be next."

Lady Aprah stood, smoothing her dress. "Who was I to deny the request of a conseleigh? I want to stress, Brothers Grime, that she told me she was to remove your father from office, not remove his head. What happened in the north was not my fault."

"It doesn't matter, *Olivia*, the north will not forget."

Luvan cringed a little at the venom in the words. To call a leader by their first name, especially in that tone of voice, well, it was clear that Whittiker meant ill.

"Like the snow falls, so too, will Gar," Canice said.

"Do you mean to make war with us? Right here in front of everyone?" Lady Aprah threw her hands up in the air. A huge man stood up behind her.

"Enough!" Luvan yelled into the microphone as he slammed his hand on the podium. "You can settle your disputes diplomatically outside of this hall. We are straying from the point."

Lady Aprah turned to face Luvan. Clearly red in the face, her arms folded over her breasts, she said, "On the contrary, Mr. Katore, I believe this is very much in tune with where this discussion about ethics is going."

Luvan arched an eyebrow at that.

Numos, seizing the opportunity, gestured a hand towards her and encouraged her to continue.

"Shortly before you visited me, Senator, Conseleigh Iycel demanded, on the orders of Guardian Eska himself, that she bring twenty-five of my men with her to depose Lord Grime and hunt down another man. Like I said before, only two of those elites returned. I lost half of my force due to whatever this scheme was. All of this without requesting a single soldier of Acquava. This action has endangered my nation and made us susceptible to retribution from those two." She pointed at the Grime brothers and turned to look at them. "Brothers Grime, if you wish to discuss matters further, as Mr. Katore says, perhaps we can reach a diplomatic solution outside of this meeting."

"The only diplomatic solution we will reach is your head upon a pike."

Luvan took back the podium from Numos and swiped his hand through the air. "Enough! Open threats against other families in power is not to be tolerated. Lords Grime, sit down or I will have security remove both of you. Lady Aprah, please return to your seat as well." He waited while the standoff ensued for a few more moments. Eventually, though, all three took their seats, obeying Luvan's orders, though this did little to cut the tension in the hall.

After a long exhale, Luvan said, "Now, I believe we have strayed a little off topic." Luvan gestured towards Aiton. "Lord Paen, your story hits to the deepest part of my heart. All of it, I assure you. What you have witnessed in your nine years is something that many don't witness in an entire lifetime. I am shocked to hear what has happened to the Hown, but I will say that is not of Guardian Eska's doing. The Hown were sworn to defend him and follow his orders. They took your blood under his authority and used it to find Hydro because finding him is Guardian Eska's highest priority. While you may hate him for doing that, it is not an abuse of his Power in a case such as this because of the level of risk Hydro poses."

"And when is taking someone's blood by force not an abuse?" Lord Zigarda asked.

Out of his peripherals, Numos dabbed his face with a handkerchief. They both had been underneath the spotlight of center stage for a while, and this meeting wasn't even close to being finished.

"When it concerns matters relating to the Core." Luvan looked around to Zigarda, then to Aiton, and finally to the others. "And while you all may be thinking I am defending Edwyrd right now, I am merely stating facts. And it is facts that we should be judging Guardian Eska on, nothing else. And the fact is that he *has* abused his Power in more ways than one, but not in the matter of requiring Aiton Paen's blood in the search for Hydro. As I will show, he has done graver things."

Sweaty handkerchief in hand, Senator Numos stepped in. "And Luvan Katore will tell you all about these abuses soon, but before formally handing over the floor, I would like to mention one more thing. An idea." He pointed his finger in the air. "Change."

"It is clear that these Trials have changed the participants. For better or for worse, those participants have now affected your nations in irrevocable ways. Furthermore, while each trial was made by a conseleigh, it is still up to the Guardian of the Core how arduous those trials are to be. I, too, want to remain bipartisan and unbiased in how we handle this. While I believe that Guardian Eska did not intend to break the psyche of those in the Trials, he did so. He picked up one end of the stick and must face the consequences at the other end of the stick. It is through our combined efforts as voices for our nations that we can reprimand him for the chaos and inhumanity he has unleashed on us all." Numos paused and let the final words linger over the crowd. "Conseleigh Katore, please. It is your turn now." Senator Numos bowed and then left the podium to sit alongside Neil Raiden.

Luvan felt the tension thicken in the room. Senator Numos had done his part, now it was Luvan's turn to do his. He took a second to lock glances with all of those who would be responsible for the overthrow of Guardian Eska. He clenched the sides of the podium, cleared his throat, and then he began.

"My ladies, my lords, and representatives, I must admit something to you today. I speak to you today not as a conseleigh, but as a former senator for this great nation of Mistral. Why do I mention this to you? Well, I feel as though it's necessary, as I perhaps gave the false pretense of my authority in order to gain audiences with you in the weeks prior to this meeting. But I tell you now that I am no conseleigh. I am no senator or politician with political agendas to pass. I come to you as a man, and although it seems contradictory now, an honest man if you hear me out. Especially as a man who claims we need to only consider facts in this case. But here are the facts: Guardian Eska has abused his Power, and he has annulled his vows.

"My service with Guardian Eska ended shortly after the events that occurred on Mount Volan during Pirini Lilapa. I did not resign my service to the Guardian of the Core. With such a powerful position, only a fool would do that. No, my service was terminated by the Guardian of the Core himself."

Luvan paused here to mark the severity of the statement, then continued.

"Many of you are probably wondering why he terminated my service. Well, I intend to tell you what really happened that day on Mount Volan, as the consequences of that day have brought a plethora of problems for all of you.

"That day, the Guardian of the Core asked me to do something unthinkable—he asked me for his help in sealing the Twelve. The Twelve are essential to our welfare as a civilization. As lords and ladies, you interact with them; they guide you when you feel aimless; they help you process your thoughts when your mind is vacillating; and they serve as ideals that all of your civilians look up to. To take them away not only disseminates fear and confusion among the common people, it also hinders your ability to lead. As many of you have experienced, you have had to hear countless complaints from your citizens since the aftermath of that event.

"Even more troubling is the fact that now our system of check and balances is thrown off-kilter. Without the Twelve, Guardian Eska has no one to keep him in check. Essentially, he is invincible. And what has he done to all of you? He has made *you* go out and tell your citizens about the annihilation of the Twelve, wishing to sow discord between you and your people." Luvan pointed towards the upper rows where the lords and ladies sat. "As Guardian of the Core, is he not supposed to protect Gladonus instead of endangering it? By insisting that you serve as the messenger for his news, he only protects his own interest and not those of the people he is supposed to care about. He has made you look weak in the eyes of your citizens, for it is your power, after all, that once upon a time put the Guardian of the Core into the position he is in now."

Garrett Omyon stood up. "Senator Katore, tell me something. If you were Guardian Eska's conseleigh at the time of the incident on Mount Volan, why did you not offer up an alternative solution? Guardian Eska's job *is* to protect the citizens of Gladonus, and he was doing that by halting the moon's course, even though the aftermath is rather unfortunate. Your job as conseleigh is to offer advice. Why did you not offer any?"

"Conseleigh I was, yes, but before that I was a senator of Mistral. Of course, my solution would have been diplomacy. And that is what I suggested."

"And diplomacy failed?"

"Guardian Eska has more authority than us. He never tried this tactic. Instead, he decided to pull out his sword, and he and his dragon leaped into the fray while his apprentice searched for the jewels."

"So Guardian Eska had no conversation with the Twelve before the battle? I find that hard to believe."

"Guardian Eska had a conversation with them about the chief obligation of his position, to protect the Core, which the Twelve had wished to see upended for their own personal gains."

"It seems to me, Mr. Katore, that if anyone has repudiated their propriety, it was you by not choosing to obey Guardian Eska. He tried diplomacy. That did not work. The Twelve were in the midst of a battle, and he could delay action no further. And with no alternate solution present, he did what he intended to do, save many, although he would harm a few." Lord Omyon sat down.

"If you do not see this as an opportunity for a power grab, then that is your prerogative, Lord Omyon. I cannot force you to see it from my point of view. All I can do is offer you what I know. And what I know is that with the Twelve absent,

Guardian Eska is now nearly an untouchable force. Furthermore, he acted recklessly in his actions that day. Whether you know it or not, he has put you all at extraordinary risk."

"What do you mean, Mr. Katore?" Lady Liliana Voux stood up to ask this question.

"Many of you forget that this was not Guardian Eska's first Pirini Lilapa. In fact, it was his second. The first one involved Deimos, a monster that delivered death upon all of your nations. Eska never *killed* Deimos. His solution was to bind it, and he used the Power of the Twelve to help him do so. With the Twelve now sealed away in jewels, they are defenseless. If they are captured by the wrong person, they could be killed and the spells holding Deimos those weakened."

"How plausible is that?" Lady Voux asked. "Do you know where these jewels are? Surely they are at the Core?"

"I do not know where they are. But let us think about the possibilities. If Eska did have them within the Central Core, then they are all gathered in one location. Guarded as it is, the jewels are still in one place. With the recent, and most unfortunate, news of the Hown's demise, the only protector of these jewels then is Guardian Eska himself. And while he is most certainly a force to be reckoned with, hubris is the weakness of many men, and Eska is very proud. But, for a moment, let us assume that he did scatter the jewels. What if those jewels are found?"

"Who would find them? And how would they be found? This hypothetical is nearly impossible." Lord Omyon stood up and projected his voice. "You, Luvan Katore, are grasping for threads that are simply not there. I am not fooled by your rhetoric. You are here not on behalf of us, the families in power. You are here for your own political agenda. Since Guardian Eska has stolen your credibility, you are now seeking to regain your authority. This is nothing more than your attempt to win back influence and power by using our political position to strip the Guardian of the Core of his own. I do not need to hear more." Lord Omyon began walking towards the exit on the seventh floor.

Luvan glared at the man. "My bias is your own bias, Lord Omyon."

Lord Omyon stopped. "And what would you know of my bias, Luvan Katore?"

His voice was smaller now that he didn't stand in front of his microphone, but the room naturally amplified it enough to be audible.

"I know that you mentored Edwyrd Eska before he became the Guardian of the Core, and that is why it is so hard for you to see any wrongdoing. Not only that, but you sponsored him for acceptance into his own Trials. Although you have been in Guardian Eska's presence since he became apprentice to Guardian Crevon, that is still less time than I have been at his side. Whether you like to admit it or not, Guardian Eska has changed, and he is not the same boy that you trained, so I implore you to return to your booth."

Luvan didn't break eye contact with the old man, watching as Omyon stood there deciding what to do. Nor did Luvan speak. The key to winning this contest was to let the other be the first to falter.

The tactic worked.

After another moment of silence, Lord Omyon went back to his booth. "Very well, Luvan Katore. Carry on."

"Many of you will not know this. In fact, I believe that only you, Lord Omyon, or you, Lord Zigarda, would know, but the Guardian's Power does not derive solely from the Twelve. Guardian Eska is more powerful than that. In truth, it stems from four different sources: the Twelve, his dragon, the piece of cloth around his head, and the darknether glove he wears." He paused, letting the lords and ladies process this information. "It is the third of these to which I must call your attention. Although I am not privy to all of its functions, I do know a majority of what this item can do. The cloth on his head is called a reimaje, and it allows any wearer to recall *any* memory *any* Guardian has ever experienced. Not only that, but it functions as its own wormhole."

"Its own wormhole? Can you please explain?" Lady Aprah spoke. "How is that possible?"

"While I am not sure of its logistics, Lady Aprah, I am sure of its function. I have seen Guardian Eska use it, and I saw him use it on that day on Mount Volan. As Victor mentioned earlier, the previous Guardians of the Core picked up the contestants individually before the Trials even began, and my guess is that this was made possible through the reimaje. That is why he was able to quell the brawl so swiftly. As Deimos ravaged the lands, that is how he kept up with the beast. And that very item is now what puts all of Gladonus at risk. While Eska remains competent in its use, I have a different opinion of his apprentice. In fact, Epoch's testimony only adds to my concern, knowing that Eirek Mourse behaved so illogically while being hosted by Lord Evber and his family. During his training with Guardian Eska, he will surely be using the reimaje's Power. What if this training causes his already-fragile psyche to break? He now has instant access to the locations of all the jewels, and I know that Apprentice Mourse possesses an Ether Weapon; I saw it during the weapons tournament during the Trials. With those tools, he has the power to release Deimos into the world. Senator Numos has already painted a picture of the threat to his psyche. It is not a matter of *if*, it is a matter of *when* it breaks.

"I believe this is something for which none of us are ready. Again, Guardian Eska has failed in his duty to protect us." When his echo died, he continued. "As a loving husband and a father of two, I cannot allow that beast to ravage our lands yet again. The last time he did, Mistral almost became nothing more than a moment in history. Lady Voux, we cannot allow that to happen again." He turned his attention. "Lord Kapache, when the beast breaks, whose lands will be struck first? Where is the beast chained now?" Luvan looked up at the families of Pyre. "Lord Omyon, with the Twelve now defenseless and their lives at stake, who will rise up to protect us from Deimos? Can you still fight as well as you could when you were on Gladima?" He gave the rhetorical question more than enough silence to produce a reaction in the man. That reaction was silence. "Who here could stand to his might? This is not an issue of the present, but I implore you to make it one, as it certainly will affect us in the future.

"Furthermore, if I have not swayed you yet into believing in Guardian Eska's incompetence, then I must tell you about his betrayal to you all. On the day of his own Coronation, Guardian Eska took an oath, just like the Guardians did before him and just like Apprentice Mourse took on his own day. That oath, lords and ladies, has been rejected.

"By what Senator Numos and I have described above, he has not given Gladonus his fullest. Not when there is so much more that he can offer us. He has shown favoritism to planets. Lady Aprah herself has given evidence of this. Why did he demand elites from her but no Acquavan soldiers to accompany Conseleigh Iycel? And we have the example of the Trials. Nations of Pyre, how many of your eligible contestants who applied for the Trials were accepted?"

Rhagoh Requart stood up. "None."

Lady Scule of Lurid joined in the gesture. "None."

Garrett Omyon sat silent.

"That is right. None were accepted from Pyre, but three were accepted from Agrost. Three were accepted from Myoli. And with a total of eight available places, only Onkh was given consideration for the final two. Why would Guardian Eska do such a thing? And to the planet he had called his home, too? It is not fair.

"Finally, his vow to remain abstinent from love I believe is called into question as well." Luvan paused, letting the severity of his words yet again gain attention. "I have noticed for some time while I stood by Guardian Eska's side that he has showed a certain affection towards Conseleigh Tundra Iycel."

Lord Omyon rose to speak. "You said you wanted to make this case about facts. Do you have proof of such a transgression?"

"I do not have physical evidence condemning Eska, no. All I have is my verbal proof. I hope, however, that by this point you trust my words as I have not come to lie to you today; I have come to warn you about what will happen in the near-distant future.

"As conseleigh, we are *all* responsible for giving the Guardian advice. When it came to Conseleigh Iycel, he and she constantly discussed matters privately, without informing the rest of the conseleigh. When he determined it necessary to speed up the boy's training, it was not Conseleigh Aprorum who was tasked with this, it was Conseleigh Iycel. Why the favoritism when Ethen Aprorum was a weapons instructor for Chaon and Tundra Iycel was only Lady of Sereya before Lord Grime?

"To further showcase this favoritism towards Conseleigh Iycel, I ask you all this. Who is it that spent time with the apprentice during the investigation of possible sabotage for Trial participants? I was already dismissed at this point, and Conseleigh Aprorum had suffered an injury on Mount Volan, but Eska could have sent Conseleigh Inferno to guide the apprentice. Instead, he chose Conseleigh Iycel.

"Certainly, she has more years on Eska's council than all of us, but we are all competent. That is why we were selected for such a position."

"And then certainly Apprentice Mourse was selected because of the same standards?" Lord Omyon stood. "Surely his integrity and good will cannot be in question in the manner suggested here today."

"Aye, but that is where you are wrong, Lord Omyon. Eirek Mourse was never chosen to be apprentice. In truth, it is Lord Vangle's nephew who originally was chosen to be the apprentice."

Gasps broke out in the room. Whispers swelled from every lord, lady, and politician. Luvan grinned. This is what he had planned for.

"Abraham, is this true?" Lord Omyon asked.

Lord Vangle nodded his head. "Apprentice Mourse told me this when he and..." Lord Vangle doubled over, gripping the railing with one hand and his heart with another. His son clung to his side. Luvan could hear them muttering on the microphone, but nothing discernible.

"Lord Vangle, are you well? Should we call for an adored?"

Lord Vangle straightened. Sweat beaded his face. His breathing had intensified so much that even from the center stage, Luvan could see him inhaling and exhaling deeply. Everyone in the hall looked at him now. The microphone had been shut off and he now talked with the attendants around him, then he left without another word, his son at his side. Luvan's gaze trailed them out, and as he opened his mouth to speak, another voice came from the Ka'Che section.

"Lord Vangle needs to leave immediately. I am sorry, Conseleigh Katore. He has given me authority to speak on his behalf."

Luvan blinked, trying to regain his position. His flow had just been disrupted. Where had he been?

"Conseleigh Katore, I believe you were saying something about the apprentice."

"Yes." Luvan shook his head, embarrassed at losing focus so easily. "Yes, I was." He blinked and put a fist up to his mouth. He coughed, clearing his throat, ready to begin anew. "Zain Berrese did originally win the Trials, but he turned the opportunity down.

After Zain Berrese turned down his chance at apprenticeship, Guardian Eska called his conseleigh together to discuss an alternative solution. He seemed disinterested in all the suggestions besides his own: a riddle. He posed the riddle to both Hydro Paen and Eirek Mourse, and Eirek Mourse is the one who answered correctly. Guardian Eska did not mention this to you before Coronation because he probably felt it would weaken his selection. Apprentice Mourse has no recognized name behind him. He did not do well in combat. Why, the only way the boy won was because of his intellect and a few lucky stars, I am sure. The negation of this fact can be seen as further incompetence from Guardian Eska.

"As Lord Zigarda mentioned earlier, the previous qualifications were strength, Power, and wisdom. Apprentice Mourse still lacks in all three of these categories, and now that this system teeters on the precipice of such a dangerous cliff from the aftermath of Pirini Lilapa, we would do well in having a more competent Guardian of the Core. One who doesn't consolidate his Power. One who doesn't show favoritism to planets nor his conseleigh. Can Gladonus afford more mishap and mayhem? I say no. I say it is better to start over fresh and remove them both. Although Guardian Eska believes his Power makes him invincible, we can send a clear message to him today that we will not continue to live in his shackles of tyranny. We will not fall victim to his proposed propriety, a propriety that he, himself, fails to uphold.

"It is now or never. We are the architects of this great republic that your fathers and forefathers have built since the end of the Great War. Let us vote to bring him here and stand trial for his actions and wrongdoings. Let us vote to bring him here for those missteps by his conseleigh. And let us bring him here to remind him that he is not invincible and that he needs to account for the seeds of discord he has sown throughout this universe of ours. United, there is nothing that we cannot do, there is nothing that our combined voices cannot say. Divided, our voices fall mute, and his actions continue to pull us into this quicksand of injustice. Can I receive a second?"

"I." Lord Victor Zigarda stood up without a moment's hesitation.

One by one, each of the families in power threw up their support in an exclamation of defiance. Level by level, it went. First the families from Ka'Che. Second, the families from Onkh. Those from Agrost were next, and to Luvan's surprise, even the man from Cresica tossed in his support. Luvan looked up to the last row of individuals, those from Pyre. Rhagoh Requart gave his whole-hearted support. Lady Farah Scule then echoed his condemnation. Finally, it came down to Nova. Regardless of what the man said, they already had enough votes to move forward, but Luvan wanted to see just how effective he had been. He wanted this victory to be his most decisive victory in this hall yet.

"And, you, Lord Omyon, how do you stand? Are you with us or against us?"

Lord Garrett Omyon stood. "I, the reigning family in power on Nova, motion to bring Guardian Eska before us all and answer questions directly. He will face possible impeachment for his actions and the allowed actions of his constituents."

Luvan's eyes lit up. He smirked. *Unanimous.* He licked his lips. He and the senator's plan would advance to stage two. "I, Luvan Katore, then call this meeting to a close. Guardian Eska will be brought before us and allowed to give testimony on his actions and the actions of those under him. Following this, we will vote whether to uphold his authority or to remove him and begin anew. The meeting is adjourned."

He didn't have a gavel, but in his proudest moment in the Hall of Voices, he brought his fist down upon the podium, then watched the others leave, thinking to himself all the while: *Unanimous. The vote is unanimous.*

EPILOGUE

H is shell had passed out after the realization of his identity. Not something he had wanted so soon, but this place, this crystal palace, hadn't been anything like he had seen before. Somehow it let his shell see him, recognize him. It showed him his soul. And he hadn't finished planting his claws in deep enough to fully control the young man yet. His host was strong, much more competent than he could have hoped for, but it also meant the man had greater willpower. He had already defied him while with his brother. That time, he could have died. Did he know what Purge could do? Ridiculous question. Of course, he didn't know. Neither of them did. Otherwise, he wouldn't be here.

And then there was that moment in the forest, when the man's bonded animal had appeared. Normally, he wouldn't want to stand in the way of a bond, but this animal had threatened to disrupt his own, and he couldn't allow that, especially at such an early stage in their bonding process.

But the time that troubled him the most was when the connection *had* been lost. The time when the host was captured by those men in black. The black net had severed the connection. He hadn't been able to feel the man at all. He hadn't felt anything. For once, he was Powerless. No, for the second time. It had been similar, he realized, to his time within the Zas Labyrinth. He had no host. No consciousness to feed on. No Power to consume and turn into his own. He was merely there. Existing. But with no purpose or potential. He was dead.

He was unsure what his host had done while captured, but whatever it was, he approved. They were together again and now, with another jewel in his possession. They were one step closer to the endgame.

And while he might be his father's favorite, more powerful, larger, and stronger than all of his sisters and kin, that didn't make him completely disrespectful of those under him. One good deed deserved another, so he picked up his host's body, taking control of it fully for the first time, and awkwardly shepherded him out the crystal doors, back to the chill of the outdoors and the ship. There were still more jewels to seek, and their adventure was far from over.

The large mass of liquid metal was an oddity that he couldn't quite comprehend. How could it speak? Or fly, for that matter? It had no wings and no mouth. From what he can sense, it couldn't use Power, so what *did* power it?

Using the muscle memory of his host, he put the ship into the same mode he had seen many times before—autopilot. It was a magic that allowed this vehicle to think for itself. Why anyone would want to give such autonomy to something they controlled, he couldn't understand. But, then again, he wasn't human and would most likely never understand the idiocrasies of human beings or this grand system his father had helped build. He tried snorting, but it came out as a sigh. He shook his head and massaged his temples.

Right now, none of that mattered. He would be reunited with his master soon enough. They would find each other again, and everything would be as it should.

Ajid Volintasey Fuan.

Word-of-mouth is crucial for any author to succeed. *If you've enjoyed the book, please consider leaving a review on Amazon and Goodreads and other book retailers of your choice! Even if it's only a line or two, any review is greatly appreciated and would be a tremendous help.* Thank you so much, and I hope that you have truly enjoyed the novel. Keep reading to get a sneak peek of the next book in the series located in the back of the novel.

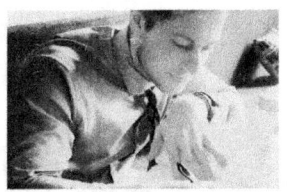

ABOUT THE AUTHOR

Michael E. Thies currently is an English educator living in Suzhou, China and is completing an online master's degree from the University of Florida in Digital Strategy. Also, he is currently completing Holistic Health Coach Certification through IIN because fitness and food is another of his passions. He is a gym enthusiast, a never-ending Chinese language learner, and somehow manages to make time to continue writing fantastic stories for all of his fans. To keep up-to-date with him make sure to visit his website www.michaelethies.com.

CHARACTER TREES

This section of the novel is designed to give readers a sense of reference for the characters in the novel. Each nation will be displayed along with the ruling house and their sigil. Those who make up that house will be noted below. In certain cases, some characters in the story will not be directly related to the house, in that instance, their relationship to the house will be explained on the page. It's important to note that I only listed the houses that are pertinent to this novel so as not to overwhelm you more than necessary.

After making your way through the nations of importance and the families in power, a few pages will be taken to detail the two prominent academies in the story and those who attend them, along with a few of their sayings and beliefs. Finally, a brief history on how the Twelve came to be and a list of their attributes will be shown at the end.

Thank you for reading and I hope this helps you as you make your way through the book.

THE CENTRAL CORE

G UARDIAN EDWYRD ESKA, Guardian of the Core for 185 years. Bonded to a dragon named, VESEL. Has one sister, ALICIA, deceased. Was sponsored to participate in his own Trials by LORD GARRETT OMYON from Nova. Has four respective aides called his conseleigh:

- TUNDRA IYCEL, conseleigh of the planet Onkh. Before being an aide for Guardian Eska, she was Lady of Sereya. He has been in Eska's service for thirty-five years.

- LUVAN KATORE, conseleigh of the planet Agrost. Before being an aide for Guardian Eska, he was a politician for the nation of Mistral. He has been in Eska's service for thirty years. He is now currently dismissed from his duties for disobeying the Guardian's orders.

- ETHEN RORUM, conseleigh of the planet Myoli. Before being an aide for Guardian Eska, he was a weapons' instructor and trainer for the Lord of Chaon, Zalos Kapache. He has been in Eska's service for fourteen years.

- RIAGAN INFERNO, conseleigh of the planet Pyre. Before being an aide for Guardian Eska, he was Lord of Therus. He has been in Eska's service for eight years.

- CRONOS, one of the four Sages, and is the only one who speaks. Is of First Blood and helps train the apprentice after Coronation. Very versed in the language of Power.

- COLIN, the oldest, most respected and trusted servant for Guardian Eska.

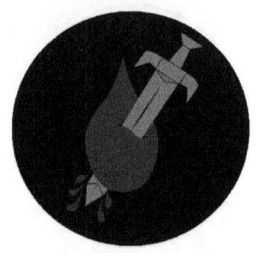

NATION OF ACQUAVA

A ITON PAEN, Lord of Acquava. Son to HYDRO PAEN THE FIRST and ATESIA. Has two siblings:

- HYDRO THE SECOND, heir to Acquavan throne and also participated in Guardian Eska's Trials.
- ANYA, deceased.

Figures of Import:
- DARIEN DORNELL, receiver to Lord Paen.
- LEN POSAIR, advisor to Lord Paen.
- ELIAS WARD, lead adored to Lord Paen.
- KORTH CENTELL, head acqua guard, from the Hart Isles.
- YUNVA YIGYR, one of Lord Paen's acqua guards.
- KENT POIL, one of Lord Paen's aqua guards.
- CASSIUS FRAUSTER, one of Lord Paen's acqua guards, deceased.
- HOLDEN HAUGHTER, one of Lord Paen's acqua guards.
- PROFESSOR IGNIS HARUKO, private Power instructor for the family.

Marquises of the Lesser Houses in Acquava:
- ROY TITYLE, marquis of the Katarh province.
- MARQISS PUWL, marquis of the Rhemu province.
- HEKTER SIGURD, marquis of the Roil province.
- ALYN BLOCTER, marquis of the Summer Isles.
- CADELL PERIWINKLE, marquis of the Hart Isles.
- SETH AXYEL, marquis of the Talyn province.

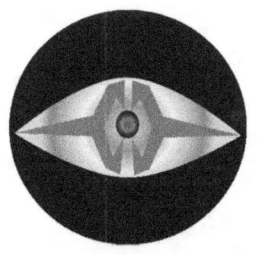

NATION OF GAR

O LIVIA APRAH, Lady of Gar. Only daughter of the deceased VISIS and AUTUMN APRAH.

Figures of Import:

- HORM DUBHALEN, head elite for Lady Aprah

- CORRIGAN BRIGGS, second in command to Lady Aprah's Father of CADMAR BRIGGS, a contestant who participated in Guardian Eska's Trials currently completing The Passage.

- Jöðurr ELDREDGE, advisor to Lady Aprah.

- Gøti LANAM, receiver to Lady Aprah.

Marquises of the Lesser Houses in Gar:

- ROWAN BERNAL, marquis of the major city of Nore.

- WILLIAM CREAZON, marquis of the major city of Brockstun.

- ROGER LUTEN, baron of the minor city of Roan.

NATION OF SEREYA

A STOR GRIME, Lord of Sereya. Had two wives, both deceased. First wife was named NEVA gave birth to WHITTIKER, currently a weapons instructor at the academy of Storm Academy. Second wife, WYNTER gave birth to CANICE, currently studying the Adored Arts on Pyre.

Figures of Import:

- KALEN KATARH, advisor to Lord Grime.
- JEL PARON, receiver to Lord Grime.

Marquises of the Lesser Houses in Sereya:

- NICHOLAS COLDEN, marquis of Eurador.
- CONNER ERTICH, baron of the minor city of Soya.

NATION OF CRESICA

L INN CLAYSE, Lady of Cresica. Lives in the capital, Syf. Single. Her father is RYBERT. Mother, LYNDA, deceased.

Figures of Import:

- AERYN SHIREWOOD, advisor to Lady Clayse.
- EMBRY KNOSSOL, receiver to Lady Clayse.
- ROLAND, personal guard.

Marchionesses of the Lesser Houses in Cresica:

- ALBONY EVENGALE, marchioness of the major city, Stynt. Has two children OSWYN (older) and EZRA (younger), now deceased.
- MARA SURG, marchioness of the major city, Lisyn.
- TIPHANE TALHEND, marchioness of the major city, Cruxe.
- MELODON SHEER, marchioness of the Triangle Islands.

NATION OF EPOCH

D AVEN EVBER, Lord of Epoch. Lives in Castle Thoth, in city it was named after, Thoth. Married to DAWN. Has one son, CAIN, who participated in Guardian Eska's Trials.

Figures of Import:
- NATHAN ALAOIS, advisor to Lord Evber.
- FINNIAN LUGUS, receiver to Lord Evber.
- CASTOR LEELAN, head of the owl guards.

Marquises of Lesser Houses in Epoch:
- EDYM LANGOL, marquis of the major city, Ambit. Has one son, JOSHUA.
- CHRISTOPHER SOLLEN, marquis of the major city, Briarwood.
- SOREN MESH, marquis of the major city, Vale.
- ROGER YOUNG, baron of the minor city, Lorian.

NATION OF KA'CHE

A BRAHAM VANGLE, Lord of Ka'Che. Son of TYON. Lives in Pelopon, the capital. Married to SHAYNA. Has four children: KYLAN of twenty, TREV of fifteen, and LIQUA and LEDLA who are twins at twelve.

Abraham has three other siblings:

- LUKAS, an older brother who is Denied.

- ELORINE SESSO who is married to RAMSEY.

- BRISINE BERRESE, the youngest, married to LARON. Have two children and one adopted child:

- JAMAAL, oldest son. Married to REINE. Has two children, AMAYA, four years old, and KALANI, six years old.

- ZAIN, a student at Gazo's Academy. Also, a contestant who participated in Guardian Eska's Trials.

- ZAKK SHIREN, adopted son of Brisine and Laron. Family murdered at the age of six. Taken in at the age of twelve. Another contestant who was accepted to attend Guardian Eska's Trials but never ended up participating.

Figures of Import:

- ERRION VESK, advisor to Lord Vangle. Nicknamed ERIE and the LORD'S EAR.

- OWLEN MANSEN, receiver to Lord Vangle.

- AENEAS KHREOS, captain of the Sea's Commander.

- BERN DENARDI, first captain of the Sea's Commander.

- GERALD STARSHINE, a royal guard in service to Lord Vangle, deceased.

Marquises of Lesser Houses of Ka'Che:

- RAMSEY SESSO, marquis of the major city, Cotterall.

- BRRYN ROPIS, marquis of the major city, Callumbra.

- DARAN MOXXIE, marquis of the major city, Mox.

NATION OF EMPORA

VICTOR ZIGARDA, Lord of Empora. Lives in Mendeck. Never married. Had one younger brother, RENAUL, now deceased. Renaul's legacy was carried on by three children:

- HAYDEN
- SELBY
- MEADE

Figures of Import:

- EDWYN LYZE, advisor to Zigarda.
- YUAN SHIMES, receiver to Zigarda.
- DR. GENUS CERE, lead scientist for Zigarda.
- ZAKK SHIREN, lead bodyguard for Zigarda.

Marquises of Lesser Houses in Empora:

- PILLIAN DESMIER, marquis of the major city, Lokigh.
- SHEAMOUS STRONGHAND, marquis of the major city, Soeco.
- MYCKEL CRUNE, marquis of the major city, Rydel.

THE TWELVE

The gestalt that is the Twelve are the warriors who survived the Great War and managed to escape before Gladima sealed itself away. Born on Gladima and endowed with First Blood, the Twelve used their Power and authority of birthright to claim home to the other planets as their home had now vanished. By showcasing their strength and ability, many citizens view them with awe and wonder and have surmised that they are deities sent to rule over Gladonus in the absence of the Ancients. Those belonging to the Heavol Tribe were created by Ancient Lyoen. Those belonging to the Evolic Tribe were created by Ancient Bane.

Rivals towards one another, and tensions still high after the Great War, a constant feud ended with them needing to quell the events of the first Pirini Lilapa (year 150 AGW) together. What's more, a prophecy floated upon the air that spoke of the Twelve's loss of Power. The considerable effort it took to stop Pirini Lilapa and the vulnerability that it exposed them to, along with their heightened sense of paranoia due to the prophecy, made them realize they would need to create a role to handle such an occurrence if it should happen again. The first Guardian of the Core, Jorey Raule, fulfilled that role in the year 165 AGW (After Great War).

The Heavol Tribe

- Fueoco = God of heat and fire.
- Orekus = God of underworld.
- Myethos = God of the suns and day.
- Saeluste = Goddess of mental health, wisdom, and intelligence.
- Trema = Goddess of the lands and harvest.
- Lucine = Goddess of birth and peace.

The Evolic Tribe

- Pearl = Goddess of water, seas, and oceans.
- Anemie = Goddess of the sky, lightning, and Axiumé.
- Luenar = God of the moons, night.
- Theothe = God of physical health and beauty.
- Crestal = Goddess of cold winds and winter seasons.
- Tomahawke = God of war and death and suffering.

BOOK 4 PREVIEW

F or over a day, Cain had walked through Kane. The notorious firelands never dissipated in heat, as if beneath the black that covered the land magma boiled, keeping it warm to the touch. With each clacking of hooves, Cain expected someone from his father's company to have tracked him down, but it was always just a firehorse. They galloped freely, manes and tails of fire flowing behind them in the wind like unraveled ribbons.

The freedom of his disappearance, or the apparently inconsequential nature of it, stirred Cain. *Why hasn't father sent anyone to take me yet? Surely he must know about my absence by now?* Cain kept his thoughts to himself, hoping they would remain only thoughts, but the more that he walked with Stannon, the more Cain recognized how akin they were. The height, the hair, even a similar lanky body type, told Cain that he was muscular underneath the fiery shirt that made him look more like a walking flame than a guide who escorted him through the firelands. Cain supposed a flame and a guide were of the same thing; both lit the way for those in darkness, and perhaps following him would answer some of Cain's questions.

"How much further?"

"Brother, we are almost there."

Cain stopped. *That word...* It annoyed him more than it should. It called back memories from twelve years previous that he didn't want: The weight of his father's axe in his hand; the voice of pleading leniency that he couldn't oblige; the gust of wind that struck him simultaneously as he brought down the axe upon the man's neck; the blood that abraded his face afterwards.

Cain crumbled to his knees. "No. I cannot do this. I cannot. I need to leave."

"Brother..."

Cain whipped out his baton and sprung forth his axe. His chest heaved up and down with heavy pants. "I *am not* your brother." He stared at Stannon's face, trying his best to ignore the similarities. He pushed himself up and turned around to leave.

He took a few steps.

No one followed him.

Then he took a few more, expecting Stannon to come pleading back to him, but he never did. Cain continued walking until he stopped on his own volition. Emptiness lay before him. Complete darkness engulfed him now. No one was on the horizon to come to his rescue. No one had been here to rescue him. And with dusk fast approaching, he knew another dawn would rise before there was any hope of finding him.

Defeated and alone, Cain looked back over his shoulder. His guide still waited in the same spot Cain had left him, his outfit a lantern in this overwhelming abyss of blackness. With a heavy breath, Cain turned around and went back to him.

"There is nothing back there for you, brother."

"I will come with you, but please do not call me brother."

Stannon bobbed his head in silent acquiescence and continued forward. Cain trudged on, following the man to whatever destiny the Ancients would bring him to, not bothering to count hours anymore, not bothering to feel emotions anymore. What did it matter? By the time anyone found him, it wouldn't make much difference. The feelings he thought in Lorian fell like rain into a chasm so deep that Cain couldn't care to try to find it.

At the first glimpse of lights and fire and the chants and murmurs of unrecognizable voices, his senses awakened.

Stannon led Cain through a village made of red clay houses and roofs of black straw. Cain started fascinating impossible, yet plausible, ideas at the same time. That

the straw on the roof may be the leftover branches of the Yggdrasil tree that fell on their land. That perhaps the red clay was earth at one time, but now was permanently red with fire from that infamous day. He also couldn't help but notice how very similar it looked to Blen when he had visited the town during the fourth trial. But that couldn't be possible, could it?

Paraded in front of them, Cain fell prey to whispers and gallant, orange eyes with flakes of fire inside burning with intrigue. The fiery eyes matched their hair. Most of the men were tall, some even taller than Cain. Even the shortest, though, stood taller than Cain's father. Hundreds came to see him, lined up in families with the shortest child in front, and the tallest man (or woman) in back, but positioned in a way that none missed the opportunity to observe this foreigner.

At the end of the village stood a man, perhaps half a hand taller than Cain. Like Cain, he held the same lanky body corded in columns of lean muscle. Like Cain, there was no stubble on his clean-shaven face. Like Cain, glasses sat at the brim of his nose.

Five paces away, Stannon stopped, and so Cain did as well. The elder in front of him, arms crossed over his chest, surveyed Cain up and down, evaluating him like he was to be some sort of slave. The orange eyes scrutinized him, meticulously dissected his physicality, and even pierced him inside on a deeper level, as if determining his worth. They were the eyes of a leader, and a passion sat inside them that could not be easily extinguished.

For the first time in this valley of fire, Cain felt chills run up his arms.

Arms still crossed, the man looked at Stannon. "Thank you for bringing my son home, Stannon."

Cain shivered and gulped. *Son?*

He turned his attention to Cain. "Come inside, Cain, there is much we need to talk about." He turned and entered a larger house, similar in material to the others.

Cain's eyes widened, and he pushed Stannon aside. "How do you know my name?"

The man bent low at the threshold of the house. "If you want to know, then come inside."

Cautiously, Cain eyed the man who went into his hut, leaving the open door as an invitation for Cain to enter. Susurrus from behind him, and a gentle shove from Stannon beside him, pushed him to the doorstep. He looked inside, cautious of stepping over the threshold, as if doing so would propel Cain into the unknown. Sweat dampened his hands, and he tried to rub it off on his tunic and pants.

"Cain, come." A voice called to him within.

Cain obliged. He bowed his head, ducking under the door's threshold, and entered. "Why did you say that?"

"Please, the door. Then come and sit here across from me. We have much to discuss." The man stared at him. His hands were folded together nicely on the table. On his left arm, a scar ran across the entire length of his forearm.

Hesitant to come further into the dwelling, Cain searched for any traps or signs of anyone else.

"No one else is here. And I'm not armed."

A sconce aglow helped Cain realize the man spoke the truth. Well, almost. While Cain knew the man carried no weapons on him from outside, he quickly noticed a long spear that hung on the wall placed upon two skulls behind where the man sat. Keeping one arm on the baton to his left hip, he closed the door and entered, taking a seat in front of the older man.

"How do you know my name?"

"Your mother told me about you."

"My mother? How do you know her?"

"Dawn came to me twenty-five years ago."

His mother's name sent tingles up Cain's arm and neck. He rolled his shoulders, trying to relieve himself of the sensation. "My mom has never been to Kane."

The man smirked. "As far as you know, Son. But she has. She came alone and afraid. Why she came here? Well, only the winds of fate know that, but perhaps she did not want to be found, and so she thought Kane would be the best place for her."

Cain gulped and took a deep breath. Could this be the story that his mom had alluded to but never explained? "Go on."

"When three men came to collect her, I protected her. Not one of them survived."

Cain glanced at the lance on the wall. Focusing on the object more, his eyes widened. *An Ether Weapon!* The skin of the lance held the amethyst coloring coated with swirls of what looked like gray clouds.

"What is its name?"

"*Protector.* It has been passed down in my family since the Smiths forged the weapons when Gladonus was created. Did you know that each planet had a native king chosen for it, back before the Great War?"

Instinctively, Cain shook his head. But then he bit his lower lip. Did he know this? It sounded familiar, but where had he heard it?

"Each king had the skill, the stamina, and the strength to rival that of anyone in any of the Ancients' cabinet. And the only reason they were never included is because they lacked First Blood. In fact, because of their lack of First Blood, they were not ever acknowledged by the Ancients Lyoen or Bane. They became powerful, however, after receiving a necklace that granted them the ability to bond with mighty creatures, the Four Creatures of Legend. When the Smiths were banished from Gladima, they stole some of the Ether Weapons and knew that nothing would upset those of Gladima more than giving it to those kings and teaching them the words of Power. So they did, and almost overnight, the four kings became more powerful than even the Twelve. In fact, with the ability to bond, they rivaled the lineage of the Ancients."

More shivers crept into Cain. There were too many things to process and digest. Where to start? Fumbling for something, anything, Cain massaged his temples. "Are you telling me that the Ancients had offspring?"

"They most certainly did. One of them helped the people of the first king of Pyre escape death. That is a story for a different day, however. What is important is that because of the actions of that man, a group of Pyre's people ended up here, in Kane. And for more than 750 years now, we have kept the lineage of that first king alive. The True Kings."

Cain gulped. His breathing intensified. His posture straightened. That is what Eirek had told him about before the stump. Before his feet had carried them there, as if fate was guiding him all along. "Did you say True Kings?"

The man's eyes widened. "So you know?"

"I…" Cain shook his head again. "No, not really. I only heard it in passing. In books that I used to read," Cain lied.

"You and I are what remains of that bloodline."

If you want to be the first to know when Book 4 is going to be released, sign up for my monthly newsletter, The Trials we Face. In it, I give exclusive insights into what is happening in my author life, book recommendations, and I showcase stories of adversity from all over the globe because we all go through trials. Sign up by visiting my website: www.michaelethies.com

Also By

The Trials of the Core (Guardian of the Core Book 1)
The Curse of Pirini Lilapa (Guardian of the Core Book 2)